Arkham Nights

Tales of
Mythos Noir

Glynn Owen Barrass

and

Ron Shiflet

Celaeno Press

2016

Arkham Nights: Tales of Mythos Noir
Copyright © 2016 Glynn Owen Barrass and Ron Shiflet
This edition copyright © 2016 Celaeno Press. All rights reserved.

Cover art © M. Wayne Miller

Publishing history
"A Man Called West" – *E'ch Pi El 5* (Rainfall Books), *Two Against Darkness* (H. Harksen Productions)
"Big Boss" – *Strange Detective Tales 1* (Rainfall Books), *Two Against Darkness* (H. Harksen Productions)
"The Lady in Yellow" – *Strange Detective Tales 2* (Rainfall Books), *Two Against Darkness* (H. Harksen Productions)
"Redemption" – *Strange Detective Tales 3* (Rainfall Books), *Two Against Darkness* (H. Harksen Productions)
"The Kingsport Desk" – *Strange Detective Tales 1* (Rainfall Books), *Two Against Darkness* (H. Harksen Productions)
"The Glass Jaw" – *Two Against Darkness* (H. Harksen Productions)
"Skin Flick" – *Strange Detective Tales 3* (Rainfall Books), *Two Against Darkness* (H. Harksen Productions)
"Last Chick Standing" – *Strange Detective Tales 2* (Rainfall Books), *Two Against Darkness* (H. Harksen Productions)

ISBN: 978-4-902075-81-6

Celaeno Press
www.celaenopress.com

Table of Contents

Cthulhu's Big Sleep

I suppose it can be said to have begun with Raymond Chandler's Philip Marlowe tale, "The King in Yellow." My eyes widened when I caught sight of that title on the table of contents. *What on earth?*

Well, it turned out to be no more—but also no less—than a wink to the reader "in the know." Marlowe saw the sprawled out corpse of trumpeter King Leopardi swathed in his lemon silk pajamas and quipped that it reminded him of a book he'd once read, and we know which one he meant. (Suppose he'd lived in a later decade and the corpse reminded him of a particular rock band. The story could have been titled, "Ded Leppard.") Oh yes. What is it that began with Chandler? The hybridization of hard-boiled detective fiction with the Cthulhu Mythos. I specify "hard-boiled" (or *Noir*) detective fiction because Lovecraft himself had earlier utilized detective protagonists in "The Lurking Fear" and "The Horror at Red Hook" which I once unthinkingly recommended to an Italian friend as his introduction to HPL! Thomas Malone was indeed a hardened detective who had, he supposed, seen it all, but he hadn't seen nuthin yet! And there was no tough-as-nails, world-weary, jaded interior monologue narration, the essential feature, as I view it, of hard-boiled detective fiction.

The first Lovecraftian *Noir* fiction I remember reading was C.J. Henderson's "You Can't Take it with You," which I believe premiered in *Eldritch Tales*. I reprinted it in my Chaosium collection, *The Innsmouth Cycle*. I found it very impressive and consider myself quite lucky to have belonged to the vanguard of Chris Henderson fandom. He was, as you know, a master of the genre. He wrote both horror fiction and detective stories (among others) and then combined them seamlessly. And of course there have been other equally adept practitioners. Joseph S. Pulver's first novel, *Night-mare's Disciple*, was a classic. And there are more—like Glynn Barrass and Ron Shiflet, whose work you are getting ready to read right now!

At first glance, the two genres combined in these stories may seem very different; so different, that to combine them would seem inevitably to produce parody, like Steve Allen sonorously reciting the lyrics to Donna Summers's song *Hot Stuff.* But that expectation would be mistaken. How can they fit together so well? I think it is because the logic of the Lovecraftian tale is that of an intrepid investigator on the trail of a mystery. The difference is that the "detective" is a scholar researching a fascinating enigma, one which looks increasingly dangerous the closer he gets to solving it. And yet that does not deter our protagonist, for he is by that point a moth headed for the flame. It is downright Faustian! Knowledge loved better than life itself—or at least better than peace of mind.

And here is another difference: Lovecraft's protagonists begin with a fairly rosy worldview, then become disillusioned to the point of nihilism or even planned suicide. The unlikely heroes in the hardboiled detective stories (especially Barrass's and Shiflet's), are well past that point going in! When they encounter the supernatural horror, it may be disgusting and daunting, but it is pretty much just a new take on an old type of crime. While nowhere near as extreme as the pulps' blind, hemophiliac or otherwise cripple 'Defective Detectives', many Chandlerian protagonist-narrators have obstacles they must struggle against within as well as without. Towers and Barnes are both former prizefighters, neither a stranger to killing men, indulging in the occasional torture-interrogation. They even confess themselves surprised to discover they possess a rudimentary moral sense, and this only when compared to the incredibly vile bad guys they are fighting. Shocking revelations cause HPL's characters to faint dead away, but these guys fight themselves to cope with booze and floozies.

As a result, these guys have hangovers, stupors, and crippling gunshot wounds to fight before they can even get to fighting the villains and crooks. The torments they have undergone serve to harden them, to reinforce their iron mettle.

However, the balance struck by Barrass and Shiflet between the hard-boiled private eye and the three-lobed burning eye is not what one might expect: the detective genre conventions are not merely employed as a frame for Lovecraftian goings on. Rather, the Mythos elements have become strictly secondary, though still crucial. These are crime stories, more of the underworld than of the netherworld. In these stories, important Lovecraft characters like Herbert West and Wilbur Whateley take the roles of mob doctors and thuggish enforcers. Resurrected Zombies become hit men who keep on coming no matter how many times you kill them. Contraband stocks of bootleg whiskey are replaced by canisters of West's reagent. And it all works!

So work up your courage and knock on the pebble glass window of the office of Shiflet & Barrass Detective Agency. If you don't have an eldritch case on your hands when you walk in, believe me, you will when you walk back out!

Robert M. Price
April 18, 2016

A Man Called West

1   A Chance Encounter

I had only been working for Dr. West a few days when it became apparent that he lived in great fear of being discovered by someone or *something*. Our first meeting had occurred one lonely night on the Falmouth beach as he was being set upon by a young gang of hoodlums. It had been a chance encounter and much to his advantage.

Having been released from prison only days earlier, my first instinct was to mind my own business. Trouble was the last thing I needed but my blood began to boil as I watched the would-be toughs kick and pummel the smaller figure.

"Well, Riley," I said, "here's where you put your foot right in it."

With a sigh of regret, I clenched my fists and went charging down the sandy embankment, into the center of the melee. Instead of yelling or crying out a warning, I came down on them in a storm of fists and well-placed kicks. Two of the surprised punks went down bleeding before they realized what was happening. A quick glance at the victim revealed a stunned look of amazement and gratitude.

"Look out!" he yelled, as one of the attackers swung a large piece of driftwood at my head. West's warning saved me a headache as the weapon glanced off my shoulder.

I buried a right fist up to the wrist in the careless fool's belly and grinned as the breath was knocked out of his lungs with a loud "whoosh!" He fell to his knees and a kick to the face finished the job. Three of the attackers were now out of commission and the remaining two backed away warily with their hands in the air.

"We're leaving, Mister!" cried one as he turned to run.

I laughed heartily as the battered youths struggled to their feet and staggered off into the night. Turning to their harried, tow-headed victim, I said, "Looks like they bit off more than they could chew."

The smaller man smiled, wiped sand from his glasses and said, "My name is Dr. West and I'm immensely grateful for your timely intervention."

"A saw-bones huh?" I asked, extending my hand.

"I've been called worse than that," he replied. "I hope you haven't suffered any injuries on my account."

"Nothing that a stiff drink won't fix."

West looked me over appraisingly and chuckled. "You're a large fellow. In what line of work are you employed?"

I wanted to lie, but there was something about West that caused me to blurt out the truth. "I'm without a job. I just got out of prison."

He seemed completely unfazed by my admission.

"I suppose at one time or another that we've all done things not sanctioned by society."

"Yeah," I agreed. "Let he who is without sin . . ."

"Don't worry Mr. . . . uh?"

"Barnes," I supplied. "Riley Barnes."

"Well, Barnes, Herbert West is not one to cast stones."

"Glad to hear it, Dr. West," I said. "Did you get hurt in the ruckus?"

"I'll live," he replied. "Now what say you we get that stiff drink you mentioned?"

"Lead the way," I happily replied.

If only I had known then what I know *now*.

West led me to a summer house, vacated for the season by its rightful owner. It was just one of the many things I didn't know about Herbert West back then.

He fixed me that drink—several actually—and before the night was over had offered me a job. It didn't pay too well but it wasn't as if I had any other offers lined up at the time. Most people just aren't too eager to hire a jailbird.

"Barnes," West said, pouring another drink. "You've been honest with me and I think it only fair that I respond in kind."

I nodded and let him continue.

"I'm currently working on medical research that will be a boon to all mankind. However, there are certain members of the medical community who are insanely jealous of my early successes and desire to eliminate me at all costs."

"Eliminate as in, rub you out?" I asked incredulously.

"Yes, I know how unbelievable that sounds," West replied. "Then again, success breeds bitter enemies and there are just as many unscrupulous crooks in my field as in yours. . . . which was *what* again?"

"Dock-worker, boxer, leg breaker, take your pick," I laughed.

"Well, maybe *almost* as many in my field," he chuckled. "Still, you're just the type of man I can use. You're strong, not a stranger to violence, and can obviously take care of yourself judging from what I observed back there on the beach."

"They were just kids," I said modestly.

"Five very large kids," West answered. "So, I'll get to the point: I need someone to act as bodyguard and run occasional errands for me since it's imperative that I keep a low profile. In return, I can offer you room and board and a small check each month. Your contributions will allow me to work unfettered on the important research I mentioned earlier. So what do you say, Mr. Barnes?"

"I'll take it!" I answered.

My first week in West's employ was a piece of cake. I didn't do a hell of a lot and spent the majority of my time listening to the radio or reading the pulps. West insisted that I take periodic walks around the windswept dunes and be on the lookout for any suspicious characters. I often got a laugh out of this last request since we were the shadiest pair in the place.

These outside jaunts gave me the chance to escape the noxious fumes that frequently drifted downstairs from West's upstairs laboratory. He hadn't given me a tour of *that* part of the house and had rebuffed my hints to have a look at it.

"It's really pretty mundane," he told me. "But once things progress, I'll be glad to show you."

I couldn't say if things were progressing or not but loud thuds and bumping sounds often emanated from the lab. When I'd ask about the racket, he'd just say "lab animals" and leave it at that. Maybe so, but I wondered what type of lab animals would cause my employer to cry out in alarm and fire off three rounds from a .38 revolver. I always meant to ask him, but I decided to drop it. It was his ugly business and not mine.

2　　Stalking West

All said and done, the human face can really take a lot of damage, and what you see in the movies about some guy knocking a bozo out with one punch is pretty much bullshit. But when you see some poor drunken bum in the street with his face smashed up from a bar fight but still conscious and wandering round? That's the truth of it, really.

I'd been working the guy over for quite a while, concentrating all my punches on his skinny, ugly face. The problem with pounding a guy though, is that, after you've turned his nose to mush, plugged one eye (making sure you keep the other in working order) and busted his teeth into the wet, groaning mess of his mouth, all you're eventually doing is bruising the knuckles beneath your leather gloves and whacking numbed muscle and weeping flesh. The guy had even peed his pants around halfway through my interrogation, which I took as a sign that he was ready to talk, but nothing but the stink of urine was coming from that gibbering little mess I'd been working over.

Beating up on a guy till his face is a pulpy lump will only get you so far. If you want to get the right answers off of him that is.

That's why I'd brought along the pruning shears.

Anyway, before I get too ahead of myself I'd maybe better explain why I was in that tiny room in that roach-pit hotel almost torturing to death a guy I'd met less than an hour earlier.

My name is Trevor Towers, I'm an ex-marine with too many medals to mention and an ex-wife I don't like to talk about. Since I left the army I've been making my bread by hiring myself out as a bodyguard, man hunter and general heavy-handed thug for people that can afford me.

The man I'd been hired to track down had been leading me on a merry chase for just over three months, ever since he disappeared without a trace from a little town called Arkham near the Massachusetts coast. But, like all scumbags with closets full of skeletons, this fella didn't stay hidden for long. A month after he went missing he resurfaced in Boston, and after picking up his trail I managed to track his wanderings all through the coastal cities of New England till I finally got a-hold of his assistant in a sunny little town called Falmouth on the edge of Nantucket Sound. Not the best of leads, but a lot better than the ghosts I'd been chasing for so long.

And try not to get too mushy over the guy I just told you I beat into a pulp. Trust me, if you knew even half of the awful things he'd done with his boss you'd be egging me on to get a bit rougher with the dope.

As it was, I was a bit pissed at him anyway, mainly due to the fact that after I'd snuck into his hotel room, one of those cheap two room affairs with a bed and a kitchen in one room and a shower in the other, he'd jumped me from behind and tried wrapping his high-grade silk paisley tie around my neck. Why the idiot thought I'd just let him strangle me instead of shoving my elbow halfway into his gut I have no idea. He went down with his face all red and surprised, and I turned round to snarl at the silly little twerp. After I'd closed the door behind me, we got down to a little quiet conversation.

My would-be assassin gave up struggling soon after I booted him in the chest a couple of times. Getting the wretch up into an armchair and tied up using his pretty silk tie was accomplished quicker than I can say it.

Anyway, the reason I was whaling on this guy was because he had information my employer was desperate to find out. I was going to use any means necessary to get that information from him.

Which brings us right back to the pruning shears.

I'd already stuffed his sock in his mouth, not only to curb his screams but also to make sure he didn't bite through his tongue from the pain I was about to inflict. I indicated, mind you, mimed if you will, what I was going to do to him before I did it. I'm not a totally heartless torturer and I wanted to give him the chance of getting out of there in one piece. But when my chopping motions didn't seem to get through his thick skull I got right down to business.

Trouble and torture are my business.

Holding his left hand down against the chair arm I proceeded to dig into his pinky finger with the cheap hedge clippers I'd purchased from a hardware store. He squirmed like hell as I cut through to the bone, and me being a bit out of practice with that type of coercion I made the mistake of slowing down as I finished getting through the flesh. I succeeded in snapping through the metacarpal bone, just above the knuckle. Because I hadn't made a clean cut, the bone splintered, inflicting far more pain than I'd intended. The guy passed out on me and good God do I hate the stink of raw bone marrow.

Now nothing hinders an interrogation more than your victim blacking out on you, an unconscious man being about as much use as a dead one. With this problem in mind I wiped the blood off of my gloves and onto his jacket, and after stuffing a tissue onto his hand to stifle the blood flow I walked over to the dirty little kitchenette to get a mug of water to splash in his face.

Pissed at being unable to find a clean cup, I grabbed a dirty one from the dishes piled up in the sink, filling it to the brim before heading back to my prisoner with the intention of chucking it over his blood-soaked head.

All that accomplished was to wash away the blood dribbling from his cheeks and chin. I was about to go boil up a pan of water to see if that would work better when the guy finally awoke.

Soon after, his one good eye blinked open and as I set to work removing his ring finger the fella started spluttering behind his gag, finally looking like he wanted to talk to me. Shears still in hand, I pulled the rag down from his mouth to let him spit out the bloody white sock stuffed up there. It slipped down his shirt accompanied by a couple of shards of cracked yellow teeth. They looked a lot like almond slivers.

While he slavered and panted I pulled his head up by his greasy hair, waving the clippers threateningly before his one unswollen eye. Before he had chance to whine or beg for mercy I again asked him the question I'd been torturing him about for the last hour:

"Where the hell is Herbert West?"

3 Rude Awakening

On my first supply run into Falmouth, I saw Trevor Towers, an appleknocker I had once fought to a bloody fifteen-round draw in the prize ring. While hiding behind a shelf of canned goods, I heard him question the clerk.

"Do you know of a Herbert West who might be living around Falmouth?"

Doctor West's reaction to my news of a man inquiring about him was a bit of a shock. His already pale pallor became whiter and his eyes almost bugged out of his sockets. I knew of his concern but honestly believed it to be overblown. I mean people in medicine just don't go around offing the competition. It would play hell with the Hippocratic Oath if nothing else.

"Did that dolt at the grocer's tell your Trevor Towers anything?"

West's tone irked me and I snapped back at him. "He ain't *my* Trevor Towers. Let's get *that* straight at the outset. *You're* the one he's looking for and *no* I don't think he learned anything."

"Are you certain?" West asked, his fists clenched tightly.

"As sure as a man can be hiding out behind the canned goods."

"Where did he go when he left there?" West continued.

"Into his car and out on the road," I answered.

"And you don't know where he went?"

I looked at West in dismay. "With no car, he was sort of hard for me to track."

"Yes, a car," West replied, crestfallen. "We'll need to do something about that. There's a serviceable one in the garage but I only drive it occasionally."

"And I don't have a license if this state requires one."

"I don't think that's going to be a problem," West replied.

"There *is* something I've been wondering about," I said.

"Yes?" West asked warily.

"Before I arrived, how did you run errands without the locals being wise to your presence?"

"Oh, that," he answered, looking uncomfortable.

"Yes, that," I replied.

His face took on a faraway expression as he paused for several moments. It gave me the creeps in a strange sort of way.

"There *was* an assistant before you," West said. "He even assisted me in the laboratory and was damn near indispensable at times. He left shortly before your arrival, due to certain complications."

"What kind of complications?" I pressed. "I need to know what I'm involved in here."

"For Pete's sake, man!" he exclaimed. "It was nothing illegal if you're concerned about that."

"Then ease my mind," I replied.

West sighed. "Well, I guess you should know." West sighed, pausing to dramatically dab at his eye with a hanky like a hammy theater reject.

"Your predecessor was injured rather severely in a lab accident," West said. "He suffered extensive injuries and was sent out west so his family could be near him during the recuperative period. In light of this tragedy, you can certainly understand my prior reluctance to give you a tour of my laboratory."

"Sure, I can see your point," I answered, though I felt he was giving me a load of crap. Still, I let it drop and decided to go along with him. "So what would you like me to do next?"

"We'll continue as before, for the time being," he answered. "Keep your eyes and ears open. Perhaps nothing will come of this."

"Maybe," I agreed, though I had my doubts if Trevor Towers was involved.

The following day I was introduced to Doctor West's "service-able" automobile. After taking a gander at it, I could understand why it was kept out of sight. West's vehicle was a hearse, a beat-up 1920 Lorraine Twelve-Column carved-panel job.

"What do you think?" West asked as I walked around the meat wagon.

"It's a hearse," I said, stating the obvious.

West frowned and said, "I can see you know your automobiles."

"Sorry, Doc," I replied. "It's not my idea of discreet."

"It runs superbly," West beamed. "I inherited it from a dear friend."

"Some friend," I muttered. "You drive around in *this* and you're damn sure going to attract attention."

"I don't believe anyone in Falmouth has seen it yet."

I walked around the macabre object and suddenly stopped. "There's a goddamn coffin in the back!"

"Calm yourself," West chuckled. "It's presently empty."

"Inherited as well?" I asked.

He nodded and I clammed up about it.

"It's a stroke of genius really," West stated. "If someone ever stops you, just show them the coffin and tell them you're running late!"

"That's one hell of a stretch, Doc," I replied doubtfully.

"I just wanted you to see it," West said. "I may well take it out for a drive late tonight. I do that from time to time . . . one of my little eccentricities."

"Will you be needing me to come along?" I asked.

"No," he replied. "I would prefer you to remain at the house, especially in light of Mr. Tower's recent appearance in town."

"Whatever you say, Doctor West."

West left the house around eleven 'o-clock that evening. It was a moonless night and I thought the entire thing was pretty screwy but hey, it was *his* eccentricity. I sprawled out on the downstairs sofa and relaxed to a whangdoodle show from New York on the radio with a couple of beers. Before long, I was so drowsy that I drifted off to sleep.

Something woke me. I looked at the clock and saw it was three-thirty. West was still gone but I had the unsettling feeling that I wasn't alone. I sat upright, with the hairs rising on the back of my neck.

"Get a grip, Riley," I mumbled. "Probably just had a night-mare."

I settled for this explanation and was feeling better when a loud thud came from upstairs. As quietly as I could, I hurried to the fireplace and grabbed the poker. I hefted it in my arm and crept toward the stairs. I'm usually a light sleeper and it unnerved me to think that someone went past me and upstairs without waking me.

On a hunch, I walked to the front door and checked it. It was still locked. No one had gotten past me unless they had locked the door behind them. Another thud came from above rapidly followed by more. The hairs on my neck were standing again and I regretted not having the .38 that West kept in his possession. Deciding that I'd have to make do with the poker, I hurried up the stairs. I reached the top landing and held my breath. The silence was ominous as I stood in the dimly lit area.

I finally exhaled and that was when the thuds started again. Someone was pounding on something hard enough to wake the dead and I determined that the noise was coming from West's laboratory. Racing to the door, I stopped, realizing that the room was locked and only West had a key. "Shit," I muttered, glaring at the wooden door. Having few options, I stepped away from the door and readied myself for what was to come.

My shoulder crashed into the wooden obstacle and sent it crashing inward. I staggered after it, nearly losing my balance but managed to grab onto a steel table and steady myself.

And then someone grabbed *me.*

I yelled in surprise, instinctively pulling away from the icy grip on my wrist. Still half-blinded by the laboratory's bright lights, I blinked and tried to get my bearings. It took a few seconds for me to realize what I was seeing, as I stared at the huge fist pounding on the cold steel slab. A large naked man was restrained on the table, his face and upper body terribly scarred from what appeared to be chemical burns. His face—if you could call it that—was a ruin, a mess of burnt and fused meat. Saliva foamed from his tattered lips and an eye socket was completely covered with shiny scar tissue. The pathetic wretch's nose looked like a smashed lump of clay with only ragged slits to function as nostrils.

"Holy Christ!" I raged. "West, what the hell have you been up to??"

The thing kept pounding on the slab, causing my ears to ring. I spied the loose wrist restraint and decided to reapply it. The pounding alone was driving me crazy enough as it was. I grabbed the figure's cold arm and gagged as a layer of putrid skin sloughed off in my hands. Pushing past my own terror, I finally managed to secure the offending arm after a hell of a struggle.

I turned from the slab and found West smiling coldly at me. "You've done well," he offered. "I now expect that you would like an explanation."

I started to charge the little bastard but quickly noticed the .38 he was pointing. In his left arm he clutched a cloth-wrapped object against his chest and shoulder. I stared closely at the bundle and then lost my supper.

Clutched in West's hellish embrace was a dead child, surely no more than four or five months old!

4　　The Hellbound Heart

Have you ever loved someone so much it physically hurts when you think of them? Such an awful aching of the heart and mind that you freeze up in the agony of lost love? That's how I feel about her. Every time I see a woman who resembles her, even slightly, my heart aches for the love I once had. And trying to form a relationship with another woman has been as impossible with her as the yardstick to compare to.

We were high-school sweethearts, and engaged and married soon after our graduation. Then the war came along, and I joined up to do my bit like all the other dumb, loyal Americans. After two awful years of blood and mud and death I came back only to find that things just weren't the same between us. I wasn't the same; the war and the things I'd seen having changed me to a different man from the one she married. There was just something inside of me, something bad that her love and tenderness couldn't exorcise. Six months after that, the divorce went through.

That's life for you.

Now I know I said I didn't like talking about her, but this is relevant to the rest of my story, so hear me out.

That love I was telling you about? I never did stop feeling it. I went off the rails when she left me, losing myself in blood and violence wherever and whenever I could find it. It's like she's haunting me, see? What's made it worse is that every night, without fail, my dreams are filled with our lovemaking, our holding hands, and all the rest of that soppy stuff I don't have time for anymore. And as a man who likes to be in control of every facet of his life it's a real curse having to suffer these nightly confrontations of what can never be.

Because she's gone for good.

When she died, it was the fifth time I'd lost her. The first being when I joined up to go to war, the second and third being when we separated and divorced. Her marrying her rich bozo of a boyfriend was the fourth, and her death in a car crash a year later was the fifth. I guess you could say there was no happy ending destined for us.

Fuck destiny, my life is my own.

I lost her a sixth time after that; taken from her tomb by some evil son of a bitch. Do I need to tell you his name?

Doctor Herbert West, M.D.

Her husband was horrified, of course, possibly even more so than I. And with a lot more dough than I could make in a lifetime, and a chip on his shoulder almost as big as mine (poor little rich boy didn't like his toys taken away), he had enough cash to fling around to find out who'd taken her corpse and enough rage to want the guy stone dead.

To add insult to injury, he contacted me to find that grave-robbing son of a bitch. He'd heard rumors I was a man that could get things done. What can I say, shed loads of cash from the man that stole my woman and a chance to get even with the sleazy pervert that robbed her from her grave? I signed up, lock, stock, and smoking barrel.

Now there's something to be said for a man that would rather die than give you the information you need; something more to be said for the one who could invoke such fear in another human being.

Herbert West's assistant felt that kind of fear towards his former boss and mentor. I'd had a hell of a time getting West's whereabouts out of him, and by the time I finished, he was happy for me to end his miserable life with a bullet through the skull.

Happy to die without the fear of Herbert West coming after him.

I wish in retrospect I'd tortured that grave robbing scumbag for a little bit longer, but being a professional, I had a job to do and no time for distractions.

What he told me before I ended his pitiful existence was that West had been lying low for a while. The man had been spending time in Falmouth, but also helping out in a church mission somewhere up in Boston. This was a good enough start for me, and would you believe that before he died he begged me to burn his body? Having never witnessed such a pleading expression in another man's face, I gladly obliged him, setting the room alight before leaving quietly and hitting the fire alarm on my way out.

I still have some morals left in me after all.

My return visit to Falmouth didn't prove helpful, but having the address of the Mission had me driving to Boston that same night. Before long, I found myself driving through the city's early morning grayness, coasting along its streets in search of my destination. The place I was looking for was a dump called the Gill Street Mission of The Resurrected Father. Quite a mouthful. After driving round for an hour or so, I eventually located it through the directions of a newspaper stand setting up shop for the day.

The Mission itself looked like a closed-down clothing store, enclosed behind a pair of big, dusty, flyspecked windows with a glass door between them. Above the door was a sign reading FREE SOUP, and there was already a row of bums queuing outside—probably with a sprinkling of war veterans like me filling their ranks. Well, like me if my life had turned out a little worse, anyway.

Leaving my Ford parked down a nearby side street, I shoved past the line of human refuse and stepped inside the soup kitchen to look for the people running the joint.

The inside of the place was your typical haven for down and outs, filled with cheap metal tables and old wooden church pews for chairs. As I walked in, the stink of boiled cabbage and sweat hit my nostrils, a sour mixture that smelled like loss and despair. A few bums were already lined up at a bench set up as a soup stand, adding their mingled stenches of piss and misery to the room's rank atmosphere.

Pushing past the derelicts and receiving half-hearted threats and pokes for my trouble, I asked the man behind the bench where I could find whoever ran the place.

No such luck.

The man behind the counter, standing rigid while he mechanically poured thin, greenish soup into a chipped bowl, was the biggest guy I'd ever seen in my life. He was black, at least six foot nine, and towered over me and the other little people lurking in the soup kitchen. Now there was a big and ugly bastard, his dull expression adorned with two bullet-hole scars. One of these was embedded across his left eye and stitched in such a manner that the upper eyelid was permanently pulled down over the lower. The other scar formed a gouge in the center of his dark forehead. How anyone could survive such injuries and function was completely beyond me.

His prizefighter arms, each as wide as my head, were knotted tree trunks. I could tell by the knuckles on his huge scarred hands that he'd been a boxer at some point in his life.

Asking who ran the place, and if he'd ever heard of West, evinced no response from his big expressionless face. Whether he was deaf, reticent, or just a bit backwards I had no idea. So I just stood there, like a moron, until one of the bums being served paid enough attention to my plight to help me.

The guy, his face pockmarked and dirty, flashed me a genuine smile, and spoke in a mellow Irish accent.

"It's the Fadder you want," his smile widening to reveal chipped brown teeth, "Fadder Murphy's up the stairs."

The polite, disheveled Irishman then pointed towards a wide staircase at the rear of the room, a staircase that had probably looked regal once upon a time, before the dust and the woodworms took over. I thanked him and left the soup stand, and saw the place steadily filling up with bums of all creeds, colors, and sizes as I climbed the stairs. Apparently, everyone is equal at the bottom.

As I'd suspected, the building had been a clothing store in its more prosperous past. The cavernous upstairs room was filled with empty clothing racks, naked mannequins, and other miscellaneous trash.

"Hello . . . Father Murphy?" I said, clearing my throat within the congealed atmosphere of dust and decrepitude. Silence greeted me from the maze of junk and plaster bodies, and after twiddling my thumbs for a minute, I was about to give up when a noise to my right made me turn around.

"Over here," the voice said, a strong Texas accent betraying the small-framed man who hopped towards me. Father Murphy hobbled forward, in his black outfit and white collar, a crutch tucked under his right arm. His right leg was missing above the knee. "So what can I do for someone so obviously not in need of soup?"

The small, thin, gray-haired man was unshaven, with bright blue, intelligent eyes. He approached me with a smile on his face and joviality in his voice.

"Sorry, young man, I was just in the john. I have a bit of trouble sometimes." He indicated his trouble by banging the base of his crutch heavily on the floor.

"I'm here about a doctor that used to work here, a Doctor West, do you know him?"

As soon as I spoke the bastard's name, the Father hobbled closer, raising dust from the floorboards as he slammed his crutch down again, the sound vibrating through the floor. When he got closer I noticed a strange smell about him, an odor like mold and something I couldn't quite put my finger on.

"Looking for the good doctor, are we?" he said, nodding his head in smiling contemplation, "a fine man and a great aid in the Lord's work."

"I was told that if I came here, I might find out where he is." I was starting to feel a little creeped out by the way he stared at me.

"You should be careful what you wish for, my son," the Father replied, and backed away without elaborating.

A second later a pair of huge, thick-fingered hands wrapped around my throat. They lifted me up, making my feet dangle about a foot over the floor. It didn't take a genius to realize the Father had used his crutch to signal the prizefighter downstairs. But me, I was too dumb to realize it until I felt his big brown paws throttling me. As I hung there choking, struggling uselessly to free myself from the iron grip, the last thing I saw was the holy man limping off through the mannequins. From the corner of my eye, I noticed that the back of his head was caved in as if from massive blunt force trauma. Then, everything went black.

I don't need to tell you who I dreamed of while unconscious.

5   The Errand

I stared into the barrel of West's revolver and realized that I had been duped. West was not at all what he claimed to be and I should've known that his job offer had been too good to be true. God knows what I'd gotten myself into.

"So do you shoot me now?" I asked, trying to remain as calm as possible.

"You *could* help me *dead*," he answered, "but you're much more valuable alive."

I frowned. "What makes you think I'll help you?"

"Do you wish to end up like him?" West chuckled, gesturing toward the figure strapped to the steel slab.

I stared in horror at the pathetic creature and then turned to West. "Was that your previous assistant?"

He shook his head and smiled. "No. That was a squeamish little fellow that upped and vanished. *I'll find him, though.*"

"Then what's the dead kid for, you sick bastard?"

"Raw materials," he answered. "You'll need to accustom yourself to such things."

I glared at West in silence, trying to find a way out of this nightmare. Nothing feasible came to mind at the time.

"This is quite a shock to you," West said. "You're currently at a loss as to how to proceed but soon you'll begin to get ideas. If *anything* should happen to me, I've made arrangements with an associate to release certain papers of mine. These papers implicate you in my endeavors and will result in your incarceration. So, it is in your best interest to ensure that nothing unfortunate happens to me."

I spat on the floor. "Blackmail, Doc? That's low, even for you."

"Spare me the clichés," West replied. "Just be certain that you understand your situation."

"Oh, I understand all right," I answered. "Just remember, West, that every dog has his day."

"Not for a long time," said West, lowering the pistol. "Now get over here and take this cadaver off my hands. In the corner you'll find a refrigeration tank. Undress her, drop her in, and lower the lid."

I felt sick to my stomach but did as West demanded. For all my threats, I was really over the barrel and had little choice but to follow orders until I could somehow get the drop on him.

I slept poorly after that and kicked the sweat-stained sheet off me. Relieved that I had escaped some pretty bad dreams, my stomach clenched up when I remembered that nightmares were the least of my problems.

West had laid out the facts the night before and given me my marching orders. I was to follow his instructions without question and if things went well he would release me from his service after a few months. I found his assurances hard to swallow, thinking of his former assistant and what had become of him. I longed to strangle the perverted little bastard but needed to protect myself in the process. I only half believed that an associate was prepared to implicate me if something happened to the good doctor but wasn't prepared to take any chances.

After getting dressed, I went to the kitchen and made coffee. West wasn't around—apparently still in bed after the late night—but I still didn't have much of an appetite. Still, I needed the caffeine for the task ahead. West had a big job for me. A job that I dreaded.

It seems that West, from one of his mysterious associates, had received word that Trevor Towers was in the Boston area asking questions about his whereabouts. My job was to find Towers, subdue him and bring him to West. That would be easier said than done. I wasn't afraid of Towers but the guy was a tough bastard when it came down to a fight. I would have to become as ruthless as he if West's plan had any hope for success.

I downed the mug of coffee in one gulp, sighed, and mentally reviewed my plan of action. I was to drive the Lorraine to Boston, go to an address West had given me, and talk to a man named Father Murphy. I had really been a dope to get involved with West and hoped to God I'd be free of him the first chance I got. Maybe I could stumble across some useful information on my trip to Boston.

My drive to Boston was uneventful and I found the address West had given to me with little difficulty. As soon as I was in town, I stopped over for a quick visit to get a gun off a shady jailbird I used to know. A few minutes later I discovered that Towers was already in the clutches of West's associates and all that remained was for me to transport him back to Falmouth. Towers was unconscious when I saw him and looking pretty much the worse for wear. I wasn't surprised in the least after taking a look at the ugly mugs who accompanied Towers with me on the return trip.

I had managed to get myself in a hell of a bind but it seemed a minor matter compared to what was probably in store for Towers. I was damned glad to not be in *his* shoes. My only plan was to keep my fingers crossed and hope that an opportunity would arise for me to help him before it got any worse. I had no doubt that things would *definitely* get worse.

6   Ties That Bind

There's no greater cliché for a man in my line of work than waking up in the clutches of the guy he's been hired to catch. That was the scenario I found myself in when I awoke, minutes, hours, or days after the nap the black man and his one-legged friend had sent me to, and like hell could I do anything about it.

I'd been through worse; at least this time, tied to a chair in an unknown room, I wasn't surrounded by sour-faced Huns. Seeing the pure look of evil in the eyes of the man sitting across from me stopped that from being much of consolation, though.

Small, thin and blonde, I recognized him as none other than Herbert West. He stared at me like a predator from behind the large, thick lenses of his spectacles. If it hadn't been for the red smears on his lab coat and the abattoir he called a lab behind him, he could have almost passed for a real doctor. He even had a clipboard and stethoscope, for God's sake.

The whitewashed walls around us were covered with anatomical diagrams pinned alongside yellowing page fragments covered in writing that looked like Arabic. Below these were shelves full of test tubes and beakers, jury-rigged together with orange rubber hoses. Specimen jars filled the shelves to the brim, the one closest to me containing a pair of pale, dainty feet flaking apart in some clear fluid. Another held dozens of human eyeballs, bunched together like grapes.

Two metal tables, located roughly at the center of the room, stood behind West's seat, their contents hidden by brown-stained sheets. Of all the things it could or should've smelled of, the room was filled with the stench of overdone bacon. Of course, I wasn't alone with the good doctor. The one-legged padre and his big black friend were also present, blocking the only exit, standing guard like dead-eyed automatons. Whatever pretense of normality they'd had at the Mission was gone. I briefly wondered whether the winos were missing their soup.

As West had been watching me for some time, I decided to drop the act that I was still asleep and began to tug at my bonds. Naturally, my chair was bolted to the floor and the ropes were tied tighter than a mosquito's ass. From the expression covering his nasty little face it looked like West was enjoying my predicament, so I stopped struggling and settled for just swearing my head off at him.

"You dirty little tow-headed cock gobbler," was the best insult I could think of on the fly, before I started rambling on about his whore of a mother.

When I was finally good and hoarse, West cleared his throat and began reading from his clipboard.

"Mr. Trevor Towers" he said in a quiet, mellow tone, "ex-husband to Mrs. Jayne Towers . . . or should that be Mrs. Jayne Smith?" he grinned a mouthful of tiny white teeth at me, as I choked on my own bile.

"You're nothing but a croaker, you creepy little toad." I spat this out with more anger and venom than I'd used in a long while.

West finally rewarded me with a reaction, smacking me violently across the face with his clipboard. It was worth knowing I'd actually riled the little freak, even if it did cost me a loose tooth and a mouthful of blood.

"What else would you call a grave-robbing monster?" I sputtered through split lips, steeling myself for another clipboard slap. I was surprised when all he did was stand up from his chair. He then turned towards the metal bench before addressing me again.

"I can see how an illiterate snoop like you would think that, especially with his lost love involved."

I took a slow deep breath at this attempt to rile me, staring daggers into his back as he reached over to retrieve a small metal case from the edge of the bench.

"Would you believe she was one of my greatest successes?" he said while removing a weathered hypo from the case, checking its needle in the light from the fixture above. "Far more successful than even these fine specimens," he turned and indicated the two guarding the door, as expressionless and unmoving as when I'd first awoken. "They do as I say because they think I'm their god."

I barked out a laugh, eliciting a grin from him as he continued.

"I brought her back to life and you think I'm a monster? She's out of the dirt and under the sun thanks to me."

Breaking off from my mental image of flicking his head off like a fly, I told him what I thought of his statement.

"You really are one delusional turd," I sneered.

Leaving the bench to approach my chair, West halted just a foot away, rolling up his sleeve to reveal a pale skinny arm dotted with needle marks.

"I used to have to make my elixir of life in a test tube, you know."

He jammed the needle into his arm, filling it with blood from one of his broken veins. The black color disgusted me: it flowed into the tube thicker than tar. West then withdrew the needle, waving it in my face. Pleased at the way I recoiled in disgust, he said, "But the times have changed and so have I."

Crazy little Doctor West then spun round on his heels, his sleeve slipping down as he strode towards the metal bench. He tore away its brown burlap sheet with a theatrical flourish. What he revealed beneath that dirty sheet was a half-immolated corpse as black as an overdone sausage. At least I knew where the smell of smoked pork was coming from.

The worst thing though, was that from the burned features on the dead man's face, it was obvious it was the guy I'd snuffed while searching for West. I felt like gagging when he reached over to touch the thing.

"You're a war veteran, yes?" he said while picking up the dead man's right arm, one-handedly testing the flexibility of the shriv-eled limb with the syringe still clasped in the other.

"You've done your homework, pecker-head," I replied. I was start-ing to wonder how long he was planning to let the theatrics drag on.

"Well, I'm a war veteran too," he said, "so I know what death means. I know that it is as unnatural and vile as what you did to this man here."

The little croaker then jabbed the syringe into the corpse's fore-arm, pressing down on the plunger till he'd emptied the filthy fluid into the cadaver.

"His name was Dan Kane by the way; a good assistant albeit with too delicate a stomach for our work. He ran away from me but I knew I'd get him back sooner or later. Before long, we'll have our little reunion."

I didn't believe any of his crap-talk about resurrection, but that didn't mean I wasn't going to try and escape his crazy clutches as soon as I was able. So when he began poking around the corpse's chest with his stethoscope I used the distraction to try and free myself from the ropes around my wrists. It was while the doctor was looking for the corpse's heartbeat that I found the small pen-knife tucked up beneath my watchstrap.

Not knowing or really caring how it'd got there I turned my gaze firmly from the gift horse's mouth and quickly began nego-tiating the little knife into my fingers. With that accomplished, I went to work on the ropes binding my wrists.

7   All Hell Breaks Loose

I knew I needed to get out of lookout duty and inside the lab, if Towers was to survive his meeting with West. My presence wouldn't guarantee anything but I wasn't going to sit idly by while West violated all laws of decency in his alleged pursuit of knowl-edge. If I had to get locked up again for that, then so be it.

Entering the house, I made my way upstairs and silently en-tered the lab. West and his associates had Towers restrained and a hideously charred figure was on the slab, with what I assumed was West's other monster under its tarp nearby.

The stench of burnt meat permeated the room and I stifled a gag as West went about checking for the burned corpse's heartbeat with his stethoscope.

"Guess you flunked cooking school too, huh?" I asked sarcas-tically.

"Barnes, you're supposed to be outside!" West barked.

I smiled. "Had to take a leak."

"And you couldn't find a suitable spot outside?"

"Well," I replied. "But that would be so uncivilized. Besides, no-one is interested in what's going on in here."

I saw Towers glaring at me and caught the flicker of recognition in his hate-filled eyes. "Hey, I know that bird," I said. "In fact I owe him."

Before West could respond, I walked over to Towers, bent over and backhanded him with a loud slap while mouthing the words, "I'm on your side."

Towers responded to my slap by spitting in my face. I laughed and turned to West. "Somebody did a piss-poor job of tying him."

West frowned at Father Murphy but before he could speak I said, "I'll take care of it."

Reaching behind Towers, I grabbed the penknife with which he'd been sawing at his bonds, the penknife I myself had hidden on him earlier, and began cutting through the rope while I pretended to tighten his restraints.

"There, West," I said with satisfaction. "Even a pipsqueak like you should be able to handle him now."

Then the charred corpse started screaming, a strangled, hoarse sound that had me and Towers sharing a horrified look. Then I yelled, "You damned maniac!"

"You're not squeamish, are you?" West asked, before turning back to the reanimated corpse. "Let me remove what remains of his tongue."

"I'm outta this madness," I replied. "I'm going back outside."

I walked toward the door, turned and pulled out the Browning I'd stashed away on my visit to Boston. "Time for your nightcap, you corpse-loving bastard!"

West leapt to the other side of the room. I would've nailed him easily if the esteemed Father Murphy hadn't leapt faster than greased lightning and grabbed my arm as I pulled the trigger. My bullet missed its target but grazed the shoulder of Towers who let out a string of curses that would have impressed Satan himself.

"Son of a bitch!" I screamed, turning my weapon on Murphy. I fired three quick rounds into his chest and a fourth that took off the top of his head and sent him reeling against the wall, trailing gore in his wake. During this melee, West leaped back, reaching for his own gun. Losing his balance, he careened into the metal cylinder in which I had placed the little girl's corpse. It crashed against the floor with a loud clang and the top went rolling across the room. To my horror, I saw the small corpse scuttle out of its container and make a beeline for West.

"Damn you, Barnes!" West railed, struggling to his feet. He finally managed to get a grip on his pistol and was proceeding to turn it on me when the reanimated child sank her unnaturally developed teeth into his thigh, causing him to drop the firearm.

West screamed again as the corpse child climbed up to his throat and tore at his jugular with a single bite. Blood sprayed all around as he struggled with his attacker. I was pleased to see Towers grab the fallen gun and then stunned as he aimed it at *me!*

"You ungrateful asshole!" I yelled.

Then Murphy's hulking black companion finally entered the fray. He nearly ripped my arm off as he grabbed it and slung me across the room. Thank God for unintentional allies! Towers' shot buried itself in the wall behind where my head had been moments earlier.

I somehow managed to hold on to my own weapon despite the force of the impact. I struggled to gather my wits about me amid the gunfire, screaming and general confusion. I had only one chance to escape the carnage alive. I could only pray that Trevor Towers came to his senses and realized that we must join forces. It was a slim chance at best.

8   Things Get Worse

I'd like to say I'd been in worse predicaments by that point, but that'd be a barefaced lie. I knew it, the screeching corpse I'd incinerated a few days earlier knew it, and the rest of the motley crew that had joined in on the bloody brawl probably knew it too. All except for the creepy little zombie creature chewing down on West's throat; she was too intent on trying to tear the bastard's head off to pay attention to anything else going on around her.

My mind shifted away from the carnage, to the familiar stink of gunpowder and the sounds of gunfire filling my ears. The only consolation was that the gun I'd nicked from West felt good in my hand. My shoulder hurt like hell from where West's bozo, a man I recognized as an old ring partner, Riley Barnes, had shot me. Wait, *was* he on my side? He sure shot the priest quick enough. Who the hell cares?

So I did what I always do in that kind of situation: shoot first and ask questions later.

Arkham Nights

My first bullet missed Barnes as the black bastard crashed into him. After that beefy monster had tossed him like a rag doll and he'd disappeared behind a table I decided to try and peg West as he danced about with his tiny new friend digging into his throat. The problem was, him whirling like a crazy dervish and spraying that black shit he had for blood as he went, made him harder to hit than a camel in a sandstorm. I noticed briefly that West's surviving guard was kneeling down beside Murphy and shaking him wildly, his huge dark shoulders sticking up like burial mounds. I hoped he wouldn't be waking the Father up anytime soon, but with West around I wouldn't bet on it. Thank God the ringing in my ears had dampened the noise the burned fella was making, still twisting and turning on the autopsy table.

As the jars of mysterious chemicals that'd been perched on the shelves were now smashed on the floor and mixed with West's blood, securing good footing was becoming difficult. And just as I managed to get a bead on the doctor's skinny chest I banged my knee on something hard and metallic and missed him by a mile. Instead of taking West down I only succeeded in blowing away the creature that would've killed him if I'd have left her to it. Now she was just a splattered memory on the lab wall.

"God, Christ, dammit!" I yelped, then reached down to pull out whatever was jabbing my knee. It was something out of West's medical kit, a pair of shiny steel calipers embedded over an inch into my flesh. I tugged the damn things out of me and lined up my sights, when I suddenly felt a bullet zip past my ear followed by a loud hiss from behind me. Then I saw Barnes across the room waving and shouting. If it wasn't for the ringing in my ears, I'd swear he was trying to warn me.

Doctor West was gesturing at me too, laughing giddily. I was about to take my shot when he fell to his knees with a smoking hole in his chest. The wall behind him was spattered with black and yellow goo, his own twisted insides joining the mess.

Seemed like Barnes was a better shot than I was after all.

Realizing finally that West's assistant was on the level came as no solace. Something big exploded behind me, peppering my back with white-hot chunks of shrapnel and setting my hair on fire. How I escaped the explosion in one piece I have no idea, but as the wall at my rear became a blazing sheet of fire I began crawling on my hands and knees towards the exit, dragging surgical scalpels, tools, and West's black blood under me.

The room was choked with smoke and the flames lapped at my

ass by the time I reached the door, one aching eternity later. Turning round I spied West through the black clouds; he was on his knees, juddering like an erratic jack-in-the-box as the fire engulfed his prone form. At least my hearing had returned in time for me to realize the guy on the table had stopped his yammering. I found Murphy next to me as dead as Dillinger, his face and chest burning and adding more fumes to the already eye-watering smoke. I was about to take aim to finally finish West off when another explosion sent me scurrying away with my clothes on fire, like a fleeing rat.

As I tumbled down the stairs, I saw my savior Barnes was nowhere to be found, so I had no chance to thank him as I doused the flames burning my head and backside up. God only knows where the big guy with the lovely scars had disappeared to either; maybe he'd gone to buy flowers for Father Murphy's grave. Reaching the ground floor with my best suit a singed mess I hoped sincerely that West himself had departed to whatever kind of hell was reserved for croakers like him.

Running from West's collapsing house, I paused once to look back, wondering whether or not the doctor had well and truly gone.

If I'd seen him being torn to shreds from a yard away I'd still have my doubts that evil creep was really dead. When more explosions wracked the top floor and the windows burst asunder I hoped the greasy black flames billowing up to the sky contained at least a little residue from his disintegrating corpse.

I then wondered, soot-stained, bleeding and burned as I was, where I could find the nearest, cheapest bar. God, I could go for some brown.

Epilogue 1: The Girl Hunter

I've never claimed to be an optimist, but have always been the kind of dog that's willing to learn new tricks. And two days after the 'incident' involving West I went to visit my employer, informing him that the guy who'd robbed Jayne from her grave was gone and he could finally put his mind to rest. I then tore his check up in his face and broke his jaw for good measure.

I don't think either of us saw that coming.

Just like I'd not foreseen the possibility of my ex-wife coming back from the dead. But what good old Doctor West had done with the corpse in his laboratory had been a real eye opener, and if there was a chance of seeing her again I'd take it.

That's optimism for you; even though I know it'll take a lot more than West's creepy resurrection formula to win her back to me.

So, with my car retrieved from the impound lot in Boston, my hair trimmed down to a buzz-cut to conceal the singes, and me wearing a brand new suit, I started my journey with more than enough bullets to deal with any unfortunate incidents that might come my way. Even now, after a month of dead ends and false leads, I'm still hunting for her, running down across my list of next of kin and old acquaintances.

As long as there's hope I'm going to keep on searching, and woe betide anyone who gets in my way.

Epilogue 2: An Uneasy Reprieve

I regained consciousness and cursed loudly as the pain of a twisted ankle shot through me. I vaguely remembered halfway choking to death on smoke and chemical fumes in West's lab and making a split second decision to get the hell out through the second-floor window. When I came to, I felt heat and realized that the house was being consumed by fire.

An explosion thundered from inside as I struggled to my feet and limped away. I looked over my shoulder but saw no sign of Towers, West, or his demented associates. My primary focus was to put as much distance between myself and the entire burning mess. I didn't fancy a return to prison and there was no way I could make anyone believe what had occurred in that house of horror.

I'm now working on the Frisco docks and say a silent prayer every night that West was lying about implicating me in his twisted schemes. I hope that the bastard is good and truly dead but I saw too many things while in his employ to rest easy on that score. It's hell going through life looking over your shoulder but it's a damn sight better than being dead. Or undead.

Still, it sort of eats away at me, knowing that he might still be somewhere out there and in a position to blackmail me. *That* doesn't sit well with me and I know it's only a matter of time until I pull up stakes and go looking for the little bastard. He better hope like Hell that I don't find him because he's got a *lot* to answer for. I'm usually an easygoing sonofabitch but there *are* things to be said for the Trevor Towers approach to dealing with problems; not a whole lot of good things, but they get the job done.

Big Boss

Like most stories in my life, it starts with a corpse. Except I hadn't done the deed this time . . . not entirely. You see, the low-lid that'd been sent to snuff me made the second major mistake of knocking on my apartment door. His first mistake was making far too much noise as he walked down the corridor to my room.

Also, he'd been dead once already; a zombie, if you will.

I'd been watching him through the peephole as he approached my door, holding a shotgun one-handed like the stone-cold, hard man he thought he was.

When he knocked, I edged myself to the side of the door, and pretended like I was fumbling around with the lock, just long enough to make him think I was behind it. A second later, he booted his way into the apartment, waving that cannon of his around, all locked and loaded. I noticed that his pasty-faced nose was dripping snot thick with cocaine.

A dope zombie, if you will.

I lingered just long enough for him to take me in before sticking my butterfly knife hilt-deep into his eye.

My would-be killer fell flat on his face, killed outright as the impact forced the knife up into his brain. He still danced that awful death jig, leaving an ugly stain on the carpet. No way I was getting my security bond back now, or my knife, for that matter.

My name is Trevor Towers; I'm a war veteran and all-round son of a bitch and I'd spent the past week in that hotel trying to get a bead on Arkham's resident gangster, the man called 'Big Boss.'

Once my companion was good and still, I flipped his coke-snorting body onto its back and did a little poking of my own. I first broke his shotgun open and let the shells clatter all over the hardwood floor. After tearing his jacket and shirt open, I found a litter of bullet holes across his chest, most of them mortal. They looked way past raw and had scarred something fierce.

This knuckle-dragger had been one of Big Boss's boys, dragged out of the ground to bump me off just before I sent him right back to Hell. I started shifting through his pockets for some kind of identification or a clue that might get me closer to Big Boss, when a dark form blocked the doorway.

It was just the hotel's landlord, in all his shirtless glory, with a half-full colostomy bag strapped to his chest. He didn't even blink twice as he caught me in the act of pillaging a fresh corpse.

"Dawh won't be fixed till tomorrah," he said, in his thick southern drawl and then trudged down the hall.

Right then, I was certain that discretion was the better part of valor, and decided that I had better make a quick exit from his building. After all, someone *had* told the dead thug my room number.

I packed my meager belongings and was out of my room and down that rattrap's stairs in three minutes flat. I paid the rent for the entire week plus something extra to cover for my broken 'dawh.' The flour-lover at the desk gave me that vamp wink, which offered me a quick romp behind the counter for just a couple extra dollars.

I let her down as gently as I could. She didn't take it half as well as I'd thought, so I left the hotel with her snarling some pretty imaginative abuses behind me.

The dump I'd been staying in was on French Hill, one of the older parts of Arkham—once a crumbling little town that was slowly but surely pulling itself out of oblivion and growing into a city.

Before I came to town almost every gambling den, brothel, and speakeasy had been taken over by Big Boss in a quick and bloody coup. He hit them so hard and fast that it shook the entire underworld. Word on the street was, many of the men the Boss had had bumped off were soon seen walking around with the rest of his crew.

You'd have to be off your nuts to buy that tall tale. Then again, the trail I'd been on—tracking down my ex-wife and love of my life—had gone completely cold. And believe it or not, she, like the bimbo I'd left in my room, had also been dead, before the good doctor Herbert West brought her back to life. Of course, the quack was dead; I and one of his disgruntled henchmen saw to that. But *she* was still out there somewhere and leaning on her friends and acquaintances had got me nowhere.

So when I heard about Big Boss and his supposed army of men back from the dead, I just had to check it out. Maybe there was some kind of link between him and Herbert West's only successful experiment: the one woman I'd never forget. My Jayne.

If I wanted to get some answers, I had to get to Big Boss.

He was a slippery little eel, out of sight and apparently out of reach. The only place I could find him would be Arkham, where he oversaw the bootlegging operations for the region. It was as good a lead as any.

On my first crack at him, I tried to join his gang as muscle. I was turned away at the door, despite my glowing credentials and impressive background. Then again, who could blame him: why waste your dough on living, breathing rubes, when you could just bring all your deadbeat, dope-headed futzes back to life for free?

For my next attempt I decided to piss him off so much that he'd come and find me. I started by hanging around the bars in Arkham and badmouthing him and his crew. I figured that he'd be angry enough to break cover sooner or later. Sending out feelers and being loud around the right people in certain juice joints had obviously paid off.

I finally had the sap's attention.

I had only been back on the East Coast a few days when I caught a glimpse of Trevor Towers. His stone-hard mug brought a flood of bad memories running back and I cursed the day I'd lollygagged myself into leaving my job in Frisco.

The last time I'd seen Towers, he had taken a pot shot at me shortly before the explosion that nearly cost both our lives. To this day, I can't be sure if he ever figured out who I was. I wasn't looking forward to bumping into him again; the man was a tough mug and bad news all around. I once slugged it out with him to a fifteen-round draw in the prize ring and right then and there I knew that there had to be smarter ways to make a living. I had been in an Arkham gin mill—celebrating the job offer I'd gotten from a private dick named Wade Kearney—when I saw Towers lounging at the bar. He must have come in when I had staggered into the men's room to make room for more beer. Slipping past him, I made my way to the exit and disappeared into the foggy streets of Arkham, eventually finding my way to the rat-trap I'd been staying in.

Arkham Nights

What the hell is he doing in Arkham? I wondered, flopping down on the halfway clean bedspread. The man had gotten in a hell of a lather over Herbert West, the quack I mentioned earlier. Hopefully, Towers had calmed down some, since West got blown to smithereens. I sure wasn't losing too much sleep over it, aside from the occasional nightmare of his ever-smoldering corpse coming after me. But who the hell has time for bogeymen, when you're knee deep in witch-haunted Arkham?

"Witch-haunted my ass," I mumbled, as I rummaged for a bottle.

I'd asked Kearney about it. He was more than happy to oblige with an explanation.

"Hey," he'd answered, "It's great public relations. Do you know how many Dumb Doras flock to a place like this, looking for ghosts and ghoulies and two-bit horror?"

What the hell for? Hell, the real world was bad enough without trying to dig up something worse. It was only much later that I learned that Kearney was feeding me a whole lot of bull. If his cases were anything to go by, he'd had his fill of things that went bump in the night. Enough to fill a book, maybe.

I took a swig of the bottled panther piss and winced. Kearney had found me through a mutual friend back from our time in the service, who'd put in a good enough word when the dick dug up my checkered past. He had given me an advance on my salary and a few days to get used to the town before getting on to the real legwork. Kearney had also seen my bout with Towers a few years earlier so he knew I wouldn't go yellow on him if the going got tough.

I couldn't help but laugh. How ironic, that the bruiser I wanted to have nothing to do with had helped to get me this job. I wasn't scared of Towers but I'd damn sure avoid a rematch, unless there was some dough to be made.

After my encounter with Big Boss's zombie goon I moved right into the next flea-pit motel. It was a place on Crane Street, set between Miskatonic University, Hangman's Hill and the hospital. Now there was one hell of a view. Atop Hangman's Hill, directly facing my window, stood a dilapidated little graveyard. I suppose that if I was a local I could've lived out my days in Arkham without ever having to step out of my neighborhood. Then again, this dead-end town seemed to work out pretty well, if the locals were anything to go by.

After settling into my new place, I decided I would continue kicking at the hornet's nest in every nearby speakeasy, making sure I kept well away from the prom-trotter or Mick joints. The bars that sold the cheapest, crummiest coffin varnish were the ones I'd shoot my mouth off in, letting anyone that'd listen know that I'd just whacked one of Big Boss' dumbest, hardest boys and if the man took issue to that, he should take it up with me.

Was that the most hair-brained scheme I've ever come up with? Yes. Did I want to get a lead on Jayne even if it killed me?

Yes. A thousand times, yes.

I slept in late after my first night in town. It wasn't something I did often. I decided that I could get used to this life of idle luxury, if I ever made it. Pull the other one while you're at it! After a hot shower and a shave, I left my place on Crane Street, sauntered past the Miskatonic campus and ate breakfast at a diner on Church Street. The cook could fix up a mean plate of bacon and eggs but the dame behind the counter was a textbook chunk of lead. She weighed about two-fifty, with buck teeth up to here. Prison doesn't quite rub out all your standards. I polished my plate and left a generous tip on the counter to make up for disappointing the doll. She took a gander at the tip and gave me a grin all teeth and gums. I decided it might be best to find another eatery, just in case.

The morning fog was beginning to lift as I retraced my steps and casually made my way down to West and Saltonstall Streets. I decided to drop in on my new boss and see if he had any work for me. I went up to the battered desk, but there was no one in the small waiting area. I approached Kearney's office door, peeked through the frosted glass panel and knocked.

"It's open!" he growled.

Someone woke up in the wrong side of the bed.

I entered his office, grinning like a moron.

"Morning, Barnes," he said, looking up. "Have a seat."

I parked my keister in a poorly upholstered chair and took out a pack of smokes.

"Your head cold?" Kearney asked.

"Sorry, boss," I said, removing my hat.

"Never mind," he laughed. "You look better with it on."

I lit up a gasper and took a long drag.

"I was in the neighborhood and thought I'd drop by. Just in case you needed me."

"What I need is sleep," he replied. "That and a miracle cure to this hangover from hell."

"One of *those* nights, huh?"

"Yeah," he said. "I was paid to baby-sit some college dewdropper by his rich daddy. The kid's off to Europe to see the sights before next semester and 'Pop' wanted to make sure he didn't miss his boat this morning . . . or pass out and drown in the Miskatonic."

"Sounds like a barrel of laughs."

"Oh, yeah," he said, voice dripping with sarcasm. "Between groping barmaids, he and his pals tried to impress me with their wit and erudition. If I never hear another debate about the Platonic ideal it'll be too soon."

"The what?" I asked.

"Never mind."

"So you're copasetic?" I asked. "I'll be around if you need me."

"No," Kearney replied, lighting a gasper of his own. "There's nothing doing right now and I plan to go home and count sheep. I know where you're staying if something important comes up before Monday. Still, I appreciate you asking."

"It's nothing," I said. "I appreciate you giving an ex-con a break."

He waved me off, saying "Forget it. You got a raw deal. It's the least I could do."

"Well, see you Monday," I said, getting up to leave.

I was almost to the door when Kearney laughed and said, "Get *this*. While gallivanting around last night I happened to see the old big six himself, Trevor Towers."

"Really?" I asked, feigning ignorance. "Imagine that."

Kearney cleared his throat. "I don't know if you two are getting along or not but . . ."

"Not exactly," I interrupted.

"That's too bad," he said, shaking his head. "He's going to need a friend if he keeps shooting his mouth off the way he's been doing since hitting town."

"What do you mean?" I asked.

"He's pissing off the wrong people," Kearney answered. "Arkham only *seems* all nice and boring but underneath, it's just as rotten as any other place. I know he's got a reputation for being a tough guy but he may be getting in over his head with the local dirt-bags."

I shrugged. "I'd be happy to tell him but I don't think he'd listen."

"Understood," said Kearney. "Just wanted you to know in case he was a pal of yours."

I thanked him and left the dingy office. Kearney had given me a lot of bad things to mull over.

I spent most of that day taking in the sights. Arkham was a small town going through a city's growing pains. This had its advantages but also brought with it a share of the problems that ate away at most cities. A growing economy meant good kale for the average Joe but also attracted the low-lifes like moths to a flame.

With Towers being his usual charming self, I knew that warning him would be a wasted effort. I didn't have any desire to step in *that* particular cow flop and didn't owe him anyway. Whatever shit-storm he managed to stir up would be one of his own making.

Pushing the thought from my mind, I went looking for a place to eat. I found a small café and filled up on clam chowder and home-baked bread. Fortunately the waitress was a choice bit of calico and had high enough standards not to settle for a mushy-faced ex-boxer like myself. This meant I could eat here as much as I liked, without having to worry about any necking cashiers.

After leaving the café, I stopped at a newsstand and grabbed the latest issue of *Weird Western Tales*. I was a sucker for pulp magazines and this one contained a story by the inimitable Josh Reynolds. I paid for the magazine and thumbed through it as I walked back to my hotel. "Warriors From the Nether Depths"; now there was a winner!

I soon arrived at my new *Home Sweet Home* and made my way upstairs. I poured three fingers of white lightning and stretched out on the unmade bed. In spite of Reynolds' fever-heat prose, I soon nodded off and slept until dark. I woke from a terrible nightmare, where 'Big Bertha' had me tied naked to a bed. She did 'coochie-coo' noises as she came closer, dressed in nothing but a pair of brass knuckles.

I once heard that there was a god of dreams, fella by the name of Morpheus. I made sure to remember to kick his ass if I ever came across the goof. Rubbing the sleep from my eyes, I put on a clean shirt and headed out to check up on the Arkham nightlife.

Arkham Nights

A joint called Ciro's looked interesting so I went inside and found a small table in the corner. Eventually a hard-looking blonde took my order and before long I was enjoying one of Milwaukee's best natural resources. A raggedy jazz band was getting down as hard as it could for the sake of the deadbeat early patrons. I was beginning to question my choice of speakeasies. Just as the last of the patrons were getting fed up with the band's birdbrained racket, they decided to take a break.

I decided to enjoy another brew in silence and caught bits from conversation from a nearby table. Three tough-looking birds were throwing back drinks and laughing.

"The palooka *actually* thinks he can take on Big Boss. Can you imagine the balls on that guy?" The largest bimbo of the three asked.

A baby-faced punk, hard at work trying to make himself older than he looked, spoke up. "That's not *balls*," he said. "That's a death wish."

The third man smiled. "I hear he's gonna have his hash handed to him later tonight. Big Boss can't abide by that trash talk. The Miskatonic's gonna have another tenant before morning."

It didn't take a genius to figure out who they were talking about. It sure looked like the shit-storm was forming and I couldn't help but wonder how Trevor Towers planned to survive it. The man had serious balls, but I doubt he ever harbored a death wish. Feeling sort of bad for the sap, I visited a couple more juice joints before winding my way back to Crane Street.

The night after I settled into my new digs, I found myself sat in a nondescript juice joint across the docks, talking to some old rat-faced drunkard called Brown Jenkin. A queer old duck, what with his shock of white hair and skinny little face; he was friendly enough but I knew, just by the glint in his eye, that he would sell me out in a second flat. I bought him drinks and he nibbled pretzels like a rodent, taking in every word I said about Big Boss and his crew. When I'd said my piece, I let Brown get a couple of words in, before a couple of toughs stepped into the bar to retrieve a small brown parcel from under the counter.

As they were turning to leave, my new best bum friend made up some excuse and walked up to meet them.

I couldn't make out the words or see their looks in the juice joint's light, but I got the gist of it: I'd struck a nerve with some-one important. If all went well, I'd be having a chat with Big Boss himself.

When they were out of there, I let myself loose, to sink into the muck along with the other lowlifes and drank to my lost love.

"To better days" I muttered. No one replied.

I sat there until last orders came and went, switching rotgut for snort, until I was well and truly hammered by closing.

They jumped me when I was just a few yards out of the bar, their beefy hands dragging me through the cool darkness of as-phalt into the dank stink of alleyway cobbles. I was even more surprised to know that the man that'd pulled me off the street was a cop: a big, round faced bull with his cap pulled down leaving most of his face in shadow.

The evil glint in his eyes was bad enough, but when the other copper stepped out into the streetlight's glare, I knew I was right up shit creek without a paddle. The second cop, smaller and skin-nier than his partner, tapped a nightstick against the flat of his palm menacingly.

Climbing to my knees, I raised my hands as if to say, 'what's the problem, officers?' But my mouth got the better of me and I blurted out, "You know, you're holding that club of yours all wrong."

This elicited a harsh kick to my chest and I crumpled back to the floor, upchucking from the pain. As the gorge rose in my throat I heard the big one say, "He's holding the stick just fine. Show him, Eddie," and a lightning bolt of pain exploded across my head. My vision blurred as I twitched and hacked up on the floor.

The bigger bull pinned me to the ground with one of his leather size twelve's, even as they relieved me of my wallet and my pistol. I stared daggers at him as he leafed through my wallet, with his partner pointing my own gun at me.

This was far from my proudest moment. My ear was throbbing, trickling blood onto my chin, dripping down to merge with the dribbles of vomit already hanging there. I licked my sticky lips and fought back the awful taste.

The cop holding my wallet said, "Driving license says you're one Trevor Towers." His voice was deep and mean. "What kind of a faggot name is that, Ed?"

The other cop sniggered.

He pulled the bills from my wallet before throwing it back to me empty. That was the last of my Jayne hunting budget. I struggled to find the strength to get up, but he just ground his heel against my face and said "Mr. Towers, you have been officially given your marching orders to leave Arkham. Courtesy of Big Boss."

They left the alley laughing, leaving me with the filth and the vomit. It didn't really come as a surprise that Big Boss had cops on his payroll; I never expected anything less. I just hadn't thought he would rather send them to do his dirty work than deal with me head on. He obviously didn't like getting his hands dirty.

My night a failure, I climbed up, leaving the alley with an even worse stagger. Heading towards my hotel, covered in a sticky film of my own blood and vomit, I stalked around the glare of the streetlamps and dreamt of a change of clothes and a shower.

I must have looked like quite a sight to the mostly respectable people I stumbled by on Main Street. I heard plenty of disgusted mutters and loud hoots from the motorists before I reached the relative peace of Boundary Street. Soon after I was staggering past the wide, looming form of Hangman's Hill before turning left onto Crane Street.

The Crane Street Hotel was a two-storied, gambrel-roofed affair that had probably been a lovely joint, once upon a time. The years hadn't been kind to it, though: it suffered from both the rot from the docks and the morbidity of the nearby graveyard. But, it was discreet and cheap, just the place for a broke, beat-up bum like myself. As I walked up the cracked stone steps all I could think about was taking a shower and getting some sleep before I made a flit and worked out some other means of gaining cash.

Girl hunting was an expensive business, and the only means that I had of earning cash, that of boxing or thuggery, didn't seem like much of an option, all things considered.

To add insult to injury, I found my room door hanging wide open. I walked in expecting to find the place ransacked, but instead found myself face to face with the guy I'd stabbed the night before.

He stood there staring at me with his one good eye, looking only a little bit worse for wear. The eye I'd jabbed had been poorly stitched up, and whatever my butterfly knife had done to his brain caused the right-hand side of his face to sag as if it were putty. I raise my hands up, beaten and unarmed and said "You looking for more of the same, palooka?"

The twice-dead man walked up to me, dragging his right foot behind him as he walked. Thrashing like a spastic, he lifted and pointed his pistol at my face. He slobbered and drooled, his good eye glazed over. "Boss said to finish the job." Even in this sorry state, he had me dead to rights and he knew it.

"You don't look so hot right now." I replied, edging back a little further. "Sure you don't want to sleep it off?"

"Look who's talking," he continued, sloping forwards as I stepped back, dancing our broken little windup dance. I thought of diving at him, kicking him straight in the chest, doing *anything* that would help me get the drop on him, but he'd pulled the trigger before I'd known it; there was a deafening boom and then . . . nothing. For a moment, I wondered where the hell the bullet had got to.

I opened my eyes to see him sprawled on the floor, the back of his head turned into a mangled red mess.

I turned to look and there she was: Jayne, in the flesh, looking as alive and as beautiful as the last time I'd seen her.

I honestly thought I'd died and gone to heaven.

She was dressed like midnight but was a hundred times more mysterious. Wearing a jet-black dress that hugged the gentle turn of her curves, gently sloping down to a stretch of tan stockings, ending in two shiny double strap shoes.

Jayne stepped into the room like she owned the place; she examined the décor, shaking her black, Lauren Bacall waves in grim-faced distaste. When she finally turned to me with the same look she said:

"Looking lively, aren't we, Trevor?"

I struggled to find the right words, but all I did was babble like a baby; like a goddess of lust, she glided closer, biting her bottom lip and said . . .

"You need to give it up, Trev; go stalking for a more suitable mate."

My heart skipped a beat. "I love you Jayne, I need you." I said.

She frowned as she stepped around the dead punk. A thousand years of death and longing passed by the time she stood before me.

I tried to think what I looked like to her: a filthy, mewling thing, with blood and vomit on my face and raggedy clothes, withering under her blue eyes and high cheek-boned face. Even in the light of that sickly ceiling lamp, she was just too perfect.

Her pitch-black dress drank deep from the light that spilled off her glossy hair.

"Our kinds shouldn't mix, Trevor," came her brutal reply.

I babbled my incoherent begging mess, once again. It was all I could do; the bombshell of finally seeing her had me utterly shell-shocked. I soaked in her radiance like a starved sunflower. I hadn't even noticed that she was still grasping the automatic she'd used to kill the punk.

"Get out of town," she said before slamming the gun against my already swollen ear.

I sank into painful oblivion and for the first time in years, I didn't dream of her.

I wound my way through the thick fog and finally arrived at the gambrel-roofed building that I called home. The front door was unlocked and a dim ceiling lamp gave off just enough light for me to find my way up the stairs. I stumbled only a couple of times during my unsteady climb and felt my way toward my room. I fumbled for the key, eventually managing to place it in the keyhole and let myself inside.

I was thirsty but didn't relish a trip to the shared second-floor bathroom basin. Flopping onto the bed, I groaned and started to unbuckle my belt.

Damn it, Riley, you need to take it easier with the booze.

"Put a sock in it," I muttered to the nagging voice inside my head.

The Sandman was knocking on my door when I heard the gun-shot.

What the . . .

For a drowsy half-second, I thought I was dreaming. But I'd been around enough guns and gunfire to know; there's no mistaking that sound once you've heard it. I sat up in bed, fighting back my throbbing headache. I kicked at my shoes and scrambled to grab them in my drunken stupor. I finally managed to corral them and hurried to the door.

The piece, Riley. Don't forget the piece.

I reached into the battered dresser, removed my .45 and stuck it in my belt. Opening the door slowly, I stuck my head outside and peered down the hall. A door was ajar and I did a double take when a well-stacked dame took her sweet time before she left the room. As soon as she started down the stairs, I rushed to the open door and peered inside.

I choked back a yelp as I looked inside. A much-abused stiff—dead for days by the look of him—was sharing the floor with my old chum Trevor Towers.

Who woulda thunk? You're flopping at the same hotel!

The big lug looked like he'd been put through the wringer, but he was breathing. The side of his face was bruised and battered. I didn't know *what* to make of the corpse. Pushing the door shut, I found a piece of paper in my pocket and took a pencil from the nightstand. I jotted down a brief message:

Towers,
Lose the goddamn corpse and pull yourself together. I'm going after the broad.

R.B.

I found wilted flowers drooping over a cheap vase, half filled with green water. After placing the note on Towers' chest, I tossed the dead weeds to the floor.

"Bottoms up!"

Laughing like a schoolkid, I poured the slimy liquid on Towers' ugly mug and dashed out of the room.

But where could I find the mystery woman?

I ran down the hallway and hurried down the stairs and barreled through the hotel lounge, nearly knocking the screen door off its hinges as I went. Looking down Crane Street, I saw a figure disappearing into the fog so I made after it like a stumbling hayburner. The fog swirled around me as I stumbled into the spot where I'd seen the woman disappear. Going after a quick hunch, I headed right on Boundary Street, groping blindly in the fog until I saw a figure on the steep path leading to Hangman's Hill.

By now, I was sucking wind, just like the bad old boxing days. No wonder I never did make it as a contender. By the time I neared the top of the hill, I was completely out of breath, so I stopped to wipe my eyes and stared toward the Wooded Graveyard below. Two dark figures loomed just beyond the gate. A woman—the broad I'd been after, had to be—and a big-six bastard of a man.

"Hey, lovebirds!" I yelled, like a complete goof. "We need to talk!"

The two stood silently as tendrils of fog enveloped them. Their forms shifted, becoming distorted and vague as shadows. Something large slid out from under the man's coat, expanding as it went. It waved in the air like the trunk of some circus elephant. I wanted to yell again but thought better of it. Blinking the mist away from my eyes, I looked again but the figures had disappeared. I could have gone after them. All I had to do was step into the mist . . . .

And then what, Riley? You don't even know what's behind the curtain, do you?

I stared at the empty space where the two figures had stood and shrugged. No, this was none of my business. Every single thing about Towers was beyond me, now. As I stumbled down Hangman's Hill it *also* occurred to me that I wasn't too keen on returning to the Crane Street hotel that night. Towers was going to fly right off the handle, as soon as he woke up from his stupor and that was one kind of grief I didn't need.

I slowly meandered back to Kearney's office where I planned to spend the rest of the evening. It was a good thing that he was an unusually trusting soul—especially for a private dick—and I owned a key to the office.

I made sure to avoid any cops. I'd rather settle for Kearney's couch than a bunk bed in the drunk tank. Some of the local bulls were okay but Kearney had warned me to keep an eye out for the bad apples. Half soaked from the fog, I made it to the office and let myself in. My head was pounding and my gut was sour but I knew I was way better off than Towers. This thought consoled me as I kicked back in Kearney's spare chair, removed my shoes and parked my size twelves on top of his desk. I would talk to Towers in the morning when both of us would be good and rested. I lit a gasper. I closed my eyes and dreamed.

This time, I didn't dream of 'Big Bertha'; instead, I dreamt of a waitress I knew back in St. Paul. We were just about to get into the horizontal hop, when some bastard started working on my skull with a jackhammer.

"Barnes, wake up!"

"I swear officer," I mumbled. "We're engaged."

"Get out of my chair, Barnes!"

"What!?" I continued, "I'm marrying the broad!"

"Ugh!" I moaned as cold water splashed across my face and soaked into my shirt. My eyes shot wide open and I saw a confused Wade Kearney holding an empty cup.

"Sorry, boss!" I croaked, struggling to my feet. "What time is it?"

"Late afternoon," he said. "I've been looking for you all over the place. I hadn't taken you for the bumming type."

He lit a gasper and grinned. "Didn't I give you enough for a room?"

"Too much going on back at my place," I explained.

"Define 'too much'," he asked, taking his usual place behind the battered desk.

"Gunfire and corpses," I stated.

He ignored the remark, reached into his desk drawer and took out an envelope. Grinning sheepishly, I asked, "I'm not fired am I?"

"No," he replied. "But I might have a task for you, if you're up to it." He looked doubtful after taking a gander at me.

"Sure thing," I said, "just fill me in on what needs doing."

"You probably won't like it."

Grinning, I said, "That's what you're paying me for."

"Good man, Barnes," he answered.

I awoke from what had to be the worst nightmare I've ever had into a reality that wasn't any better. My room, a pokey little rat-trap at the best of times, smelled like an abattoir: the man Jayne had dispatched the night before was still there. A bleak afternoon light bled in through the rain-spattered window panes.

I'd dreamed I'd been crawling up a mountain of broken stone blocks, an impossibly slippery green that stank of seaweed and dead fish. Every time I reached the top of a block, I'd find myself right at the bottom again, facing toward the foot of the mountain where a sea of misty waves lapped at a nasty, brown beach.

My purpose in the dream had been to reach the mountain peak and save Jayne before Big Boss came to steal her from me, but the impossible dead ends drove me to the edge, made me jump out of the dream. I awoke to the dank, reeking corpse-smell all around me and my first thought was that I was somehow still trapped, unable to wake up.

I tried to pull myself up from the floor but I only made it half-way to my feet before crumbling back down. I felt like garbage and my head was ringing in pain. It wasn't just the massive earache that Jayne gave me or the cops' rough-housing—a thick cake of blood tugged my skin to its limit.

The thought of Jayne made me cringe, but at least it gave me the strength to climb to my feet and drag the ruined coat from my shoulders. I tossed it across the too-familiar corpse, hoping that it could partially snuff out that pungent, rotten smell. Stumbling around him I opened the window to allow the moist air inside so I could clear out the room and my head.

Staring down at the damp street and the hill beyond, I wondered just how the hell I'd get rid of that damned, dope-headed torpedo. I'd bet dough that no one in my building would've bothered to investigate the sound of gunfire last night, so I'd probably be safe for a little longer. I stripped myself down to my blood-soaked birthday suit and headed towards the bathroom.

The bathroom around me was tiled from floor to ceiling in an ugly shade of cream that bled into the bathtub and the other appliances. Even as I tumbled inside the grimy shower, all I cared about was drenching myself clean before sleeping for a night and a day.

The water was as cold as ice but I didn't even feel it. Reaching down to grab a bar of soap, I started washing out my matted, foul smelling hair. When I ran my hands over my ear, I nearly collapsed from the pain.

After that mistake I left the tub and started running a proper bath instead. I checked there was hot water running from the tap, before stepping towards the sink mirror to give my injuries a once-over.

I've heard of crashing: junkies in alleyways begging for a puff, dopeheads begging for the hypo even as they're getting worked over by a bunch of alleyway toughs. I always thought I was beyond these kinds of lows, until I looked at myself after my Jayne comedown. The whole right side of my head was a red-stained mess, my right ear so clogged up with blood and gunk that it looked like a pile of meat.

I shook my head, my mirror image reciprocating, rubbed the sleep from my eyes and checked my mouth for loose teeth before turning back to sit on the edge of the tub.

The bathtub quickly filled and the steam from the water tickled me as I stared at the mildew-covered floor tiles. Only then did the bombshell that Jayne had dropped finally hit me.

'Our kinds shouldn't mix, Trevor.' she'd said, giving me my marching orders as if I was another dog soldier. Looks like she was connected to Big Boss. *What the hell did she mean by her kind?* I wondered. *Can't have been the dead dopehead, could it?*

I put my head in my hands, wanting to cry, wanting to roar. Instead, I just sat there, torturing myself over how beautiful she looked. Before long, the numbness set in: a big, dark dog of a thing that settled its paws down in my gut.

I turned from my brooding to test the water just as I heard it splash over the tub's rim. When I realized it was just on the wrong side of scalding, I climbed into the tub and relished the tingling pain.

I spent just enough time in the tub to scour myself with soap before gently scraping the scabbed blood from my face and scalp, letting hot water do the rest. After wiping the steam from the mirror I examined my ear to discover it wasn't too bad; sure, it was red and swollen like a badly done slice of bacon but I'd had way worse in the ring.

I toweled myself dry and put on a fresh set of clothes before I was ready to flit the hotel. Before leaving the room, I pored over my coat; I couldn't bear to walk the streets without it, but the damned thing was so messed up and soaked in blood, that I couldn't bear to put it back on. The dead dopehead's coat got me out of the bind. It was in better condition, a dark brown trench coat that was barely one size too small, but it covered my piece and shoulder holster, so it'd have to do.

I noticed the note a moment later; it'd gotten stuck to my own coat, discarded on the floor beside my slowly rotting pal.

Written on a little slip of paper, it read:

Towers,
Lose the goddamn corpse and pull yourself together. I'm going after the broad.

R.B.

Who the hell is R.B.?" I wondered, more than a little confused. It took me a moment to realize that it had to be Riley Barnes, Herbert West's disgruntled former henchman. I followed most of his instructions: I lost the corpse and left the hotel.

My plan was simple and idiot-proof: find Jayne, get her to spill the beans, at gunpoint if neccessary and if Big Boss or any of his cronies got in my way I would just whack the bastards.

The things I do for love.

As I was heading toward the Miskatonic River, it occurred to me that Riley Barnes was only a very small piece of the puzzle; why he'd decided to get involved in my business and go after Jayne was beyond me.

Dusk fell on the rain-sleek streets and the musty smell of dispersed street filth filled the air. I was heading for my car, stored in one of the warehouses along the riverside, filled with goodies that meant Hell on Earth for anyone that pushed me too far.

Arkham, with its twisting little streets and cramped, aged buildings, is almost beautiful when you wriggle out of its tacky barrel houses and its loud business district. From far away, the Miskatonic

River looked like a wide, glossy snake from a bygone time, its watery scales patterned with the reflected moon and stars. For one silent moment, this place looked almost good enough to live in.

I'd been mulling over Jayne's words about being near her own kind. Before long, I realized that she was maybe residing near one of Arkham's burial grounds. She'd always been of the morbid sort and I didn't see it as too much of a stretch that she'd given me a clue as to where she was. Turns out, I was completely right.

I'd placed my car in storage in a guarded warehouse, the kind that charges an arm and a leg for security. This hadn't bothered me at the time; after all, my big blue Buick contained so many expensive goodies that I couldn't risk leaving it on a street corner.

After driving from the warehouse, I turned right onto River Street towards the nearest burial ground. I was going to scour around it for any sign of Jayne. Slowly, I noticed how the night had grown cloyingly warm and the streets were deserted. Everything in Arkham seemed to be holding its breath for the chaos to come.

Driving around the graveyard, a squat little place flanked by wooden fences and filled with thick, ancient trees, I checked out the surrounding buildings in search of one that seemed up to Jayne's standards. Before long, I parked up on the corner of Lich Street, keeping watch on the most likely candidate, a decent looking hotel just across from the graveyard.

After hanging tight for about an hour or so, I left my Buick to go check on my treasured stash.

There they were, all prim and proper. A shotgun, two Chicago typewriters, a case of dynamite and enough ammunition to support a small war. I was staring down at them in grim admiration when I caught sight of her walking past the intersection at Lich Street and heading down Parsonage, towards Christ Church Cemetery.

There was a man with her; had to be the tallest fella I've ever seen. Despite the fact that the rain had stopped, he still covered her with his umbrella. I felt my heart skip a beat and by the time I realized I was gawping they had disappeared down Parsonage Street. I pulled myself together sharpish. Pushing the trunk shut I climbed back into the Buick, turned the ignition with a snap and steered it, engine purring, around the street corner. There they were, two shadows moving across an empty sidewalk.

I parked and waited until they were near the end of Parsonage Street. When another car came coasting past, I drove up behind it so as to get closer without them seeing me.

The red convertible in front took a right onto one of the streets leading to the University and I slowed down as Jayne and her companion took a right at the end of Parsonage. Finally, I got a good look at the guy with her. Now there was an ugly bastard.

He was dressed in a black suit, looking mean as hell even from fifteen feet away. His face was mostly concealed under a thick black beard surmounted by a shock of dark curly hair that stuck out beneath an ill-fitting hat. He had a pale, devilish face, so long it looked goat-like. I reckoned he must have been seven feet tall, a mean ass bodyguard if ever I saw one. Still, his stature didn't mean squat against the load I was carrying.

I slowed the Buick until they were out of sight before I followed the route they'd taken, taking a wide berth through Washington Street. I steered to a halt with the long sprawl of Christ Church Cemetery to my right and my quarries silhouettes moving across the buildings facing it.

I left my car and ducked down, using it for cover before darting across the street towards the cemetery to try and get a bead on where they were going. It wasn't long before I saw they were heading to an old hotel across from the cemetery's front gates. At least half a dozen men stood guard, armed with long-barreled firearms.

The building was a four-story brownstone, with the majority of its windows boarded up except for those on the first floor. A pale yellow glow filtered out from them and the entranceway, spilling its sickly light out onto the puddle-strewn curb.

With the cemetery fence looming over me, I sat crouched in what I hoped was complete darkness. I watched Jayne talking to one of the guards and found myself itching to blow the lot of them away before staring Jayne right in the eye, just so I could say: "Remember me, honey?"

I've never said that my obsession was a healthy one.

The mugs guarding the brownstone began leaving their posts and started ambling towards the cemetery. I knew that going in from the front wouldn't be such a hot idea. Creeping back towards the Buick, I decided to collect a few choice weapons from the trunk before making my way to the rear of Washington Street.

Wade Kearney was one hell of a clairvoyant. He was dead on the dough when he said I wasn't going to like the job. Apparently, the former Mrs. Trevor Towers had paid him a visit shortly after

I left the day before. It seemed like she had her ex-husband on her tail and wasn't too hot about it. She was involved with some unsavory characters—but what did I expect; she'd married Trevor for Pete's sake—but didn't want any harm to come to him. She'd asked Kearney about assigning someone to keep an eye on him and lending a hand if things got tough. Someone who was rough enough to cut it.

Guess who Kearney picked.

I'd planned on seeing Towers anyway but I damn sure didn't plan to let him know that I'd been hired to watch his sorry ass. After leaving the office, my first stop would be the Crane Street hotel so I could grab a clean pair of threads. I couldn't really spare the detour, but I didn't have any choice.

I arrived at the hotel, ready for anything. There were no cops hanging around, which I took for a good thing so I walked right in and made my way to the second floor. The door to Towers' room was now closed and I slipped into my own room unobserved. I changed clothes and went to the communal bathroom for a quick shave. When I was good and done grooming myself, I mustered the strength to march down the hall.

I banged on Towers' door, dreading the reaction I would get. After a while, I tried again and yelled, "It's Barnes! Open the door!"

I knocked a third time but got no answer. Maybe the chump had finally kicked the bucket. I was about to turn, when I felt someone stepping behind me.

Towers is gonna cold-cock you and pound your skull into the floor-boards, the voice in my head said.

"He ran out a little while ago," a meek little voice behind me said.

I felt relieved to see the hotel's half-wit employee lingering behind me.

"When did he go?" I asked to confirm his statement.

"Less than an hour ago," he replied. "Skipped without paying."

I decided I ought to ask about the corpse "Was there any trouble around here last night?"

"Just the same crap as usual," he slowly drawled.

Apparently, 'usual' in this place meant bullet-riddled rotting corpses and gunfire. With Towers gone, I went down the street to the small lot where I'd parked my flivver. It wasn't anything to write home about but I didn't plan on going after my mark on foot. I'd had enough walking the night before to last me a lifetime.

I drove around Arkham for a long time before I even caught sight of Towers. It was just blind luck that I spied him running out of a parked Buick near the Christ Church cemetery, before he concealed himself against the shadows of its wall. "What's he up to?" I muttered, pulling to the curb and cutting my lights. From where he'd positioned himself, he seemed interested in the decrepit brownstone building across the street. Deciding to check it out, I left my car and drove through the back streets to approach the building from the rear. A low-wattage bulb near the service entrance didn't do much to dispel the darkness. That could work to my advantage, as soon as I'd figured out just what the hell Towers was up to.

I was mulling over my next move when I caught someone stalking me from the corner of my eye. Used to be, Mother Barnes's favorite bouncing boy wasn't all that slow on the uptake. How times change.

"Well, if it isn't 'Bad Penny Barnes' skulking in the dark."

"Jesus Christ, Towers!" I hissed. "You trying to give me a coronary?"

He just stared at me.

"What the hell is this 'Bad Penny' shtick?"

"Can't get rid of you, now can I?" he replied. "I got your note. How come you didn't come around later?"

"You'd split by the time I got around to it."

"Well, here I am," he said. "Where did the broad go last night?"

"I followed her to the old wooded cemetery on Hangman's Hill," I answered.

"And?"

"There was this big, scary-looking sonofabitch with her."

Towers smirked. "I'm pretty sure that's 'Big Boss.'"

"Don't know about no Boss but the bastard sure was huge."

"So how come you're here?" Towers asked.

"Let's just say this place stinks about as bad as Falmouth."

Towers grinned. "I almost shot you in Falmouth."

"Yeah," I said, "That was a load of laughs. You think you wanna give it another go or should I just help your screwy ass?"

"Tough choice," Towers said. "But Jayne's with those assholes, so you *might* come in handy."

"Ain't that the bees knees," I replied. "What's the plan?"

"The plan is," he answered. "I get to have a little talk with her and kill anyone who tries to stop me."

"Sounds solid."

"We'll split up and search the place," he continued. "If you spot her first, come and find me. You'll know where I am."

"So I just follow the trail of bodies?" I asked.

He smiled. "For a start."

All things being equal, my encounter with Towers had gone better than I expected. I took the first floor of the brownstone building, while he proceeded to the second. My initial search yielded nothing but dusty rooms, broken furniture and moldy carpeting. It had been some time since anyone had used the hotel for its intended purpose. I heard the floorboards creaking above me and wondered if it could have been Towers. Probably not; he was sneakier than that.

"Rats. It's gotta be rats," I whispered, using the flashlight I'd stuck in my coat earlier.

Shifting though the decrepit rooms, I wondered how Towers was making out. I hadn't heard any gunshots yet but I bet that the bastard was good with a blade. God help any fool between him and his Jayne. I thought he was on a madman's quest but I couldn't help but sympathize, especially after the mess back in Falmouth.

Herbert West and Falmouth were a part of my life I would never forget, try as I might. I still had nightmares about what happened there and if I were the praying type, I'd have chalked it up to being my first *real* encounter with evil. If what was happening in Arkham was even remotely like that—and I was beginning to suspect that it was—then I'd have no choice but to go all Alamo with Towers. Even if we were just a couple of amoral shits, we couldn't let that kind of thing happen anywhere ever again.

I'd pretty much covered the first floor of the building when I saw a battered door at the end of the hall, the word BASEMENT written on it in faded lettering. I didn't like the idea of moving to the higher floors until I was certain that the place was good and covered. I tested the door and was surprised at how easy it opened.

"Someone's been here," I mumbled.

I shifted the flashlight to my left hand and took out my automatic.

Somewhere in the half-dark of the space below, there was the glow of light. I padded cautiously down the steps and stopped. In the far corner, a man was nodding behind a wobbly desk, a bundle of newspapers at one corner barely keeping it from tipping over. He was the baby-faced punk I'd heard running his mouth back at Ciro's. A nearly empty bottle of gin rocked on the desk and the girlie magazine he'd been perusing was spread out nearby. Steel canisters were stacked against one wall. The words *H. West Formu-*

la #241 were stenciled across their sides.

My blood ran cold as I made out the words.

"No fucking way," I whispered, as I made my way to the nodding punk.

I guessed that explained why 'Big Boss' had picked a building so close to the cemetery but God only knew what a bunch of hoods planned to do with West's resurrection juice. Nothing good, that was for damn sure.

I was tempted to put a bullet through the punk's brain but held back at the last second. A gunshot could screw everything up, but there were more than one ways to kill a sleeping man. I pocketed the automatic and stepped behind the snoring guard. Grinning viciously, I flicked the catch on my switchblade and kicked his chair legs from under him.

He barely had time to realize just how royally he'd screwed up. I watched him frantically grope for his weapon before securing his head with my left arm and slitting his throat. The bastard grabbed his throat and thrashed around, spraying a gush of hot red blood all over the place as he went. When he was good and still, I let him lie in his own mess and went up the stairs to find Towers.

The second floor seemed clear, almost eerily corpse-free, even though Trevor had probably just gone over it with a fine-toothed comb. Taking the stairs, I became grimly aware that things were too quiet, even under the circumstances. No blood, no gunsmoke lingering in the air. All too clean and easy for my taste. I wasn't Trevor's biggest fan but the man was a damn sight more agreeable than the thugs we were after.

I treaded cautiously, making sure not to trip over furniture or debris. After reaching the third floor, I traipsed down toward the double doors at the end of its narrow corridor. Even behind the reinforced wooden panel, I could hear the rumble of angry voices, followed by a loud thud like someone being bounced off a wall.

"This must be the place," I chuckled, cocking my gun.

I stepped to the double doors and kicked them wide open. Trevor was talking to Jayne, his gun trained on Big Boss. His speech was all hoarse. Something must have happened to his throat. I barely had the time to take it all in before a large, blood-spattered figure rose from the floor and pointed its machine gun at my partner.

After we'd split up, my reunion with Riley soon led to nothing more than a dull search of the derelict hotel's empty rooms. The floor I'd taken revealed nothing as I searched for Jayne and Big Boss.

In the darkness, every part of the hotel was the same uniform shade of gray; I couldn't imagine the place being that much different in the daylight. Walking slowly up the staircase and towards the next floor, with the threadbare carpet beneath my feet and the peeling wallpaper against my back, I sided myself against the musty wall. This was a place for the long-since dead, a dump for the old bones, when the cemetery got too packed for comfort.

I arrived on the third floor landing as quietly as possible and noticed something different.

Like the rest of the hotel, the staircase opened up on a corridor lined with doors. This floor however, bore a far shorter corridor, with a double door at its furthest end. A faded light filtered through the gap. I held the Tommy gun tightly, fighting back the shakes as I made my way across the corridor.

Kill Big Boss, make Jayne face me. I repeated the plan like a mantra as I stepped down the corridor towards the light.

Halfway there I could make out their voices: one as coarse as gravel, another mean and loud. The third one, an angel's silken caress.

My angel, Jayne.

I reached the door and knelt in front of the dark wooden slabs. Through the cracks, I peered into a room filled with flickering glow of candlelight.

It was a dining room, dark and grimy despite the glow of the candelabra arranged around the round tables. Near the center of the room, I found the sources of the voices. There were three of them, sat around a table covered in dog-eared ledgers.

The huge black shape moved to sit directly across from me, obscuring most of my view. This had to be the giant goon I'd seen with Jayne earlier. She sat facing me, across from him to his left. She looked resplendent in the black dress I'd seen her in the night before.

Sitting beside Jayne, almost completely hidden by the big man's head and shoulders, was the man I assumed was Big Boss. All I could see was a pair of wide shoulders connected to the thick arms of a body clad in a too-tight gray suit. His voice resonated deeply as he spoke. He sounded like a big palooka, alright.

"Eighteen cases to Kingsport, same to Rhode Island. On second thought, Wilbur, double that, you hear?" Big Boss said.

The man called Wilbur opened his mouth, letting loose his thick swamp yank accent.

"Ayuh, Boss," he said. "I wuz just thinking."

Jayne's voice chimed in like a tinkling bell. "He thinks we might have been followed, Boss."

Wilbur continued. "I swear it, there's some peeper on our trail. I jus' know it."

"How's your ex, Jayne? All good and done with?" Big Boss said.

She replied with, "He'll stay out of our hair," and it almost sounded like she was covering for me. Big Boss chuckled, a loud purring noise that made the hair stand up on the back of my neck. "We turn make gold out of paper and soldiers out of dead men, come hell or high water. Isn't that right?"

Wilbur pushed his huge frame out of his seat before heading towards the right-hand side of the room, out of view.

"Peepers, Boss," he complained, "we need ta leave taown. I been havin' too many bad dreams."

"We stay. In Arkham, we'll drink deep of humanity's suffering," came Big Boss's reply.

Wilbur grunted something unintelligible and I heard a door open then slam shut.

"Wilbur's right, Boss," Jayne said. I could see her clearly now. She seemed to be staring right at me. "We should move while the going's good."

With Wilbur gone, I knew this would be as good a time as any to get to Jayne. With neither of them armed, I had the element of surprise.

I stood up, and took a deep breath before kicking the door wide open.

I got a quick look at Jayne's surprised look and Big Boss's face—oddly fuzzy and distant beneath his wide hat—just before I was lifted up by the throat and pushed against a wall, cracking the plaster as I went. The wind blew out of my lungs in one long gasp.

So much for the element of surprise.

Wilbur, his snarling mug pressed up against me, held me up in one hand and tore the gun from my hands with the other.

Struggling against his grip, I heard Jayne say, "Oh, Trevor, why did you have to do that."

"It seems I owe you that jerk soda after all, Wilbur," said Big Boss.

From up close, I took in Wilbur's strange features. His pupils were wide, almost seeming to melt in the compound black of his eyes. His dirty, bushy beard was streaked with white. He smelled ripe, like wet roadkill. His mouth was a nightmare of pointed brown teeth.

"Peepers, Boss," he sneered. "Buzzing 'round us like horse-flies 'round dung."

I tried to suck in air, even as Wilbur clenched my windpipe shut. Even as my vision began to fade, I tried to look up at Jayne. Blood pounded in my ears and through it all I could hear Big Boss say, "We snuff him and then put him through the process, make him more amenable."

"Aw, kin't I rip his bawls off an' feed' em to him?" Wilbur drawled.

With my consciousness slipping away and my options running low, I knew I had to act now or forever hold my peace. From the looks of it, neither Jayne nor Riley Barnes were going to come to my rescue. Reaching into my waistband, I unstrapped my trusty butterfly knife.

With one weakened hand, I grabbed hold of Wilbur's jacket for support, and drove the knife up to the hilt through his white shirted chest and with my last ounce of strength, I twisted. Wilbur fell to the floor, releasing me as he crumbled in agony. My Tommy gun clattered on the floor beside him. I let it lie there, for now.

Hopped up on adrenaline, I tugged my necktie loose and sucked in a long breath of air before stepping over the dying hillbilly.

Jayne stood almost ten feet away, with Big Boss beside her and I could swear that she almost looked like she was pleased to see me. In the blink of an eye, I had my pistol out and pointed at Big Boss. Jayne put up her hands and backed away, but the big palooka held his ground.

"Jayne," I croaked through my bruised voice box, "you've got yourself mixed up with some real rotten eggs."

"Says you," she muttered sullenly.

I glared at Big Boss and he stared right back at me, unflinching and there was something just so off about his face I can't begin to explain what was wrong with it. Even close up it looked all jumbled and wrong but I'd been through too much shit to care; right now, all that mattered was that I had a gun and all the aces in the goddamn deck.

"Guess you got me," Big Boss muttered, his shifting pink face changing by the second. He raised his big hands into the air.

I was a hair's breadth from pulling the trigger when a loud

voice called out behind me. I spun on my heels to face the fresh threat.

"Towers, move!" Riley shouted. I dove as I saw Wilbur, shooting up on his feet, my machine gun pointed right at me. In a split second, Wilbur's shoulder and then the side of his head exploded into a fine black mist. Riley, from his half-cover beyond the doorway, had saved my bacon once again.

Wilbur staggered back a couple of steps but didn't go down. I found myself ducking for cover as the machine gun spewed its chopper-fire in a wide arc above me before his huge, gangly form finally collapsed into a heap.

Riley charged into the room but I ignored him as I heard Jayne moaning in pain. Even as I turned I knew that the worst had happened; Jayne was slumped on the floor, clutching at her chest and twitching in agony.

Big Boss was laid out a few feet from her but I didn't care; she was dying. I'd ran myself ragged and gone through hell to find her and now she was dying all over again.

I fell down to my knees and pulled her up into my arms. It didn't take a doctor to know what those tearing, seeping wounds across her chest meant. Even as she sagged into my arms I leaned into her. Her chest heaved, her lips moved but all that came out was a liquid gurgle. Her bright wet eyes looked up at me as she went.

Jayne was going, going . . . .

From a hundred miles away, I heard Jayne's voice. "I'm going, Trev. Please, let me go," she gasped, struggling even as she choked on her own blood. "And make sure I stay that way."

Jayne gave me the kind of smile she knew I'd die for, just as the light left her eyes. "I love you hon," I sobbed. After wiping my hand clean of her blood, I closed her eyes and eased her gently to the floor.

All over again, Jayne was gone.

I'd just nailed the big lummox called Wilbur when I noticed Towers cradling his ex-wife. The woman looked shot all to hell, long past gone. Everything stank of blood and cordite and something *else*, something utterly wrong. I moved past Wilbur's corpse and made my way to the 'Big Boss,' killed by his dying henchman's last machine gun burst. The .45 rounds had really done a number on him. 'Big Boss' had been finally put out of commission.

"Two dead bogeys right here." I said. Towers didn't respond.

Looking around the room, I noticed the ledgers piled up on the tabletop. "What have we here?" I said, as I flipped through the pages.

Towers eased Jayne's body to the floor and croaked, "What?"

"Looks like registers," I answered. "I bet the authorities would have a field day with these."

"Yeah," he replied. "I bet the *right* people would."

"There's more than just the ledgers here," I said. "There are whole canisters of West's zombie juice in the basement."

"What, just laying around?"

I grinned. "No. There was a guard. He's out of commission."

"Jayne's gone," he said.

"I'm so sorry."

Towers sighed, looking exhausted. "I need to make sure that she stays that way."

"We could blow this place to Hell," I suggested. "Get rid of the zombie juice and . . ."

"And Jayne, too," he finished. "All right."

Towers went to his car to retrieve the explosives, leaving me alone with the three stiffs. It's not that I'm squeamish but I'd gone through too much crap to be at ease. I lit a gasper and motioned for Towers to move his ass. He might have lost everything in the end, but he'd hurt a whole lot of people on the way. I wondered if he'd stop, after this. Hell, I wondered if we would *ever* stop. I walked to the double doors and waited for him.

He arrived not long after, with a crate stuffed to the gills with dynamite.

I stepped back to give him room. "It was nice seeing you," I said.

He smirked. "Now there's something I don't hear every day."

Something bubbled and gurgled.

"You need a soda or something?" he asked.

"Not with my cast iron gut," I replied.

We turned and stared at the floor where Wilbur's corpse lay. "Jesus Christ," I mumbled, as I watched the bastard slowly dissolve in front of my eyes. His flesh bubbled and popped, releasing a cloud of noxious fumes into the room.

"What the hell is *that*?" Towers asked.

"Beats me. But I bet it ain't good." I said. *Nice, Riley. At least it beats screaming your head off.*

"You think Big Boss . . ." Towers began.

We turned to the big bastard, just in time to catch his eerie transformation.

Somehow, the big dead man in the pinstriped suit had begun to squirm and bulge obscenely. Crunching like dry leaves, his body quickly ripped and split itself open from head to toe. We backed away as something long and glistening shot out of Big Boss's bloody shell, a thousand beady red eyes blossoming across its sinewy form.

"Holy shit," I managed. Towers settled for a loud, gagging moan.

Long, leathery wings exploded out of the thing's back. It hissed at us, even as it writhed inside the bloody red roots that used to be Big Boss.

"Bastards!" it screeched without a mouth, its eyes blazing with a brilliant flash.

He'd got us there.

"It looks pissed," Towers said.

"Yeah, well I *am* pissed," I said, raising my pistol. I had just squeezed the trigger, when something wrapped around my ankle and threw me off balance. My shot went wide, the bullet smashing the fly-specked window of the room. I landed in a heap and stifled my scream as the soggy remains of Wilbur's dissolving hand spilled into my pant leg. I was scuttling backwards when Towers pulled his gun and drew a bead on the slithering horror. The creature flapped its massive wings, letting out a deafening squawk. In the blink of an eye, it had shot off the floor towards the broken window. I heard the gunshot ring out and saw a small hunk of flesh splatter against the wall as whatever the hell that creature was smashed its way through the lingering shards of glass and disappeared into the night.

"Well ain't that peachy!" Towers spat in disgust. "What the hell do we do now?"

Towers was shaking, barely holding it together. I decided to comfort him best as I could.

"Now," I said. "We do what you do best."

"The hell is that supposed to mean?" he asked, staring at me.

"We throw all caution to the wind," I replied. "We turn down every sane bit of advice we ever get and go after the palookas—stomping any chump who gets in our way—until we've cornered the rats behind this and killed every last one of them."

Towers smiled. "You've been taking notes."
"I always was a fast learner," I replied.
"Are you sure you want to go through with this?" he asked.
I extended my hand, saying, "Come hell or high water."
Towers grinned and shook my hand.
"Let's blow this place to kingdom come."

Unlike most stories about my life, this one ended with more corpses than I could ever care to count: Big Boss's death instigated a domino effect of decimation that left every single one of his animated goons sent back into Hell, where they should have stayed in the first place.

Arkham's city hall made sure to cover up the incident. The sudden deaths of Big Boss's grunts were chalked up as a freak outbreak of tuberculosis. The destruction of his property was written off as a disastrous gas main explosion.

As for me and Barnes? We made a pact that day that put us on our path to thwarting and destroying every creeping, crawling thing that Big Boss had left behind no matter where or when we found it.

Six months after our encounter with that inhuman bastard posing as a mob boss, our mission is still going strong. Jayne still lingers in my mind, her memory fading away in degrees every time that Barnes and I strike a blow at those slippery little bastards.

From the heart of Arkham, BARNES AND TOWERS INVESTIGATIONS stands against the things that go bump in the night, growing stronger by the day.

Abandon hope, all ye monsters who fuck with us.

The Lady in Yellow

I stared out of my office window at a view as dull and uninviting as a nun's underwear. Arkham's dark, cobbled streets and its scruffy little buildings did little to inspire me. Beyond the lazy, tar-black stretch of the Miskatonic, the town lay like a sleeping serpent, under an evening sky dotted with stars.

But I—one of the few and proud enlightened with a pulse— knew that beneath Arkham's doddering façade lay unimaginable horrors, ready to pounce on any poor fool that wandered too close. Me and my business partner, —ex-marine and former boxer by the name of Trevor Towers—had come face to face with Arkham's deadly underbelly on more than one occasion. After surviving our first encounter with its evils, we'd decided to go into business together as private investigators, operating in the very heart of the seedy little town.

Say what you will about old Arkham, it sure knew how to pull you in.

In the few months we'd worked in Arkham we'd succeeded in thwarting the plans of an alien monster that posed as the new Mob Boss, and solved the case of a man that vanished in degrees, only to be replaced by something inhuman. There was the odd kidnapping, of course, the usual extortion cases, and the sordid little jobs that came our way.

It was a hell of a way to make a living.

I turned away from the window and checked my watch. It was already a few minutes to six and I guessed my client would be knocking on the door at any time. I pulled a chair behind my desk and wondered, for the hundredth time, just who this mysterious john was that wanted to meet me without even disclosing his name.

We'd certainly made more than a few enemies since dispatching Arkham's otherworldly crime-lord. That's why I kept a Colt Automatic under the desk to keep away any prospecting torpedoes, as I hopefully waited for the next paying gig. Being careful goes a long way in this business.

Our office was situated in the newer part of Arkham, just across the river from old town, in a building that was barely classy enough to let us skip rent every other month. My office, white-walled and laid with a gaudy blue carpet, could've almost been sparse if not for the huge antique desk before me. Hewn from dark brown wood and paneled with decorative scallops on each corner, it was filled with drawers, some of which were still stuck like Hell. We'd bought it for a song in a yard sale in nearby Kingsport.

That was where my partner was at the moment, working a surveillance gig and judging by the way he sounded on the phone, also wrestling with one bastard of a hangover. Trevor couldn't work unless he'd gotten absolutely smashed the night before a job. Besides, he was a big boy; he could deal with it. Who was I to judge the man who saved my life?

A huge shape darkened the office door's frosted glass pane. I didn't need to check my watch to know that the knock came at six o' clock sharp. Looked like this john was prompt, at least. He let himself in without a word from me. He seemed oblivious to the gun I pointed at him, too hip to the jive to even consider that his next action could get him killed on the spot.

He was a huge black fella, just tall enough to clear the door, wide too; so wide he had to squeeze through the door frame. Thankfully, he seemed to be unarmed. Smiling at him, I said "Wish you'd called ahead; I would've had the door widened."

He grunted before shutting the door behind him. I gave him the once-over: this wasn't your usual spade. He looked dead serious, dressed in the spiffiest pinstriped suit I'd ever seen. Every single thing on him, from his black leather brogans all the way up to his yellow cravat, reeked of orchids.

He wore a black bowler hat that ended just above his dark, beady brown eyes. There was a weariness in those moist and jaundiced eyes, as if he'd walked a million miles to reach me. Curiouser and curiouser, as the caterpillar said.

At least the john looked like he could afford me, so I tucked my gun into the desk holster and stood up to shake his hand when he reached the desk, and invited him to sit.

My hand was engulfed in his big brown grip, then he squeezed his wide behind into my two-sizes-too-small chair. I cringed inwardly as he sat, expecting it to break like kindling. Thankfully, it held.

He introduced himself, saying, "My name isn't important. All you need to know is that I need help and I got all the heavy sugar you need." The man's voice was thick like pea gravel. Once he'd said his piece, he stared around the office, and said, "This doesn't seem like the kind of place a couple of shamus's would work from."

"Oh, this is my thinking desk," I replied. "We keep the filing cabinets and secretaries on another floor."

He grunted and stared at me morosely with those big, sad eyes.

"I'm here because I know you and that hard-boiled mug, Towers, took out Big Boss himself."

The man had done his homework, apparently. I bet he even shifted through every dive and asked all the right jailbirds, just to make sure. I asked, out of professional courtesy, "So you know my partner?"

He put both hands on the edge of the desk and I guessed that if he really put it into his head, he could've probably snapped it in two without even breaking a sweat.

"I saw him kill a man in the ring once," he explained. "Cost me a whole lot of dough, too."

"That's Towers, alright," I said. "A right heartless bastard."

Ignoring my joke, he continued, "I need you to pay attention. This is important."

Realizing he wasn't after any sweet talk, I pulled a notepad and a pencil from the desk drawer.

He continued, "Soon after Big Boss was done with, there was a vacuum that a whole lot of folks rushed in to fill."

I nodded. This one wasn't just a loaded daddy-o; he was educated enough and smart enough not to waste time.

"Many of Big Boss's operations were ripe for the picking," he continued, "so my underlings and I took over some of them. I suppose I should thank you for that."

I saluted and started doodling on my pad.

He said, "I need a whole lot of things done that I can definitely afford."

I smiled politely, saying, "My associate and I will do anything to assist you, within the limits of the law."

He grunted again, his little shorthand for distaste to my little attempts at humor.

The hulking man reached into his jacket pocket and produced

two objects. The first was a big brown envelope, the second a small photograph. He dropped them on the desk and pushed the envelope towards me, checking up on the photo one last time. In his big fingers, it looked more like a postage stamp.

"One thousand dollars," he said without looking up, "and ten extra, too, once you've got the job done."

The envelope seemed one hell of a lot more important all of a sudden. I never thought I'd see that much dough from a simple peeping job. After he'd slipped the photo towards me, I realized that maybe the pay was nowhere near as good as it had first seemed.

The photograph was a mug shot of a blond-haired woman. She was beautiful.

"That's my wife," he said, "She's been abducted by a cult."

At this point, I started to wonder just what the hell I had gotten myself into.

The abduction by a cult part: water off a duck's back; but a black man, married to a white woman? Now there was a proper can of worms.

I started getting some serious notes as we went through the details of the case, my eyes constantly drawn back to the thick wad of cash concealed in the envelope.

I just had to wonder what Towers would make of it all.

Slouched back as comfortably as my Buick's seats would let me, I kept my eyes on the job while daydreaming of a time when I wasn't going through the hangover from Hell.

I'd left my apartment as quietly as possible, hoping I could maybe sneak past it and lose it in traffic. No dice: the damn thing shot off its dark little corner, sank its teeth into my brain and reminded me that beer and a Welsh bearcat by the name of Rhian mixed far too well together.

I'd left her asleep in my bed, looking as sweet as an angel and smelling twice as nice.

You ask me, it ought to be illegal, making a man work after a night like that.

But, the gig Barnes gave me was a simple one: following some dame around whose husband suspected her of infidelity. That's what I'd been doing as the afternoon slowly turned to evening, driving around the streets of Kingsport before I finally parked my keister across from a row of houses, one of which I'd seen her wriggle her perky blonde ass into.

To the left of me, the row of houses were big-bricked, cottage-like affairs, arranged behind a row of pepper trees that gave me lots of camouflage as I searched them through my binoculars.

Tailing her so I wouldn't be noticed had had me lagging way too far behind her, so I hadn't been able to see which house she entered. It wasn't that big a deal, all things being equal, but my slip-up had me spying on all three houses instead of just the one.

To my right stood a high, white fence, beyond which lay a sloping field that led straight into an unlit country club, which made me seem inconspicuous. When the odd pedestrian walked by I pretended I was reading my paper—just some bozo with nothing to go home for.

Sat there, all neat and cozy with my head still pounding and my body aching like I'd been stretched on a rack the night before, I waited to see just what the bird was up to, if anything.

The wait paid out, eventually. I discovered two important pieces of information. One, that the first house in the row was owned by an old geezer. I'd caught him puttering around in his front garden, holding a kid-sized watering can in his claw-like, arthritic hands. Two, the house at the end of the road was shuttered up and quite probably empty.

The first two were well lit for the night, so I deduced the woman was either inside the old guy's house, somehow humped to death by the octogenarian stud. That, or she'd just gone for the one at the center, which had kept its doors and curtains good and shut since she'd gone, to guard her from prying eyes.

I looked back at the old man, shrugged, then turned to the center house.

Around six, I started to wonder how my partner was doing with our latest potential client. All told, we might have gotten ourselves a pretty sweet gig, but the kale wasn't always a given and some of our jobs weren't exactly cliffhanger material.

Take our latest case, for example: a rube in Kingsport, some well-to-do banker type with more mullah than sense, had gotten in touch with Barnes worried that his wife was getting busy behind his back. I hadn't met the rube, but according to Barnes, he'd been a stuffy old goat who acted like the whole world owed him rent.

He paid us what we thought *we* were owed for taking the job and although I spent the day following his hustling wife from one dull location to another, it did seem like she was up to something *fishy*.

I was reaching for my thermos, fit to burst with black coffee laced with about a pound of sugar, when that something finally happened.

The window on my side of the Buick was wound down slightly, just enough to allow some of the night air in and my coffee breath out. The loud sound of a door slamming shut meant that, since the little old gardener had been gone for a while, something was going on next door. I mentally crossed my fingers in the hopes I wouldn't have to stick around here any longer than I'd have to.

A minute after the door shut, the blonde came strolling into view, heading out of the middle house's front garden with a tall, dark-haired man in tow. Going by the way they handled each other, stepping off the sidewalk before turning to embrace, I knew they weren't just old pals playing catch-up.

I would've liked to use the camera but the flash would definitely blow my cover. Not that it would have mattered, as it turned out.

I'd tucked myself into my seat and made some notes on my pad. Going by the address she'd gone into and the time she arrived, I wrote down how long she'd spent there before making a brief note of her lover's description.

While I was at it, the pair began necking something fierce, with her leaning against the car her husband had probably got her. When they finally split, she turned to climb into the Cadillac and I found myself surprised she'd actually held off from jumping his bones in the middle of the street.

The Caddy started with a tiger's growl and sped down the street. Soon as the man turned back to his den, I decided to finally call it a night.

I got my stuff together and chuckled. There went another rich man's trophy wife, sneaking out of her display cabinet to get some take-away nookie, when I heard a loud, angry tapping against my window.

I didn't have my gun on me. After all, what was the worst that could happen on a stake-out? I turned to look at the schmuck thumping at my window and wished I hadn't. It was the blonde's lover boy, looking all good and pissed off as he pointed at me through the glass.

His other hand held a tire wrench.

Forcing a smile, I rolled the window all the way down and pretended to put up my innocent bystander act. Turns out, the gigolo must have noticed my camera so my gig was well and truly up.

Up close and personal, he didn't look like much. He had a too big nose for his pretty boy face and I could smell the fruitcake perfume he had slapped all over his prissy self.

"Did that old bastard put you up to this?" he growled. "You better tell me or I swear to God I'll bash your stupid mug in. Then your stupid car."

From the sound of his voice, the lollygagger couldn't string a threat together to save his life: his voice wavered too much and his face kept switching between a snarl and a frown.

"Public decency inspector." I said, friendly as you please, still eyeing the tire iron. "Just patrolling the streets to make sure no one makes a mess on the sidewalks."

This made him lean into the car, his pointed finger almost pushing up against my nose. "Why you. . ." he snarled, then yelped like a pup as I grabbed his finger and twisted it all the way back.

I leaned into him even as he retreated, grinning as he dropped the wrench and fell down to his knees.

He twisted like a little dervish against my grip, trying to rescue his pointing finger against my hold.

I caught his wet gaze and snarled "Stop playing with other people's toys. And never, *ever*, approach strange men in cars!"

I released him after this, leaving him to fall flat on his ass.

I wound the window up without bothering to check whether I'd made him cry.

Sometimes, the job is its own reward.

For the next hour, my mystery john told me his little sob story, about how he'd gotten to know a young, down-on-her-luck dancer and saved her from a life of streetwalking. Soon after meeting, they fell head over heels for each other before getting married in an odd little coastal town called Innsmouth. I knew it as a place full of bad news and ugly truths.

He went on to say that while he spent his time running his empire, she kept herself busy with a lot of hobbies that would keep her mixed race wedding out of sight from the rest of society. One of them, the seemingly innocent pursuit of antique books, had got her involved with a bunch of book-loving kooks that went so far as to worship one work in particular, by the name of *The King In Yellow*.

Arkham Nights

The last time he'd seen her, before she fell off the face of the Earth, was five days ago, when she left for one of their meetings in Boston.

He scoured the place for her, naturally: every single person that was there that day, from the manager of the hotel where the meeting took place, all the way down to the bellhops and the cleaning lady, had been given the third degree and then some, without much success.

After picking up a few names and some vague descriptions of the cult's leaders that led him nowhere, he decided to hire a professional. Someone with a taste for the weird and the bloody: two dicks going by the name of Towers and Barnes.

I was flattered that he picked me, especially considering the amount of dough he decided to throw my way. After I reassured him that he'd be updated on a daily basis, he left me his number scrawled on a piece of paper. A half hour later after he was gone, I was still staring at his wife's photo, laid out beside that big wad of cash, and wondered where on earth I should even start looking for her.

In my opinion the whole book angle was nothing but hokum, and she'd just dumped him for a fresh start elsewhere. Then again, I sort of wished that wasn't the case. He didn't look like the type of guy who could take getting dumped like that all civil like.

I was knocked out of my reverie by the shrill ring of the telephone. I picked it up, only to hear Towers' gruff voice on the other end. After he'd finished telling me how the tailing had gone down, I went on to inform him about our latest gig. True to form, he'd worked out a lead before I'd even finished speaking.

"Well, a daddy-o got hitched with an offay. Heavens above." Towers muttered, squinting through the glare on the car's windscreen. He fumbled for a pair of sunglasses before continuing. "I guess it *does* take all kinds."

I smirked. "Says the man who raised Hell just to talk to his ex-wife."

He snarled in reply, not taking his shielded eyes off the road as he peeled rubber towards Boston.

It was a few minutes past nine, and he was in a real foul mood for being dragged out of bed so early; probably wouldn't have bothered if it weren't for the big wad of cash that'd just been thrown at us. He'd just picked me up in his Buick, his angry, hulking form barely covering the glint in his eye.

Apparently, Trevor knew his weird books. *The King in Yellow*, Trevor informed me, had something to do with a writer fella from Boston.

"Weird cults and fan clubs and books with weird names," he'd said, "That's right up Justin Geoffrey's street. He writes about that bushwa all the time." Towers had met Geoffrey through his ex-wife, which didn't come as too much of a shock; after all, the woman had been dead, reanimated and then killed again. Even so, he was all too eager to drive us up to our only solid lead.

It was a typical hot-day road-trip, with the two of us baking in the car, counting bug-stains as they splattered across the windshield. Not a bad day to make a thousand bucks.

One thing I had found out through our contacts was the client's surname, Wallace. Towers brought it up as we drove through a patchwork world of fields and trees.

"So, what we got on the guy? Besides half his name?"

I looked back at him, saying, "They tied the knot up in Innsmouth."

Towers swore, shaking his head in disgust.

"Innsmouth? That freak show town?"

"I guess so."

"Makes sense," Towers said, "Where the hell else would they find a priest damn fool enough to marry them?"

Innsmouth was Arkham's smaller, creepier, fish-infested suburb, a place that had given birth to half the bogeymen in Massachussets. Apparently, the place had been bombed halfway into dust by the Navy, with the majority of its inbred hick natives carted off to some government freak show, only to be replaced by more of the same.

Towers continued on the same tact, "What about our stoolies, Blind Eddie, or Brown Jenkin; did you get anything from them?"

"No more than what he told me," I replied, "He got most of Big Boss's rackets and everyone else got the shaft."

A truck filled with hay suddenly overtook us, leaving a cloud of dust and exhaust fumes in its wake; Towers gave it the finger before saying with a laugh, "Which lets our daddy-o hire two torpedoes like ourselves for an open-and-shut missing persons case."

"If we find her," I said, spoiling the mood.

"That's one big if," he said sourly, then added, a touch more giddy, "Spent any of our little wad yet?"

"Got us a filing cabinet and a hat rack for the office. Soon as we get the rest, I was thinking we ought to hire a secretary too." I said, staring back at the scenery.

"Lemme guess: blonde with tits about . . ." Towers paused for a moment, before asking ". . . yay big?"

"I was thinking scrawny and bald," I replied, grinning. "You know, the working type."

"Hey," he said, "As long as you don't marry the bug-eyed Betty."

The Buick kept picking up speed as we went, making the fields speed as if running for their lives.

Looking out of the windscreen, I finally noticed: Towers had caught up with the hay truck.

He grinned wickedly and I guessed he was about to give the driver a crash course in polite motoring.

Slamming his foot down on the gas, Towers said, in that creepy little tone of his, "Hold on to your hat."

I rolled my eyes, took hold of my hat, and muttered, "Here we go again!"

After giving the truck driver hell for a while, I finally settled down. Besides, the truck had turned off in the direction of a nothing little village and we'd almost reached the outskirts of Boston. And man, did I like Boston.

Riley, looking a bit green around the gills after my little show-off, looked relieved when I eased up on the gas. Unfortunately for us though, as we reached the city proper, we got bottlenecked something fierce. Still, I loved this town with its skyscrapers and bustling crowds, its crooneries its speakeasies, its commercial streets fit to burst with the ritziest things you could hope to find. If Arkham was a sullen old hag, this was a bearcat fresh out of Catholic School and dripping Greek fire.

After the drive we were absolutely famished, so we decided we'd hit the first place that was close to Geoffrey's. I knew his address by heart: 80 Bay State Road, just across the street from the Charles River Reservation and half a stone's throw from Boston University. There were bound to be restaurants around there somewhere.

As we wound our way through inner Boston, I noticed Barnes idling. Guess he was scouring though the crowds looking for potential secretaries. I decided to tell him just what I knew about Justin Geoffrey.

"He's a bit of an odd duck, this feller we're about to meet," I said, as I led the Buick through a jam on Brookline Street. "He looks screwy, I'll give you that. He twitches and mumbles to himself but his brain's as sharp as a razor."

Barnes laughed, saying, "So you guys clicked from the start, huh?"

I ignored him and said "He's probably the only person who could know anything about that thing Big Boss turned into; Hell, he's the only one that might have an idea about that funny lobster thing we saw floating down the Miskatonic."

"I don't think we ought to know, if you ask me," Barnes said. I silently agreed.

Mercifully, the traffic thinned out and before long, we were traveling down Brookline Street at a decent pace before crossing the bridge across the Charles River Reservation.

From then on, we took a right turn on Storrow before another right at the university and into Bay State Road. With this done in what I could only describe as record time, I filled Barnes in on the rest I had on Geoffrey, giving him the juiciest tidbits I had about the man.

"I remember Jayne telling me he was locked up in an asylum once," I continued. "He'd been abroad, somewhere in Eastern Europe I think. Things got . . . weird over there."

Barnes said, "Ain't that just peachy."

"Well, it seems he got it into his head that some cult or another was out to bump him off, because, at least that's how I heard it, he apparently let some secret from one of their books out."

Having spied an eating-place just across from the University, I finished up my tale while pulling up at the nearest parking meter.

"So when it comes to ghosties and ghoulies and witchcraft, the guy knows his stuff. When he isn't lollygagging with four-flusher poetry, that is."

Bay State Road stretched out between two rows of tall but cramped apartment houses, each flanked by wide sidewalks with a sparse treeline. It didn't seem like the kind of place a mad poet might live in.

After stuffing our faces with Boston's finest fare, me with a plate of ham and eggs, Towers tackling two plates of the same accompanied by a cheddar cheese apple pie, we decided to take a leisurely walk over to Geoffrey's. Walking a few dozen yards along the side of the street, Towers soon led us to a tall, beat-up red-bricked house.

"Nice haunt," I said, but Towers didn't answer.

I followed his lead up the front steps to a wide green door. Towers banged at it without bothering with the greenish lion's head brass knocker.

Towers was about to say something when a half dozen latches rattled open to unlock the door. I guessed the owner was still keeping an eye out for cultists. It opened just enough to reveal a thin man in his glad rags: sleek black suit with a white shirt, a black bow tie and a look of complete contempt in his pinched, pink face. A thin layer of jet-black hair was slicked across his shiny head, complimenting his pencil-thin mustache.

He gave us the once-over before saying in a clipped English accent, "I do believe you have the wrong address."

Towers, looking annoyed, said, "No, busboy, we don't. Go tell Justin that Trevor Towers is here to see him."

The man leaned forward, scrunching up his nose. "Oh dear, it *is* you," then added, "A moment, please," and the door slammed shut at our faces.

"Nice fella," I said, before adding, "Still, next to Geoffrey, he's almost normal."

A moment later the door opened again, and our sour-faced friend admitted us into a lobby of black and white marble floor tiles, flanked with high walls made from gilded wood planks. There were two small doors on either side of the lobby and a pair of wide, walnut double doors at the end. There weren't any staircases, so I assumed that one of the doors led to one or hid a service elevator.

The skinny little busboy led us across the lobby before halting at the double doors and turned to us with his trademark sneer.

"Master Geoffrey will see you now," he warbled as he opened the door with a flourish. I didn't know whether to salute or curtsy.

Towers led the way into the room, a long rectangular hall that looked like it had been ripped straight out of Buckingham and into the middle of Boston. Everything smelled of some strong, sharp incense that I couldn't place for the life of me.

The room had a thick red carpet, patterned in golden Inca designs, its nauseating design bleeding into the striped red and yellow wallpaper, obscured for the most part by the tall oak bookcases lining the walls. They seemed to reach all the way up to the pink ceiling, where a twinkling chandelier hung from its center.

Now there was a room fit for a weirdo. Then again, Towers didn't seem to mind; he just strode towards the man at the other end, sat behind a long wooden desk covered by books and a typewriter, a pair of thick red velvet curtains at his back.

The man, whom I thought had to be Justin Geoffrey, was a testament to poor taste.

The stick-thin man was dressed in a double-breasted powder blue suit. He waited for Towers to get near before nervously shooting out from behind his desk toward him. He took us in with jerky, bird-like glances, staring at us through those deeply gray pools he had for eyes, set in his gaunt handsome face. His hair was a shock of ginger, and, together with the light dusting of freckles on his nose, made him appear far younger than he probably was.

Tiptoeing across the carpet towards us, he stopped before Towers and cleared his throat before saying in his quiet voice.

"Towers, the years haven't been kind, have they?"

Towers crossed his arms, sneering. "You're looking as spiffy as ever."

Geoffrey quickly retorted with, "There is a portrait of me, up in the attic, that would beg to differ."

Towers shrugged as he followed Geoffrey's remark with, "What the hell are you even talking about?"

Geoffrey said, "Never mind," before getting straight down to business, "Who is your friend?"

Introductions were made all around and Geoffrey offered us drinks which we had to decline before heading back to his desk. There were a few empty seats scattered here and there; carved ebony framed affairs padded with green fabric and covered in a gold-thread urn-and-griffin pattern.

We watched Geoffrey retrieve a small silver box from the desk drawer, opening it to remove a thin black smoke.

He offered us one of the same, which we again turned down, before he lit his from a ritzy-looking desk lighter, puffing at it as if his life depended on it. This seemed to ease his jitters and we watched as he trailed the smoke on its way up to the ceiling, before snapping his head down toward Towers.

He said, "We both know you're always bad news, Mr. Towers."

Towers shrugged and said, leaning into the cluttered desk:

"You won't turn down an old friend, right Geoffrey? Not without squaring your debt first."

Geoffrey gave me a quick, nervous glance before saying, "What, that's it? Just this and we're done?"

Towers shot him a grin that was all teeth, his big hands arching up into steeples as he went on. "I'll be on the road and out of your hair for good, Geoffrey," he said.

Geoffrey positively beamed. He continued with, "Your request is my command, gentlemen," and I began telling him the score.

Geoffrey listened quietly as we went over the finer details of the case. In the five-odd minutes it took us to go through it, he went through two more smokes that blanketed even the sickly incense smell. Geoffrey went all bug-eyed when I finally mentioned *The King in Yellow*.

He puffed away at another smoke, but that didn't seem to help; his free hand kept rapping at the desk the entire way through.

When we finished, he began with, "Well, *The King in Yellow* is a play dating back to the 18th century, and as far as I know, it is a story merely of political and royal intrigue set within some mythical city." He paused to light another smoke, then, "According to legend, it's cursed."

Towers interrupted him, "Cursed how?"

"Cursed as in, literally," Geoffrey said, "haunted, blighted, blasted and voodooed, worse than the Wandering Jew."

Towers and I shared a disbelieving look. Geoffrey quickly added, "Some who read it go insane; others are haunted by the supernatural entities that the play describes. The lucky ones just die outright."

"Who the hell would go after it then?" Towers asked.

"Nobody, of course" Geoffrey said, "The book just . . . *seduces* them."

Even in light of everything else we'd gone through it sounded like a load of bushwa, but I pressed on. "Okay, so where does that leave us? How does this help us find the crackpots that got the girl?"

He was eager to continue. "Every cult, like every religion, has its own gods and focal points of worship. If they worship the play, that means that they need to enact it, every now and again; acts, put on during Sunday Mass. If your damsel in distress has been whisked away by these types, then her days are well and truly numbered. So are theirs, if they keep poking at the unknown the way that they have been."

"They sound more like a bunch of kooky two-bit actors to me," Towers said, not caring too much about Geoffrey's phonus balonus.

But I'd *seen* the thing that had burst out of Big Boss; I'd seen West making the dead walk, and the thing that floated down the Miskatonic, and I knew that there was something awfully wrong about the case. Justin Geoffrey might *look* like a dewdropping futz, but he looked like he knew his stuff.

"So what can we expect? If they do have her, I mean," I asked, not too keen to hear the answer.

"Anything," he said, staring me in the eye with a clear, intense look. His twitching hand finally went still as he continued, ". . . that lies beyond the ken of man."

Our interview with Geoffrey had gone better than either of us anticipated. Barnes and I knew all there was to know about the underworld but that prissy futz had tread far deeper than either of us would dare to go.

As a parting gift, he gave us a lead on a troupe of King in Yellow worshipers that lived in a mansion in the woods just north of Boston, run by some big cheese by the name of Errin Fox. "It takes money to organize and madness to maintain the worship of the Yellow King," he said, "Errin Fox has both in abominable abundance."

Guess it was about time that fruit got new house guests.

Driving back through the choked streets of Boston, I kept myself from bashing my horn into the steering wheel by going over what we'd learned with Barnes.

"So what do you think? Did your pal just sell us a load of hokum or what?"

"He's not my pal," I snorted. "He's just a fruity little table-rapper with too much free time on his hands and if we keep at it the way we are, we'll end up just like him."

Barnes laughed, and then his voice turned grim.

"Let's just hope this King in Yellow is a lot of hooey," he said, his tone uncertain. "Then again, you never know, what with our luck so far . . ."

He was referring to the Big Boss case, an experience I was desperately trying to forget.

"Well, if we find her all chewed up by creepie-crawlies, we can always refund Wallace's payment," I grumbled, getting madder still. The car in front of me, a dark red Ford Convertible, wasn't letting up an inch.

If I hadn't been in such good company, I would've gotten out and had a word with the driver with my trusty crowbar in hand. I checked for any traffic bulls and found none. Good old Boston, never a cop around when you don't need one.

Barnes began to speak. I shushed him, putting the Buick into reverse. After making sure I had the space to leave our lane, I whipped the car to the left, taking a U turn back to the way we came.

Car horns blasted and brakes squealed; Barnes started cussing up a storm but I didn't care. Trevor Towers was well and done with Boston's traffic.

I'd decided to drive back towards Boston University, onto the Massachusetts Turnpike and toward wider, open pastures.

"You crazy palooka," Barnes said. "Are you trying to get us both killed?"

The Massachusetts Turnpike opened up into a wide motorway, out into the sparse countryside that surrounded Boston.

Barnes said, after a while, "If we end up stumbling on something that's out of our league, we could always contact Wallace, get him to send us some extra manpower."

I didn't like how spooked he sounded. Riley Barnes just wasn't the kind of man to show he was afraid; then again, I couldn't blame him, seeing the kind of things we'd gone up against.

I said, "It's either a group of rich nuts worshipping a stupid play, or it's a bunch of dyed-in-the-wool crazies. Either way, we can blow them all the way to kingdom come." I wasn't joking. I had dynamite in the trunk.

That seemed to lighten Barnes up a bit. "Dyed-in-the-wool, huh? Did you pick that up from a girlie magazine?"

"Skimmed the editorial while I was on the crapper." I said. "This is gonna be open-and-shut, Barnes, just you wait."

I reached to knock wood, just in case, barely missing a piece of roadkill on the way. As far as omens go, that one didn't look too promising.

We followed the Turnpike to East Boston, getting through it without getting into too many jams, all the way through Chelsea and onto the Salem Turnpike.

Soon enough, we'd be in the patch of woods that Geoffrey

had mentioned, located in the shadow of a lovely little town called Salem.

If Arkham was Witch Central, then Salem had to be the genuine, grade-A, primo deal.

The Turnpike took us straight into Chamber Woods, a thick wad of greenery lurking below a steep embankment on the right. I found it hard to believe that a mansion could ever have been built there. Everything looked so wild and pristine but Geoffrey wasn't one for red herrings, despite all his outright kookiness.

We made for Chamber Woods on a dirt road so thickly peppered with rocks and fallen branches that I felt like my car's suspension would go at any moment.

I drove in silence, mostly looking out for the larger chunks of debris. Barnes, staring out at the passing trees, said, "Everything about this place just screams ambush."

I nodded, saying, "It's too quiet around here; you even heard a bird since we got here?"

The 'road' continued unabated, every now and again snaking out into unexpected turns. These sections were pretty much choked with trees, with a few of their branches stripped where unknown vehicles had recently passed.

"So Errin loves seclusion," Barnes said after I'd scraped the Buick's paintjob through another obstruction.

I grunted.

"There's no gate," he said. "You'd think there would be a gate or something."

After a few more minutes, the dirt road finally led us to our destination. Hopefully, there was only one person around here that was crazy enough to build a mansion in the middle of these damn woods.

Surrounded by two acres of well-kept lawn stood a white, two-storied, T-shaped building with a square face. The mansion was set in the center of a nearly perfectly round clearing, with the thirty feet or so of gravel path I drove down ending at a square space bearing three poorly parked cars.

The mansion's front end was about forty feet high and about just as wide. Its steepled gray roof stuck out over the building's walls, festooned with gold spindly columns that reached down to touch the veranda.

Its outward gaudiness, however, didn't make the place look any less like it had been left to ruin. Most of its windows had been broken, with jagged spikes of glass poking out from the second-floor window frames. The same went for the two flanking the door on the first.

As I slowed the Buick and turned into the car park, I noticed that the building's left side was similarly damaged. The glass in the car windows had also been smashed.

I counted a bright red convertible, a black Ford station wagon and a green sedan of the same make.

I was about to turn to Barnes, when he said, in a quiet tone, "Get the feeling we might be too late to crash the party?"

I nodded.

The steps up to the veranda, leading to the dark red door centered deep within an alcove, lay just a few feet beyond the car park. It'd been left ajar to reveal a gaping blackness beyond.

Barnes was staring at the cars. He clicked his tongue before saying, "So what's the verdict Trev? Bomb? Bop party gone bad?"

My eyes felt almost glued to the house. I couldn't quite put it in words, but the thing seemed almost alive, somehow.

I bit my bottom lip and said, "Don't know and I don't wanna know, but I bet you we can take it."

I reached into my jacket to retrieve the .45 auto from my holster. It didn't help much, but it was a start.

As Barnes reached to prep his own gun, I pumped a cartridge into the chamber of mine.

I found myself grinning as I climbed out of the car. Barnes stared at me all puzzled.

He said, "What? We're just gonna barge in there? Just like that?"

"Well, if it was a bomb that tore up the place," I waved towards the cars and the mansion, "Then maybe we don't really got to do squat."

Barnes snorted before heading towards the veranda. He said, "I don't think Wallace is going to go for it; not if his wife is in pieces."

"After the shit we've been up against, who gives a rat's ass what Wallace wants," I said.

I followed him around the car knowing in my gut that death himself had cast a very long shadow over Errin Fox's shattered home. We walked up the steps to cross a veranda blanketed in shattered fragments of glass.

We crunched across the debris and positioned ourselves on either side of the door. Peeking inside, I saw that the room beyond was as dead and empty as we'd thought.

There wasn't much in the way of light as we entered, besides what was filtering in from behind us. That long, dull square however, revealed everything we needed to know.

The entrance hall was about fifteen feet wide and twice that in length. It told a story of destruction and death. The ornate oak grandfather clock and tables and chairs were smashed to bits all around us.

The dark red blots spattered across the floor were the worst part, seeming to somehow move, when I'd catch them from the corner of my eye. The walls were also spattered with blots of congealed gore.

I kicked at a piece of broken clockwork and sent it skittering towards the end of the hall, into another open door, flanked by a pair of alcoves. Steep staircases reached up beyond each of them.

Barnes was going over the carnage, whistling softly. He held his gun slack against his side and I suppose that, like me, he thought that the worst had come to pass after all.

I said, "No bomb could have done this. This is old-fashioned human ugliness, plain and simple."

We cautiously made our way to the end of the hall, raising our guns at the darkness in case the mansion had any more surprises in store for us.

We'd go through the mansion with a fine-toothed comb, if it meant that we might just get Gemma Wallace out of here in one piece.

The rest of the first floor held more of the same brutal carnage. As we searched through the other rooms we found smashed glass, cracked furniture and blood in spades.

It was after we had retraced our steps and made our way up to the second floor that we found our first survivor. In a bedroom on the western side of the mansion's 'T,' we found a man dying in a growing pool of his own blood.

The door was locked so I kicked it down. Inside a bedroom decorated in gay whites and pinks with a large double bed at its center, we found the half-naked bastard.

As we entered, he struggled to raise his revolver in his limp hands, then finally dropped it when we approached. He seemed almost relieved to see us.

We approached him cautiously He was a pale, skinny fellow,

topless with a shock of mussed, receding black hair lying atop his sweating brow. Blood trickled slowly from the multiple stab wounds dotting his red-stained chest. After taking a gander at him, I lowered my gun. He looked halfway gone.

Barnes said sternly, "You the one behind this bloodbath?"

The man coughed with a liquid sound and raised his head.

His eyes seemed to clear a little as he looked at Barnes.

"I'm afraid not," he said, obviously in agony.

"Then who the hell did this?" Barnes sounded almost about to lose it.

"Let's just say we bit off a whole lot more . . ." the man said, spitting blood. ". . . than we could chew."

"We know about the King in Yellow, if that's what you're getting at." Barnes said.

The man chuckled, another gurgle rising from his throat.

"They came for us after the second act. The Stranger and his mask . . ."

He was wracked with coughs, bloody spittle flying out of his mouth. He had a few more minutes left in him, if that.

I said, "Listen, we're looking for the Wallace girl."

His eyes focused on mine. "Some of our troupe fell in with the King's phantoms. The rest . . . didn't make it through the act." He laughed and pointed at his gun. "They got me before I could pull the trigger . . . ."

Barnes went on, fighting back the wave of nausea that creeped into his voice.

"Who are 'they'? Where the hell are the rest of you?"

"What about the Wallace girl? Come on man, the least you can do is give us that!" I said.

He grinned at me widely, revealing a mouth full of blood-stained teeth.

"One last good deed, eh?" he swallowed back a mouthful of blood and said, "The unturned women were restrained. The men were slaughtered."

"Then . . ." I began to say but was quickly cut off.

"I escaped just as they began tearing out the men's hearts. They almost got mine." He pointed at his mangled chest. "What's left of them is probably scattered in the woods. The phantoms told them to eat the hearts."

"God damn," I said.

Barnes frowned, obviously disgusted.

The man groaned before saying, "Fox and Madson have a place

in Kingsport, on the docks near the cannery. You may find the woman there, if you're quick."

Barnes turned to me, "Looks like Geoffrey was right on the money."

I said, "Kingsport isn't too big. She shouldn't be too hard to find."

I turned back to ask the dying man, only to find that life had left his eyes.

I crossed myself. Barnes didn't bother.

We stood in silence and turned away from the corpse. Barnes began heading towards the door.

"You think we should let the bulls know or something?"

Barnes shrugged. He paused for a moment before replying. "Let's just wipe down the place and leave this mess up to someone else."

We did just that.

The carnage at Fox's mansion stuck with us all the way to Kingsport.

I was coming to terms with the supernatural angle, while Barnes was chalking it all up to drugs and madness. We were about to leave the Salem Turnpike when Barnes spoke up.

"I get it now: Kingsport, as in, 'The King's Port.' You think that's why they chose the place?"

I nodded. "Sounds kooky enough for a pack of freaks to cling to. You still working the drugs angle, aren't you?"

Barnes snarled. "No way around it, is there? I mean, who the hell else could have done it, except for some big six junkie, off his head on dope?"

I wanted to remind Barnes about the kinds of things people *can* get up to when they're not on dope. When they're stuck in the trenches, for example, trapped behind a gas-mask, hands shaking from not letting go of the trigger for two days straight, when they find themselves knee-deep in the dead, screaming at a radio that's gone dead with the Krauts shelling the world above into dust . . . .

I held on to the supernatural angle instead.

The drive to Kingsport was fairly uneventful, all things being equal. Towers managed to avoid running over anyone and I was only teetering at the edge of another coronary. The traffic had been worse than expected and Trevor wasn't having it. In all fairness, my attitude may have—hard as it is to believe—made Trevor a bit nervous. I tend to keep it together most of the time, but this case was really rubbing me the wrong way.

What we'd seen at the Chamber Woods mansion had really shaken me. Yet, after all we'd experienced in the way of supernatural bogies it was mild by comparison. Our conversation on the road had been standard fare, but I still couldn't keep the anger that was bubbling in me from showing. Trevor made sure he gave me as much space as I could stand. He cracked, fifteen minutes later.

"You want to tell me about that bug up your ass?" he said, flipping the bird at a hot-rodding college boy.

I scowled, so he pressed on.

"Come on, Riley," he said, "it's not like we haven't had worse."

I lit a gasper and breathed it in, before staring out the window.

"Look," he said, "I don't enjoy sticking my big nose in your business but we're partners, goddamn it. Don't clam up on me."

"Skeletons in the closet," I mumbled.

"What?" he asked.

"I said there are skeletons . . . in my closet."

Trevor scowled. On any other day, he would have looked almost funny.

"I had a sister," I said, "emphasis on *had*."

He nodded and actually slowed the car down.

"This was back when I was still boxing," I continued. "I'd been training for the big leagues and I let Lisa get . . . loose."

"How old was she?" he asked.

"Nineteen," I answered, "but you wouldn't know it, looking at her. She was just a kid at heart."

"She was about my age," he continued. "When they sent us to the trenches, that is."

"Yeah, you either wised up fast or you weren't around to worry about it." I smiled grimly.

"Anyway," I continued, "it seems that while I'd been busy, Lisa had gotten involved with some no good types in college."

"College, huh?" Trevor said, "She sounds like a smart girl."

"Yeah, Lisa got the lion's share of the brains in the family. Ma worked like a dog to pay for the tuition and I chipped in however much I could."

"What about your old man?" Trevor asked.

"He was worthless," I replied. "Ain't that just the thing?"

Trevor nodded.

"Well, Lisa came to me one afternoon at the gym and really nagged me, all sweet like, to take her to the pictures."

"And you didn't take her, did you?" Towers asked.

"Hell, no," I answered. "Riley Barnes was going to be *the champ* some day. He couldn't be bothered to waste any time with his kid sister."

I was shocked to find my eyes watering. I choked back the tears.

"Look," Trevor said. "It's okay if you'd rather not talk about it. I know I pry sometimes."

"No," I said, "this has been a long time coming."

I ran my shirtsleeve over my eyes and said. "Damned wind's messing up my peepers."

Trevor kept quiet as I pulled myself together. After a while, I went on with my story.

"Lisa didn't go to the pictures that night. She hooked up with some college rowdies and went to a party instead. There was dope and brown and she just couldn't turn it down. We never figured out exactly what happened but some old couple found her dead by the side of the road. She'd overdosed and her *friends* had dumped her like so much garbage."

"Jesus," Trevor whispered.

"Damn near killed my Ma," I said. "She held on for a year after that, just wasting away."

"I'm sorry," Trevor said.

I barely held back a smile. This had been the first time Trevor had ever said the word. "I did just fine for myself, though. Made it all the way to my first big bout and got KO'd just the once in my entire career. Not that it meant a damn, in the end."

"I must've fought you before that," Trevor said. "You seemed to care *plenty* when you were in the ring with me."

"Nah," I replied. "I just hated your stupid mug."

He laughed and I couldn't help but smile. "Since then," I said, "Dope dealers tend to drive me off the deep end, you know?"

"Makes sense."

Time seemed to pick up the pace after I'd spilled my guts to Trevor. We spent the time telling dirty jokes, having our little gross-out pissing contest as we went. I was halfway through telling the raunchy story of the vicar and the toothless whore, when

Trevor took a right into Kingsport and steered the Buick into a shadowy little spot on the dock.

"So she says 'I guess you just don't love me anymore' . . ."

"We're here," he said, nodding toward a gray, tall building.

"Nice place for a bad deal," I replied. "Bet it blends right into the background."

"Not that anyone would look for it, going by the place."

"We did," I replied. "Time to bust some heads."

"Soon as we get the schmucks," Trevor affirmed. "We rush them."

"Got any cards with you?"

Trevor shook his head.

"Ain't that a shame," I said, pulling a rolled-up magazine from my pocket.

Trevor rolled his eyes and smirked. "What's that? Latest version of McClure's?"

I held up the copy of *Thrilling War Stories* and grinned. On the cover, some overly patriotic doughboys were going over the top with bayonets at the ready. They looked almost constipated, if you asked me.

"Jeez," Trevor moaned. "What, the Somme wasn't enough for you?"

"Oh, the Somme is gonna last me for a lifetime," I answered. "But at least in these stories the good guys win for once."

Trevor stared at the warehouse. "You think we're the good guys in this story?" he said.

"Who the hell else could we be?" I answered. "We got the Tommy Guns and the trenchcoats and the crappy rat-trap for an office, don't we?"

In my heart of hearts, I prayed that I was right.

It had been two hours since we began our stakeout and there was still no sign of our quarry. After the first hour, our conversation had slowly died down. Since then, Barnes had sat reading from his magazine while I looked for another way to waste my time.

After failing to keep myself busy, I'd set my sights on a small black beetle that kept attempting to climb across the windscreen. Each time it reached the halfway mark, it slipped and tumbled back down the glass to land against the wipers.

I was sat watching it go through its hundredth attempt, when the bad thing happened.

Barnes yawned and I couldn't blame him. I was beginning to miss all those hours I'd wasted during trophy wife stakeouts. At least there, nobody got seriously hurt.

Everything went weird at the blink of an eye.

I noticed that something was wrong when Barnes, after I saw him with his arms still stretched a good minute into his yawn. He sat there in that pose, as if he was stuck in place.

I only noticed the change from his reflection on the windshield, as my eyes were stuck on the bug, stuck in mid-step.

It took me a good few blinks before I even noticed the stillness.

I was about to turn and ask him just what was going on, when I realized that I couldn't move my head a single inch. I tried to speak, but found my lips locked shut.

My whole body seemed inert, or just about. I was unable to turn my head. My hands were stuck across my lap. I could wiggle my fingers and toes a little, but that was about it.

Fear began to creep in.

Before long, I realized that I could move my eyes. I couldn't see much past Barnes or the warehouse through the windshield, but that would have to do.

The terror set in about a thousand years later, creeping into my mind at an almost geological pace, while we were both frozen in place.

It moved in as slowly as an ice floe, an invisible cloud of rage that pushed the sweat down my brow and spine. I've been good and scared and helpless before, but this one took the cake.

Barnes must have been going through much of the same. His breathing was coming in bursts, matching the bebop of pure terror that beat in my chest.

I felt my heart was about to fly right out of my ribcage, and I knew that was just the beginning.

The 'worst' came riding on its loud hayburner. It made the Buick rattle as it went by, shooting a cloud of exhaust fumes through the half-open window.

I couldn't see too well on account of my frozen viewpoint, until the big six took a sharp turn and halted in front of the warehouse.

It was an old issue army Studebaker with its white star logo long since peeled away. The cloth covering the cargo bed looked like it had seen better days.

I'd ridden in one of those myself, back during my tour; they had been stuffy and cramped and too slow for their own good, but none of them had ever felt so truly, palpably *evil*.

Sweat trickled down my brow and my heart pounded like a jackhammer. Barnes was still paralyzed. The bug looked just as helpless as we did.

We were caught in a web of invisible, cloying strands waiting for the emperor of spiders to waltz in and sink his teeth in us.

I fought back the fever pitch of my own rising horror.

The truck's side door opened; its passenger, a man in long yellow robes, climbed down from the cab and made his way to the rear, pulling up his yellow hood. I couldn't see the driver but I assumed he looked about the same.

Before long, the driver joined him and they both began undoing the clasps at the truck's rear.

If I could have screamed, I would have done it until I'd gone hoarse.

Even more figures climbed down from the truck, all covered in dull yellow robes from head to toe. Going by their height and the cut of their shoulders, I'd have to guess they were probably all male.

They dragged their tired, sobbing birds behind them. There were half a dozen of them, framed by a dozen weirdos, but that wasn't all.

A swarm of . . . things, looking only halfway real, danced all around them like a cloud of locusts.

They were twisting, dancing devils, sprouting and retracting bits and pieces all over the place. Their faces were warped and skull-like, almost looking like they were screaming in rage. Swimming above and among the abductors and their victims, they seemed to almost *radiate* hate.

Their pure evil poured through my feeble, mortal frame, burning through my veins and heart, looking to sink its crooked claws into my heart.

Beside me, Barnes had begun to shake violently. The bug on the glass did a quick jitterbug, before it fell from the windscreen to lie dead on its back.

My time, I knew, was up.

When it rains, it pours. Typical. One second I'm having a stretch and watching Trevor gawping at a beetle on the car windshield, the next I'm stranded helpless in a nightmare. I thought this was another nightmare, tried to tell Trevor to *just wake me up* goddamnit, but no dice. He and the beetle were all stuck in place, as helpless as I was. The three of us, playing green light-red light with the forces of evil.

Trevor says I read too many pulps; that these things are gonna rot my brain. Who'd a thunk that all this sword and sorcery hokum would ever catch up with us? Ghoulies and ghosties and creepy-crawlies were one thing but this . . . this was *sorcery*, clear as day. And I knew I couldn't deal with sorcery.

I was reassuring myself when a passing Army truck near rattled me out of my seat. The truck screeched to a halt in front of the warehouse and I saw the whole robed weirdo posse filing out of the back. Others joined them and they began herding female prisoners inside the gray building. We'd hit paydirt, but that didn't help our situation any.

I fought against the mystical bondage that held me in place, but that didn't do squat. As I stopped to catch my breath, I caught sight of the yellow mist that hung over the weirdos. Sweat was trickling down my forehead and pooling into my eyes. I blinked it away, keeping my eyes glued to the bizarre entourage, when I realized that the yellow fog was actually a *swarm*.

They twisted in the air, waving their limbs all over the place, each bursting out of the mass of their bodies, branching out as it went, before receding back into the mass. Their faces were things of pure evil that sucked all hope out of their pathetic captives. Not that I was doing any better, mind you.

I wriggled my tongue and let out a useless, gurgling moan, as I noticed Wallace's wife among the captives. Mustering all the strength I had, I flexed the muscles of my mind and pushed back against the charm, feeling it go, inch by inch. From my neck, down to my shoulders, wrapping around my skull to my jaw until I finally let out . . .

"Trevor!" I hissed. "Can you move?"

His eyes were open and I could see that he was still struggling. I grabbed him by the shoulders and shook. Trevor just stared daggers into my eyes.

"Fight it, Trevor!" I urged. "We still got some bastards to snuff!"

Trevor didn't move, so I decided it was time I got some more drastic measures. If I couldn't give him the strength he needed with my words, I'd let him draw from his own, unexhausting rage. Grabbing Trevor by the shirt, I said, "I'm doing this for our own good."

I smacked him in the jaw with a hard right jab. Trevor began to howl through his clenched teeth, staring daggers at me, breaking out of the spell in a single flex of his red-hot mind. I knew for a fact that he was going to be okay when he groaned "Barnes, you sonofabitch."

I slipped back to my own side of the car, watching Trevor as he slowly regained control of his own body.

"Looks like your beetle buddy is okay," I said, watching Trevor rub his jaw.

He glanced at the windshield and grimaced. "Did you pop *him* in the jaw too?"

"No, I just gave him your digits," I said.

"Good," Towers said, "that beetle needs a real man."

I shrugged and said, "Let's get to work."

Creeping toward the warehouse, I felt the side of my face where Barnes had hit me already starting to swell. For a pulp-reading nerd, he still knew how to throw a proper punch.

We wound our way around the truck and what little foliage grew around the warehouse, skulking for cover the entire way.

I pricked up my ears and heard no alarm. Peeking from a corner, I noticed that there weren't any guards posted, either.

We were ten feet away from the warehouse, when I stopped to take the place in. It was a dump, no way around it, its many, dusty windows staring down at us from their rotting frames.

The chanting sent shivers down my spine.

I couldn't make out the words, but I knew the intent—every single jigaboo word of it was thick with venom. It seemed to waft out of the warehouse, twisting in the air like some living thing.

Barnes tapped me on the shoulder, whispering, "Ain't that just the bee's knees."

A loud, wailing scream cut through the litany. It was muffled out before we even had the chance to get around the truck and through the entrance.

So much for sneaking our way in, not with a dame in distress. We charged past the truck and booted our way through a pair of wide, faded blue doors, only to slip into madness, with a yellow-clad evil at the head.

The cultists didn't even look up at us as we burst through the doors, guns at the ready.

In the dim light, we saw it all: the wide chamber had a flat, dusty concrete floor flanked by distant, peeling walls. The cracked rafters from the high and distant ceiling seemed as long and wide as a giant's ribcage.

We gawped, like terrified ninnies, at the awful things inside.

The group of chanters were on their knees around a row of large wooden blocks, arranged into an altar, just thirty feet away. The rest of the yellow-clad weirdos were bent down in prayer, with their hooded heads facing the altar and their backs to us.

The women were arranged to the left of the altar, choking back tears. One of them had been laid out across it, her pale body naked with her chest ripped through from the navel up to the collarbone.

Barnes said, "Those filthy fucking butchers. It's a goddamn chopping block."

I just nodded, absolutely dumbstruck.

Another hooded man, the one that I assumed was the big cheese, stood behind her limp form. He held a bloodstained knife in one hand, something red and dripping in the other.

We were about to charge in, guns blazing, when something else slowly faded into view behind him.

This wasn't a phantom, this much I knew. Not a swarm of howling ghosts or any creepy crawly that we'd ever seen before.

We watched as the big cheese offered his still-beating offering to a yellow praying mantis, as big as a man.

It wore a grinning, golden mask; the claws at the ends of its arms had long-fingered, human-like hands growing at their tips, bearing large golden trays. One made a gentle, tinkling sound as the heart plopped on its glistening surface.

Another weirdo stepped up from the silent congregation and took the big cheese's place, dragging a new victim by the hair as he headed for the altar.

I recognized this one; Wallace's wife was headed for the chopping block next, so we sprang into action.

Like a penny dreadful villain, the man dragging Mrs. Wallace paused and pointed at us, shouting, "Usurpers!"

Every head turned in perfect sync to stare at us, shocked as they watched two charging private dicks coming at them.

I have to admit, I didn't feel too bad about crashing that particular party. The bug-thing—their King in Yellow—looked absolutely livid.

Waving his Thompson around, Barnes said "On the ground, hands up where we can see them." Then, "You there, let the girl go."

The man dragging Gemma Wallace let go, without thinking twice about it.

I covered Barnes, sneaking worried glances at the bug-thing. How he could look past that monster was beyond me.

We were a few steps away from the cultists when the thing dropped its golden plates. They went clattering down to the altar, the still-beating heart in one smacking the concrete.

We pointed our guns at the thing. It made a noise from behind its mask, a guttural alien screech that might have been a warning.

We froze on the spot, just like back in the Buick.

Son of a bitch had us all wrapped up and ready to serve.

I stared daggers into the mantis-thing's mask. It stared back with grim and golden contempt. Whatever lay beyond those slits for eyes made me feel feeble and small.

Around us, the cultists began to rise, muttering nonsense as they reached for us.

The man on the altar addressed them, his words dripping with malice.

"See the gift the King has brought us? Fresh cattle to add to the pile!"

From the back of my mind, I knew I'd heard this voice before. I filed this away for future reference, closed my eyes and focused on my trigger finger, making it wriggle by sheer grit. Thankfully, I mustered enough strength to pull it all the way back.

A spray of red-hot lead flew, getting the King square in his misshapen, yellow head.

My body sprang back into action, with Barnes following suit, pumping a good dozen rounds into the charging weirdo's chest.

Hail to the King.

Everything turned out as usual, as soon as we burst into the warehouse. We were outnumbered and scared half out of our minds, but we still gave the bastards one hell of a fight. We'd saved Wallace's bird, but she wasn't out of the woods just yet. When the King in Yellow struck us with his binding magic, Trevor broke the spell by tearing the thing's head clean in half.

I had just downed one of the King's main flunkies, when the wounded creature began to scream. It flailed around and its unholy shrieks made me feel as if my skull was splitting in two. I clutched my head with one hand and was about to finish the freak off when it suddenly collapsed into a sprawling mass of wriggling meat. It looked almost helpless for a moment, until it outright *exploded*.

I was about to mouth a warning when the yellow phantoms we'd seen earlier burst out from the gory remains of the King, flitted about the room and then slipped through the concrete floor. A black stain, shaped like an odd three-pronged sign, bled through the floor where each creature had disappeared.

The weirdos started to run. Trevor dropped more than a handful in one long, weaving spray. I made for Wallace's wife, who seemed to be suffering from major shellshock. I had almost reached her when the yellow-robed loony I'd just shot jumped up on his feet. He seemed all riled up, despite the sucking wounds across his chest. He raised the knife, ready to plunge it into the dame.

"Gemma, move!" I yelled, raising my gun. She fainted and I guessed that'd have to do.

Another burst took the bastard out for good. I made my way to the Wallace woman and checked her pulse, rubbed her wrist and slapped her cheeks gently, just for good measure. She was still out.

Towers was still firing at the stragglers. When his cartridges were good and spent, he made for the other women, all huddled together in a corner. After making sure they were alright, he turned back to me.

"Some of the bastards got away," he said, grinning. "The girls are shook up, but they'll live."

"Maybe that'll teach them to steer clear from weird books," I answered.

"I guess."

A gurgle bubbled out from the bloody yellow heap nearby. I stared at the cultist I'd almost cut in half already. "Jesus Christ, how are you still alive?"

"Shit, Barnes, good thing you never tried to be a hitman." Towers laughed, before adding, "Hey, I think I know him."

Wallace's wife slowly returned to consciousness and I tried to comfort her. Towers walked over to the dying cultist and tore his garish mask off. "Well, isn't that something," he said. "That's lover boy." He walked over to the sacrificial victim and grimaced. "And *this* is the runaway trophy wife."

He walked back to the moaning cultist and stood over him. I'd seen that look in Trevor's eyes before. Our rescued captives had had enough horror without having to watch all the awful stuff that Trevor was going to put the man through.

"Trevor! I'm taking these gals out of here." I said.

Distracted, he answered, "Sure buddy, knock yourself out."

I led Mrs. Wallace with the other women and slowly herded them out of the warehouse. I glanced back and saw Trevor kneeling beside the cultist.

I almost wished I'd shot him dead.

Almost.

I sat behind my battered desk and poured a stiff drink. It had been several days since the incident in Kingsport, with Mrs. Wallace safe and sound in her husband's arms. His gratitude would keep our creditors out of our hair but I wasn't too sure if his wife would pull through. Wallace certainly wasn't going to let her out of his sight, not after the last mess she got herself into, and let's face it: she wasn't going to stay put when she snapped out of it. But that's marriage for you, I guess: one part lies and nine parts compromise.

I thought of my own kid sister and regretted that this Riley Barnes hadn't been around for her back in those days. Maybe things would have turned out otherwise, if her big brother had been around. Then again, maybe I was spouting a load of bushwa. At the end of the day, people *do* change. Trevor and I sure as hell weren't the same men we'd been back before Falmouth. Yeah, we were still rough around the edges and we lacked finesse, but we got things *done*. We were pit bulls: once we latched onto something we wouldn't let go.

The newspapers reported that Errin Fox had managed to escape the carnage at Kingsport. That poor schmuck doesn't know it yet, but he's living on borrowed time. Maybe it'll be next week or next year but we'll get to sink our teeth into the bastard. Long and crooked teeth, the kind only ugly, battle-damaged pit bulls like us have.

And this time, we won't let go.

Redemption

I wiped my forehead with a grimy handkerchief and cursed at the weather. Arkham's streets were hotter than a whorehouse's sheets on this August day and my partner, Trevor Towers, had had the good sense to take a day off and waste his time at the beach with the newest waitress of the Arkham Kettle. Looking at Trevor, you wouldn't expect him to be the day-off type, but if it helped to take the edge off his strung-out attitude, then it was alright with me.

Barnes and Towers Investigations had been doing pretty well for itself since we opened shop and my old war buddy, Wade Kearney, was largely to blame. He had moved to Illinois to help his brother-in-law set up a trucking firm and had been generous enough to let us use him as a reference. Kearney had a reputation for handling the screwy cases and we sure as hell weren't strangers to *that* kind of thing. Hell, half the stuff Trevor and I had been caught in sounded like it had been ripped straight out of the pulps. Still, it was a good living. Better than a guy fresh out of the stir could hope to have. I had been framed—the wardens didn't buy it, of course—but the truth eventually came out and I was free to go. Kearney had helped me get a license and I had kept busy ever since. Then again, the license was just a formality; Trevor and I always had our own sense of doing what we thought was right. But now we were on the level, at least on paper.

Business had been so good, in fact, that we had put up an ad in *The Arkham Gazette* for an office girl to help out on a semi-regular basis. The lucky dame was a part-time college gal named Betty Polanski and she was already an hour late for her first day on the job. I figured I could overlook this breach of punctuality since we needed a bird if we were ever gonna get us some higher class john. The young lady was a bearcat and I just knew Trevor would be pleased as punch to see her.

To keep myself busy, I rifled through the looser desk drawers and took out a bottle of Old Sea Dog, pouring two finger's worth in our cleanest dirty glass, complimenting my treat with a butt straight out of my hope chest. I blew out a plume of smoke and sighed. Yes siree, this was the life.

"I'm here!" the voice came from the doorway.

Jesus, just listen to that foghorn, I thought, as I landed, face-first, back on terra firma.

"Hello?"

Stunned, I stared at the whale of a woman before me. "Lady, people in *South Carolina* heard you."

I cursed Trevor for agreeing to leave me alone in the office. Putting on my best airs, I looked at the white-haired heavy weight in our doorway and asked, "Who are *you?*" I'm real quick witted that way.

"I'm Gertrude," she answered. "But my friends call me Gertie."

"Hello Gertrude," I replied.

The woman stepped forward and extended a mitt that was almost as big as mine. We shook hands and I reminded myself to check for fractures later.

"What can I do you for?" I asked.

"Gertie," she said. "You might as well call me Gertie, since we're going to be working together."

"Come again?"

"Well, I don't know if Betty told you," she said, "but I'll be filling in for her when she can't make it."

"I'm sorry, what?"

She shook her head sadly. "For a peeper, you sure are slow on the uptake aren't you?"

"Please, enlighten me," I said.

She sighed. "I'm Betty's mother, Gertrude Polanski."

"Pleased to meet you, Mrs. Polanski, but I was sort of expecting Betty."

"She had to go shopping this morning."

"*Shopping?*" I asked.

"That's right," she said. "School starts soon and she can't just show up at work looking like a bug-eyed Betty."

"I guess not," I managed.

"You're such a *dear*, Mr. Barnes!" she said, beaming. "We

need the dough *so* bad to pay for books, tuition and groceries . . . I promise you won't regret this for one minute. You really are such a *dear* and *understanding* man!"

Maybe so, but Trevor certainly wouldn't share that sentiment, not when he laid eyes on this chunk of lead. Hopefully Betty would be in by the time he showed up tomorrow, just so I could let him down easy.

Deciding I should make the best of it, I directed Mrs. Polanski to the outer office and instructed her to organize matters as she saw fit.

"Just buzz me if any clients arrive and then send them in when I give you the word."

"What word would that be?" she asked.

"'Send them in'," I answered.

"There's a mouthful," she squawked.

God help us, I silently prayed.

I forced another knowing, lopsided grin at her and hurried back to my inner sanctum to have another go at the bottle of Old Sea Dog.

Trevor was going to have a field day with this.

The sky was clear blue, all the way from its zenith down to the horizon. It was a dome of pale cobalt that promised a day of clear weather. The sea, a pure Egyptian blue hue, rolled off toward that horizon in gentle waves, licking back at the shore where the children frolicked and the grown-ups roamed.

The beach was absolutely bustling. I sat beside a gorgeous dame whose dark pink swimming costume hinted at the gentle slope of her curves.

By all accounts, this should have been a perfect day.

Still, I couldn't help but feel embarrassed over the jagged lines of scar tissue crisscrossing my chest and sliding down my left leg. These were my souvenirs from the Great War, things that were as familiar to me as my face in the mirror. Even though my swimsuit concealed the worst of it, I couldn't help but feel like they might be one hell of a turn-off.

Her skin was flawless, lightly tanned perfection. She'd been my girl for two weeks now and looked like she wouldn't have had me any other way.

Not that it helped any.

Sun and sand were fine; I could handle waves too, on a good day. But when it came to the ocean—hell, when it came to any large body of water—I got the jitters something fierce. I don't know why that is. Maybe it's a fear of the unknown or maybe my Dad just diddled me when I was in the crib.

Who am I kidding? My dad was a saint. Now, my mother . . .

Thankfully oblivious to my existential crisis, Kate sunned herself beside me with her long red hair splayed out across our beach towel. It stood out as a halo of dark gold against the white terrycloth, putting the glimmering sand around it to shame.

She was a joy to behold but I just sat there watching everyone else come and go, like some two-bit weirdo. Sneaking glances at her, I kept checking if she was ready to hit the road.

No such luck; she looked about as happy as a cat before a warm fireplace with a bellyful of tuna. When she finally caught me sneaking glances at her, she just smiled.

She rolled around to face me, pushing her thick black sunglasses up the gentle slope of her nose. I took a whiff of her and glory be, she smelled good enough to eat.

Her lips made a tempting proposition as she spoke in a lazy, mellow tone.

"You fancy taking a dip, hon?"

I shook my head, saying, "Too crowded for my taste. Besides, I like the view."

This seemed to satisfy her and she lay back on the towel, stretching provocatively. She raised her knees and tucked her legs back, giving me a full view of her perfect calves.

She said, in her low, husky voice, "You can get an even *closer* look if you join me for a dip . . . ."

If she'd asked me to put my hand over an open flame, punch a bull straight in the jaw, hell if she'd asked me to eat a brick for her, I'd have done it, but not that. Never that.

The magic was dispelled as someone started screaming. Kate sat up, tilted her sunglasses up onto her forehead and squinted her green eyes to the source of the noise.

I turned to look and my jaw nearly dropped.

"What the hell is *that*?" I said, climbing to my feet for a better look. I could see a girl in the water, struggling against the waves, not twenty feet from the shore.

Kate was quick by my side. "A shark; it's gotta be."

I began running towards the girl with absolutely no idea of what to do next.

A few people had already stopped dead in their tracks to gawp at the drowning girl. Falling into the drill sergeant routing, I took control of the situation.

"Shark!" I shouted, waving my arms as I ran past a couple and their kids.

The man turned to me saying, "You a lifeguard?"

"You wish," I replied then added, "just a concerned citizen."

I turned from him to look at the girl. I was two steps from the water when she was pulled under the waves.

Everyone began to scramble out of the sea, running around like chickens. A teen-aged boy, thinking he'd go ahead and be a hero, headed right back in. I ran at him and grabbed him by the short hairs before he did something stupid.

He skidded to a halt and turned to look at me, his freckled face flushed with determination. I knocked him back down to earth.

"Kid. If you want to help, go up to the café and call the coast guard."

He gawped at me before doing as he was told, heading for the cafeteria on the raised area of grassland behind the beach.

I took a deep breath, realizing I'd drawn in a crowd. The few dozen people on the beach were now gathered around me, speaking in hushed tones. Some of the smaller children had run to their parents, bawling their eyes out.

I felt Kate's hand slip into mine and I turned to look at her; sure enough, she had been rattled. I couldn't blame her.

Probably everyone on the beach was worse off than she was. And the waves just kept lapping at the coarse sand, without a care in the world.

Some of us kept our eyes out for a sign of the shark. Maybe a fin, or a flash of teeth or the sight of some severed limb in the flotsam. Suddenly, the hushed tones around me were shattered by someone's frantic yell from my left hand side.

The beach was enclosed on either side by two rocky outcroppings leading up to green-topped cliffs. I turned to see a lanky, gray-haired man dressed in a cream shirt and matching shorts, running toward us. He had a bulky pair of binoculars hanging from his pencil neck that swung wildly as he ran.

The man skittered to a stop near the center of our group. He looked around frantically before darting for the water. I was on him in an instant, grabbing him by the shoulders to keep him from making the dive.

"What the hell is your problem, huh?" I said, looking at the back of his twitching head.

A child behind me said, "You can't go in there, mister. There's a shark!"

"No shark. Can't have been," he howled. He shook in my grasp and I held onto him for dear life. "I was watching from the rocks," he continued, "it looked human... almost human."

Someone sniggered at the old man. I glared at the crowd before turning to face him.

"Just what the hell were you doing up there mister?" I asked. "What were you looking out for?"

"Jen, the girl in the water." he said, fighting back tears. "She's my daughter. Massachusetts state swimming finalist. Top of her class."

Very gently, I relaxed my grip. Just enough to keep him from panicking, so he wouldn't try and plunge back into the water.

"Sea monsters? Christ." some mug behind me said.

I glared at him but he looked too scared to notice.

"No such thing," I said. "Probably a Great White. Gotta be."

I then said, "All of you, keep out of the water, you hear?"

A dark, muscle-bound man, his arm wrapped around a little blonde dame, said, "We're not too far from Innsmouth, you know."

Everyone took another step away from the water at that.

Turning back to the girl's father, I said, "My name's Trevor Towers and I'm a PI. Now, how about we take it easy, okay?" I let go of his shoulders and was thankful that he stayed in place. The poor fella looked exhausted and terrified and about to keel over.

Kate said, almost reading my mind, "Mister, let's get you away from here." She had our beach towel in her hands, which she draped around the man's quaking shoulders.

We led him away from the scene, towards the embankment. The cafeteria patrons had gathered around for the show. Bad news travels fast, especially when there's blood involved. The freckled kid was with them, waving his arms wildly, obviously reveling in the attention he was receiving. The beach crowd began to break away, as if they were following my lead.

The coastguard and an ambulance would be here soon enough. By my count, they'd probably be too late for Jen, if a shark was involved.

I entered the office to begin another red-letter day in the life of Mother Barnes's little slugger. I took off my hat and glanced at the receptionist's desk, pleased to see that Betty Polanski had finally showed for work. She scrambled for an apology and I told her to "Forget about it."

She just gave me a *killer* smile that all but brought me to my knees. "I hope Mother wasn't too much of a handful yesterday."

"Barnes and Towers have gone through worse," I said, though I doubted that Trevor would survive this. "Still, it's all well that ends well."

I gave her the three-cent orientation on greeting prospective johns and then retreated to my inner sanctum. After taking my place behind the desk, I lit a gasper and mulled over Trevor's phone call the night before. There had apparently been some nasty business at the beach after a girl disappeared, possibly snatched by a shark. Trevor had talked to her distraught old man who had the wild notion that his daughter had been abducted by something stripped straight out of Doctor Caligari. I guess the man did what he could to cope.

I puffed my gasper down to the butt, shuffling through a stack of mail that was either bills or some type of dough-grabbing scam. If it were up to me, these people would have been booted to Antarctica by now. I sighed and chucked most of the envelopes, bills and all, into the metal wastebasket.

I was snubbing out my smoke and reaching for another when the intercom buzzed shrilly. "Hot damn!" I said, almost shooting out of my seat. "Now there's a crooner."

My fingers twisted the volume control to a more tolerable level and then said, in my best big-shot impression:

"Yes?"

"Mr. Barnes, there's a gentleman here to see you."

"Send him in, Betty," I grinned.

"Right away, sir," she replied.

I swear, if it wasn't for her Momma, that girl would have had us all looking classier than Pinkerton.

A tall gawky fellow with gray hair opened the door, and looked around as if lost. "You Detective Barnes?" he asked.

"Private Investigator, more like. Not affiliated with the Police Department."

"Good," he said. "Bunch of knuckle-draggers, if you ask me."

"Sir, you're preaching to the choir," I said. "Have a seat and tell me what's bothering you."

He pulled up a chair and said, without further ado, "My name's Abernacky. I need you to find my daughter."

Christ! I thought. *That's the crazy Towers told me about.*

"We excel at finding folks," I said. "But how come you haven't turned to the police?"

"Why should I?" he barked. "'So they can laugh at me through their hats and call me crazy? I know what I saw, damn it, and now I got a note that proves it!"

I shrugged and decided to humor the man. After all, how crazy could this whole mess be, after what Trevor and I had been through?

"Let's begin at the beginning," I said. "Why would the police think you're crazy in the first place?"

"Did you hear what happened at the beach yesterday?" he asked.

"I understand that a girl drowned," I said.

"That's what the police would have you believe."

"And you have reason to think differently?" I asked.

"Damn right I do," he barked. "That girl, she was my daughter and she *didn't* drown, goddamn it."

I was about to ask how he could be sure when the intercom buzzed.

"Yes?" I asked.

"Mr. Towers is here," said Betty.

"Send him in," I replied, then turned to the man. "My partner should be here presently."

Towers stepped inside, positively beaming after he'd seen Betty Polanski for himself.

"Trevor," I said. "I'd like you to meet Mr. Abernacky."

Abernacky turned to Trevor and said, "I kept the card you gave me. Decided to take a chance."

"I'm really sorry for your loss," Trevor commiserated.

"Let's hope you're wrong on that count," Abernacky said.

Towers raised his eyebrows. "That's a hell of way of looking at it."

"What was that about a note, Mister Abernacky?" I prompted.

"Here," he said, reaching into his jacket pocket. He took it out and tossed it onto the desk.

I picked up the crumpled piece of paper and read the plainly printed words.

Your daughter is in Innsmouth. The Marsh clan has her. Act soon or you will never see her again.

"Did you show this to the police?" I asked.

"They just thought it was some sicko's idea of a prank."

Trevor looked at me and shrugged. "Mr. Abernacky *did* mention a . . . creature . . . carrying off his daughter. Unfortunately, there weren't any witnesses from his vantage point so you can imagine why the cops are reluctant to take the note seriously."

"What did you *see*, Trevor?" I asked.

"Not much until after the fact," he replied.

"I *know* what I saw!" Abernacky exclaimed.

I looked at Towers but said nothing. He returned my gaze and said, "I can't be sure that a sea monster was involved but this note is worth checking out. I've had my fair share of looking into twisted pranks, but I'll go by my gut and say that it's legitimate."

"So that's it?" I asked. "Didn't you get anything else? Like a ransom demand?"

"Just the note," Abernacky replied.

Towers looked at him and asked, "You're sure this is a monster? Couldn't this have been just some weirdo in diving gear?"

"'No. Can't have been."

Abernacky sighed and then continued. "I told you the police tried to write it off as a sick prank. Maybe it is so, but you saw those people at the beach, how spooked they got when someone mentioned Innsmouth."

I looked at my partner and said, "What do you think?"

Towers was a hard man but he would never settle with leaving a desperate old man on his own. Neither would I. Towers looked at Abernacky and said, "I think my partner and I should take a trip to Innsmouth."

"Thank you! Oh, thank you!" Abernacky said, looking almost relieved.

I decided to be as honest as possible. "We can't promise that your daughter is okay. But if she's there, we'll find her and bring her back."

Towers was clenching his fists, probably going over his own recent loss. He took a deep breath and said, "You can *bank* on it."

Abernacky left us with a flimsy lead to go by. Barnes was poring over the note for a good few minutes before he finally placed it into one of the desk drawers.

He looked at me and said, "What do you know about Innsmouth? Besides the fact that it's probably swarming with kidnapping, inbred hicks?"

"Not much," I replied. Then it came to me. "Let me make a call. I might know someone that can shed a little light on the situation."

Barnes got out of his seat and headed to the other side of the desk. I plopped myself right in his seat, making myself comfortable.

As I picked up the phone, he said, "Who's your source, Trevor?"

"Justin Geoffrey." I said.

"Jesus Christ, not *that* fruit again," he groaned, leaning back to plant his heels on the desk.

I put the phone to my ear and said, "It'll be over in two shakes of a lamb's tail. You'll see."

Barnes snorted and put his hands behind his head. "I don't know. Is the lamb a spastic junkhead?" I silently agreed with him and dialed the number by heart.

The phone rang twice before it was picked up; a stiff, too-thick British voice answered, saying, "Epson residence."

I knew I got the right place, recognizing the busboy's snooty little tone right away. Geoffrey was just dodging calls, as usual.

I said, "Tell Justin that Trevor Towers wants to speak with him. I *know* I've got the right number."

The voice said, "Quite, indeed, sir. Please hold."

There was the rattle of the receiver, followed by long, unending silence. I snarled and swore under my breath to while away the time. Barnes seemed to enjoy every second of it.

Geoffrey picked up and did not sound pleased, speaking in his usually sarcastic tone.

"Mister Trevor Towers," he said, pronouncing my name in a slow, condescending manner. "If I remember correctly, you had reassured me that our score was settled."

Last time we had seen the dewdropper, Barnes and I had also been looking for a girl that had been snatched by a crowd of murderous book lovers, in service to a bug-eyed monster.

Thanks to Geoffrey's leads, we'd managed to thwart the cult before things got out of hand. I'd lied to him to get that juicy tidbit, telling him that it had been enough to square his debt to me.

I went on the offensive, snapping into my no-bushwa tone, "We were settled up until you sent that Ashton Smith fella our way. That loon just about got us killed!"

That case was a particularly harrowing tale that neither I nor Barnes ever wanted to go over again.

"Tell Geoffrey to suck it up," Barnes shouted from across the desk. "Or we'll give him a special house call."

Geoffrey heard Barnes, loud and clear, gulped and said, "Point taken."

I got down to brass tacks and told him all about our case, from the sorry tale of Abernacky and his daughter all the way up to the weird guff about Innsmouth.

He was quiet until I mentioned the town, then said, "You fellows should try looking for cushier jobs. Have you ever considered lion taming? At least that covers dental."

I put a hand over the mouthpiece and told Barnes, "What do you know, he's heard of it." Barnes grinned and I went right back to Geoffrey.

"'Hardy har har pal," I said. "So come on, spill it. What's the skinny on Innsmouth?"

"There's nothing much to go by but rumors." Geoffrey's sounded hesitant, his arrogance fled. That snooty little bookworm's reaction made me feel better somehow.

"Towers," he said, "the only useful advice I can give you is that you should stay out of Innsmouth. If you can't help yourselves and you don't just want to drive yourselves into an early grave, then I suggest you pay attention."

I looked at Barnes and found him staring at me, looking worried.

Geoffrey's voice got deeper, more confident as he went on. "Keep in mind, this is for your own good. Not that I'd miss you, Trevor, but there are things going on in Innsmouth that would turn your hair white."

I didn't argue with him.

"The Marshes, and the Esoteric Order of Dagon, they run the place. Don't stay there after dark," he said. "That's when they *really* let loose."

I have to admit, I was creeped out. Then again, that's Justin Geoffrey for you.

"Like Orpheus, don't eat or drink anything they offer you and *keep away* from those that have the Innsmouth look about them. You'll know them when you see them. Also, keep away from the warehouses near the shore, and watch your back."

I interrupted him with, "What about the note?"

He said, "If that note *isn't* a trap, she might just be alive. I sincerely doubt it, though."

There was a long pause and I was about to hang up, when he added. "You're armed, aren't you?" I told him that I was. "Drop them," he said, adding a kooky little twist to his string of bad omens. "Bullets . . . may not be as much use as you'd think. Think fire; lots and lots of fire."

I thanked the man and reassured him that this time, we were done for good. He hung up immediately after. Barnes pulled away from the desk and leaned in.

I told him everything Geoffrey had said. Barnes waited until I was finished, then said: "Sounds like a pretty welcoming place. You think we should risk it?"

"It sure as hell won't be the first freak show we've had to shut down." I replied.

Barnes got out of his seat, stretching his arms before saying, "We should draw up a plan over at Denny's."

Denny's was a barrel house just around the corner from our building. The place served nothing but coffin varnish, but it'd have to do.

"Damn straight," I said.

Outside, Arkham looked dark and wet and foreboding but hey: at least it wasn't Innsmouth.

We arrived on the outskirts of Innsmouth just before dawn. We knew it as soon as we rolled down the windows and choked on the smell of fishheads, rotting by the thousands on the shore. We were parked on a narrow road that wound its way through the sandy dunes of the surrounding area.

"Christ," Towers growled, "who'd stand to live in this place?"

I lit a smoke and grinned, catching a glimpse of Trevor's scowling features. "Nobody *human*, that's who, if your pal Geoffrey is anything to go by."

"Pal?" Towers said. "You're a real riot, Barnes."

He lit a smoke and continued scowling.

I grinned and said, "Better put on your vamp act, before you scare off any potential sources of information."

He put up his best mad dog grin and said, "What do you think?"

"There we go," I said, "there's the lady killer I know."

We smoked and whiled away the time, until the eastern sky began to lighten. I started the car's engine and drove into the town proper. We eased through what passed for the downtown area and spotted a hotel called The Marsh House.

"You think we ought to check in there first?"

"Why not?" Towers answered. "We might as well stomp our feet, see what sort of pinheads come crawl out of the woodwork."

"Place looks pretty quiet," I said. "What the hell did Geoffrey mean, about the *Innsmouth look?*"

"Who cares?" Towers replied. "I don't give a shit what the locals look like as long as we get what we're here for."

"Amen to that."

I turned down a narrow drive off Main Street and found the hotel's small parking area. Towers looked at the empty clamshell lot and said, "Business is booming this time of year."

"Bet they'll be thrilled to see us," I chuckled.

Towers smirked. "Most people *usually* are."

"At least someone around here was nice enough to send Abernacky that note."

"Well," Towers said, "I hope the sonofabitch shows himself before too long."

I parked the car and said, "That would be nice, long as he's made sure he's covered his own ass."

The man at the hotel desk didn't seem too pleased to see us. If anything, he looked downright spooked. I walked up to the counter and said, in my best Swamp Yankee impression, "Howdy friend; you got room for a couple of fish peddlers?"

"Howdy?" Barnes mumbled. "Look at Barnes, hamming it up."

I elbowed him in the ribs. Trevor just stared daggers into me.

The desk clerk looked at us through bulging eyes and seemed to struggle with the words.

"Err . . . ah . . . We don't get many tourists this time of year." he wheezed.

"Yeah," Towers interjected, "we can see that. But what do you mean 'This time of year'? It's summer, for Christ's sake!"

"We err . . . don't usually get any guests. Ever."

"You *do* have rooms, right?" I asked.

"Not at the moment, I'm afraid . . ."

"What's that supposed to mean?" Towers asked. "Is the place booked of not?"

"No it's . . ." the clerk muttered. "Maintenance. That's it. Rooms need maintaining. Also, we're booked. Local function."

Towers growled. "So you *have rooms*, except no one can live in them, unless it's people who already live here."

I reached into my pocket and took out my wallet, shoving a twenty on the counter. "There," I said, "that ought to cover maintenance costs for a couple rooms."

"But the function . . ."

"Hey, fellow!" Towers growled. "You trying to gyp us here? You want me to get *Life* magazine on the phone and let them know about your little racket? I can get two dozen journos crawling all over the place here before you know it."

The clerk cringed.

"All right," he croaked. "I guess I can spare two rooms."

I smiled. "We really appreciate it."

The clerk gave us a look of unfathomable misery and pushed a dog-eared register across the bench. "Fill this out and everything should be ready in an hour or two."

"Thanks, friend!" I said. "You're real swell, you know that?"

After signing the register, we headed out to the car. Towers could barely keep himself from laughing. "So that's the Innsmouth look, huh?"

"Yeah," I answered. "Creepy as all get out."

"No argument there," Towers replied. "I get the feeling we won't be seeing the welcome wagon around here."

"Who cares?" I said. "Not you, with your journo friends over at *Life*."

Towers nearly bust a gut laughing all the way down to the pier.

It was the damnedest thing. In all of Innsmouth there wasn't a living soul who would rent us a boat. Apparently, they were all either already spoken for or being repaired. Towers tried to tell them that he'd spotted a couple that were seaworthy but their owners didn't seem to go for it and told Trevor to scram. It didn't help that Trevor got into a fight with one of the froggier-looking fools, who went definitely cross-eyed after getting a right jab right in his bulging peepers. Towers was quick to tell the few locals who would listen just what sort of lucrative business opportunity they were turning down, for all the good that did. It was pretty obvious that

Innsmouth wasn't going to be opening up its doors to us anytime soon. Towers said that it didn't matter; sooner or later, by brain or by brawn, we'd wriggle our way behind their locked doors and get the answers we needed.

We walked back to the center of town and plotted our new approach.

"I think it's safe to say," I said, lighting a smoke, "That they've caught wind of us by now."

"Don't bet on it. Bet those half-wits don't even know how to start a rumor, never mind spread it."

I offered Towers a smoke. His hope chest had been crushed during a disagreement with one of the boat owners back at the pier. He lit up eagerly.

"Barnes," he said, smiling, "Where does a person usually go if they want to get the lowdown?"

I immediately knew where he was going with this. I answered it with another question. "Would it be a place where horn-dogs get together to get their privates wet and feed each other lines until they're fit to burst?"

"I was thinking of a speakeasy," he said. "But a whore-house is fine, too."

We laughed at that and went looking for the raunchiest juice joint we could find. After a short walk, we spied a place called The Kraken's Mistress and headed for the door. The place was far from crowded. There were a couple of Chinamen, a Russian and three Swedes, mixed with a smattering of local seadogs.

We caught the dirty looks and heard some mumbled curses as we stepped to the bar and ordered our drinks. "Nice little shithole you got here," Towers said, loud enough for all to hear "Really brings out the best in this town."

"Keep it down," I whispered. "We're looking for a lead, not a fight."

"Lead? In this dump?" he said. "These surly bastards ain't gonna spill anything but their drinks."

"Point taken," I answered.

I finished my drink and ordered another. Downing it in no time flat, I grinned at Towers. "Yeah," I bellowed, "I hear that if you wanna get laid in Innsmouth, you're better off kidnapping a girl from Arkham."

"For crying out loud, Barnes," Towers mumbled, then added, "Can you blame them? I mean would you risk dipping your wick in a slimy glob of frog eggs?"

Behind us came sounds of chairs, roughly kicked away from tables. We turned to greet our fellow drunks.

The big Russian said something in some gobbledygook language and all the foreigners suddenly decided they had places to be. This left us facing five of the local bad-asses, each hell-bent on murdering us.

"Trevor, do you think we went too far?"

"No," Towers replied. "Everyone knows that folks from Innsmouth are suckers for honesty."

A big lug—not as far gone with the Innsmouth look—smashed a whiskey bottle into a makeshift shank and stepped forward.

"You think you're so fucking clever, don't you, townie?"

Towers spat on the floor and laughed. "It doesn't take a brain surgeon to see what's been going on around here. Bet you degenerates have to steal a dame every once in a while just to spice things up. There's only so many times a fella can screw his mother before the novelty wears off."

The young tough roared and came charging forward, right on cue. Towers tensed up, ready to throw down. I watched the young man slash blindly, going for Towers' face, so I grabbed his arm and twisted it up.

The man screamed and flailed helplessly, before collapsing on the floor behind the bar. Towers followed up with a shot to the young thug's kidney that would have him pissing blood for the next couple of weeks.

Towers grinned and said, as the other seadogs charged us, "See what happens when you talk trash about Innsmouth?"

The barroom brawl lasted only a couple of minutes. The Innsmouth rowdies had the brawn, but they lacked the brains. Me and Towers weren't exactly world-class boxer material, but we'd picked up enough tricks to outdo any run-of-the-mill street brawler.

We left six badly injured men lying in the bar and strolled casually down the street. Our current plan was getting us nowhere and we had to pick up the pace if we wanted to find the Abernacky girl. Turning to Towers, I asked, "Did Geoffrey give you any hint about where to find the head honchos around here?"

Towers rubbed his chin and looked thoughtful. "He gave me some bushwa about an 'Esoteric Order of Dagon' running the place."

"Sounds like a lodge," I replied.

"Sounds like a clubhouse for nutjobs."

"I don't get it," I said. "Seems like half the nuts we deal with feel the need to go off and form their own religion."

"Geoffrey once told me that most of these so-called new religions we've come across are *actually* ancient."

I raised my eyebrows and grinned. "'Look at you, Mister fancy academic. I hear the dean's chair at Miskatonic U is up for grabs, if you want it."

"Screw you, Barnes."

I was about to reply when a noise came from the boarded-up shop window we were walking past. We stopped and squinted at the pitch blackness between the planks.

"Probably wharf rats," I said.

The door creaked open just a crack. "Psssst!" a voice said from inside. I reached for the piece in my shoulder rig but Towers shook his head.

"You talking to us?" he said, looking at me as if we were having a conversation.

The voice from inside answered. "I was the one who sent the note. I know where the girl is being kept."

"Could be a trap," I whispered.

"Or," Towers answered, "It could just be the break we're looking for."

Towers continued to smile at me and said, "Just so you know: if this is some kind of a set up, we're going to find you and stomp on your skull until it's lopsided. Are we supposed to come in?"

"No!" the voice hissed. "Not from the street . . . too many witnesses."

"Okay, where from then?" I said, looking at Towers.

"Behind the store. There's an alley door. It'll be unlocked."

"Wanna give it a shot?" I whispered.

Towers grinned. "We got nothing better to do."

I was relieved to discover that we *hadn't* walked into a trap. A young man holding a kerosene lantern ushered us in and locked the door behind us. He seemed fidgety, the kind you get when you're either hopped up on dope or scared half out of your mind. He didn't quite have the *Innsmouth look*, apart from the bulging eyes. He caught me giving him the once over and said, "Yes, I'm like the others."

"You know where they're keeping Jennifer Abernacky? Towers asked.

"Yes," he said. "My brothers are holding her in the basement of Dagon Hall."

"Your brothers?"

"My name is Ronnie Marsh," he answered. "I'm . . . the black sheep of the family."

I extended my hand and said, "It's good to meet you, Ronnie Marsh."

He reached out for my hand, but pulled back at the last second. I looked at it and saw that it was dry and covered in scales, with the webbing beginning to sprout between the fingers. I reached out and clasped it. Looking Marsh in the eyes, I said, "We tend to go beyond skin-deep."

"Most don't," he answered, looking sad.

Towers said, "That's all real touching. How about you put a lid on it until we've saved the Abernacky girl?"

"You're right," Marsh agreed. "Time is running out."

"How long do we have to get her out and what's the best way to go about it?"

"There's a secret entrance into the hall," Marsh said. "I know the way in. They plan to sacrifice the girl at midnight."

"It's always got to be midnight," Towers complained. "God forbid any of these weirdos would get anything done sooner."

Turning to Marsh, I asked, "Not that we don't appreciate it, but . . . how come you're helping us?"

He smiled. "The Marsh name was respectable, once. But over the years, my family have brought our name low and degraded our people. Just a few years ago, their carelessness brought the Feds down on us. The town has . . . lost its luster, since."

"What's in this for you?" Towers asked. "Seems to me that you're signing your own death warrant."

The flickering light reflected off tears welling up in the young man's eyes.

"Redemption," he whispered.

We left the boarded up shop with instructions to return to the Marsh House. Ronnie Marsh didn't believe that anyone would go after us before dark but he warned us that our car would have likely been disabled by now and that we would probably need to find another way out of town. Fortunately, he provided us with an alternative. There was a rattletrap bus that went into Arkham every couple of days and the key was kept inside the unlocked vehicle. The hayburner was conveniently parked in a lot next door to Dagon Hall.

"Do you think Marsh will still be alive to lead us to the girl?" Towers asked as we paused in the alley.

"We'll make do, with or without him."

Towers grinned. "Works for me . . . not that I'd want anything to happen to the kid."

"Sins of the fathers," I replied. "Ain't that the way it usually is?"

"At least he's doing something about it. That's more than most people would do."

A wooden crate came crashing to the pavement, narrowly missing us by inches. I reached for my gun but Towers moved like greased lightning, aiming at one of the forms perched on the roof above us. His first shot thundered in the alley and a deformed figure went windmilling off the roof, to land in a heap on some garbage cans. My first shot winged another attacker, but it was obvious that we were outnumbered.

"We got to get out of this alley!" I shouted over the racket.

Crates were raining down on us and it was impossible to draw a bead on any of the bastards.

"I've got a plan!" Towers shouted, before dropping another Innsmouth citizen.

I was really eager to listen to Trevor's plan but then the lights went out.

I woke with a splitting headache and slowly opened my eyes, dreading whatever it was that I'd have to face.

"That's better," said a familiar voice, just as a wet cloth was placed against my head.

I squinted through the pain and said, "Marsh?"

"The one and only."

I started to sit up but he put his hand on my chest. "Easy there, mister. You're safe for now."

I looked around, at what appeared to be a quaintly decorated room.

"Where's Trevor? Where the hell am I?" I asked.

"You're in Marsh House," he answered.

"Hold on pal," I growled. "If this is a trap . . ."

"Don't worry," he said. "I took care of the desk clerk. I'm the only one that knows you're here."

"Where's Trevor?" I demanded, grabbing him by the shoulder.

Arkham Nights

I saw him wince and relaxed my grip. "Sorry," I said. "He's my partner, is all."

It's funny how things come to you at the damnedest of times. Once upon a time, I'd have rather shot Trevor on the spot than talk to the mug. Things changed, since I got to know him. I guess a guy never *really* gets to know another man but you can learn to like them, if you go through enough shit together. I didn't plan on leaving town without him *or* the Abernacky girl. How did that old line go? 'All for one . . .'

"They've got your friend at Dagon Hall as well," Marsh said. "I doubt that he and the girl are together. The ground beneath the place is honeycombed with rooms and passages."

"Can you get me in?"

"Yes," Marsh answered.

I looked at him and said, "You're one brave man, anyone ever tell you that?"

"A *man*." Marsh said, looking wistful. "That's all I ever wanted to be."

Trevor was going to be pissed about the locals slashing his tires. At least Marsh had retrieved my partner's bag of goodies from the trunk and brought it with him. I unloaded it on the bed while Marsh looked on.

"Your friend must be a very violent man."

I grinned. "He likes to think of himself as cautious."

I began to count through Trevor's stash of guns, his assortment of knives and his stash of DIY explosives, when I caught Marsh looking at our mini-armory. I offered him one of the automatics.

"You trust me?" he asked.

"Sure. Why wouldn't I?"

He beamed as he pocketed the weapon.

He was still grinning when the harpoon crashed through the window and buried itself in his chest. Stunned, I turned to the window but no one was there. The bad guys were onto me, somehow.

"Son of a bitch!" I roared, rushing to check up on Marsh.

He looked up at me, smiling through the pain. "There's a map in my pocket . . . you're going to need it . . . tell the girl I tried . . ."

His words were lost in a long, choking gurgle. I knelt beside him and took his rough, scaly hand.

"I'll tell her that a *man* gave his life for her."

Marsh held my hand until the light fled from his eyes.

I took the map from his pocket and covered him with a bedspread. It seemed like the good folks of Innsmouth had been having a merry old dance at our expense. I took the case from the bed and smiled.

"Keep dancing while you can, you bastards," I whispered. "It's time to pay the piper."

Waking up tied to a chair was nothing new. It had happened to me, funnily enough, during my first encounter with the supernatural.

Déjà vu is one major bitch.

Back then, I'd been at the mercy of a man that could re-animate the dead, a quack by the name of Herbert West. With this in mind, waking up to the sight of Peter Lorre's uglier older brother and his giant toad-thing boss was an improvement, all things considered.

I checked the bonds that held my hands and found that they'd be wound as tight as a vice, so I decided to suck it up.

I took a deep breath and steeled myself for the worst. I could handle the stabbing pain from my bruised eye, the sting from my split lips and bleeding gums, but getting a noseful of that awful Innsmouth stench was almost more than I could bear.

I looked around and found that I was being held in a low, gray-bricked room, all glistening with damp. The only illumination came from a bare ceiling bulb and going by the dampness in the air and the grit under my feet, I could safely assume that I was held in some musty, forgotten old cellar in God knows where.

Still, it suited my captors well.

One was a big six Innsmouth specimen, all balding and chinless with those bug-eyes and flakey skin that Barnes and I had gotten to know far too well. He had on a two-sizes-too small dark gray suit, his lumpy head and overly long arms making him look like some troll straight out of a fairy tale. He wore a rawhide belt complete with gun holsters, each bearing a big, mean-looking Colt between pouches dotted with copper shells.

It wasn't the guns that scared me though; it was the look of pure malice that came from the big cheese, all the way at the other side of the room.

The big cheese sat behind Lorre Senior on a throne-like seat carved from dull white coral, its skin looking all slick and black from under the ends of its ragged sleeves and neckline. It was dressed in a long crimson robe, covered in weird gold symbols and fishy-looking patterns. Its paws, so much like the bloated hands of a week-old corpse, were covered in scales, with claws sticking out from the tips.

Its face bore the Innsmouth look in all its naked glory; a scaly and rubbery face, sloping to a pair of perfectly smooth holes where the ears should be. Slitted pink gills flared from its long neck and its eyes were two solid black pebbles that glared at me with an alien malice.

The creature stopped, halfway through talking to its deformed cronie and peeled back its lips to reveal multiple rows of jagged white teeth. I guess that's what passed for a grin, as far as it was concerned.

I didn't have to speak their gobbledygook language to know what was going on. This wasn't an interrogation. After a brief conversation, Lorre Senior's calloused fists mercilessly knocked me unconscious.

They hadn't bothered to ask me any questions.

Obviously he'd continued beating me while I was out. I could tell, by running my tongue over the chipped mess that used to be the left side of my jaw and the bloody mess I'd made all over my shirt.

I'd like to say I'd had worse, but I'd be lying.

The big toad was speaking to my interrogator in that Innsmouth gobbledygook when I came to. It stopped mid-sentence and Lorre Senior turned to look at me, his face twisted in rage.

"The master wants to know what you're doing here, boy," he said. "Tell me, so I can kill you."

He released one revolver from his holster, pressed it against my forehead and said "Speak and I will make it quick."

He hadn't mentioned Barnes. Maybe the old slugger had slipped away from their ambush. I swallowed some blood and then said, "What are you talking about? I'm just a fish-peddler; honest."

The big cheese chuckled: a loud, sinister purr that made me shudder. Lorre Senior didn't seem to get the joke though and settled for smacking me across the head with his revolver.

The impact nearly took my head off. My vision wobbled, everything going hazy before snapping back into gonzo focus.

I saw my old trainer, Spiky Joe, five years dead from cancer, standing next to Lorre Senior, screaming down at me over the din of an invisible crowd.

"Come on, Two-Gun," he said, his eyes pleading. "You got this mook."

I wanted to smack Tompkin one right across the mouth, but it couldn't have been him, in the ring. We'd fought fifteen bouts, worn ourselves down to the bone before I finally got the son of a bitch to give up the ghost.

Everything seemed like a dream, all bent the wrong way and mangled. The cellar around me bled into a ring, surrounded by ropes. I looked at Tompkin and there he was, leering down at me and waving a gun in my face.

"I'll kill you!" he snarled.

"I'll die!" I laughed, spitting blood as I spoke.

I looked back and there was Joe, the lights of the arena glistening across his bald, black head. He egged me on, howling like a madman but I just couldn't find the strength to go on.

I'd gone fifteen rounds with Tompkin and was dead on my feet long before the bell had rung. My knees had turned to jelly. One of my eyes was already swollen shut and the other was going.

There was no way I could go on. Hell, I couldn't even put up my hands.

"Come on, man," Joe shouted. "Just take a swing, he's dead on his feet!"

"I can't do it, Joe," I muttered through my shattered teeth, my split lips turning every word into agony. I had no idea where my gum shield had gone.

"Bullshit," he said, so close to me I could drown in his big, sad eyes. "I didn't come back here just to have you quit on me. Suck it up!"

The bell rang. Tompkin came at me ready to bury that big gun of his right into my skull.

I tried to raise my hands but there was nothing doing. Joe was fading away, whisked into nothing and I knew that I was going to have to get off my ass and on with the job.

I flexed the muscles in my arms, drawing strength from everywhere at once.

My arms tore free, tearing away at wood and hemp as they went, showering me in splinters. I howled like the Devil himself, as I landed a swift left hook at Tompkin's fat pudgy nose.

The crowd roared all around me.

I was back in the cellar, my arms aching like bastards. Lorre

Senior was doubled over in front of me, bleating like an animal as he clutched at his ruined nose.

Grabbing at his pistol, I reached for the other in its holster, before giving them a single hard twist. He let go, so I fired a single shot into his belly, the thunder of the gun sending the crowd back to the nonsense mist it had sprung out of. All that was left was the dull roar in my aching head and the sound of that ugly bastard bawling as he died.

It would be a good while before he died. Plenty of time to knock that fish-faced big cheese off his throne and on his ass.

It looked almost terrified, before it pounced. A long golden blade flashed in its paw as it lashed at me, aiming for the jugular.

The big cheese was fast, but wasn't no Two-Gun Towers. In the blink of an eye, I cocked back the hammers and pulled both triggers at once, turning its howling face into red and green mush. It fell back onto its throne, staining the coral with whatever stinking gunk it had instead of blood.

"Ooorah!" I snarled with glee.

There was no time to waste; the ring from the echoing gun blasts had barely faded, before it was replaced by a set of hurried footsteps closing in from behind the door.

I turned, only to find my feet still tied to the chair legs. I tucked one of the guns into my waistband before bending to let myself loose. With that done with, I twisted around to greet my new challengers.

The door was a worm-eaten, wooden thing, about as old as Davy Jones's locker. Someone was scampering frantically for it, getting closer. I cocked back both barrels and took a deep breath to steady myself.

You better believe that Two-Gun Towers was out for blood.

I made my way through the burrow-like tunnels that wormed beneath Dagon Hall. Marsh's map had been a godsend and my goose would've been cooked a long time ago if he hadn't stashed Tower's miniature armory away for me. I'd emptied three clips into the fish-men that went after me through Innsmouth's twisting streets and I knew that there would be more a'coming before long, hot on my trail as they followed the corpses.

I was close to the underground entrance when I heard gunfire echoing out from the depths. My head still pounded and my knees were halfway turned to jelly but I knew that Towers and the girl had to be close. My cheap wristwatch had been smashed but one look at the night sky told me it must be about midnight. The beam of my flashlight danced across a wooden door and I slowed my pace. Approaching cautiously, I took a deep breath, gripped my gun and booted my way in.

The door flew off its hinges and I almost fell flat on my face, only to find myself staring up at a pair of barrels held by Trevor Towers himself.

"Again with the shooting . . ." I muttered.

Towers tried to grin with what was left of the red ruin that used to be his mouth.

"Got the girl yet?" he said.

"I just got here."

"What about Marsh?"

"He died . . . saving my life."

"Another favor we owe the bastard," Trevor said.

I pulled myself up on my feet and said, "At least he died knowing that he did right by folks."

"More than most of us can hope for, I reckon."

I looked at the piles of twitching meat that lay in the room. "Who were those guys, you think?"

"Who gives a shit. We got a woman needs saving," he answered.

I was too glad to get out of that stuffy cell; those two looked worse dead than they ever did alive. I was almost glad for the damp dankness of the tunnel Barnes led us through.

Made up of greasy square slabs, it stretched out from the door at an angle and sloped down on our left. The walls were coated in layers of slick moisture, with a row of dim bulbs attached to a thick black wire trailing across the curved ceiling.

"Nice digs," I said.

Barnes said, "Bet you'd fit right in with your face the way it looks now."

I was about to give Barnes a piece of my mind, when we heard someone running up the corridor. There was the sound of footfalls and voices barking out what had to be marching orders in the Innsmouth gobbledygook.

Barnes swore and led us out of the tunnel. Before long, we were running deeper underground.

"Barnes? Do you even know where you're headed?" I said. When Barnes didn't answer, I hissed, "Barnes, for Pete's sake, where are we going?" We turned left at the next intersection when he said, "Ronnie hasn't steered us wrong so far. The map should take us right to where they're keeping Abernacky's girl."

The tunnel sloped down a slippery decline, and we slowed down, holding to the walls for dear life. The Innsmouth posse seemed to be getting closer, their rabid screeches getting more distinct by the second.

We passed by a closed wooden door just before it came crashing open. Barnes stopped in mid-run, pivoting on his heels like a ballerina from hell. I turned around, only to see a massive, black-skinned fish-man snarling at us.

Now there was a face even a mother couldn't love.

It crouched in the corridor, its misshapen head scraping across the ceiling. Its sleek skin was pitch-black, save for the white streak that ran across its belly. Its eyes hung in the air like free-floating pools of silver. Letting out a whine that soon turned into a roar of anger, we watched its lips pull back to reveal two rows of jagged yellow teeth.

We pulled our triggers in unison, my shots going a little wild. I was coming down from my adrenaline high, and my hands shook something awful.

The fish-thing took our bullets like they were nothing, even as they tore into his scaly flesh. I'd just about emptied my guns when Barnes shifted his aim slightly and went for its eye just as the thing got a little too close for comfort. The bullets tore into its face and buried themselves into its skull, making the fish-thing drop dead in its tracks.

Barnes spat, and kicked at its head savagely. "Stay down you rotten, stinking bastard!"

"So I guess we just go for the head?" I suggested. Barnes nodded.

Checking my guns, I realized that I was fresh out of ammo with the legions of Innsmouth almost breathing down our necks.

As if reading my mind, Barnes handed me the green canvas sack he'd had slung over his shoulder. It was my stash, with every single gun and bullet in its rightful place.

"Hope you got enough ammo in there for everyone."

"And then some," I said, breaking into a big, snarling grin.

The horde of fish-things came barreling at us through the corridor, snarling like mad dogs. Barnes and I crouched behind the dead behemoth, using its hunchback for cover.

I barely suppressed a smile, feeling almost content. Now there was something I could wrap my head around; charging madmen, a cocked Thompson in my hand with a full clip, and some solid cover.

I turned to Barnes. He was pulling out cartridges, piling them up high. I retrieved a box of cartridges that looked like they might fit my revolvers, in a pinch. The sight of the sticks of dynamite at the bottom of the sack almost had me drooling.

"Hey, Barnes," I said, pointing at the sticks. "You think we can risk it?"

Barnes, all locked and loaded, shook his head. "We do that and we get trapped here for good," he said. "I say we do this the tried and true way."

I nodded, just before we unleashed a storm of red-hot lead down the tunnel.

The first half dozen came charging at us on all fours, like a bunch of slavering dogs. Our battery sent two of them flying, to crash into the fish-things coming up from the rear.

A trident came hurtling down towards us out of nowhere and stuck hilt-deep into the dead behemoth's humped back. Its corpse shuddered from the force of the impact. Taking a step back, we kept firing away, taking a few more fish-beasts out for the count.

The air around us was thick with gun smoke and the screams of the dying.

I was going for a fresh clip, realizing that the fish-things were almost on us. The sons of bitches were faster than they looked.

I dropped my Tommy and pulled out my guns just as one of them cleared the behemoth's back, planting a bullet in its eye.

Only two of the things were left standing now, looking shaken. We'd torn the bastards to ribbons and they had nothing to show for it.

I was about to let them go when Barnes stopped shooting and said through the ringing in my ears: "Trevor, I almost forgot—one of those things slashed your tires."

The nearest fish-thing got both barrels to its crotch. In a fit of mercy, I let the other one skitter its way up into the dark, damp halls it called home, before we continued our descent.

If the carnage didn't stop any more of those bastards from coming after us, then the terrified little straggler certainly would.

The tunnel seemed to go on forever, growing colder every step of the way. Before long, we were sloshing through shallow pools of something that smelled a lot like seawater. We were heading into another intersection, when I heard the distant sound of rushing water.

Barnes stopped and rifled through his pockets for his map.

"Lost the trail, kemosabe?" I asked.

"No, not at all," he said, tapping at the neatly folded piece of paper. "It's just . . . I can't really put my finger on it."

"What's that supposed to mean?" I asked, pushing back against the terror that was creeping in.

Halfway through the intersection he said, "It just couldn't be drawn to scale. Could it?"

We took a right, moving along another corridor that began ascending after a few crooked, sloping yards. The sound of rushing water got louder by the second, until it was a roar so loud, it drowned everything else out.

The lights on the ceiling flickered, then went out for good.

We felt our way through the darkness, checking our guns as we went.

"You think we're still under Innsmouth?" I asked as Barnes finally flicked his lighter to life and checked the map.

"We're almost at the outskirts. If we turn left here," he waved at the darkness. "We should be at the chamber before too long."

I checked my watch: just twelve minutes to midnight. Let's hope that Innsmouth folk were as punctual as they were ugly.

We slowed down to a creep as we reached the turn. Hunched in almost total darkness, we listened to the sound of waves rolling gently against a nearby shore.

I let my eyes get used to the dark and saw that the tunnel ahead was getting wider, its surface covered in sand. Twenty steps ahead, it ended abruptly before a rough-hewn stairway, rising up beyond our field of vision.

The sounds of familiar-sounding voices filtered down the steps, lilting in that Innsmouth gobbledygook. I turned to see Barnes's eyes glitter in the dark, certain that we'd reached our goal.

A draft of cool, salty air rose up to greet us. Halfway up the steps, I stood on a loose stone and sent it clattering down to the tunnel floor.

I cussed at my clumsiness through clenched teeth. We waited for a while, but no one came. Maybe no one heard us or they just didn't give a damn.

The voices rose in pitch as we cleared the steps, making our way through a wide and rounded stone archway before us, fronted by a sand covered floor.

We split up in silence, so we could cover either side of it and saw . . .

Jesus Christ, where do I even begin?

The nearest, most inconspicuous-looking objects were a pair of tall stone pillars, set on either side of the entrance. They were covered in swirling engravings, coated with some darker, flaking stuff that seemed all too familiar, and wrapped in thick rusty chains.

Barnes dropped into a running crouch, and motioned for me to follow.

We entered the chamber.

The cavern was huge. Its tangy smell of ancient blood and peeling rust filled my nostrils. Ahead and above us, it faded into tar blackness, sloping down to reveal a small, round tunnel about fifty feet away to our right.

That's where the waves and the chanting came from, amplified as they boomed inside the cavern.

We peered across the corridor, at the humpbacked fish-things that lay prostrate twenty feet away.

There were about a dozen all told, praying to the biggest bastard fish-things I'd seen yet. I sneaked a glance at Barnes. He hadn't shifted an inch. Cocking my gun, I looked back at the slimy fish-thing mass.

The smallest of the three behemoths was a white, man-shaped thing that seemed to have been molded by some vicious, uncaring God. Featureless but for a black hole of a mouth, it jittered constantly, pulsing all over.

To its right was a King Cheese fish-man, sat on his stone-hewn throne and looking like the biggest daddy-o in the sea. His robe of threaded gold was weighed down under a metric ton of pure ritz.

And then there was the third one. If King Cheese and his palsy crony were bad, then this thing was a crime against nature itself. A mass of black, bloated pulsating filth, its flesh was covered in pink, shiny pustules. It moved like a cheap wind-up toy, all jerky and out of beat.

King Cheese addressed his subjects in gobbledygook. The pale creature beside him repeated the words, with the crowd following suit.

Just then, I noticed that the pale creature was a part of the bigger black thing to the right. Long tubes stretched out from its back and rear end to snake into the larger thing's bloated form.

The ritual went on. Barnes shifted from his place and started rifling through my bag of goodies, raising one hell of a racket. My hands shook as I grabbed his hand, before they caught on to us.

"What the hell are you doing, Barnes?" I hissed.

He just shook me away and said, "Help me prep the dynamite."

I checked my watch and saw that it was five minutes to midnight. "Did you see the girl?"

Bundle of dynamite in hand, Barnes said. "Girl's gone already. Didn't you hear?"

I blinked slowly and waved at the assemblage. "You mean you can actually understand that gobbledygook?"

"I guess," he said. "Don't ask me how I know, because I don't."

I struggled with the words, but couldn't come up with anything. What was the point anyway? Jen Abernacky was dead and gone.

Barnes searched through his pockets with the dynamite tucked between his knees. He said, "Best we can hope for is getting the hell out of here." Producing a lighter from his jacket pocket, he continued with, "... *after* we've blown these bastards right to kingdom come."

I nodded. Barnes had a point.

"You get those boomsticks lit. I'll lay down the suppressing fire," I said, cocking my guns with a wink and a nod.

Barnes cracked a smile and passed the bag. "I sow the lightning, you bring the thunder."

The bag was jam-packed with every last stick of dynamite in my stash. I lifted it one-handed and said, "Showtime!"

I charged around the pillar as Barnes broke cover, heading for the group, his fuse primed for Armageddon. Some ugly bastard in the fish-mass shot up on his feet and started barking orders.

I dropped him with two shots to the chest. From the corner of my eye, I caught Barnes letting his dynamite fly, so I flung my bag over into the baying crowd.

Not missing a beat, I hopped back to the tunnel behind us. I could hear Barnes keeping the pace as best as he could.

The dynamite blew just before I'd reached cover. Letting the old army instincts kick in, I made a leap of faith into the dark and landed on a bed of rubble and sand.

The next explosion rang like doomsday. The world around me shook like mad as I pulled myself around to check up on Barnes.

Thankfully, he didn't look *too* worse for wear. He was shouting something at me, but I couldn't make it out over the din of the explosion.

Barnes was helping me to my feet when my hearing returned.

A chorus of awful wails reached my ears. My hairs stood on end at the sound.

"I guess we've still got it," Barnes said, as he turned to face the carnage. I joined him with my guns cocked.

Going by the pitch of the screams and their intensity, I judged that there ought to be a few stragglers still kicking. I counted fish-men: the dead, the dying, the broken and the burning ones that pulled themselves toward the lake, like wounded soldiers crawling across no man's land.

The Big Cheese's throne was smashed to pieces, scattered across the sand along with pieces of his steaming flesh.

That's when I noticed the bloated black thing, writhing in flames, its skin peeling apart as the fire consumed it.

Barnes and I flinched in unison as it popped like a huge zit, sending chunks of foul meat flying across the cavern floor.

Checking my guns, I found that I was down to just two bullets.

One of the monster-chunks started to crawl around, inching toward us. I gave it a wide berth. I watched it shed a dozen pink eyes, sloughing off tendrils as it went.

I cocked my gun and hoped I could get a clear shot.

Barnes pushed me out of the way just as I pulled the trigger. My shot went wild.

I watched as Barnes ran to the pile of meat and started peeling away at it, revealing a naked, human girl underneath. She looked a little worse for wear, covered in monster-guts and some writhing tendrils, but she was human all right.

As I moved in to help Barnes, I snuck a glance at the remains of the broken giant to discover its pale, semi-human extension, raised up on a writhing tentacle, staring at us.

It started to howl, so I shot its head off before it could get any further.

We were rushing the girl back towards the tunnel when Barnes said, "You're Jennifer Abernacky, right?"

The girl nodded, only half-awake, stumbling around like a zombie. She spat out a white, chunky substance and said, "Where the heck am I?"

We chuckled, despite ourselves. Jennifer Abernacky was one tough customer. We led her through the tunnel, with the screams of the dying monsters still echoing behind us.

We didn't bother to check if we were being followed. Who'd dare, anyway? Instead, I helped Barnes get the girl out of Hell and into the open air.

We stepped out onto a wide sloping beach, the black sky about filled with glistening stars.

Beyond the beach and a narrow stretch of sea lay a long, dark shape that had to be Plum Island. That meant Innsmouth was off to our right, laid along the top of the cliffs behind us. We'd come one hell of a long way.

The girl started to struggle. Barnes let her go, draping his jacket around her small shoulders. It covered her right down to her knees.

Teeth still chattering, she looked up at me and said, "I know you, don't I?"

Barnes caught her by the armpits just as she collapsed. He grinned at me wryly and said, "Still the lady killer, aren't you, Trevor!" Pulling her into his arms, Barnes started heading down the beach.

I said, "Now wait a minute."

He turned to look at me. "That thing in the cave's still kicking," he said. "I think we should get while the going's good."

"What about my car? I can't just leave her back there!"

Barnes scowled at me and said, "You'd really go up against those things now that they're ready for you?"

"Point taken," I said, before following him glumly. Sure we'd killed a couple of fish-gods and we'd blown Innsmouth a new asshole, but who was going to pay for my beautiful car?

Catching up to Barnes, I said, "You know, if we keep on the left we'll eventually reach the Merrimac River. Follow that and we should reach some podunk town before long."

Barnes nodded. "I think the closest place is Rowley. We can rent a jitney from there." He paused, looking down at the girl in his arms. "We should stay out of Innsmouth from now on, okay? I sure as hell don't want to go through whatever happened to her."

I nodded. Being swallowed and almost digested by a monster was not an ambition of mine.

The coastline veered to the left to reveal a distant village, its windows lit despite the late hour.

"Don't get me wrong or anything, but if I never see another fishing village, it will be too soon. Also, I'm done with beaches. Zip, kaput, no thank you."

Barnes chuckled. "Picking vacation spots with you is gonna be a whoopie."

"I bet Jen's gonna agree with me, soon as she's up and about," I replied.

THE KINGSPORT DESK

I was way past bored as I made greasy finger patterns on my polished desktop to pass the time. Our detective agency, BARNES AND TOWERS INVESTIGATIONS, was going through a dry spell. I didn't even know where Barnes was and our cute secretary had either taken the day off of her own accord or was taking her sweet time getting here, as usual.

I wondered briefly if the dicks over at Pinkerton had to share desks, like Barnes and I did, or if they had to suffer a bunch of snooty secretaries like we did. This desk had come all the way from far Kingsport, and it was an absolute travesty of carpentry. Big and all grungy-looking (kinda like me, I suppose), it had about a dozen drawers, most of which wouldn't open; to pass the time, I'd poke at them every now and again with a nail file and a bobby pin, as I was about to do at that moment.

I'd been borrowing both objects for about a week now from my current girlfriend, a waitress working at a nearby café. I'd left her in bed on the off chance that there'd be something doing at work.

The drawer on the top left had been a major pain in my neck and I spent every spare moment trying to break into the bastard.

Seeing how I'd only ever seen lock picking done in third-rate flicks, I was secretly hoping I'd screw the lock so bad that I'd just have to resort to brute force.

I was good at brute force, but I'd decided that just this once, I'd look for a workaround. The old Trevor might have taken a hammer and chisel to the drawer, but not me, no siree.

I had the nail file rammed right into the keyhole and was twisting the bobby pin left and right when God above, the damn thing finally clicked open.

I looked at my work, pleased as punch. If Barnes had been here to see it, I'd have bragged till I was blue in the face. No such luck.

Behind me, the sun peeked out to greet me through the cloud cover, like a proud dad. I grinned before turning back to savor the spoils of my victory.

I grasped its brass knob, all tarnished around its well-worn rim and gave it a good tug. The drawer came open with a scraping creak. Must wafted up from a sheet of old newspaper that lined its bottom, almost causing me to sneeze.

The newspaper was about the only thing in it.

"Talk about let-down," I muttered, looking over what seemed to be an old sheet from a French newspaper.

I'd been to France during the war and had learned to hate the place. Shifting through the drawer, I found some more trinkets rattling around in the dust.

Poking around, I retrieved a thumb-sized orange pencil eraser, half a dozen pencils of odd lengths bundled up in a rubber band, and what looked like a pawn ticket.

The receipt was for a local shop—Arkham Pawn and Jewelry— hand-written in a chicken-scratch scrawl. The place was just over the other side of the river. I checked the date and grinned.

Maybe the day wasn't wasted, after all.

Leaving a note for Barnes, I locked up and left the office with a spring in my step and a happy little bee in my bonnet.

Apparently, the gaudy little receipt had been written just last week, which piqued my interest. After all, we'd had this desk for months now and this was brand new by comparison.

Unless Barnes had gotten the drawer open without telling me and snuck the receipt in, I had quite the mystery on my hands.

And mystery was my specialty.

The day was a sluggish, misty thing, an early sign of New England creeping into winter's cold little turf. I took deep gulps of fresh air and sped across the river onto Garrison Street.

Garrison's tail end sank into the mist, giving the town an almost fairy-tale look. Church and Main seemed just as enchanted as I passed them by on my way to the university.

I walked past wrought-iron fences and mist-tinged lawns into a section built out of sandy walls and Romanesque windows that made Miskatonic U look more like something out of Ivanhoe than a place of learning. A gaggle of girls in knee-high skirts were hanging 'round the entrance, adding their own beauty to the freshness of the day.

I tipped my hat at them and sprang past the gates and into the side streets leading up to Miskatonic Avenue, where the mystery pawnshop was to be found.

I passed by shuttered shops and scruffy tenements, fronted by scruffier people. The air turned cold and my good mood soured at the sight of this decaying street and its pathetic tenants.

The avenue seemed to have taken a turn for the worse since I'd last walked down it, a mere two months earlier. Arkham might be a place of deep history and untouched mystery, but it sorely needed a cleanup.

God only knew where our taxes went. Then again, they probably went down the same sinkhole that the Town Hall had been sucked into six months ago.

I neared the store and was not surprised to notice that it had probably seen better days. It stood next door to a fleapit hotel with a sign over it saying, 'Coloreds Only.'

I sneered in disgust. Some of those 'Coloreds' had fought and died for their country as hard as any white boy, but they still couldn't catch a break.

Arkham Pawn and Jewelry had grimy windows partially concealed by a row of second-hand jackets. I passed a group of black fellows leaving the hotel as I approached it. I gave them a reassuring smile and got nothing but suspicious looks and muttered slurs for my trouble.

I shrugged them off but could not ignore that dark cloud that seemed to gather around me. The door opened to gloom and must and a tinkling bell.

Like a devil's workshop ripped straight out of the funny pages, the place was cluttered with junk, and impenetrably dark.

The counter was located to my right. I had to tiptoe around guitars and golf clubs and even a suit of armor to reach it.

It was a glass affair, with its top shelf brimming with discarded jewelry, second-hand guns and poorly maintained knives. The man behind it, with his pits stained under each rolled up pale blue shirtsleeve, was hard at work stuffing a greasy BLT into his mouth. He only acknowledged me after he'd worked the thing into his maw.

He chewed slowly and stared at me all bug-eyed. One masticating eternity later, he finally blessed me with a crooked little smile.

"Good day, sir. How can I help you?" he said, his voice surprisingly well-groomed. Feeling jittery, I got down to brass tacks and showed him the ticket.

He grasped it in his greasy fingers and looked it over.

"What the!" he said, staring at me all worried, before finally mustering a sickly sweetness in his tone that I did not approve of.

"Yes sir. Quite so, sir. Please, wait here while I fetch the item."

The man turned to unlock a steel cupboard out of a row that lined the wall behind the counter. I kept up my con act in silence, whistling a tune until he was done shuffling about.

The man banged around beyond the counter, mumbled and tutted a few times before going, "Aha!"

He shuffled back to me before thrusting a small cardboard box in my direction.

Smiling sheepishly, almost as if he were afraid to ask, he said, "That'll be twenty dollars, sir."

I pulled the wallet from my pocket and handed him two tens.

I raised my head to find him leering over the cash in my billfold.

"We have some quality goods just released this morning that you may be interested in, sir," he said, almost drooling. "Some Prussian helmets in near-mint condition and a few Chambers originals, if you're looking for something more . . . grisly."

"Who is that?" I muttered, as I palmed the cardboard box.

"Chambers, sir," he continued. "Surely you are a man of books."

I shook my head, acting all ambiguous and turned to exit the shop.

The futz said: "I'll see you soon."

Pausing in the threshold, I turned to say, "Let's hope not," and let the door clatter shut, its eerie bell tinkling behind me.

Finally out of the shop's stuffy clutches, I went back to my usual routine of acting wary all the way across Miskatonic Avenue.

I walked back the way I'd come without acknowledging the blacks this time. They just hissed and swore.

The mist over Garrison had grown thicker, looking as if it was about to choke Arkham in its pillowy mass.

I stuffed the box in my coat pocket and headed the other way, looking for a way out of the Avenue. Reaching the turn into Garrison, I had to step over an unconscious bum sprawled out on the sidewalk, hopped up on Arkham's finest coffin varnish.

I turned right and felt a strange, nonsensical terror: it seemed to me as if the street was watching me. Not just the people walking across it, mind you, but the very bricks in the walls and the glass within the window frames themselves.

I undid my tie, my fingers slipping uselessly along the knot.

Beyond the unreality of Garrison, I told myself, was the river and the safety of the office. I picked up the pace, trying to outrun the paranoia that had gripped me since I'd left the shop.

I broke into a run, my feet slapping on the dew-soaked pavement. I noticed another sound: the gentle clicking of talons, the soft clop of hooves and the skittering of things I couldn't quite put in words.

I reached the university and turned left, looking to lose myself in the buildings past the gate. I half-slipped on the slick cobbles wondering just where the pretty girls had gone off to.

Everything was thick with fog, with the university wavering behind a wall of shifting white.

Panting and sweating despite the cold, I realized that I had taken one hell of a wrong turn. A row of coarsely hewn buildings peeked out from beyond the mist, their peaks coming together to form a horizon of ugly, twisting spires.

I'd stopped and turned back too late: my assailants had reached me.

I left the Arkham Kettle and headed back to the office. Towers was restless, what with the recent dry spell, and I had gone out looking for him. He and the bearcat he'd been seeing were an item apparently and I wanted to let him know that our cash flow situation had greatly improved after Abernacky's check had cleared. After talking to Trevor's gal, I was surprised to learn that Trevor hadn't been in the entire day. I asked her to have him drop by the office if he should show up later and told her he ought to treat her to something fancy, first chance he got.

Back at the office, I winced when I found the door unlocked and the front desk deserted. I checked up on the front desk, looking for Betty Polanski, our occasional secretary and just found a note that told me she'd be out for the next couple of hours. I briefly considered letting her go, but only briefly; if she left, I'd only have Trevor's bent little mug to look at, every time I went through the front door. Sighing, I walked into my inner sanctum.

I plopped down on the swivel chair behind the battered Kingsport desk and cringed as an ancient spring protested loudly. "Yeah well, suck it up pal," I mumbled and eased into the desk. I leaned forward to pick up my half-empty pack of smokes, when I noticed that the top left drawer of the desk was *open*.

"Would you look at that," I said. "Trevor finally got the best of it."

Smiling, I looked inside the drawer and was disappointed to find nothing but a brief note.

Barnes,
I finally beat the bastard! Would you believe all I found was a lousy pawn ticket? But get THIS: it was given in receipt of an item sold to the pawnbroker only a week ago! I'm going to pay them a little visit and see what sort of screwy crap is going on here. Probably won't be back today.
Ta-Ta,

Trevor

"Trevor can do cursive, huh?" I mumbled, honestly surprised. I was definitely intrigued but I'd have to suck it up until Trevor came to gloat, first thing tomorrow. I wasted the next couple of hours getting some billing statements in order until Betty Polanski finally showed. With everything looking peachy, I took the rest of the day off and caught a matinée at the Arkham Bijou.

I didn't get back to the office until ten the next morning. Betty was hard at work on her nails but had at least brewed me a fresh cup of coffee while she was at it.

"Any news from Trevor?" I asked.

"I haven't seen Mr. Towers all morning," she answered. "But he's a big guy. I bet he can take care of himself."

I smiled and said, "That's Trevor all right."

I sounded more confident than I felt. True, Trevor could take care of any run of the mill toughs with one hand tied behind his back. But we didn't deal with toughs; we dealt with ghoulies and ghosties and things from beyond the grave and those were more than a handful, even for Trevor. What if one of those had come back for a rematch?

I went back to the Arkham Kettle at noon and found that Trevor was still a no show. From there, I started scouring through his usual hangouts. After drawing another blank, I decided to pay a visit to Arkham Pawn and Jewelry, seeing how that was his last known destination.

The pawnshop was an oddity, even for Miskatonic Avenue, but

I figured it was about time I had a chat with the people that ran the place. I walked through the door and smiled as the attached bell tinkled my arrival. The pasty-faced man behind the counter frowned as he saw me walk in. I glanced at his wares and found that most of them were just piles of halfway rusted junk.

"I ain't here to buy. Ain't selling either," I said, putting both hands on the counter.

"Sorry, sir," the man rasped, "I'll have to ask you to come back during business hours . . . ."

I could tell that he was so full of bushwa his eyes were brown.

"Closing down? In the middle of the day?" I asked.

He struggled with the words. "Inventory check, sir. Only employees allowed."

"All right then. I'll make you a deal," I said. "Help me find a missing bit of inventory of my own and I'll keep out of your hair."

"I don't follow."

"Need a hint?" I said. "My business partner came to your shop yesterday. Been missing ever since."

The man stared up at me, looking terrified.

"Were you on shift yesterday?"

"Yes, sir," he said.

I reached into my pocket and took a snapshot of me and Trevor from my wallet. Betty Polanski had taken the snapshot, after we had gotten ourselves properly smashed after the Innsmouth case. I laid it down on the counter.

"The one on the right is my partner," I said. "Was he in here yesterday?"

The man shook his head, making his jowls wobble like jelly.

"Look closer," I said. "You can't have missed him."

I looked at the man's hands as he fumbled with the picture. They looked like fat rolls of dough, pudgy with scabbed over nails. I hoped like hell that whatever he had wasn't contagious.

"He certainly wasn't here yesterday," he said, lying through his teeth.

"I'll keep that in mind," I said, smiling as I stared into his bloodshot eyes. "Good luck with your inventory."

I turned my back to the freak and headed for the door. I heard him snickering as it closed behind me.

On my way back to the office I had to squeeze my way past a crowd gathered around some scholarly weirdo who called Hitler 'a godsend to Germany'. It just goes to show how quickly people forget how bad Huns can get, when you let them fly off the handle.

"Nuts," I grunted, and headed back to the office all good and pissed. In the end, I decided I was better off making an after-hours return visit to the pawnshop later that evening.

The fog provided plenty of cover when I broke into Arkham Pawn and Jewelry, through the back entrance, sneaking past the burglar alarm in no time flat.

Closing the door behind me, I reached into my jacket and took out a heavy-duty flashlight, keeping its beam aimed low. I swept the back room, scanning through cardboard boxes brimming with books. There were a few other boxes filled with random junk but nothing that really caught my eye. Stepping lightly—or at least, trying to—I made my way to the front of the shop and looked around.

I was about to leave, when I decided to check out the counter drawer just under the cash register. By the way it hung, halfway open, it almost seemed to beckon. Shielding my flashlight's glare from any stray passers-by, I looked inside and immediately spotted a BARNES AND TOWERS INVESTIGATIONS card. We'd had a bunch of them printed up shortly after going into business and it was a good bet that the one I was staring at had been from Trevor's personal stash.

I palmed the card and put it in my jacket pocket. Tomorrow, I'd put the pasty-faced sonofabitch through the wringer for lying to me. I wiped my fingerprints from the counter and drawer and made my way to the back room. I decided to take a last-minute peek at one of the book-filled boxes, so I bent forward and pulled back a cardboard flap.

"Jesus Christ," I whispered, staring at the title printed across the spine. "*The King in Yellow.*"

There was a rustle, a raspy chuckle and then a brass candlestick put me out like a light.

I awoke on a beach mumbling, "Where the hell am I?"

Waves gently lapped against the shore but I couldn't hear them for the jackhammers pounding inside my skull. I reached for the back of my head and felt the large goose-egg that was sprouting out from the dried blood and matted hair.

It took a few moments to gather my wits but I finally remembered what had happened. The freak at the pawnshop had gotten the drop on me while I was rifling through his books. And not just any books, mind you, but copies of *The King in Yellow* itself. Me and Trevor had seen it before, when we went up against a bunch of lunatics that worshiped the work in its pages and the alien king that starred in it.

With great effort, I struggled to my feet and gazed across the water. My geography was a bit rusty but I knew that I definitely wasn't in Arkham. I had to wonder if I was even in Massachussets, for that matter.

Turning away from the water, I peered into the distance. I could see mist-laden buildings slowly coming into view, laid out like pictures out of a children's book. Sighing, I rubbed my head and started walking toward the unknown city. Maybe there would be someone there I could ask for directions.

Or maybe I could just catch the next Jitney out of Fairy Land to Arkham, while I was at it.

Out-manned and outmaneuvered, I raised my hands, palms up, to the shadowy group around me. A tall, naked thing with hooves for feet and a pair of twisted horns stepped out of the mist to meet me.

Ain't that just the bee's knees.

It snorted, but kept its distance. I caught sight of the leather collar fastened to a long steel chain and sighed with relief.

A man appeared holding the chain. Bald, he was dressed in a black robe, beneath which he wore a suit of medieval-style armor. He held a wicked-looking spear in his other hand.

"Ah-ka-me ku-se?" the satyr giggled, just as the other shapes stepped into the light, to reveal a row of armored, spear-wielding, scowling weirdos.

"Look guys," I said, trying to play it cool in the face of abject insanity. "I know it's nowhere near Halloween yet. But if you're doing something, then I don't wanna know about it. How's that sound?"

The satyr cackled, and said, in his scratchy voice, *"As geht-mey cat cu-hul!"*

A pair of strong hands shot out of the mist and dragged me down by my arms. A moment later I was pushed roughly to the floor, my hands cuffed behind my back with steel shackles.

Looking up at the wall of spears around me, I decided to sit perfectly still and let the satyr start digging through my pockets, until he finally found the cardboard box.

He turned to his entourage and showed them his prize.

I said, "Anybody. Speak. Fucking. English?"

The satyr said, "Every girl's crazy 'bout a sharply dressed man."

"Well I'll be goddamned," I muttered.

I looked up to see a bald rube pushing out from the crowd, wearing a metal skullcap with a peacock's tail feather sticking out from the top.

The man kneeled close to me with the box in his hands. Without hesitation, he began to rip at it, revealing the small, carved effigy of a lion's head inside it. It was red, about the size of a tangerine, the king of the jungle himself wreathed in a crown of living snakes.

"What's that supposed to be?" I mumbled.

You'd think that being trapped in a strange city at the mercy of sinister men would teach me subtlety. Then again, what good is subtlety when you're stuck in a place full of weirdos?

"You have been summoned by the King," the man said, his accent pure Brooklyn, before barking the word, "*Udo!*" at his entourage.

Once again, I was dragged to my feet and turned to face the array of misty buildings that spread out where Arkham should have been.

Suddenly the penny dropped.

"Shit, the King, THE KING IN YELLOW?"

I was dragged forward, flanked by two spear-wielding toughs.

No one had bothered answering my question so I twisted around to see where the English speaking man had got to. He stood behind me, walking side by side with the satyr. The creature poked its tongue out at me.

I asked, "This is about the King in Yellow, isn't it?"

The man nodded.

We walked in silence for what seemed like hours, as we made our way through the city, trudging through the puddles that had formed among the cobblestones of the rain-soaked streets.

I tried to take in the city around me, checking the crooked curve of its clay and wooden buildings, trying to peer at the shapes that writhed behind the tinted windows, when I finally turned my eyes up at the sky.

It was a dull, bone white dome, flecked with black stars.

"Madness," I said, shaking my head.

An eternity later, we finally stopped in the middle of what must have been a square. Not that I could have known, with the fog laid as thick as it was.

"What? Are we taking a piss-break or what?" I asked and for the first time I realized one of the shaven-headed spear-bearers was a woman.

She smiled, looking halfway decent while she was at it. Then the man with the Brooklyn accent started to shout in that weird gobbledygook of theirs and the female guard spun me round on my heels.

I was facing the satyr. It gave me a grin that was all teeth, and said in a clipped, English accent that sent shivers down my spine, "You heard the man! Stop and rest!"

Then Brooklyn voice and the beast keeper proceeded to pull barbed daggers from their robes.

I thought they were going to come at me. I froze, waiting for the inevitable, when they suddenly leapt on the satyr and started hacking at it as if it were a piece of meat.

It screamed and giggled, dragged down to the floor even as it was hacked to pieces. I stepped back, looking away until its wavering voice had finally mewled away into nothing, trying my damnedest not to gag as the smell of shit and offal struck me. I thought about beating it, maybe running as far away from my captors as possible, when it hit me: *Where would I run and where would I hide, in the city of the Yellow King?*

The scampering sound of hurried feet and shuffling bodies snapped me back into unreality.

I felt about to upchuck and couldn't hold it down. The satyr, its pathetic body torn to bits, seemed to glint in the pale mist as it lay in a pool of its own black blood.

The leader of the guard and the rest were on their knees around the dead beast, dipping their fingers into its blood and entrails to paint symbols onto their chest pieces.

"What the hell are you doing?" I sputtered.

The leader approached me, another baldie taking his place beside the corpse.

He said, "It's a spell, to get us where we need to be."

The dark, dripping symbol on his chest was that of a dot surrounded by three twisted spokes.

"What the hell is that supposed to mean?" I managed, even as I tried to wriggle away from him.

"Behold, we have arrived," he said.

I turned, only to see the mist finally part to reveal a massive structure that I knew hadn't been there before.

A huge castle loomed before me, almost skeletal in design, its walls shaped out of ribbed columns and pointed arches that formed elegantly fluted windows and doors. The two corners facing me, a few hundred feet apart, were each topped by a slim, pointed turret.

I backed up to take the place in, finally coming to face a gigantic lion's effigy that had been hewn into the wall. A mane of stone serpents twisted around its triumphant, roaring face.

"Just like that fruity little trinket," I whispered.

The leader of the guards waved his hand and my shackles clattered on the floor.

"We were sent out to retrieve the man bearing the icon," he said.

"Great. Curiosity, nail files, and bobby pins," I grumbled, rubbing my wrists. "The bane of my existence."

I let my captors lead me into the building.

I was led up a wide stone staircase, through a double-wide black timber door, into a foyer walled with black granite and carpeted in tatty, stained, red material.

Iron chandeliers lit the place. Trudging across the carpet, I found myself led through another door into a large room set up like a dining hall ripped right from a DeMille flick.

The clatter of booted feet echoed through the hall as we made our way to the staircase at its rear.

The staircase was wide and richly carpeted. Its gaudy gold banisters made the rest of the plain stone hall appear sparse by comparison.

Slowly, it hit me. The place wasn't just *like* something ripped from a storybook. It probably *was* a world in a storybook, a world ripped right out from the pages of *The King In Yellow*.

Two guards, one male and one female, flanked me at the foot of the stairs. Three newcomers closed in from the right: a pale, raven-haired woman surrounded by two bald, dark-skinned men. Like the rest, they wore suits of armor under their black cloaks. Their chests held the same crooked sign as the soldiers, but painted in bright yellow. The woman gave me the once over before addressing my former guards in the usual gobbledygook.

"*Het hy gesien die geel teken?*"

"Keep going," a voice said behind me. I did as I was told and we made our way up to a second floor balcony.

Just the pair of guards flanked me as we walked up the stairs; apparently, they didn't need the extra muscle, now that I was right where they wanted me.

We halted at a door facing the top of the stairs. It was painted bright red, like two others lining the wall to either side of it.

The guard knocked twice, without bothering to look at me.

I twiddled my thumbs and stared at the floor, feeling like a schoolboy on the way to the headmaster's office.

I still had no idea what the King wanted with me and if I was honest, I didn't want to know.

There was a shuffling on the other side of the door. It opened and a woman in a stained white dress eyed me through the gap with a twitching left eye, her lolling head adorned with a small silver tiara clasped around a shock of lank, blonde hair.

She scowled at me, then at the guard.

"Demos," she hissed, glaring at him.

"This is the Queen's daughter," he whispered, then told the crone, "My lady, is the Queen indisposed? The Stranger has come to see her."

The hunched woman looked at me, her head bobbing.

"Worse sins will lead you to worse Kings, one for each color of the rainbow," she spat.

"Can't argue with that," I said.

She let us in and wandered to the balcony, muttering as she went.

The man called Demos shook his head.

"In you go," he said, "I need to keep an eye out for the Princess. She tends to fall down the stairs."

More than a little relieved to have dodged the King In Yellow so far, I stepped inside. The door slid shut behind me.

The wide square room was a little less sparse than the rest of the castle. Its floors were fashioned from hexagonal cream stone slabs, its walls draped with dark red tapestries smothered in embroidered signs and sigils.

Before me stood a wide, red leather couch, its back toward me. The backs of two blonde heads were visible, but their owners didn't seem to acknowledge me. They were facing a gap in the wall covered by a brown, fluttering curtain that appeared to lead either to an open window or a balcony.

The only other furniture in the room, apart from the couch, was a pair of huge globes set on either side of the curtain, propped up on matching dark wood stands. Even from a distance I could see that the shape and curve of their worlds looked nothing like good old Earth.

"Hello?" I said. The presences in the couch didn't seem to notice. From somewhere behind the curtain, rose a gentle, singing voice.

Arkham Nights

> *"J'ai perdu mon amie*
> *Sans l'avoir mérité*
> *Pour un bouquet de roses*
> *Que je lui refusai*
> *Il y a longtemps que je t'aime*
> *Jamais je ne t'oublierai!"*

Before I knew it I was heading toward the source, mesmerized by the sound of the voice.

I passed by the couch and found it occupied by a pair of shriveled, blond-haired corpses. Dressed in dusty black and gray page-boy livery, they looked as if they'd been left there to rot for decades.

The curtain blew open as a draft of sea air rushed in to reveal the mysterious singer.

She was a creature of wispy, blonde beauty with an angular, regal face. Her slim figure was wrapped in a burgundy satin gown, the skirt split at the middle to reveal a pair of shapely, pink-stockinged legs. Her stomach looked heavy with child.

Her piercing blue eyes found my own, and her face broke into a pencil-thin smile. "I am Cassilda, your tyrant Queen," she said in a musical, singsong voice. "What is your purpose in my realm?"

I shook my head, still taken aback by her beauty. "What realm would that be?"

"What nonsense! What other realm could it be, but Carcosa!" she said.

I nodded and introduced myself, not bothering to bow or kiss her hand. Indicating her belly, I said, "Who's the lucky rube? Is it the King?"

"I'm not pregnant; not that the King didn't have a hand in this," she said, patting the bulge gently.

I said, trying to look and sound as helpless as possible, "I'm almost afraid to ask, but what does he want me for?"

She shook her head. "Something terrible, most likely."

I bit my lip. "Now ain't that another fine pickle!"

Cassilda bridged the gap between us. She smelled strongly of some musky, sweet perfume.

She said, "Please talk quietly; you'll wake my sons."

I glanced at the corpses and was about to make a wisecrack when the Queen shrieked in agony. Turning back, I found her lying in a heap on the floor.

I kneeled by her side and felt for a pulse. No dice. She was cold and limp already.

I began to panic, as I realized that the Queen had probably flat out died on me.

I lifted an eyelid. A blue iris, the pupil slitted like a cat's, stared up blankly at the ceiling. I was about to call for help when her whole body began to shudder and convulse.

I let her go quicker than a live wire. She was shaking like an epileptic, her pregnant belly taking blow after blow.

Her stomach roiled and quivered, expanding suddenly before the mounting pressure ripped her dress wide open.

Something dark and wet spilled out from the tear and started pooling down on the immaculate floor. Just like that, the Queen was deader than a doorknob.

Her stomach began to stretch upward. It didn't look like it was going to stop.

I scrambled to my feet and made for the door, started pushing and tugging at the knob uselessly.

It almost seemed to fight against my slippery grip. I turned back and saw the Queen's stomach already stretched out over four feet high. I made for the balcony, giving her a wide berth as I did so.

A moment later I'd torn through the curtains. I stopped dead in my tracks at the sight of the titanic horror hovering beyond the balcony.

I ducked and looked away, hoping it hadn't noticed me.

A loud wet 'pop' sounded from Cassilda's chamber. I went for it. It sure beat facing the thing above the lake of clouds.

I crawled under the curtain on my hands and knees and found myself shuffling across something wet and sticky. I opened my eyes to a floor covered in blood.

A man of pure fleshy gold towered over me. His face painfully handsome, he smiled at me with a mouth of sharp white teeth. A crown of golden spikes surrounded his bald scalp.

The King in Yellow.

He stood ankle deep in the Queen's remains. Offering a long, taloned hand to me, he said, "I am here," and smiled a smile brimming with razors.

I hate to admit it, but I was horribly, awfully lost. There had been no gas stations or anything else that remotely reminded me of Arkham. Well, there *was* the fog but all it did was conceal a spidery creature that had been tailing me for a while.

"I see you, you son of a bitch!" I yelled, as it scuttled into a dark alley.

There had been other things in the fog during my short walk to the city but they had mostly kept to themselves, appearing as nothing more than amorphous shapes. Now there was a word to live by: 'amorphous.' Made most horrors we'd come across sound almost tolerable.

It was pretty clear that a particular group of religious kooks was to blame. Seeing those copies of *The King in Yellow* at the pawnshop—just before getting knocked out—cinched it: we were in deep shit. We'd dealt with the yellow cultists before and knew that they meant business. In the past, we'd fought them on familiar terrain but now, I was probably stuck in a brave new world that worked according to their rules.

I didn't know if my partner was alive but it made sense that if so, he was most likely stuck here, just like me. Now all I had to do was find him without getting myself killed in the process.

"Where is everybody?" I growled.

I'd been walking for a long time and had yet to see anyone. Anyone even remotely *human,* that is. No vehicles seemed to be going through the cobble-strewn streets either, so calling a cab wasn't an option.

I stopped at the edge of a building and peered through the fog. The spider-like thing had been getting bolder by the second and it was about time I got some distance between us. I wasn't one to ever run from a fight, but I wouldn't go up against a beastie in an unknown world without my gun, either.

I crossed my arms and tried my best to look bored. I silently counted to three and then sprinted to the back of the stone building, before darting down a narrow alley. I hoped to lose the thing that was after me, but I couldn't be sure.

I splashed through puddles as I ran down the alley, herded in by tall windowless buildings. The fog had settled thickly in the winding pathways between the towering structures and seemed to somehow muffle my footsteps. Gasping for breath, I stopped to get my second wind when I heard a roaring sound like rushing water from up ahead.

I peered through the fog behind me, trying to see if the spidery figure was still after me. I briefly saw dark movement within the swirling mist and cursed my luck. The creature was still on my tail and there was nothing for me to do but press on.

The roaring noise got louder as I continued on my way. I'd

walked another fifty yards or so, when the fog grew thinner and I could make out a canal of rushing water that divided the blocks of buildings. The canal was roughly ten yards across and drained into a tunnel under the street. There was no way across the barrier from my vantage point, unless I headed back the way I'd come and cut across to the main street. That way was obviously out of the cards unless I could find a weapon.

The alley was sparse, without any cover. After surveying the immediate area, I found that one of the buildings had a couple of jagged cracks running up its side. It was better than *nothing* so I cut loose with some kicks hoping I could dislodge a large enough stone chunk. One large shard broke loose but crumbled into pieces as it hit the ground.

"That's just peachy," I mumbled, turning to look at the dark shape that was getting closer.

I ran back to the end of the alley and looked down at the rushing water. There was no way I'd be able to swim across and I wasn't likely to survive a ride into the tunnel running beneath the street. It looked like I was stuck with trying to get by my pursuer and knew the outlook was grim.

"Well, Riley, it's been nice knowing you."

Every condemned man is entitled to one last butt so I reached into my pocket and fished out the crumpled pack. I set fire to the coffin nail and stared in horror at the monstrous thing that was peeking out of the fog.

This wasn't your garden-variety giant spider. It was a downright ugly bastard, with the head and torso of a man atop eight tree-trunk-sized legs. The head was as bald as a cue ball and dagger-like fangs stuck out from its downward slash of a mouth.

The thing was almost upon me when it let out a series of screeching yelps, which I assumed was an attempt at communication.

"Go tell it to Sweeney, why don't you!" I shouted and gave the creature a one-fingered salute.

The monster lunged at me. I crouched in a defensive position and prepared to make a desperate leap at it, hoping that I could punch out its lights before it managed to sink those fangs into me. As far as dumb plans go, this one took the cake.

The creature was a few short feet in front of me as I got ready to leap. It was *do or die*, when a hail of lead went whizzing past my head and tore into the beast's head and chest. I was stunned and half-deaf by the thunder of the guns but managed to roll away from the creature's thrashing limbs. I did some scuttling of my own away from its death throes and stared at the uniformed figure on the other side of the canal.

"Looked like you could use a hand, mate!"

It was good to be out of the alley. It was *even better* when I realized I was in the company of Tommies who had been stranded here, just like I was. I had been trying my damnedest to get them to clue me in on just *where* I was but they wouldn't spill it until a Captain Jacobi had a chance to talk to me. I waited impatiently, smoking one butt after another and trying to find out if anyone had even seen Trevor, but no dice. Apparently I was the only *human* they'd seen in ages.

Jacobi eventually arrived on the scene. He was of average height and seemed to be in good shape. Most of his graying hair was pulled back under his officer's hat and there was a twinkle in his dark blue eyes that belied the grimness of his situation. He gripped my hand in a firm handshake and asked me to come to a small building that he was using as a makeshift command post. Inside, a couple of soldiers were poring over some documents, ignoring us as we made our way to a smaller, barely furnished room.

He motioned for me to take a seat and offered a drink from a silver flask.

"I imagine you could use this," he said, extending the container.

I grinned and said, "You have *no* idea."

Jacobi barked out a short laugh.

"What do you know? About your situation, that is?" he asked.

"Not a hell of a lot," I replied, handing back the flask. "I know I'm not in Arkham and doubt that I'm even in America . . . unless you Brits are having another crack at the colonies."

He smiled. "Nothing like that, old boy."

"I didn't think so."

"Have you ever heard of Carcosa, Mr. Barnes?"

"Not really," I said, lighting a smoke.

"What of the King in Yellow?"

I frowned. "Don't know much about the book itself but my partner and I ran into some cultists. Also, this bogeyman that we thought had to be the King."

"That could explain why you're here then," he said. "I'm part of an organization known as The Yellow Cross. We have been tasked to eradicate all things aligned with this King in Yellow."

"How come I've never heard of you then?"

"You're not supposed to," he answered. "It's all need to know but what's the harm. After all, we're in the same boat together, what?"

"I appreciate it," I answered. "You mentioned Carcosa. Is that where we are?"

"Quite so, yes."

"And I don't suppose it's on any map, is it?" I asked.

He shook his head. "Afraid not; it's in another dimension entirely."

"I'd really like to find my partner and get the hell out of here," I said. "Is that even possible?"

Jacobi removed his hat and massaged his graying temples. "We might be able to help in that regard," he answered. "But our mission comes first, you understand."

I frowned and said, "Figured as much. So what's the skinny?"

Jacobi thought for a moment and said, "Don't see the harm in that. Seeing how you're stuck here with us."

"Understood," I said. "But keep in mind, *my* priority is getting my partner out of here."

He nodded. "Our mission is to find and destroy a group of Germans who are attempting to form an alliance with the King."

"Germans?" I asked.

"You know, Hitler's lot," Jacobi said.

"The Hun? In Carcosa? God almighty," I muttered.

Jacobi said, looking grim, "The Germans are all riled up for another war. Not all the politicians have figured it out yet but it's coming. With Hitler's ascension, it's only a matter of time."

Frowning, I said, "I had a bellyful of the last one. I never bought into Wilson's 'war to end all wars' but it was something to fight for." I scratched my head and asked, "How do the Huns figure into this King in Yellow stuff?"

"Ever heard of the Thule Society?" Jacobi answered with a question.

"My partner and I have an acquaintance who's good with that kind of stuff. I think he might've mentioned them before."

"Well," said Jacobi, "They have a lot of pull with the Fuhrer. Another world war would be bad enough without bringing outside forces into the fray. The last thing the world needs is for that madman to import the King's minions . . . or the king himself into our world."

"Can't argue with that," I answered. "I'll be glad to help if you can outfit me with something that's got some kick. I figure if there's trouble brewing here, then my old pal Trevor just *has* to be in it."

Jacobi laughed. "That can be arranged. Never thought I'd run across a Yank here, much less one who's had dealings with the Yellow King."

I shrugged. Trevor and I had had enough of the Yellow King to last us a lifetime. "So you and your men are a Special Ops arm of the military?"

"Essentially, yes," Jacobi replied. "Our primary goal is to stop the yellow menace in its tracks wherever it rears its ugly head."

I told Jacobi everything concerning Trevor's disappearance, about the book crates at the pawnshop and filled him in on everything that had occurred up to the time of my rescue. I didn't bother with the details about all the other dark forces Trevor and I had come up against during our partnership. I figured there was only so much even a guy like Jacobi would believe.

"Look at you, all white as a sheet!" the Yellow King said, ankle-deep in Cassilda's exploded corpse.

I ignored the hand he proffered me and curled myself up into a ball, trying to squeeze myself out from between the devil and the deep dead sea.

"You sure know how to make an entrance," I managed, even as I crawled away from him.

My eyes locked with the Yellow King's for a moment and I saw the perfect beauty and the unfathomable terror of it all. It didn't help any.

"You look different from the last time we met." I added.

He threw his head back and laughed, a tinkling of silver bells.

"My appearance changes according to the story. I must admit, however, that I prefer this shape to that of a stinky bug man."

He spun in a circle, his feet sloshing through entrails as he proceeded to make his way to the couch. Despite myself, I rose up to follow him.

He stopped a few feet away from the corpses on the couch.

I felt tiny and weak beside his overwhelming presence. I stood there in silence.

He crossed his arms and sighed. "These were Cassilda's sons; she poisoned them."

"They're quite the bunch," I muttered, thinking of the deformed princess I'd met earlier.

The King was silent for a while, an almost palpable aura filling the room. It had a soothing effect on me, slowing my madly beating heart and relaxing the tenseness in my joints.

"Not that I don't appreciate the fact," I said, backing away cautiously. "But how come you aren't mad at me?"

He tilted his head sideways so I could see his smile. Then, turning back to the couch, he said, "This incarnation is far less savage than some others. This suits my needs. What happened with those buffoons in Kingsport is none of my concern. But it does put you in the unenviable position of . . . how did that saying go? Ah, yes, *owing me one*."

Although his expression was kindly I found myself unable to maintain eye contact. I'd defied a god and his forgiveness was just too much to handle.

I asked, almost sheepishly, "What can I do?"

The King stepped around me, heading back towards the Queen. I felt better in the company of more wholesome corpses. I stared at the two Princes, their wrinkled, empty eye sockets staring right back at me.

From the other side of the room, where the madness-concealing curtain and the inside-out Queen lay, came the Yellow King's reply.

"My beautiful world has been invaded by creatures I want nothing to do with. They first came to parley, but now they want only to conquer."

This piqued my interest.

"So what? Just kick the rubes out. Hell, just send in your cronies to kill the lot of them," I said.

"Unfortunately, that is not an option," he said. "They possess some sort of technology that protects them from our attacks. They bear *this* symbol as their flag."

The King knelt, dipping his hands into the Queen's torso to rise with his fingers dripping blood.

He proceeded to paint a symbol on his chest. It was a swastika.

This was just getting better by the second.

"Fucking Boche," I said, "I hate those guys."

The King grinned and said, "It seems that we're on the same page, for once."

"Damned straight," I replied, and my grin was as wicked as his was handsome.

The last thing I expected when I fell out of bed that morning was that I'd end up leading an army. Besides *being transported to another dimension and meeting The King in Yellow*, that is.

But, there I was, looking down at an army of men and women in glistening, clanking armor, spears at the ready, addressing the troops.

Not that I would have had it any other way.

Before Demos and Naotalba, the King's high priest, had come for me, his Majesty had informed me that because I was considered a saboteur of no little means, I would be leading the offensive against the Germans.

I'd agreed wholeheartedly.

There'd been a knock at the door and the captain of the guard, accompanied by a black man in white robes and a turban, had come to collect me. As if in a dream, their forces had already been assembled. I thanked the King but didn't take his hand, seeing how it was still covered in Queen Cassilda's blood.

At the head of the stairs, flanked by Naotalba and Demos, I looked down at a room packed with skin-headed men and women, each dressed in the black robes and body armor of their rank. I noticed the spears that they held, pathetic weapons that would get them cut to ribbons against the German offensive. I walked down the stairs to approach the army, with my companions by my side.

The army stared straight ahead except for the two at the forefront, the raven-haired women I'd met earlier and a satyr that looked like the spitting image of the one that had been sacrificed.

I reached the foot of the stairs and faced them, the woman saying, "Ek het 'n leër gereed maar ons makeer hom fronting dit."

Her words were the usual gobbledygook, but she'd been speaking to Demos anyway.

He said, "Where are the enemy now?"

"*Oor naby die speelgrond, en steeds op tot van geen betekenis.*"

She sounded odd but almost sensual. "Can you speak English?" I asked.

She tilted her head sarcastically and Demos swiftly interjected.

"Sorry, sir, I should have introduced you. This is Einal, the King's Knight. She understands but won't speak our tongue."

Aint' that just the cat's particulars, I thought, and spoke my mind.

"Einal, ma'am, do your troops have any weapons other than spears? I hope you do, unless you want to get cut to ribbons down to the last man."

She smirked and raised her right hand. Clicking her fingers

caused the troops to explode into a flurry of movement. Each of them reached to the back of their robes to present crossbows forged from some kind of darkly gleaming metal. Each weapon was loaded and as mean looking as the faces of the bastard that bore it.

"That'll do," I smiled.

Einal returned the smile and it made her look quite beautiful.

There I was again, wandering down Carcosa's lumpy, cobbled streets, surrounded by the King in Yellow's servants.

This time however, I was their leader and the two flanking me were my retainers: Einal to my left and Demos on my right.

We wore matching plate-mail chest pieces, although I'd put mine on under my jacket. They were armed with crossbows but I hadn't bothered with one. For me it was a gun or nothing.

Before we'd left the palace I'd ordered most of my army to abandon their spears and stick with the crossbows. Why bother with a bloody, useless charge when you could snip at the crowds from a distance? Who knows? Maybe we could pick them off without any losses on our end.

I'd be lying if I said I wasn't giddy at the thought of going up against the Huns again.

Germany's military ruler was apparently one evil and crafty bastard, and getting involved in the occult and The King in Yellow seemed right up his alley.

Realizing that I hadn't the faintest clue where we were heading, I squinted through the thickening fog at my troops then back at our guide. We were following that twin of the satyr from earlier, except this one bore a pronounced limp and was on a chain held by Naotalba.

The high priest had kept schtum since the moment I'd met him.

I decided to broach the subject of the satyr with Demos.

"What's the creature for?" I asked, pointing at the limping beast.

"We use them as compasses and sniffer dogs," he said. "They make herds on the shore of the lake."

I thought of the lake and shuddered, thinking that the satyr was probably one of its more pleasant residents.

Einal interrupted my thoughts, nudging me with, *"U kan nie verstaan my, maar u moet weet, u kan nie vertrou die geel koning."*

Naotalba glared at her accusingly, before turning away.

"Can you translate that?" I asked Demos.

"Only if I wanted to risk my hide."

Changing the subject, I asked Demos, "So whereabouts in Brooklyn are you from?"

"Lower East Side, but if I told you the year you wouldn't believe me."

I didn't doubt him.

We reached a junction I hadn't made out in the fog and the satyr started tugging its chain to the right. We walked in silence for a few minutes longer before I started quizzing Demos.

"So what's the lowdown on the Boche?"

He harrumphed and took the time to spit on the ground before speaking. Then, "They have some kind of aura about them produced by a machine they carry." He paused and spat again. I liked Demos's disdain for the Huns very much. "It deflects our projectiles, but we've seen them walk in and out of it."

I thought for a few moments. "Maybe it stops things at a certain speed? I guess I gotta sneak in there and turn the thing off myself?"

"You'll be provided with all the necessary cannon fodder," Demos replied.

The thought of charging Germans over a pile of dead friendlies didn't exactly appeal to me.

I said, "No. That's not how it's going to go down. When we reach them, you and Einal split the army and we'll get them in a pincer movement. I'll go in quick and low and bust their machine. You just keep piling the pressure."

Demos looked at me with admiration.

"The classic pincer movement." he grinned. "I learned about that in military school, back in 3053."

"What a world we live in, huh," I muttered, then the satyr stopped in its tracks, sniffed the air a little and said, "We're getting closer."

Naotalba halted straight after and turned to nod at Einal.

I watched her raise an arm and the army came to a halt as one.

It was time to square my debt with the King.

The streets of Carcosa were like a damned maze. Sure, Jacobi and his men provided some comfort but my enthusiasm was somewhat curbed by the fact there were only twenty of us, myself included. Jacobi had admitted earlier that he had no idea how many Germans might've made the dimensional leap into the yellow realm and they hadn't the foggiest about the manpower or the intentions of the King's forces.

As our reconnaissance man checked out a cross street ahead, we stopped between two towering buildings and lit up. I turned to a young soldier named Oakes and said, "You boys must be real bad asses if this is all they sent to go up against Hun *and* the King in Yellow."

He just grinned and shrugged.

"Well," I said, "I just hope there's enough of us to get the job done and go back home."

"That *would* be nice," he said. "We don't usually get to have both."

I frowned as the truth dawned on me. "This is a damned suicide mission, ain't it?"

Oakes just smiled.

I cursed my luck, jokingly punched Oakes in the arm and said, "Don't sweat it, kid. I know for a fact I'm covered. See, a gypsy woman once told me I was gonna marry and raise ten kids."

Oakes chuckled and asked, "You married?"

I held up my ringless left mitt. "Nope. Out of the woods still."

The lad was starting to tell me about his folks in Bruxton when another soldier ran up the street and said, "Barnes, Captain Jacobi would like a word with you."

I winked at Oakes and said, "We'll have a jar in Bruxton."

He gave me the thumbs up and I left to see Jacobi.

Jacobi was huddled with an imposing figure I hadn't seen before. This sort of threw me; there was no way I could've overlooked someone like him. I made my way to the two men and Jacobi looked up.

"Please join us," he said, motioning me closer.

"What's up, Captain?" I asked. "Any news on the Huns or my partner?"

"No, but we're damn close," Jacobi answered.

Jacobi's companion—a completely bald man with dark piercing eyes dressed in a gray robe with constellations stitched into it—turned to me and nodded. "I can sense the imminent spilling of blood."

"That don't exactly take a genius to figure out considering where we are," I groused.

"Point taken," Jacobi replied, "but Aleister has what you might call a knack for these things."

Aleister ignored my comment and spoke to Jacobi. "The enemy is less than half a kilometer ahead. But to reach them we must first traverse a nasty little area fraught with peril."

It occurred to me that Justin Geoffrey would just love this Aleister guy.

Jacobi looked at the bald-headed man and asked, "What is the nature of that danger?"

"A type of sentinel," he replied. "Even with the cloak of invisibility I can briefly provide, getting past will be dangerous."

"Well then, nothing new in that regard," Jacobi said. "Do you have everything that you need?"

The man nodded. "If you can spare a couple of men, I'll take them with me and send one back once we reach the obstacle."

"That seems acceptable," Jacobi replied. Then turning, in a firm but quiet voice he instructed two men to accompany Aleister.

I watched the three of them move out.

"That Aleister fella looks familiar."

"He should," Jacobi answered. "Aleister Crowley is notorious in many circles. Still, don't believe that rot about him being the most evil man in the world. He's really one of the Crown's most valuable assets."

Jacobi left to confer with an aide while I double-checked the firepower the Brits had loaned me. I couldn't help but wonder if I'd jumped out of the frying pan and into the fire.

We double-timed it through the cross street and were soon in another narrow lane between towering buildings. Crowley had sent a man back to give the lowdown to Jacobi and we had moved out shortly after. We were split into three groups and maintained a distance of roughly fifty yards between. I was in the second group but could readily see the first group in the street ahead. They crouched before what appeared to be a wall of fog before taking turns disappearing into the mist.

Hanging on to a Tommy gun, I waited for our signal and moved out with the Yellow Cross soldiers when it came. By the time our group of eight reached Jacobi and Crowley the other men had safely made it past the danger zone.

"Listen closely," Jacobi said, upon our arrival. "What lies beyond this barrier is extremely dangerous but not exceedingly intelligent."

I started to say something but Jacobi waved me silent.

"Once you pass into the mist," he continued, "you will find a grotesque and many-limbed creature. According to Crowley, it is visually oriented and can neither hear nor smell you. Each one of you will operate under an aura of invisibility which can be maintained for no more than a minute or so. It is imperative that you make your way past this creature without it becoming aware of your presence. In short, that means move fast but damned carefully. The first group has made it through without incident and I expect the same from you. Is that understood?"

A chorus of enthusiastic "Yes sirs!" resounded and a line was formed.

Jacobi turned to me and said, "No offense, Barnes, but I need you to go last. If something unforeseen happens to Crowley—not that I expect it—I need as many of my men as possible to make it through."

"The story of my life," I replied. "Nobody loves me."

Jacobi smiled. "After you go in, Crowley will teleport us safely across."

"The privilege of rank," I chuckled.

"Actually, it's a damn queasy business," Jacobi answered.

The men ahead of me entered the wall of mist at approximately one and a half minute intervals.

"We don't want them getting in each other's way," Jacobi explained.

I waited impatiently and finally Oakes—the soldier from Bruxton—entered the mist. That left only me, Jacobi and Crowley.

Jacobi looked at his watch and counted down the seconds.

Crowley appeared deep in concentration.

"Okay," Jacobi said, "It's go time!"

I nodded, clutched the Tommy gun tightly and ducked into the mist.

I felt only a brief spritz of dampness and emerged a couple of feet further down the path we'd been traveling. The only difference was another vale of mist about seventy-five yards further up the street. Well, that and the ugly bastard of a monster that was supposed to stop our passage.

It was squat and greasy-looking. Tentacles about the width of fire hoses swept slowly across the lane as if trying to sweep up anyone foolish enough to attempt passage. Well, Riley Barnes was just such a fool and judging from the absence of soldierly body parts, the men that had gone ahead of me had made it past without incident to pass through the obscuring mist at the end of the street.

Feeling cocky in my apparent invisibility, I started to lope forward figuring it would be a piece of cake to avoid the slow-moving appendages. I had only gone two or three steps when a loud curse rang out.

"Christ, it's got me!"

I searched for the source of the cry but couldn't see anything. The distraction almost landed me in trouble as I hopped over a thick, questing tendril at the last moment.

"Where are you?" I shouted, seeing a curled tentacle waving about only yards from where I stood.

I heard the sickening crack of a bone snapping, followed by an agonized groan.

"Barnes, forget about me . . . and get the hell out of here . . ."

"Like hell, Oakes!" I shouted. "I don't plan on drinking alone in Bruxton."

I unslung the Tommy gun and fired a short burst into the center mass of the creature. It didn't have a recognizable head and I was probably just whistling past the graveyard if I thought I could kill it.

"No gunfire!" Oakes moaned. "You'll alert the enemy."

Ignoring his statement, I started to fire off another burst at the monster but stopped as Oakes began to become visible. I managed to avoid another sweeping tentacle and raised the weapon in hopes of blasting the appendage rapidly crushing the life from Oakes. I was squeezing the trigger when the poor guy's head literally exploded from the pressure.

"Damn," I muttered, lowering the Thompson.

I started to fire another burst at the murderous creature but remembered Oakes' warning. No point in getting his pals killed as well. I had truly done crapped in my mess kit concerning the gunfire and might as well have erected a big sign saying, "Come and attack us."

I was pissed at myself and even more pissed at Jacobi for not utilizing Crowley's abilities to transport the men past Oakes' killer. I planned to voice my opinion in no uncertain terms once I made it to the other side. Glaring at the monster, I spat in disgust and sprinted toward the wall of mist at the other end of the street.

"What the blazes happened back there?" asked Jacobi as I staggered through the misty vale. "There was to be no weapons fire."

"Oakes bought it," I answered, glaring back at Jacobi. "*He* didn't have a damned wizard to teleport *him* across."

"Look, there's a reason . . ."

Crowley interrupted and said, "You're under no obligation to provide explanations to this fool."

"Why, you dirty sonofabitch!" I growled, rearing back to unload on him with my right.

Strong arms grabbed hold of me and kept me from decking Crowley.

Jacobi looked at me and in a soothing voice said, "Listen, Barnes. I don't like it any better than you. Oakes was my man and *my* responsibility. Aleister has extraordinary abilities but there's a limit to what he can do without depleting his energies. We're going to need him to expedite our return home when the time comes."

"Don't you mean *if* the time comes?" I asked.

"I plan on seeing that it does," he answered. "We may be few in number but each man here is highly trained and extremely motivated. What happened to Oakes is tragic but it's the cost of what we do. The best we can do for the lad now is see that his life was not given in vain."

"Yeah, I guess you're right," I mumbled. "Sorry about going off all half-cocked. Truth is, I'd like to find my partner and go home."

Crowley smirked but said nothing.

"Apology accepted," Jacobi said. "Please understand, I have every intention of ending this rotten business and getting my men home safely. With luck, we'll find your partner along the way and return him as well."

"Good enough," I answered.

We shook hands and Jacobi gave the order to move out.

We hadn't traveled far when we noticed that the buildings we passed on each side of the lane were no longer towering but now one and two-story structures. Jacobi's reconnaissance reported that Huns had been spotted a short distance ahead. We made our way forward waiting to see the German things we had come to stop. Well, the Yellow Cross had come to stop them and I was along for the ride in hopes of locating my wayward partner. Still, what was going down in Europe didn't sit well with me and I was more than happy to lend a hand.

I didn't know exactly how Jacobi expected to get the jump on our German friends—especially after my noisy display in Oakes' defense—but my unspoken question was almost instantly answered as a thick fog descended over the area.

Jacobi looked at me and grinned. "Courtesy of Aleister," he said.

"But can we see *them* in this wet blanket?" I asked.

"It can be dissipated when needed," Jacobi answered.

"I guess wizards are good for something," I begrudgingly admitted.

"We'll approach until we meet up with my point man," Jacobi continued. "At that time the fog will lift and we'll come down on the bastards like a ton of bricks."

"That's my kinda strategy," I answered, giving him a thumbs up.

We moved out and reached the point man in a matter of minutes. Jacobi conferred with the soldier and then addressed the rest of his men. "Listen up, everyone," he said. "We're about to enter the alley on the right. It runs for only a short distance and leads to a courtyard where our targets are deployed. Hanson reports there is quite a bit of debris in the area so take cover and engage the enemy when the fog dissipates."

We had our orders and soon reached the courtyard. Our point man had left a sentry with his throat slit behind a pile of cracked masonry, which seemed like the best way to leave one of them in my eyes. Our little group was locked, loaded and waiting for Crowley to lift the fog.

Crowley spoke with Jacobi and nodded. He mumbled some gibberish that was Greek to me and made some weird gestures with his hands. The fog began to slowly clear and we got a hint of what the kraut-eaters were up to. Through the thinning tendrils of mist we watched them remove materials from their backpacks to begin constructing a spindly tower of sorts.

"What the hell are they doing?" I asked.

"Based on what I've seen before," Jacobi answered, "it may be a portal device to summon reinforcements."

"You guys got something like that?" I asked.

Jacobi shook his head and frowned. "Just Crowley, and his power has its limitations."

"*That* ain't good," I replied.

I started to wisely point out that we should definitely end their efforts, when we were all shocked by the sight of some strangely garbed men leaping from the nearby roofs and emerging from between doors.

"Hold your fire!" Jacobi barked to his men, who were tensed and ready for action.

I watched in surprise as the medieval-looking arrivals let loose a volley of crossbow bolts at the Germans. The enemy held their fire and laughed.

"Who are those guys?"

"Carcosans would be my guess," Jacobi answered.

"Well, they're a nice diversion for sure but they don't seem to be having much effect. Some damned thing is repelling their shafts."

Jacobi peered through the remnants of fog and cursed. "See that soldier with the globular device strapped on his back?"

"Yeah," I replied.

"It's emitting a force field that the Carcosans can't breach. Someone will have to go in from the rear and take that bastard down."

I was all set to volunteer for the job when an unexpected sight greeted my tired eyes. "I'll be damned," I laughed. "Jacobi, I think your problem's about to be solved."

Trevor Towers was charging in from the rear with a wicked-looking blade in hand. I'd seen that look in my partner's eyes before and didn't envy the globe-toting Hun.

At a signal from Einal, one of the soldiers left the group to disappear down the street. His movements were as silent as a shadow's, and after we'd waited in silence for a while, he returned, panting quietly, to address me in an eager voice.

"Twenty tetrons down the street and then eighty to the right of the adjunct, they've stopped to do something."

I glanced at Demos, "Tetrons?"

"Say feet give or take."

"Right," I thanked the soldier before turning to face the others.

"My knowledge of this area is shit, so you need to work on your own initiative a little." It felt good being the leader again but I tried not to let it get to my head.

"I want you to split up into two groups and get around the Germans, using any camouflage that's good enough. I'll sneak up behind them, and at a whistle from me you open fire on the bastards."

Everything went quickly, with Einal and Demos dividing the troops between them. They then marched off, giving me appreciative nods and making strange salutes as they passed.

I didn't bother returning a salute I didn't know how to repeat. As the final few men and women passed me by, I turned to follow but was stopped by a pat to the shoulder.

It was Einal, paused at the rear of her group. After looking round, she said, "There is more to this than you know, and things you should be told but haven't."

She hooked her crossbow onto her belt and stepped up to me, placing her arms around my neck to give me a kiss that tasted warm and sweet.

After too short a time she drew back, whispering, "Someone has your back, though. Trust me."

She turned and was gone, my eyes following her until she disappeared into the mist.

It felt good to know Carcosan women, some of them at least, were still women after all.

I pulled myself together, recalled what the scout had told me, and chose my path accordingly.

Running twenty tetrons soon had me at the junction the scout had mentioned. The right-hand path looked hazy after about thirty with just a hint of the departing soldiers beyond.

Ignoring this, I continued forward, looking for another junction so I could double back on the enemy.

Shit, I was beginning to hate Carcosa. Why on earth would anyone want to invade the place, let alone live here?

After another fifty feet/tetrons of running I found another junction. I turned onto it and almost tripped over the corpse blocking my path.

I'd stumbled across a satyr, its open chest spilled of guts, most of which trailed off to my right. A look in that direction revealed the high priest Naotalba, huddled down in an open doorway. His robes were bloodstained and his hands were thrust deep into a steaming pile of entrails.

He looked at me and grinned. His lips and chin were bloody and I didn't like to think why.

"I've divined the future," he said, lifting hands full of dripping guts. "It does not bode well for either of us." Then he laughed, a dirty cackle that stalked me down the street as I continued with the plan.

The plan: join the pincer movement from the rear and charge a group of heavily armed Huns with nothing but a whistle and a song. I'd gotten through worse in the war, but nothing so bizarre.

With the pincer in mind I ran faster, knowing I had another forty feet to go before I reached the target. Seconds later I was brought to a stop in the worst possible way. No, not a Hun ambush, it was much worse than that. I'd reached a dead end, the street ending in a tall, shadowy building.

I didn't stay still for long, for the building had a big, open doorway.

I stepped in there quietly, into a small dark foyer bearing another doorway filled with fitful illumination.

I walked quickly through the doorway, into a room that bore the first sign of habitation I'd found in a city as dead as it was bleak.

The illumination came from a wood-fueled fire surrounded by four disheveled men. They were warming their hands, all of which appeared to have way too many fingers. None of them paid any attention to me. I snuck past them and through another door I hoped would lead me out of the house.

I was almost right: I entered another room with an exterior doorway lining the facing wall.

The exit was filled with foggy light. This encouraged me but also illuminated the sheet-draped form before it.

I started to run and made a leap over the sheet's now shifting occupant, a form that appeared way too misshapen to be human.

Whatever it was grabbed at me as I left the threshold. I now found myself on another street with a fog-shrouded courtyard at its end.

I slowed down, heading towards the right-hand corner and thinking that if I'd calculated right, I'd be directly at the enemy's rear.

I wasn't let down.

Whispering, "Damn, my old pals, all together," I took in the hazy forms of men in jackboots and green uniforms, their bobbing heads covered in gray chamber-pot helmets.

It felt weird, seeing them in this alien world. Still, they fouled it with their presence.

They were positioned two by two, with the ones nearest me, just twenty feet away, looking jittery, their rifles raised. Those beyond them were messing with something on the ground.

I took few deep breaths, put my fingers to my mouth, and whistled.

My reply came an instant later; from either side of the Germans, volley after volley of whizzing projectiles came pouring down.

Then came my turn.

Charging forward, I kept my head ducked but my eyes on the prize as I rushed the confused men. Each was covering his head despite the fact the Carcosan projectiles were falling short against their invisible barrier.

I reached the enemy hoping the barrier's hoodoo wouldn't do the same to me. It didn't, but I did experience a moment of resistance. I barged past the yelling men without a care for anything but my target.

Some of the Huns, ones that had been busy constructing a spindly metal machine, were crouched with their guns raised while shouting in babbling tones.

One of them had a device formed from throbbing globes strapped to his back. Drawing the knife Demos had given me, I leapt on him without a thought of the consequences.

My lust for battle was back with a vengeance.

I fell on him with a snarl, slipping the knife into his chest. He was dead in a second. Hearing angry shouts around me, I twisted him round to begin punching and tearing at the device on his back. Soon fists pummeled down on me and I heard guns being cocked.

I laughed as I smashed globe after globe, tearing my hands up in the process.

I didn't give a shit about the pain or the blood.

Then came the gunfire.

The Yellow Cross boys and yours truly opened up on the Germans as soon as Trevor smashed the force field projector. I stitched one of the jack-booted thugs from crotch to sternum with a burst from the Thompson and watched his guts fall at his feet. Other Huns cursed and fell in agony as they were pin-cushioned by shafts from the Carcosan crossbows and decimated by my British companions. These *Master Race Wannabees* hadn't counted on much of a fight and their shock at the unexpected turn of events made an organized stand next to impossible. The battle was short, intense, and gory while it lasted. I was kept busy trying to watch Trevor's back and at the same time avoid the undisciplined return fire from the Germans.

Before I had time to let things sink in, the gunfire stopped and all seemed right with the world. The Germans—far more than Jacobi had originally estimated—were now worm food and my partner, Trevor was alive and kicking. I didn't know how he'd managed to forge an alliance with the Carcosans and could only guess that even the King in Yellow had his fair share of rebellious malcontents. I was soon shown the error of my ways.

I was moving forward to join Trevor in celebration when Crowley knocked me aside and sent me reeling into a wall, causing me to lose my balance and land on my ass. Seeing red, I jumped to my feet but stopped suddenly upon catching sight of the crossbow shaft he held in his fist. The dour old sonofabitch had plucked it from the air before it could skewer me.

"Uh, thanks . . ." I stammered in confusion, surprised that Crowley would've made the effort.

He smiled coldly while Jacobi's voice ordered everyone to take cover. "Boys, hold your positions and return fire!"

"Don't hit the big ugly guy in the trench coat!" I yelled frantically. "He's my buddy."

Crowley sneered. "Your *buddy* better gain control over those Carcosans or all bets are off."

I felt like decking him but thought it would seem mean since he'd just saved my life. That and the fact that he could snatch an arrow in flight made me less than certain that I could touch him.

Through the haze of smoke and mist I could see Trevor yelling and waving his arms in an effort to stop the violence. *That's* a phrase I never thought I'd hear myself using in regard to my partner. His effort had no effect.

The Carcosans continued to direct their fire at our positions and to make matters worse, were stripping the Germans of their weaponry and using it with deadly effectiveness. Two of the Yellow Cross soldiers were killed and a third was seriously wounded. Our return fire was taking a heavy toll on the Carcosans, but their sheer numbers made it clear that we were in deep shit.

"We're running low on ammo!" cried someone nearby.

German bullets continued to gouge holes in the surrounding walls and bounce around the courtyard, occasionally striking a Carcosan. This pleased me to no end but it wasn't whittling down the odds enough to make a difference.

Jacobi glanced at his watch and turned to Crowley. "Can you get us out of here now?"

Crowley sighed, saying, "I'll need a few more minutes."

"Okay," Jacobi replied. He looked at me and said, "Barnes, it's nearly time. I don't know what the situation is with your friend, but we can't tarry to sort it all out."

"Yeah, I know."

"We'll withdraw into the alley!" he shouted over the gunfire. "A couple of my boys will cover our . . ."

"I'll be one of them," I interrupted.

"Look," he urged, "no point in throwing your life away."

"Trev would wait."

Jacobi tossed me another drum of ammo and yelled orders to his men. Turning, he said, "Good luck Sir! Catch up to us if you can."

I nodded grimly and took my position alongside the soldier I knew as Hanson. We laid down suppression fire as the other Yellow Cross men withdrew into the alley. A score of Carcosans fell under our withering fire while Trevor continued to rage wildly at his companions.

"Time to go, mate!" Hanson said once the last of his comrades had made it to the relative safety of the alley.

"Make tracks, kid," I answered. "I'm right behind you."

I made the Thompson sing as Hanson hit the alley. I was on the verge of making a suicidal dash to drag Trevor away from the Carcosan maniacs, when to my surprise the one nearest him grabbed his arm and pushed him toward my position.

I started to yell and felt strong hands pulling me back.

"Damn it!" I raged, thinking that the last thing in the world I needed was some do-gooders trying to drag my butt to safety. Hanson and two other men pulled me toward the alley as I watched Trevor and the unknown Carcosan head towards us.

"You were supposed to be following me," accused Hanson.

"Look, kid, this is my problem! Get the hell out of here."

"Hey!" a soldier yelled. "That's your pal and one of them Carcosan bastards."

"Let go of me and cover them!"

They released me and began to fire. I joined in and yelled for Trevor to hurry. Even my foghorn voice failed to carry over the deafening noise but it was beginning to look like things might turn out well. It was about that time that I watched in horror as Trevor staggered forward, apparently hit.

The gunfire I'd been preparing for appeared behind me, instantly felling the Huns about to gun me down. As Einal had promised, someone had my back.

Their corpses fell around me and for the moment I was too surprised to take a look at who'd arrived to save my bacon. And besides, my main concern now was in grabbing hold of the nearest gun so I'd at last own a weapon I was familiar with.

One of the fallen Germans, an officer no less, had ended up facing me with a leer of agony frozen across his face. Pushing him away I proceeded to remove the Luger from his grip before crawling to my knees to finally see who my saviors were.

Would you believe it? Not far distant I saw what looked like a group of British soldiers. They were crouched, taking cover at each street corner. With them was a man who looked exactly like my partner, Riley Barnes.

But shit . . . that couldn't be right, *could it?*

My double-take was interrupted by footsteps all around me. My Carcosan comrades, having succeeded in killing the Huns, were now rushing my way.

My congratulating them for a mission well done evinced nothing but blank stares.

They were no longer mine to order.

My sinking feeling began as they retrieved the German guns. It deepened as they utilized them to open fire on the British. The Carcosans, spear bearers and bolt throwers both, had no problem cocking and firing the German machine guns and rifles.

My orders to cease-fire came to nothing. Apart from maybe shooting the ones nearest me point blank, I was totally at a loss.

The words, "Hold back, they're on our side!" didn't help, and the British soldiers who'd saved me in the nick of time were returning fire, but seemed utterly overwhelmed by the barrage.

Added to this were the crossbow bolts of those that hadn't picked up guns. I stood helpless while my double-crossing troops continued their war against the good guys.

I looked around in panic and found a familiar face beside me. It was Demos, armed with a crossbow, his face wild with the heat of battle.

"I'm sorry sir, I really am," he said, "the King wants the German tech and what *he* wants *he* gets." He nodded towards the broken device behind me before continuing. "You're a good man though, and you deserve to get out of this."

At this, he grabbed my arm and indicated I should follow him. He headed right and pushed me before him saying, "Run! I'll be right behind you!"

So I ran, with arrows and bullets whizzing past from every direction and the British soldiers just in reach. And Barnes, I mustn't forget him.

I was almost upon them when a scream from behind, followed by something heavy, slamming against my back, sent me staggering.

I turned, gun raised, to find Demos falling into my arms, his mouth dripping blood. He'd been shot, by bullet or arrow I didn't know, until I glanced up to see Einal with her crossbow raised.

The bitch was smiling. Demos died in my arms and I found myself filling up with rage.

"You double-crossing…"

I lowered him and aimed squarely at her face. She was going to die for her treachery.

I pulled the trigger and the gun clicked empty. The next thing, strong hands were pulling me back as I looked on helplessly at Einal's evil face.

She re-loaded the crossbow with a smile and popped an arrow right into my chest.

I watched Trevor reel wildly and sort of lost it.

Without thinking, I charged recklessly forward before Hanson and the others could stop me. After only a couple of steps I figured that my partner wasn't hit but had staggered from a Carcosan that had fallen against him. His ally had been felled with a crossbow shaft fired by a coldly smiling woman. Trevor managed to regain his balance and catch the dying figure who had spurred him away from the treacherous Carcosans.

I raised the Thompson to cut down the bitch. Before I could shoot, a ricocheting bullet struck the barrel and managed to crease my thick skull. Seeing stars, I cursed a blue streak while searching the ground desperately for another weapon.

Trevor cursed the murderous woman and I stopped my clumsy fumbling long enough to watch him aim a Luger at the killer. "Take the bitch down, Trev," I whispered, wiping blood from my eyes.

His pistol clicked empty.

"Let's go, Trev!" I yelled. "We *need* to get out of here!"

I lurched towards him but was grabbed from behind by Hanson. "Jesus, Hanson!" I roared. "You got a crush on me or something?"

"We're all going *now*, Yank!"

At least Hanson's Yellow Cross comrades had latched onto Trevor and were dragging him away from the carnage. My spirits began to lift until I saw the crossbow bolt sticking from the center of his chest.

We disappeared into the alley, keeping our eyes peeled for pursuing Carcosans. Trevor was able to travel under his own weight but kept worrying at the shaft poking from his chest.

"Leave that damn thing alone," I said. "We'll be meeting up with some other Brits that can lend a hand."

"It's not that deep," he answered. "The armor under my coat stopped most of it." He grunted in pain in spite of himself. "And *what* the hell are you doing here?"

"It's a long story," I replied.

"It always is."

"Glad we found you," I said, "even if you *do* look like shit."

Trevor smiled, saying, "Yeah, well if I was *you* I wouldn't go prancing in front of no mirrors."

One of Hanson's fellow soldiers rolled his eyes and said, "Christ, they're worse than me Mum and Dad."

"I know," said Hanson, "maybe they'll declare war on the Germans and *talk* them to death."

Trevor managed a laugh. "Those are sure some smart-mouth kids you're hanging around with."

"Well at least *I* found some *Limeys* to pal around with, instead of signing up with the Yellow King's army."

A dark look of regret crossed Trevor's face. "Yeah, I'll tell you about *that* later."

I grinned and said, "If we ever get back to Arkham, there's a certain pawnbroker I intend to look up and have a word with."

"So, you met him too, huh?"

"Yeah, and he better hope I don't meet him again."

"This is all because of that damned Kingsport desk," Trevor groused.

"I figure our old friend *the King* should shoulder the blame."

"Yep," Trevor agreed, "One of these days I'll settle his hash for good."

"These fellows who saved our bacon are sort of in *that* business," I answered. "I wonder why those Carcosan goodwill ambassadors ain't following us?"

Trevor looked distraught and growled, "Why should they? I helped them get practically everything they wanted."

"Look at the bright side, mates," Hanson piped. "Any chance of an alliance between the Carcosans and the Huns is probably on hold for a long while."

"Damn I hope so," Trevor muttered.

We finally reached the spot where Jacobi and his men were gathered. They stood bunched together inside a powdery circle that Crowley was pouring on the ground around them.

"Who's baldy?" Trevor whispered as we straggled towards the group.

"Aleister Crowley," I answered. "Our ride home."

"Makes about as much sense as anything else that happens to us. Should we get his autograph for Geoffrey?"

"Let Justin get his own," I answered. "Crowley's a bit on the grumpy side."

Jacobi, pleased that we hadn't been followed, ordered Hanson and the rest of us to join them. "Be mindful that you don't break the circle, boys," he cautioned.

We started to cross and Jacobi spied the arrow protruding from Trevor's chest.

"Crowley, take care of that man," Jacobi ordered.

The magician gave Jacobi an expression as pleasant as sour milk and stepped to where we stood. He looked curiously at the arrow and then smiled coldly. "This will hurt," he said.

"No shit," Trevor growled. "It hurt going in *too*."

"Have no fear, Mr. Towers," said Jacobi stepping forward. "Once Crowley is finished you'll be good as new."

I chuckled. "That's not saying much."

"Screw you, Barnes," Trevor answered.

Crowley stood in front of Trevor and placed his hands lightly on the crossbow shaft. I saw my partner tense, waiting for the pain that was sure to come.

"Shouldn't we cut away the armor?" I asked.

"No need," Crowley answered. He mumbled a few words and his fingers began to dance up and down the shaft. Sweat broke out on Trevor's face, now becoming pale as Crowley did his magic. Suddenly the wizard pulled forcefully and Trevor groaned in pain.

I watched dumbstruck, as the crossbow shaft landed on the ground, seemed to quiver for a few seconds and become a greenish haze that quickly dissipated. Trevor reached for his wound but was shocked to find it healed.

"How in the hell did . . ."

"No time for explanations now," Jacobi interrupted. "I believe our *friends* are finally in pursuit."

"Into the circle," Crowley intoned.

The enemy's rifle fire and crossbow bolts were ineffective.

While safely within the confines of the circle, we jeered and made obscene gestures at our foe until Jacobi put the kibosh on such shenanigans.

"Spoilsport," I muttered, then grabbed my belly as a wave of nausea washed over me.

Crowley was taking us home and the trip was anything but pleasant. Still, it was a damned sight better than being left in the Yellow King's domain. At some point everything went blank, after a brief bombardment of bizarre colors, headache-inducing sounds, and brief glimpses of things and places I'd be hard-pressed to describe. We eventually arrived back in England—not where I wanted to be—but better than the alternative. We had just enough time to gather our wits, bathe and get a hot meal. Jacobi had a mission for us.

It seemed that the Carcosans were so keen on playing with their newfound technology that they decided to put it to use soon after we'd escaped their world.

Jacobi had heard from the powers that be that some strange-looking characters had appeared at a nearby town called Dewsbury to cause all kinds of carnage. And there was me wanting a drink to the memory of Oakes.

We departed the barracks Crowley had brought us to, armed and ready for another encounter with the Yellow King's men. And women. All through the journey Towers groused and griped about getting his revenge on a woman called Einal.

Quaint little place, Dewsbury, at least until we got finished there. Trevor did get his revenge through. But that's another story.

The Glass Jaw

I was minding my own business in a dive called *The Kettle of Fish* when a weasel-faced shrimp slunk over to my table and cleared his throat. I shot him my best go-to-hell look and said, "Whatever you're collecting for, I gave at the office."

The weasel looked confused for a second, then smiled.

"You *are* Riley Barnes?"

"You taking the census, are you?" I asked.

"The boss said you was a wise ass."

Sliding my hand beneath my coat, I asked, "Did he tell you about my awful habit of shooting the messenger?"

My inquisitive pal took a step back and raised his hand as if to placate me.

"Hey, I'm not worth it," he stammered. "You'd go to jail and lose your license."

"I'm not that attached to it," I replied. "Now what the hell do you want?"

"Mind if I sit?"

"Yeah," I answered. "But do it anyway."

The weasel was short and skinny as a string. He sweated heavily even though the night was cold and clammy. His pupils were about the size of saucers and whatever monkey was riding his back had definitely gotten the upper hand.

I downed my beer and pushed a large jar across the table.

"Pickled egg?" I offered.

"No thanks, my appetite ain't what it should be."

I rolled my eyes and said, "Do tell."

The weasel lit a smoke, his shaky hands jerking the flaming match so bad that it looked like he was trying to flag down a train.

"It's obvious that you're not really up for making social calls this evening. Why are you here?"

"Lost the draw," he answered.

"Huh?"

"Yeah," he replied. "Somebody had to give you the message and I'm the sap that lost."

"Well, I'm no prophet but I'm getting a vision of me being pissed off. I tend to become unpleasant and lose my charm when that happens."

"Yeah, I've heard that about you," he said. "But see, this isn't coming from me but from Boss Logan . . . so please don't take it out on me."

"Boss Logan!" I laughed. "Don't tell me that little pissant has developed delusions of grandeur."

The weasel looked around all panicky like and tried to shush me. "Please . . . someone might hear you and start trouble. Then I'll be in deep shit for not warning you off."

I admit that I didn't like the sound of that one bit.

"Warn me off *what?*" I growled. "You can tell that sonofabitch that . . ."

"Please!" the weasel squealed, attracting attention from the dive's other unsavory patrons.

I glared at the drunks at the bar and said, "Go back to your drinking. My pal's upset because I ate the last pickled egg."

Turning to the weasel, I said, "Okay, spill it and then get the hell out of here."

I was seeing red when I left the bar. I decided to run by BARNES AND TOWERS INVESTIGATIONS before returning to the small but clean room I rented from Mrs. Bordon, a nosy old widow with a heart of gold. I knew my partner Towers was out on the town with his girl but if I felt the urge to put my fist through a wall then better our office than at Mrs. Bordon's. That wall-punching urge was becoming a damn sight stronger after hearing what the weasel had been sent to tell me.

It seems that me and Towers were to make sure that a protégé of ours threw an upcoming boxing match. That was the word from Boss Logan, a former bootlegger and heretofore two-bit hood. Failure to throw said bout would supposedly result in some very unpleasant consequences for both the boxer and his family.

My partner and I had been back in Arkham only a few weeks since our adventures with those Yellow Cross boys over in England. In that time we had taken an interest in a young heavy-weight fighter named Eddie McCoy. The kid was talented and hungry as hell. He had the finesse that me and Towers had lacked in the ring and a killer right that could send a giant to the canvas. All Eddie McCoy really lacked was experience and the confidence that comes with it. And as for throwing the fight, that just wasn't going to happen. No way in hell.

I hoped that the stooge from the bar could get my point across to his boss. It's sort of hard to talk when your teeth get knocked out. And to make matters worse, I had to hit the hophead twice since Towers wasn't around to put in his two cents worth.

The foggy night air seemed to tamp down my rage to a more manageable level and I was relaxed to the point of carelessness on the way to the office. Two blocks from my destination a giant of a man stepped out of the alley and was wielding a blade that had me debating whether to call it a knife or sword. I started to reach for my gun but a voice behind me said, "I wouldn't do that."

I made a point of showing my hands and waited patiently for whatever fresh hell was coming down the pike. The big man in front of me grinned and said, "That was some performance you put on back at *The Kettle*. You shouldn't have punched a little fellow like Nate. Yeah, some performance."

I managed to cough up a loogie and spit it within an inch of his brogan.

"Then you'll just love my *next* one," I bluffed.

"Yeah?" he challenged, his voice dripping with menace.

"Yeah," I answered. "In about thirty seconds I'll be pulling my size twelve shoe out of your ass."

The thug cursed and raised the blade. About that time I heard something drop behind me like a sack of potatoes and a big ham of a hand grasped my shoulder and pushed me to the side. "It's a hell of a night to be out walking," said the unexpected voice of my partner, the inimitable Trevor Towers.

Tower's was pointing a .45 still dripping blood from where it had cracked the skull of the second hood whom I had heard but not seen

The blade-wielding tough stopped in his tracks seemingly flummoxed by the unexpected turn of events. I admit—not proud-ly, mind you—that I took advantage of the fellow's momentary distraction to step forward and kick him in the balls.

Towers shook his head and smiled. "Classy move, Barnes."

"And you, pal of mine, have impeccable timing," I answered.

"Be glad my date had a headache," said Towers. "Though I would like to have seen how you planned on getting out of *this*."

"A good magician never reveals his secrets."

"You heading for the office?" Towers asked.

"Yeah," I answered. "You want to give me a lift?"

"We took Kate's heap tonight," he replied. "I'm on foot as well."

Laughing, I said, "I don't guess the exercise will kill either one of us."

Barnes slammed the receiver down, the phone ringing shrilly as it settled into its cradle. I sat quietly, staring towards his scowling face while waiting him to speak. Well, his mouth opened to spout cuss-words that probably sent a few nearby saints tossing in their graves, before throwing me a glare that would've sent most folks blood cold. I'm a cold-blooded bastard anyway—just ask my bookie—so I took the glare with aplomb.

"You kiss my mother with that mouth?" I asked, giving him my best, most cheerful 'how ya doing pal,' grin.

Barnes growled. Grabbing the telephone up in both shaking hands, he threw it against the wall. It rang sharply as it bounced, complaining again as it landed on our frayed green carpet.

As Barnes sat glaring towards it, I said, "I'm not picking that up," followed by, "Feel better now?"

He looked at me and that evil expression cracked just a little. Sighing, giving me a slight smile, he slumped back into his seat.

"The fight we've got Friday . . . it's true that Logan owns the guy. The punk's also grown in stature since we last dealt with him. He's got mob boss aspirations to boot."

Dealt? Yeah, you might say that, Barnes flushing the little shit's head down a toilet—where it belongs, I might add. He performed this little act after witnessing Logan getting a little too rough with a girl down at Annie's, a bar we frequented.

I sat forward with interest.

"So the Whately guy's his . . . who'da thunk it."

Noah "Iron Man" Whately was one big, ugly boxer our guy Eddie had just fought his way up to. And some cheap scumbag like Logan thought we would throw it? No wonder my partner felt so pissed. Me, I was taking it easier because I wasn't the one he'd approached with this ridiculous threat.

"Two ideas," I said, "Let's see what you think of them." Barnes leaned forward, clenching both hands under his chin. "One, we go find 'Boss' Logan and make him wish he'd stayed in that toilet you shoved him down." Barnes chortled; it was good to hear. "Or two, we grab this Whately fella, tie the bastard up, and send him off on a boat trip far, far away."

Barnes' hands slapped against the desk. "I like it, pal, I like it!" he said, his face beaming like a kid's on Christmas Day.

"So which one's it to be?" I asked, thinking I already knew the answer.

"Both," Barnes replied, and that happy smile became something sinister.

"Sir," I replied, standing from my seat, "you're a pleasure to work with."

Before leaving the office, Barnes retrieved the phone, hoping it'd forgive him the roughhousing. It did, so he called up Eddie to make sure everything was okay. Good kid that he was, Eddie was already in bed, dreaming innocent, big slugger dreams, no doubt. So, not wanting to upset the applecart, Barnes told his mom we'd see him in the morning.

A lovely lady was our Ma McCoy, a widower who'd single-handedly brought up Eddie and his three sisters after her husband failed to return from the war. Always greeting us with a friendly smile, Eddie's mom would fill us with cheer and freshly baked pastries. It broke my heart to see how poor they lived, but Eddie's successes were helping fix that, fight by fight.

We loved her, and our protégé Eddie, which is why Barnes felt so mad and why I was willing to do anything possible to set things right that very night. Sometimes though, having the will isn't always enough.

Once outside the office, me and Barnes went our separate ways. Settling who'd do what hadn't proven difficult: it was plain as day that the chip on Barnes' shoulder was itching the merry hell out of him. This meant he'd be the one giving Boss Logan a little visit. Me, I was off to find the Whately fella to see if we could remove him without violence. I wasn't holding my hopes up, and that suited me fine.

Arkham Nights

We left the office and again emerged into the foggy Arkham night. Being a glutton for trouble, I looked forward to having a little not-so-friendly chat with the overreaching scum known as Boss Logan. We had sort of a history and it wasn't the kind that made the bastard want to send me a greeting card each Christmas. Shoving a guy's head in the toilet is not the recommended way of winning friends though it can *definitely* influence people.

The thought of that punk having the nerve to insist that Eddie McCoy throw a fight really had me steamed. Eddie was a good kid and had worked like hell to reach the point where he was in line to earn some decent dough, provided he kept on winning his fights. I planned on seeing his winning streak continue at least until someone beat him fair and square.

As for the so-called 'Boss' Logan, men of that type are like roaches. It seems like every time you stomp one under your shoe than two more crawl out of the woodwork. Me and my partner had been doing our best to exterminate such pests in Arkham for the better part of a year, which is roughly when our partnership began. It's a never-ending struggle and one that can be damned depressing at times. Still, it helps me sleep good at night. Most of the time.

After Towers and I separated I worked up a sweat walking through the thick fog and became chilled in the damp night. Welcoming the sight of the sign proclaiming ANNIE's, I approached the familiar establishment and quickly spied one of Logan's men loitering at the front of a nearby alley that ran alongside my destination and the building next door. Fortunately he had his back turned to the street and hadn't spotted me yet.

I grinned, impressed that Logan was sharp enough to have someone posted to alert him of the shit-storm heading his way. Maybe he *had* gotten smarter over the years. I veered away from the club's entrance and took a parallel alley to the rear of Annie's and peered around the back of the building. The coast was clear so I made my way through the blanket of fog until reaching the other side of the building. Stopping at the alley, I cautiously looked toward the street and could just make out the shape of Logan's sentry. With any luck I could ambush him from behind and send him to dreamland before he wised up to my presence.

I took a deep breath and moved cat-like through the swirling mist. Having almost reached my target, I managed to stumble into an ash can and lose my balance. Okay, by cat-like I was referring to how a drunken tabby might fare in a room full of bowling balls.

Logan's man turned in surprise and yelled, "Who da hell's there!"

I barreled toward him—impressed by my quickness—and hit him with a shoulder block that sent him reeling into the brick wall. I caught him on the rebound with a right cross to the jaw and watched him sag to the floor. Taking a strand of clothesline from my coat pocket, I quickly hog-tied the lug and left him dreaming.

A metal staircase beside Annie's led to the second story where Logan and a couple of fly-by-night operators had established temporary offices. I made my way up the stairs and entered a door opening onto a wide, dimly lit hall. The floor was covered in worn, puke-green carpeting and made me wonder why I'd bothered to wipe my feet upon entering. Just good manners, I guess.

Logan's office was located at the end of the hall on the right. I checked the artillery in my coat pocket and smiled at its comforting presence. I hadn't a clue as to how many of Logan's thugs would be with him but didn't plan on taking unnecessary chances. I would lay it all out for the bastard and leave no room for doubt concerning our position in the matter of the upcoming prize fight.

Harsh light spilled into the hallway from Logan's office and I could hear him kibitzing with someone on the phone as I approached the open door. Logan was alone—his keister parked behind a big oak desk—and I was frankly surprised when he looked up and smiled as I filled the door frame with my not insubstantial bulk.

"Later," he told the party on the line.

"Barnes," he said shaking his head, "I wondered how long it would take you to find your way here."

"No trouble at all," I replied. "I got directions from some punk in the alley. I would've brought the Good Samaritan along but he's tied up at the moment."

"You think you're real cute, don't you Barnes?"

"No," I answered. "What I *think* is that you're going to need more muscle . . . especially if you don't deep six this idea you've got about Eddie McCoy taking a dive."

Logan reached into his shirt pocket and fished out a pack of smokes. He lit one, inhaled and blew out a smoke ring. I glanced over my shoulder and began to be wary. The piece of crap in front of me was a certified coward and there was no way he would be trying to get my goat unless he had a contingency plan to save his ass.

"If this is the part where you threaten to mop up the floor with me then I think you'd best reconsider," he said.

"And why would I want to do that?" I asked, playing along with him for the time being. Glancing over my shoulder, I said, "I don't see any sign of the cavalry."

"Don't need them," he replied.

"That's right," I said. "It's an ambulance that *you're* going to need."

My fists were clenched tightly and I was about a second away from deconstructing Logan when the phone rang. I paused as he grinned and said, "Saved by the bell."

He picked up the receiver and handed it across the desk to me.

"Barnes," said a woman's sultry voice. "I have someone here who'd like to speak to you."

Glaring at Logan I started to describe what I planned to do to him but was interrupted by a child's voice on the line. The child was crying but I could tell that the voice belonged to a little girl. She was sobbing the entire time but I could still make out the words with only a little trouble. The child was pleading with me to come get her and take her home to see her Ma, sisters and brother Eddie. I was trying to reassure her that everything was going to be okay when I heard the sound of an open hand striking flesh, followed by a high-pitched wail and the sound of the receiver being slammed down.

It took all of my will power to hang up the phone and release my grip on the .45 in my coat pocket. I glared at the grinning thug and whispered, "You're dead."

Turning away from Logan, I walked out the door. My entire body trembled with rage as his gloating laughter followed me down the hall and into the night. I kept telling myself it could be a ruse but in my heart I knew the truth. I had to find Towers and tell him what had happened.

Whately wasn't hard to find. After drinking a quick malt in a bar the boxing fraternity used, I was informed by a guy with barely a tooth to his name that Whately was training like the devil over at Aldo Marin's gym, across the river. Well, no one said being a snoop didn't demand a little legwork, and this being personal, I walked that extra mile.

That mile took me across the river and left at River Street, then past the docks before heading towards French Hill. Soon I reached the line of box-shaped, decrepit buildings at its base.

Aldo's Gym, the second building along, had a sign proclaiming its owner and function above a wide-open doorway. Walking towards this, the sounds of heated combat reached my ears, familiar from a hundred bouts of my own. A few moments later I stepped inside the gym's bright interior.

Aldo's Gym—been there before, probably be there again—but as I glanced around I saw nothing of the man himself. White-washed walls aplenty, lots of dumbbells and punching bags, but no sign of the big, grinning black man with the impressive gold dentistry in his maw.

Directly before me were the gym's two rings. The one to the left stood empty but its partner bore the source of the noise, two guys going at it there sparring. Well, not exactly sparring. One stood dressed in protective gear whilst the other guy pounded the living shit outta him.

A couple of fellas stood watching this one-sided battle, the one to the left a little guy in a cap. His jacket lay hung under his arm, a pair of bright red braces holding the pants up against his skinny ass. The other, a big ape in a suit, looked like he'd probably been through a couple of bouts himself.

"Attaboy!" 'Braces' hollered as Whately knocked his smaller opponent to the canvas. Now that the meat pounding was over my presence was finally noticed, all heads turning to me.

Oh yeah, the guy doing the punching was Whately, a wild-haired giant of a man, six foot five in height and not far from that in girth. A thick red beard matched the shock on his head, matted and dirty like the rest of him. His skin looked as pale as death in the overhead lights, his thick ginger eyebrows furrowed upon a sloping brow. Panting from the fight, he stood shining with sweat.

I smiled, tipping my hat while musing over how healthier he'd look with a tan. Did hillbillies have passports? I didn't think so, and not that he's need one. Then I turned my gaze to the stooges beneath the ring.

Braces and the ape glared daggers as I paused before them. The other guy, Whately's partner—he was out for the count despite his protective headgear.

Braces had a pale, scrunched-up pip of a face, his partner one both wide and flabby, just like the hands he'd begun clenching beneath the sleeves of his too-tight suit.

His ears were cauliflowered, his nose a mashed-up relic above a pair of saliva-slicked lips. Compared to him, Whately was a pretty boy.

I didn't like the way his beady eyes glared at me, not one bit. Then he opened his mouth, making me like him even less.

"Take a hike, bozo." His voice phlegmy, the ape grinned sourly, revealing a mouth of chipped yellow teeth. Raising his fat paw he indicated the door behind me.

I gave him a generous smile, was about to reply when the squirt interrupted me. "You heard the man, peanut, now scram!"

Peanut? Braces' voice was thin and reedy, me wanting to snap his skinny little neck for being so rude as to interrupt a gentleman at his words.

I took it however, ignoring Braces completely as I addressed the ape. "I've come to see your man, I have a business proposition that involves some travel."

In way of reply, Whately issued an enthusiastic 'Hurr.'

I briefly wondered whether he'd even learned to speak.

The ape smiled his wet nicotine smile, breathing on me foully. "That kinda thing goes through the Boss, sweetheart."

Peanut? Sweetheart? These guys sorely needed better material.

Folding my arms I said, "It's a one-time only offer, and I need to speak to Mister Whately in person." Whately seemed to like being called 'Mister,' for he sent another happy grunt my way.

"Realllllllly," Braces said, my urge to smash his face growing. Then a groan appeared from the canvas behind Whately, meaning his playmate was about ready for another pounding.

The ape nudged his companion and said, "Go help Frankie out."

"But, but. . ." Braces said, looking from me to his pal in panic, but the ape hissed loudly, Braces sending me a dour look before heading to the ring.

The ape grinned before saying, "Okay, pal, just give us five and he'll see you out back."

Braces, up in the ring helping Frankie to his feet, snorted and laughed.

I ignored this and looked to Whately. Still smiling, slivers of drool fell to his matted beard. No evil intent there, just the distinct, moronic friendliness of a damaged mind.

I found myself hating Boss Logan even more now. Returning Whately's smile I said to the ape, "Five minutes, okay," the ape grinning like I had 'sucker' painted across my forehead in bright red letters. I nodded and headed left, stepping between the rings towards the gym's back entrance. On the way, I removed a pack of smokes from my inside pocket. While inside my jacket, my fingers unclipped the holster on my .45.

Eyes glared into me as I headed towards the rear door. Searching through my jacket I found a box of matches, lighting my smoke as I stepped into the night. I heard Braces snickering as the door slid shut behind me.

Well, Towers' old momma didn't bring up a sucker, which is why I stood behind the gym just waiting for trouble.

With the door a few yards to my right, I stood there looking as casual as possible, my hands stuffed deep inside my pockets. My trigger finger was itching, my hands, balled into fists, clenching back and forth beneath the fabric of my jacket. To my left lay an old stone wall, tall and gray in the twilight but black where coated in moss. The smell of fresh nature filtered across the wall, soured by the nicotine pouring from my nearly exhausted smoke.

I spat it out as the door opened, the light hitting me in a flash as two dark figures stepped outside. The door slid shut again and my eyes adjusted. Before me stood Whately and the ape, the former in a suit as ill fitting as the guy's beside him. Wrists dangling from his sleeves, his pants at half-mast on a suit crumpled, threadbare and stinking of sweat. It seemed Whately wasn't gaining any dough from his fighting endeavors. The next thought saw me grinning: they probably paid him in raw meat.

The ape scowled in the darkness, saying, "Funny man, eh?"

"I aim to please," I said, turning back to Whately. Towering over me, the red-haired giant continued to smile his moronic smile.

"Just had words with the boss," the ape continued.

I interrupted him sharply with, "Boss Logan that'll be?"

"Yeah, now you're a clever girl." He breached the gap between us and stepped forward. "The boss says beat it the hell out of here or never be seen again."

This sounded like a threat, and this, coupled with the fact he was invading my personal space, saw me saying, "Okay . . . well I can see where I'm not wanted." I went to turn, before decking the bastard with a single sock to his face.

The ape staggered backwards, his hands clenched around a dripping mouth.

"Dastard," he said from between bloody fingers, "you broke my dose!"

I shook my hand free of cramp and tipped my hat, saying . . . nothing, for at that moment a fist came crashing against my head, sending me flying sideways towards the gym wall. The impact nearly dislocating my shoulder, the wall hit me like a second iron fist—an iron fist from 'Iron Man' Whately to be sure. I saw sparks and slumped down its rough surface, tasting copper and cracked teeth as I fell flat onto my ass.

Turning, blinking my vision back, I pressed my back against the wall. The ape, on his knees now, dripped blood as he said, "Kill the dastard, snap his neck. Gaah dat hurts!"

A huge shape stepped around the ape. Whately, still grinning widely, loped towards me with deadly intent.

Well, considering my current situation, I reached into my jacket, retrieved my gun, and shot him. Not much a sore loser, I aimed my bullet towards his left shin. The discharge, drowning the ape's complaints, sent Whatley staggering back. But only slightly, that slug of mine having the cheek to pop from his leg without leaving a mark.

I swallowed blood but not my panic. I looked to Whately's face and found him smiling, of course.

"I think 'Oh shit' are the words you're looking for," Braces said, the punk having stepped out into the alley sometime during the commotion.

Although still wanting to snap his neck, I found myself agreeing with his words. As Whately loomed closer, I realized saving my own neck came first.

I hurried back to the office only to find that Towers hadn't yet returned. I wisely opted to use my car this time instead of plodding through Arkham on foot. Beside myself with rage, I started the heap and rushed off to find Trevor but only after availing myself of some heavier artillery. I wanted to avoid gun play and the Thompson I'd taken along for the ride often had an intimidating affect on two-bit punks. I had a pretty good idea where to look for my partner, figuring he might still be searching area gyms in an effort to find Logan's boxer and talk some sense into him. Knowing my partner's idiosyncratic definition of conversation, violence was a foregone conclusion.

If Eddie's sister was really in the hands of Logan's crew it would be necessary for us to proceed cautiously. Admittedly that was a different approach from our usual, and meant that we'd have to be more selective about who we killed, and *when*. Hopefully I could find Towers before he managed to knock off any of Logan's thugs. This was one of those cases where rescue must come before retribution.

I had visited two gyms in a fruitless effort to find Towers and was steadily driving towards French Hill when the sound of a gun-shot grabbed my attention. It tends to do that and it didn't take a brain surgeon for me to realize that my search was nearing its end. I drove in the direction of the ominous sound and hoped like hell that Towers hadn't killed anyone yet. I parked in a small lot outside Aldo's Gym and got out of the car. There were only a couple of other cars around and no one standing out front.

I placed the Thompson beneath my long coat and let it hang loosely beside my leg. Cursing my arthritis and the general Arkham dampness, I flatfooted it to the rear of the brick building and found pretty much what I expected. Towers was holding the proverbial smoking gun and entertaining some new friends. One big bruiser with bloody face and flattened nose seemed plenty thrilled at the prospect of what his even larger compatriot was threatening to do to Towers. It didn't take a quiz kid to figure that the wild-haired lummox with the matted beard was Logan's fighter, Whately. We'd had dealings with at least one other member of the backwoods clan and this guy carried a family resemblance that just screamed intelligence.

Whately was being egged on to acts of violence by a third shrimp of a character sporting red braces. I'd seen the little guy before working as a cut-man for some bottom of the barrel stumble-bums on the New England fight circuit.

I stood in the shadow of the building and watched the proceedings with a curious eye. Whately grinned at Towers and lumbered towards him.

I could see Tower's grip tighten on his firearm and decided to make my presence known. I coughed loudly and said, "Hey, Trevor."

The Thompson had somehow appeared from beneath my coat and I now had the attention of everyone present.

"Hey, now just a minute," said Braces, his hands outstretched in a placating manner. "I'm sure we can talk this over."

"Oh, I'm *sure* we can," I replied.

Turning to Towers, I said, "My heap's around front."

I tossed him the keys which he snagged with his free hand. He gave me a questioning look, obviously not understanding my eagerness to leave. "We'll talk plenty once we're out of here," I said.

Before leaving, he turned to the trio and said, "Later, ladies."

Whately started to make a move towards him but was swarmed on by his frantic companions who were none too eager to dance to the tune my Thompson would play.

I held the machine gun on the trio as I slowly edged around the side of the building. Finally, I heard my car cough to life and made a fast exit from the scene. Once safely away I began to tell Towers what I'd learned and suggested we drive by Eddie's home.

He nodded and took on a demeanor that I'd seen a couple of times in the past. It didn't bode well for anyone foolish enough to get in his way.

"We'll get the girl back safely," I said, though I hadn't stopped to figure out how yet.

"Yeah," Trevor replied. "And then someone bastard's going to bleed."

I agreed but couldn't help wondering how much of the blood was going to be ours.

Eddie sat across from me clenching and unclenching his fists above the table's blue-checkered cloth.

"Damn," and for Eddie, this was a strong cuss word, "what kind of people live in this world?"

"Scum is the word I use," I replied. and tears fell from his eyes in two long streaks.

I felt for the kid, I really did: it wasn't that long ago I was dealing with a guy that lost his daughter to a kidnapping, in a nearby town called Innsmouth. A shitty case that one, but not as shitty, or as close to home, as this.

"Eddie?" I asked, keeping my voice low, "do you need a belt of something strong?" I could have done with a drink myself, least of all to ease the ache from Whately's pounding. I fought it.

"Eh? Oh I dunno," he said and I wondered just how he was handling things *this* well. Better than Ma McCoy, that was certain, still upstairs being looked after by his sisters and . . . Barnes, where the hell was Barnes already? I stood, pushing my seat back, and after another look at Eddie headed for the door. I opened it to the darkened foyer and found Barnes stood whispering into a telephone.

Up those stairs I could hear Eddie's ma still sobbing, accompanied by his sisters voices. Damn, those two were strong gals. Barnes, speaking quietly into the receiver, turned to face me, nodded and said, "Yeah, yeah."

A door opened upstairs, followed by footsteps heading down

the staircase. It was Tricia, Eddie's eldest. I followed her wet face as she descended towards us, opening my arms when she stopped before me.

"Mom's just about asleep," she whispered and the dampness of her cheek made me feel sad and angry at once. As she burst into sobs I patted her shoulders, saying, "Hey, hey, it's okay," although I knew things were far from it. I let those sobs wrack into me for a while and as she finally pulled away I said, "Listen hun, you got anything strong in that kitchen, liquor-wise?"

Tricia nodded. Letting her shoulders go I said, "Go make Eddie a stiff one, and one for yourself if you need it." I wanted her out of the room, as gently as possible, because behind her Barnes, his phone call finished, stared at me in a way that shouted privacy.

Tricia left us to it, sniffling as she went, and after the door closed Barnes and I stood silent in the near dark. Behind me, the sounds of cupboards opening and moving crockery indicated Tricia was putting those strong drinks together.

"Anything?" I whispered.

Barnes leaned against the staircase, his arms folded. He sighed, this being the last sound I needed to hear. "Logan owns any number of hideouts around town. We really would be looking for a needle in a haystack."

This made me hiss. So now the dirty rat had holes all over town to boot. "So," I stepped nearer to Barnes, my voice becoming a hoarse, angry whisper, "we grab one of his punks and beat the information out of him." I leered in the darkness, "You know I'm up to it." I was serious.

Barnes stared at me sadly. "We can't risk it, not with that little gal's life on the line."

I shook my head. "What are you saying pal?"

Barnes stood straight, breaching the gap between us. He spoke just inches from my face as he said, "This is more than a kidnapping now and we both know it."

"Whately, yeah?"

"Yeah," Barnes answered.

We were referring to Whately's invincibility, that little aspect being far from the norm. It would be to most anyway, but me and Barnes had some experience in that direction. I had a thought, and Barnes did too.

"Justin Geoffrey!" we said together. He was after all, the occultist in the know.

Now Geoffrey had helped us before, through all kinds of misadventures, and if it involved the occult, it was a sure bet he could help provide some kind of answer.

After some words in the kitchen, we left Eddie and his sister to head through the side streets towards Peabody Avenue, Justin's current abode.

His last house had burned to the ground, he never told us how or why, but we both guessed it was linked to one of his weird experiments. To tell the truth, the guy was one of the fruitiest nuts you could ever meet. But, this nut had the know-how and two friends who had seen firsthand how lifesaving that could be. Some months ago Geoffrey had seen us as a menace, until we helped him out of a jam with some torpedoes he'd crossed.

Justin Geoffrey, possibly ours and Eddie's savior. I had my fingers crossed, tucked inside my pockets because the night was a cold one, as we headed the short distance between Eddie's home and Geoffrey's. We reached Peabody Avenue quickly, encountering nothing but night mist on our way. This side of Arkham, to the southeast of the river and down below French Hill, seemed to like going to bed early, as the dark windows and closed curtains proved.

The brownstones of Peabody Avenue, like its companion rows, slept too, but on reaching Geoffrey's we found the front door ajar, a dim light filtering from within.

My first thought was foul play: no one with any sense left their door open at night, not in Arkham. Barnes thought similarly: I saw a gun appear in his hand as he crept towards the door.

"It's not broken," he whispered. He pushed the door further, the gun lowered to his side as he shouted, "Hey, Justin! Hey!"

Subtlety, thy name is Barnes.

With my .45 in hand I trailed my partner's footsteps, following him into the house. Nudging the door closed I examined the foyer for signs of foul play. There were none, just a narrow, dark room with a table to our left and a hat rack on our right. A door before us provided the light, and sounds of ticking and chanting.

Bare floorboards creaked beneath our feet as we continued. I felt a bit more relaxed now: it was Geoffrey's voice we heard, omming and droning away. Barnes shouted him again and the chanting ceased, but not the ticking.

"Err, hello?" a timid voice said, and shuffling sounds came from the room. Then the sliver of light grew large, the man we sought opening the door fully.

A cloud of spiced incense filled the foyer as Justin Geoffrey faced us, his short red hair ruffled atop his thin face. Looking a bit surprised, he blinked and smiled before saying, "It *is* good to see you, *really* it is!" before ushering us into his inner sanctum.

Geoffrey's inner sanctum: a big room lined with bookcases and huge Turkish rugs, those covering the walls and the floor. Terracotta pots filled with salt, planted with smoking incense sticks, dotted the floor.

After scanning the room I turned to Geoffrey. Why was he staring? It was our guns of course, Barnes tucking his into his jacket before saying, "Your door was open pal, and . . ."

"And you were worried for my safety!" Geoffrey said. His face beamed as he turned from us. I forgot to mention, our fruity friend was dressed in a red velvet house-robe smothered in oriental designs, his turned back revealing a gold Chinese dragon. For a moment I thought I saw the dragon wink at me, smiling its sharp, toothy-mouthed smile.

Shoving the gun back into my jacket I followed Geoffrey towards a small circular table, this bearing the source of the ticking. Geoffrey stepped around it and turned, his smiling dragon hidden but *his* face still beaming.

You're stoned, I thought, looking from him to his most recent weird experiment. The table held four metronomes sat on a black cloth, surrounding a chunky, deformed, brown clay troll. Its leering face was surrounded by a shock of gray straw-like hair. I thought, *Heck, what a beauty.*

Barnes got straight to the point. "We have a problem with a boxer," he said.

I found myself looking at that ugly little troll, wondering if it was really staring back or I was just seeing things.

I shook my head and listened as Barnes went through our trouble with Whately and Logan.

"Logan, Boss Logan, I know that man," Geoffrey said. He went on to explain how the mob 'boss' had been seen with the Frenchman, an occult fanatic who'd probably given the Whately fella his powers.

"From what I know of these spells," Geoffrey continued, "Whately can probably be supernaturally enhanced so he cannot be harmed for an hour or so, perhaps even longer."

"Damn," Barnes muttered.

"Yeah, but the fact Eddie's sister's been grabbed, means Logan's worried despite this spell of his," I said.

"It seems perhaps that Logan knows something of your occult dealings, my friends," Geoffrey said. "Taking on one of the Frenchman's spells would be quite the challenge." He grinned, showing off a mouth of small, perfectly white teeth. "I like it, immensely!"

So, we finally had someone in our corner, with Geoffrey ready and willing to remove Whately's powers. But would getting rid of Whately get our lost little gal back? Also, a win over McCoy would give Whately a shot at one of the top middleweight contenders, a shot that by all rights should be Eddie's.

Barnes and I shared a look, him wording my thoughts with, "We need to find her before the fight is over, have Eddie win the fight fare and square with his little sis safe in our hands."

This was our only possible plan if we were to retain our dignity, ensure Eddie's future and save his sister to boot. Also, Logan was going to suffer, badly, he could count on it.

We left Geoffrey's soon after, the man poring through his books as we departed that gaudy, fume-filled room. Facing the night, filling my lungs, Arkham's air had never tasted so fine. We never did find out why he'd left his door open, and Barnes, stepping outside after me, closed it tight behind us.

A clever, gifted man Justin Geoffrey might be, but he was sure lacking in the common sense department. This is why I found myself wondering how long it would take him to burn down this latest house. Probably not long, I mused, as we headed towards Eddie's.

Regarding his counter spell, Geoffrey had told us to ring him the next morning. We had a long night ahead of us, me doubting I would get any sleep before picking up the phone for some hopefully good news.

Sometimes, being right can be a real bitch.

I arrived early at the office, having managed to sleep only a couple of hours. I'd left my partner at the McCoy house the previous evening believing it would be wise to have a hard-case like Trevor on hand in case Logan got any other bright ideas. This whole set-up had gone sideways from the beginning and we couldn't take a chance on things getting further out of hand.

Searching for the coffee pot, I nearly tripped over a loose spot in the carpet and cut loose with a string of expletives. I hated making coffee but it was way too early for our office girl to arrive—never a sure bet during the best of times—and I desperately needed something to keep me going. If things got worse I had some little white pills that could do the trick but they tended to make me a bit erratic in my thinking. I only ever used them as a last resort because guns and erratic thought processes could be a pretty lethal combination.

Finally, after what seemed an eternity, I managed to get the coffee brewing and plopped down behind the Kingsport desk to light a smoke. I listened to the coffee percolate and stared at the telephone, willing it to ring. Geoffrey had promised to call but God only knew how long it would take him to come up with what we needed. I couldn't help but smile perversely at our plight. When the success of our plans depended on a fruitcake like Geoffrey then I knew we were in trouble. But, to be fair, the strange little occultist had saved our bacon on more than one occasion. For now, I could only whistle past the graveyard and hope he was up to the task.

The phone rang during my second cup of java. I sloshed steaming liquid onto the desk top while reaching for it but finally managed to wrestle the instrument to my ear.

"Barnes here," I growled, ready to hang up on anyone not named Justin Geoffrey.

"My, but aren't you the voice of happiness," Geoffrey said.

"Yeah, that's me," I replied. "I hope you're calling with good news."

"Yes, about *that*," he answered. "I'm afraid that the counter spell I found may take a bit longer to implement than expected."

"Jeez," I groused, "can't you come up with something quicker?"

Geoffrey chuckled and said, "It just doesn't work that way, my friend."

"But," he continued, "I may be able to create a psychic compass that could be used to find Mr. McCoy's sister."

Now *that* sounded intriguing.

"I got no idea what a psychic compass is but it ain't like we have a lot of options at this point," I replied. "What do you need to create this gizmo?"

"It isn't a *gizmo* as you so quaintly put it but instead . . ."

"Look, just tell me what you need," I interrupted. Geoffrey was one of those guys in love with the sound of his own voice and we were pressed for time.

"In short," he answered, sounding disappointed, "I'll need an item of jewelry or a piece of clothing that belongs to the young lady. Something like a bracelet would be ideal."

"I'll get right on it," I answered. "The family don't have much but I seem to recall a pretty little bracelet that the girl was showing us. She mentioned only wearing it on special occasions."

"That will be perfect!" Geoffrey answered. "I can get started once you bring it to me."

"I'm on it," I replied. "Hang tight and don't leave the house. I'll get it to you ASAP."

"Wonderful!" he exclaimed. "I'll be eagerly anticipating your arrival."

I high-tailed it to the McCoy home after hanging up the phone. Geoffrey was often in a world of his own and I didn't want to give him time to become distracted and wander off into another dimension or burn the house down around himself. I didn't know how Trevor would react to this Plan B regarding the psychic compass but we were at the end of our rope and had to get the girl back, or at least learn where she was, before we could continue with other aspects of the plan.

The days leading up to the fight were a blur of frustrated searching. We had nothing, and with Barnes and me knowing Arkham like the back of our hands, this was no mean feat as far as Logan was concerned. Sending feelers out beyond Arkham proved useless too, so wherever Logan had Eddie's little sister hidden, it was a damned deep hole.

Throughout this, Geoffrey had been hard at work, his hoodoo voodoo methods coming to no fruition either.

Me being unable to use my usual information gathering methods meant Logan's men survived with their ears and fingers intact. God was I boiling by the time we reached that fateful day, my mind and fists just itching to tear Logan and his lot to tiny, bloody pieces.

I awoke that morning with my fists clenched and my teeth gritted, pulled from sleep by my landlady tapping on my door telling me I had a call. Usually, I would cuss at her under my breath, sometimes a bit louder, for spoiling my much needed beauty sleep. Today being a day where phone calls saved lives, I quickly climbed into my pants and dressing gown without a word.

I left the room with my hair an un-groomed mess and rushed downstairs while trying to ignore the rude comments the old dame was making.

"Why, the sight of your bare chest has me positively swooning!" she said, the last word drawn out by her thick southern drawl.

"Gaah!" I said, her retorting with, "I'll go make breakfast then."

I reached the telephone in the lobby, put the receiver to my ear, and said a gruff, "What?" into the mouthpiece. A gentle, melodious voice, the complete opposite to my own, replied with, "Why, good morning, sleepyhead!"

"Geoffrey!" I growled, "It's . . ." raising my arm I checked my watch, "half past six in the morning. How come you're so bright and breezy?"

"Been up all night, chum," he replied, his cheery, pleasant tone grating on me, "and I'm surprised that you weren't, considering."

Pure mental exhaustion had been the solution to my sleepless nights. Lucky me.

Geoffrey's ability for not getting to the point had me squeezing down on the receiver. He must have heard the phone creaking, ready to break, or maybe my teeth grating down the line, for he continued, "Well, my counter-spell is finally good to go."

"It's about time, pal," I replied, followed by, from Geoffrey, "Would you have rather done this yourself? I can go into the intricacies and dangers of dealing with otherworldly beings right now if you wish."

I shrugged, trying to shake off my frustration. *My* anger wasn't *his* fault. "Listen Geoffrey, I mean Justin, I'm sorry, pal." Eating humble pie wasn't something I was used to, but I did my best. "I value your work, fella. We need you."

I imagined the smile on Geoffrey's face grew large enough to slice his head in two.

Catching a movement in the corner of my eye, I turned to see my landlady heading down the stairs, off to make breakfast, I assumed. My stomach growled.

"And that other thing?" I asked, worried that he hadn't mentioned it already.

"Good to go as soon as one of you charming fellows arrives here to receive it."

This ripped my face in half with a big, beaming smile. Damn the guy was good.

"Gimme half an hour," I replied, "and would you mind giving Barnes a call next?"

Replying in the affirmative, Geoffrey then said, almost hesitantly, "And my fee . . ."

"A crate of apricot brandy?" I replied with a chortle.

"God bless you, dear sir!"

In the nick of time, it seemed our day was actually going to be saved.

The sound and smell of sizzling bacon reached my ears. I turned towards the kitchen, deciding to toast my luck with coffee and breakfast.

I'd received an early call from Towers and was now on my way to meet him at Geoffrey's place. We'd both been on pins and needles because the day of the boxing match had arrived and we'd made no headway on finding Sonia. Needless to say, Eddie's mind had not really been focused on getting ready for the upcoming bout and I secretly worried that he might blow it even if things were on the up and up. At least now we'd have Geoffrey's mystic compass and could hopefully grab the hostage before the fight. Time was running out fast and I soon pulled up in front of Geoffrey's place though I'd broken more traffic laws than you could shake a stick at.

I pulled into the circular drive and watched Towers come to a screeching halt in my rear view mirror. Leaving my heap, I watched him exit the vehicle and nod at me. He carried the promised case of apricot brandy for Geoffrey and appeared to be in a hurry to get rid of it.

"This better work," he mumbled.

"Geoffrey won't let us down," I said, with more confidence than I felt. I took the crate off his hands and watched him barrel ahead of me and make his way through the unlocked front door.

Our mystic ally had a vast assortment of junk along with priceless artifacts but never locked his door. I guess he figured it would send the wrong signal if a reputed occultist needed locks to protect his accumulated swag.

Geoffrey was in his usual state of disarray but greeted us affably. We entered the cluttered foyer and did our damnedest not to trip over the array of items littering the area. Our host led us deeper into the house and seated us in his study, which explained why the foyer was so cluttered. It was difficult to find a place to sit but we managed.

Towers shook his head in dismay and said, "Damn, I thought you'd never finish."

"It wasn't something I could purchase at the five and dime, you know," Geoffrey replied, thrusting the object forward.

In all honesty, it *did* look pretty much like something you'd get at the Woolworth's toy department. It consisted of a small compass that was glued to a piece of wood and covered in transparent green stones that looked like costume jewelry.

"You're sure this will work?" Towers asked.

"Probably," Geoffrey answered.

"Wow, now *that's* a real ringing endorsement," I said.

"Look," Geoffrey complained, "it isn't my fault that I've never had occasion to use such a device prior to now."

Geoffrey was on the verge of getting steamed but I headed it off.

"It looks good to me Justin," I said. "How close does the girl's bracelet have to be to the compass to get an accurate reading?"

"There's no specific limitations mentioned in the tome but I would recommend you keep the two as close as possible. The compass point will be drawn to the girl. Really, it's so easy even a pair of lunks should be able to use."

I smiled, took the bracelet and attached it to the compass. "That ought to do it," I said, beaming at my common sense approach to the problem. Towers just smirked and said, "You're a regular Einstein, aren't you?"

I nodded and handed the bracelet to Towers. Geoffrey had already opened the crate of Apricot Brandy and was in search of a clean glass.

"I hope like hell this works," I said.

Towers frowned and nodded toward our host, "It better, he's not gonna be any good to us once he gets started on that."

We picked who'd do what on a coin toss, one of us going to search out Sonia's whereabouts, the other taking care of the match. As I'd much rather be out and about than cooped up dealing with the ring-work, I felt I won that toss, Barnes and I separating outside Geoffrey's place with few words but a concrete understanding: after finding and securing the girl, I would contact him immediately.

And this time, I didn't need reminding to tread carefully. Logan's fellow rats wouldn't hesitate in blowing a hole between poor Sonia's pigtails if I went in there cannons blazing. A gentle approach would keep Sonia alive, and we'd made a vow to Eddie we'd do so.

With the needle on my bizarre compass pointing west, wavering slightly to the north, I turned left. Leaving Peabody Avenue I stepped down College Street, heading in the direction of Hangman's Hill.

The time on my watch read eight thirty, giving us a good nine hours before the fight started.

The Arkham around me stood quiet at this time of day, the air warming as the early morning mist finally began to clear. A sudden chill hit me as I crossed the Parsonage Street intersection.

The reason? Arkham's witch house stood to my left, once demolished then miraculously whole again a year later, but this wasn't why I shivered, pulling my collar up. It was because of the tales I'd heard as a child, plus a dare I'd accomplished when only a little boy in shorts.

Sneaking in one night to pinch a stone from the yard, I'd grabbed the nearest one quickly, jittery to return to my friends. My prize in hand, I'd been about to leave when I heard an ugly tittering from the window facing the yard. What I saw there gave me nightmares for months.

Feeling easier after leaving it behind, I reached the university campus. The sight of that huge array of buildings, surrounded by flowering cherry blossoms, cheered me up no end, as did the group of students entering the campus.

I envied their happy, innocent lives, the world to them still a fresh, exciting place.

My expression turned sour as I left the campus behind. I checked the compass and found the needle hadn't wavered, meaning I would soon be passing Arkham and entering the fields leading towards Billington's Woods.

Windblown cherry blossoms filled the gutters at me feet, turning brown in the amassed filth.

Cheers, Arkham.

When I reached the university hospital I had a choice of either returning for my car or walking further. With neither plan that appealing, I chose a third option. I stole a car.

After breaking into a nearby, copper-colored 1920 Buick, I drove past the hospital then down Boundary Street before turning left onto Aylebury. With the Miskatonic flowing to my right, I departed Arkham, my compass, on the Buick's dash, pointing northwest.

The river being my companion for a good while longer, I didn't like the direction the compass, or my day, was taking.

Soon after I came upon Billington's Woods, lying thick and deep ahead and to my left. The road veered towards them and me with it, and damn did I hope my drive wouldn't be a long one.

An hour later and I was still hoping, the Buick's poor handling an added burden as I drove along wishing I'd picked another car, or even returned for my own devilishly fast Coupe.

After Billington's Woods the road turned worse, ruts and stones appearing with abandon. The Buick's handling following suite with little sympathy.

Another hour of tortuous driving followed.

As I drove, the ground grew higher, the stone walls bordering the road growing tight as the ruts and debris increased beneath my wheels.

Even the landscape was going against me. As the road tightened, curving like some crazy, wound-up snake, I slowed my stolen chariot even further for fear of hitting something. A wandering cow was a thought, or possibly even a fallen tree. The ones I passed were old and diseased, their dark, heavy branches leaning across the road with an evil intent. I felt glad I'd kept the roof up.

I was now about seventy miles northwest of Arkham, not far from the border to Vermont. Already well past Dean's Corners, I was slowly but surely closing in towards Aylesury Pike. It appeared the compass had one destination in mind: the decayed village of Dunwich.

Dunwich was one of the last places Barnes and me would have thought of looking. I suppose that's where the beauty lay. Dunwich was a tiny farming community in an area that had once housed lumber mills, before its decline.

Declined, inbred—these two words suited Dunwich down to the grimy ground.

I crossed the pike and the landscape around me remained unchanged, the forests hiding much of my view as the road's wild curves continued.

As the forest finally started to thin, the road began to widen.

Beyond I spied farmland, barren as it was, gaining a better view as the trees disappeared. The increasing dilapidation of the walls followed the road's widening, the brambles flanking it growing thicker and wilder as Dunwich loomed ever closer. I supposed so anyway, for so far I'd seen very little in the way of buildings, just the odd derelict-looking homestead, built from scratch and slowly falling back into it.

One of those ruins might house Sonia, I realized. Removing my foot from the gas pedal I pulled up beside a decrepit wall. I came to a halt before checking two things in order.

The time on my watch: twelve oh two. The direction on the compass needle: northwest, still.

It was time to walk. I took the compass in one hand and removed my hat with the other. Placing the latter on the passenger seat I stepped out onto the road, stretching my arms and legs. A stretch felt good for the soul, even in a dump like Dunwich.

After some indecision I retrieved my hat, pulling it down over my brow.

I left the Buick and headed forward, checking the compass constantly as I stepped deeper into Dunwich country.

The fields grew shoddier. The houses, becoming larger but no tidier, were built closer to a road now without its barrier wall. These squalid places looked deserted, or, if not, I couldn't imagine what folks could live in such decrepit hulks. The windows were gaping holes of darkness, with rotted boards or dirty sheets spotting many.

I stepped warily, conscious of my surroundings at all times.

Dunwich was a ghost town, like the old west but without any romantic charm.

The road started to rise again, approaching and disappearing towards the mountains lining the horizon. The stone pillars crowning those had never been part of Mother Nature's designs.

I sighed, looking towards the deep dark woods surrounding their base. Sonia could be there as far as I knew, hidden away in some dark little cabin within a maze of stubborn boughs.

Ten more minutes and my feet began to ache. I encountered a river, trickling away beneath a wooden bridge, and guessed this was the upper reaches of the Miskatonic. The compass took me off the road and across the bridge.

My anticipation grew as I walked upon stony grassland no kinder on my feet than the road. A cluster of gambrel roofs lay between the river and the mountains. Dunwich proper.

The compass wavered as I walked, hinting I might be getting somewhere. Closing in on the mountains, my worries concerning distance returned. I had a long, wearying walk ahead of me.

Deserted as it was, I eventually reached the village. I wavered in my resolve but this was where the compass wanted me. And who was I to question Justin Geoffrey's nifty piece of enchantment?

I soon entered Dunwich's deep, rotted heart, a village formed from ugly homesteads matching those I had passed on the road.

Somewhere within that sprawl I spied a church steeple, sagging and ugly against a sky rippled with gray. As it appeared to be at the village's center, I headed that way.

The smell of decay grew in strength, becoming a positive stench as I stepped between a pair of log-built houses. Soon after, rubble, rotted food and suspiciously large bones started to hinder my footsteps. The ground lay as messy as the buildings surrounding it.

The village was a different world, a dimension where decay held sway. That decay filled my lungs, had me feeling contaminated, unreal even.

The compass helped maintain my grip on the world I knew, and for that I felt thankful. Entering and searching a few dust-filled, rotted houses had me gripping the device tighter still. In my other hand, my gun felt loose in my sweaty grip. Their obvious abandonment had me wondering whether Sonia was held even further beyond Dunwich's confines.

I hoped not, for the clock was ticking and my time was slipping away.

The village's rundown state started to weigh even more heavily on me, so much I felt I might never leave, or if so, I would do so as a shambling, skeletal pile of rags, a victim of Dunwich's diseased, decrepit unlife.

My knees growing weak, I walked shoulders slumped, my arms dangling at my sides as my footsteps fell heavy and leaden upon the filth-covered ground. I felt sure this place would be my end. Soon I would drop, becoming so much slimy, decaying mulch.

I turned a corner, staggering more than walking, and glimpsed something that cured me in an instant.

Conspicuous on a street of garbage stood two shiny black cars, a Chrysler Saratoga accompanied by a Ford Continental. Both were far from old, far from damaged. To be exact, they stood out like two sore, shiny thumbs.

I checked my watch. The time: one thirty-two.

My balance returning with each nervous breath, I snuck towards the house they stood before using the shadows of another, taking extra care to avoid what lay beneath my feet. My approach soon brought voices to my ears. *Paydirt*, I hoped. A minute later I halted before a window covered in damp wooden boards, the latter filled with knots and gaps. I used these to see just who the voices belonged to.

The room I peeked into, formed from bare plaster walls and not much else, held two men.

And was I surprised! Why, I was actually taken aback. The last of my earlier, Dunwich-fueled funk dissipated as I clasped eyes on Braces and the Ape. The latter sat with his nose bandaged from our earlier encounter. Braces had replaced his bright red pair for ones of a more sober brown.

Hung somewhere in that room, a gas lantern flickered and hissed, illuminating their ugly mugs. Sat before a long, uneven table, I'd caught the two mid-conversation.

"If we're gonna kill the brat anyway, why not now?" Braces said, his words sending my teeth snapping down against my lower lip.

"Boy, if you wanna get along in this world, you gotta learn to follow orders." The Ape's voice, clogged and nasal, brought a vicious smile to my lips. "Plus," he continued, "what if the boss calls back, wanting to speak to her?"

"Hell," Braces replied, "I'm sure Rosie could put the kid's voice on if need be."

The Ape grunted in agreement and stood, pushing his chair back. Following his movements I watched him head right before he paused before a weird looking object.

Half-hidden behind it, he said, "I'd love to know how this thing works."

The object was formed from a cluster of pale creamy cylinders of uneven height and width. Braced together by metal strips, the tallest stood topped by a thin, zigzagging metal pipe. The cylinders disappeared into a dark wooden box, this forming the base of the device. Like a radio, it had dials and switches built into its surface.

A thick black wire, trailing from the object, was connected to a telephone.

"That Frenchy sure is clever," Braces replied.

So telephone lines just weren't needed, here in Dunwich.

I left the scumbags to it and made my way to the side of the house. Passing the door to their room, I went in search of another.

Within a dark, cramped alleyway I discovered the door I wanted. With a slow turn of the handle, I found it unlocked.

I opened it up and was faced by sheer darkness. I dropped the compass into my pocket and cursed silently as the door continued inward. It creaked loudly, the racket filled the black air. Fumbling in the dark, I found and retrieved the handle to stop the door mid-movement. I held my breath, listened intently, and tried to hear whether my entry had been noticed.

I heard a low mumbling somewhere off to my right: Braces and the Ape talking away, ignorant to my noisy entrance.

I stepped into the darkness, making slow, careful steps while waiting for my eyes to adjust. A minute or two later I realized the scene wasn't in any hurry to change.

A wall stood a few yards ahead of me, sheer blackness forming the spaces to my left and right. Stepping carefully, for the floor held a symphony of wooden creaks, I headed right.

I was forced to follow the wall like a blind man, my fingers trailing damp plaster as I followed the muffled sounds. They grew louder as I walked, and I was beginning to discern words when my hand fell through nothingness.

I reached out my foot, finding one elevation, followed by another. I'd come upon a staircase. Sonia was somewhere up there, my gut said in a whisper.

I paused, briefly, then went for it, making my slow way up and towards a light source.

When I got top I found that the light issued from somewhere to my right. I went into a crouch and turned to discover an open doorway. Within, an uncovered window provided the illumination.

This was the first decent light I'd seen in an age. My excitement grew as I heard a voice that sounded like Sonia's, a child-like humming from beyond the doorway.

Still I crept, slowly but surely, calming my breath to stem my excitement. Eddie's little sister was still far from safe.

I reached the doorway with barely a creak and bent to my knees, taking a sneaky peek inside.

What I witnessed there both gladdened and pained me. Ahead and to my right, in a room of bare plaster walls and uncarpeted floorboards, sat a little girl in her nightgown, cross-legged upon a pile of grubby looking mattresses. The dirt-stained window lay directly behind her. I recognized the humming girl playing with the corn doll as Sonia instantly.

Seated on a stool before Sonia was a blubbery whale of a woman, in a gaudy, flowery dress that probably would've made a fine two-man tent.

She sat leafing through a magazine, but stopped to stare at Sonia's sad little form. "Child," she said, in a pleasant tone that betrayed her ugliness, "if you don't pipe down you're gonna get another slap."

Sonia froze up and began to sob quietly.

I'd seen enough, and with the whale's loud, asthmatic breathing masking my entry, I sneaked in towards her. Sonia, noticing my approach, looked down again as I placed a finger to my lips.

Quickly behind the whale's heaving form, I put her out with a crack to the head, easing the monstrosity to the floor in case her fall alerted the two downstairs.

Hah. Maybe if I'd let her fall she would've gone right through the floor, crushing the two bastards.

With the whale bested, Sonia jumped up off the bed and shouted, "Uncle Trevor!"

I hushed her, leaving the girl stood confused, the little doll dangling limply from her hand.

"We have to stay quiet for now, hon," I whispered, grunting as I lowered the woman to the floor. Still on my knees, I beckoned Sonia towards me. She hugged me hard enough to crush the breath out of me. Tears formed at the hell those bastards had put her through. And not forgetting Boss Logan, now there was a bastard I wouldn't be forgiving anytime soon.

"Now listen honey," I said, taking hold of Sonia's tiny chin, "you're gonna have to cover up your ears while I go downstairs. I need to frighten those nasty men away with my gun."

"But . . ."

"No," I interrupted, "I do this and soon you'll be back home with your mamma."

Sonia smiled and nodded in understanding.

The happy little tyke even helped me tie Rosie up, grabbing me a pair of fallen, raggedy curtains to use on her flabby arms and legs.

Then, leaving Sonia stood with her hands over her ears, I headed back downstairs, to go "frighten off" those nasty men.

I took Braces out with one to the head, putting two through his chest for good measure. The Ape, crafty in his jungle ways, got a bullet off before expiring. But, with half his face missing, he found aiming difficult. His bullet hit the table, smashing out two of that fruity contraption's cylinders.

I checked the phone but it didn't work, which meant giving Barnes and Eddie the good news would have to wait until I could get back to Arkham.

We left the whale still bound and gagged, escaping in their very own Ford Continental. Little Sonia sat grinning away beside me as I drove. Her day had definitely taken a turn for the better. Mine too, as it happened.

I checked my watch. It read one fifty-two.

I mopped my brow with a less than white hanky and screamed at Eddie McCoy. "Have you got mud in your ears, kid?"

He glared at me and mumbled something derogatory which might have hurt my delicate feelings were I not so worried about the whereabouts of Towers and Eddie's kid sister, Sonia.

It was necessary to scream over the noise of the fight crowd—most of them stewed—and even more necessary to convince Eddie to stay away from the devastating power of Noah Whately's iron right hand.

"Lay off the kid," grunted Eddie's corner man, Max Brandywine. "He'll make it up in the next round."

"It won't go past the next round," I growled. "Not if he don't box from the outside and work his jab instead of trying to slug it out with the creep."

The sixty-second rest period was ticking down and so was my patience.

Slapping Eddie on the shoulder, I tried my best to grin. "You got to trust me, kid. Towers won't let anything happen to your sister. So please, just dance around this ogre until he gets here. And don't even think about taking a dive for that scum Logan unless I give you the word."

My efforts to get through to Eddie were stopped by the clang of the bell signaling round two. Across the ring I spotted Logan and a couple of his monkeys take their seats at ringside. I guess he was determined to see the results of his handiwork in person. Well, fine. If Eddie had to toss the most important fight of his young career then I'd make damn sure he wasn't the only one going down.

I watched the two fighters approach the center of the ring and cursed. Eddie didn't stand a chance unless he took my advice and finessed Whately. The crowd cheered as Eddie snapped a couple of stiff jabs to Whately's chin and then danced away. Whately grinned as if to say he ate such punches for breakfast and tried to unload with a powerful right cross that caught nothing but air, causing him to stumble awkwardly and look foolish. The crowd jeered derisively and a dark expression of rage settled over the larger boxer's face.

"Good job!" I bellowed. "Stick and move . . . just stick and . . ."

Someone tugged at my sleeve and I turned to read them the riot act. It was one of Logan's boys who quickly raised both hands in a don't be alarmed manner.

"What the fuck you want?" I asked, gripping the cold steel in my jacket pocket.

"The boss says he don't care how long the kid drags it out just as long as you're clear on what happens if he don't eat the canvas."

"Oh, we ain't forgetting," I said. "I promise you that we ain't forgetting a damn thing about this."

"Well then, see you around, Barnes," he replied, heading back to his seat.

"Yeah," I whispered to myself. "You'll be seeing me all right."

I turned my attention back to the action and smiled at Noah Whately's feeble attempts to cut off the ring on Eddie.

"Looking good!" I yelled as Eddie again peppered Whately's face with jabs and then danced out of range.

It was impossible for Eddie to put a hurt on Whately while the red-headed behemoth was protected by the Frenchmen's spell. On the other hand, there wasn't much that could happen to Eddie as long as he followed instructions and boxed at long range. The big problem with this strategy is that Eddie's a scrapper and prefers to mix it up with an opponent rather than win a dance contest. I can't say that I faulted him for that but my main concern was keeping him in one piece until Towers returned and until Geoffrey could hopefully work his magic and counteract the Frenchman's hoodoo. Even if the spell on Whately remained in effect it was still possible for Eddie to win on points once it was clear that Sonia was safe.

Now this was all good and well as long as Eddie stayed cool and didn't try to make like the knock-out artists he worshiped. During the remainder of the round he kept his poise and easily outpointed Whately. That left eight rounds or roughly thirty-two minutes for Towers to show up like the cavalry and save the day. Barring that, I was afraid I might be looking at Barnes' last stand.

Three more rounds flew past and Eddie was looking good. He continued to out-box his larger and stronger opponent without getting himself too banged up. At the end of each round he returned to the corner and looked to me for word on his sister's safety. I could only encourage him to have faith in Towers while trying not to show my own concerns in the matter. I muttered a quick prayer under my breath and then watched as things turned to shit during Round Six.

Things were going according to plan for the first third of the round as Eddie hammered Whately with a continuous barrage of punches while remaining untouched in the process. Then for reasons known only to himself—pride would be my guess—the kid decided to go toe to toe with his magically protected opponent. The crowd was on its feet as the two fighters traded a series of heavy blows that echoed through the smoke-filled arena. During this exchange Eddie was staggered and the only thing saving his bacon was the fact that Whately was so blown from chasing the kid around the ring that he couldn't press his advantage to a conclusion.

Eddie was in bad shape but managed to stay away from Whately until the bell ended the round. His left eye was badly swollen and his handsome face was bruised and battered.

"Jesus Christ, kid!" I yelled as he collapsed onto the stool. "You trying to ruin everything?"

"What's the use?" He mumbled as Max Brandywine and Nicky Spitz the cut man worked on the kid's face with icy bars in a desperate attempt to alleviate the swelling. "If I got to lose to save Sonia then I at least want to go down swinging. I'm tired of running away from Whately."

"Look kid," I growled, "Just play it safe a couple of more rounds. There's still plenty of time to get yourself killed if that's what you're wanting."

I glanced at my watch and wondered if Towers was going to make it. There were a whole lot of things that could've happened and most of them weren't good. Still, my partner was an unstoppable force and I had to believe he would show no matter the odds. With that in mind, I spent the remainder of the rest period beseeching Eddie to keep boxing and not get himself kayoed for nothing.

The bell sounded for Round Seven and Eddie rose from his stool with determination. I just hoped he would follow my instructions and play it safe for as long as possible.

The first few seconds of the round quickly dashed such hopes. Hell, nobody else ever listens to Riley Barnes so why should Eddie McCoy be any different?

I watched in frustration as Eddie went straight toward Whately. He threw the by-now obligatory jabs which had scored so many points for him through the first six rounds of the fight. But instead of moving away as instructed, he bobbed and weaved in front of his foe, avoiding some big punches and generally frustrating the hell out of Whately. The angry lummox tried to land some haymakers and succeeded in only looking foolish.

The crowd was clearly behind Eddie, hooting and jeering at each flailing attempt by Whately to land a solid blow. The kid seemed energized by the vocal support and moved in close to land a wicked combination of hooks and uppercuts that would've floored a normal opponent. And therein lay the problem.

Noah Whately was incapable of being hurt while protected by sorcery. So instead of going down he shrugged off the punches and fired back with an uppercut of his own. The crowd gasped as the punch literally lifted Eddie off his feet to deposit him on his ass half way across the ring.

The referee moved in at this point and started the ten count.

Max Brandywine, Nicky Spitz and an arena full of fans screamed for the kid to rise. With no sign of my partner, I started to think maybe it was best if Eddie stayed down for the count in order to avoid the beating that was sure to come if he made it to his feet. Though glassy-eyed and unsteady, Eddie McCoy just managed to make it to his feet before the Ref reached ten.

The official allowed the bout to continue and the crowd roared its approval.

Even a lug like Whately was smart enough to go for the kill with a dazed foe in front of him. He moved forward like a tank and threw a punch that while only grazing Eddie's shoulder sent him careening against the ropes. He came off them like a drunken ballerina and managed to retain his balance by sheer luck. Only due to the merciful slowness of Whately was he able to survive the remainder of the seventh round.

The kid collapsed onto his stool between rounds and looked accusingly at me. He didn't have to ask the question because I'd been wondering the same one myself.

Where was Towers and Sonia?

I didn't know what to tell the hurting young kid in front of me. I'd grown so used to Trevor Towers doing all the larger than life things he set out to do that it was sort of a shock to find myself contemplating getting out of this fix on my own. Truth be told, I didn't plan on getting *out* of it. I planned on *payback*. If Towers wasn't back with Eddie's sister in the next few minutes then it meant they weren't coming back.

And that meant that Logan and anyone standing between him and me was going to die. I could give Eddie McCoy that much. And that glorious bastard of a partner, Towers, I damn sure owed him that.

"Look kid," I said, "don't quit now. You can still win this fight on points but you got to box. Win the damn fight and let me take care of Logan!"

He looked right through me and refused to acknowledge any of the pleading instructions given to him by his corner. The bell signaled the start of Round Eight and the kid took a beating but somehow managed to remain standing. There was no reasoning with him and he was probably behind in the fight on points after sustaining two knockdowns.

This left four minutes until the tenth and final round.

I don't know if Eddie decided to actually listen to me but he managed to box superbly during Round Nine and easily outpointed the fatigued Whately. Even with that, I was pretty sure that a knock-out was the only chance in hell he had of winning the fight and that just wasn't going to happen unless our friend Justin Geoffrey somehow managed to nullify the Frenchman's spell of invincibility over Whately.

The crowd was raucous as the bell rang to start the tenth and final round.

Eddie moved straight at Whately and landed a quick series of jabs before sliding away. At this point I wasn't sure if the kid was going to box or go out in a blaze of glory. Things definitely looked grim concerning his sister's fate and it was surprising that he was able to continue at all.

Knowing there was even a faint chance that his sister might be returned safely was all Eddie McCoy needed to decide his course of action. The kid again moved toward Whately, holding his hands low as if inviting a knock-out. His larger opponent was still under the Frenchman's protective spell so Eddie decided to offer himself up for the slaughter as demanded by Logan.

He flicked a tentative jab towards his clumsy foe and this time stood his ground instead of moving away. Even an oaf like Whately could hit a stationary target and he answered the jab with a thundering right cross that staggered the kid. I muttered a curse and watched the kid reel across the ring as a result of the blow.

A black rage rose up inside me and I gripped the heater in my pocket. If everything was in the toilet then the time had come for me to settle matters with Logan. Whately might come out of the fight on top but I could make damn sure that Logan, the crooked bastard, wouldn't be around to reap the rewards. Glancing toward the ring, I saw Eddie get nailed with another big right that sent him to the canvas. I shook my head in disgust and started around the perimeter of the ring in order to confront Logan. Half way to my target I heard a high pitched voice screaming some gibberish loud enough to cut through the roar of the crowd. Momentarily distracted from my goal, I turned toward the source of the strange disturbance and did a double-take.

Justin Geoffrey was stumbling down the aisle, dressed in a

flowing robe of canary yellow and holding aloft what resembled a sparking pinwheel. Behind him, a frustrated Trevor Towers was peering toward Eddie's corner in an apparent attempt to locate yours truly. "Barnes!" he yelled, instantly spotting me as I frantically waved my arms.

"Sonia's safe!" he bellowed. "Tell the kid!"

"And tell him to fight!" screamed Geoffrey. "My magic is stronger than the Frenchman's!"

"Jesus," I moaned. The kid was in a world of hurt having just been felled by Whately's punch. The only thing working in my favor was that the big brawler from Dunwich was too slow-witted to go immediately to the neutral corner as instructed in the pre-fight instructions given to both fighters concerning what must occur in the event of a knockdown. I hurried to the side of the ring closest to where the kid was sprawled and started screaming at him.

He peered at me through glassy eyes as I tried to get through to him.

"Sonia's safe! Towers got her to safety!"

He shook his head as if to clear away the cobwebs and said something I couldn't hear over the pandemonium around me.

"She's safe!" I bellowed again. "Now get off your ass and show these morons why you're going to be the future champ!"

By this time Whately's screaming trainer had finally convinced the big oaf to go to a neutral corner and the ref had begun the ten count.

"One . . . two . . . three . . ."

"Park it, fella!" yelled a pencil-necked geek in glasses. "I paid good dough to *see* this fight."

"Up yours," I growled, turning back to the ring. "Come on, kid!" I pleaded. "You can put this clown away *now*."

He seemed to get my meaning and made it to one knee as the ref continued to count. "Four . . . five . . . six . . ."

I was sweating bullets but the kid made it to his feet by the count of nine which seemed to have a marked effect on the stunned crowd. A few fans in the crowd began to chant the kid's name and soon the entire arena echoed to the sound of Eddie! Eddie! Eddie!

The battered fighter shot me a grin and turned to take care of business.

With less than a minute remaining in the final round, he moved straight toward Noah Whately and easily avoided a roundhouse right thrown by the bigger man. Stepping inside he unleashed a flurry of body shots that caused his foe to visibly cringe. He followed this up with a series of wicked hooks that rocked Whately back on his heels.

The kid was taking charge but was there enough time remaining for him to land the one big punch that could put his opponent away?

Eddie had heart but *that* was an intangible that exercised no control over time. And time was something that was fast running out.

I was cheering the kid on at the top of my lungs when I felt someone career wildly into me. Turning to deck the fool, I stopped in amazement as my eyes rested on the figure before me. It was Justin Geoffrey, still waving that infernal pinwheel and mouthing gibberish at the top of his voice. Spittle flew from his lips and I made out something that sounded like, "Iä! Iä! Niggurath Vhata! Dagon Shan . . . Dagon Shan!"

I shook my head in bewilderment and turned back to the ring in time to see Eddie staggered by a wild right that never would have landed had the kid not been exhausted. With precious seconds ticking away, Geoffrey pushed past me and jumped onto the ring apron.

"Noah Whately! Dagon Shan! Dagon Shan!" he screamed.

As crazy as it sounds, time seemed to stop for a handful of seconds and the atmosphere became electrically charged. There was a blinding flash and I watched Eddie McCoy get his bearings and load up for one final punch as time resumed its normal pace. The kid ducked under a straight left from Whately and seemed to reach down to the ring canvas for his return punch. And what a punch it was. I even managed to hear it land over Geoffrey's maniacal screams behind me.

What happened next is still being debated to this day. It's become part of the strange lore that seems to keep the town of Arkham front and center in the minds of those who try to explain the unexplainable.

Eddie's punch landed about as hard as any punch *could* land. To say that the kid destroyed his opponent with the blow would be the literal truth yet still an understatement. Noah Whately's head—once impervious to damage thanks to the Frenchman— seemed transformed into something akin to delicate crystal. Eddie McCoy's Hail Mary punch to the jaw shattered the head of Noah Whately into a thousand shards of glass sending the now headless opponent down for a ten count from which he would never rise.

Silence hung over the arena like a deathly pall but lasted only moments. I sort of think it was broken by Boss Logan's scream of pain and terror as Trevor Towers grabbed hold of him. The punk's banshee wailing—coupled with the scene of horror in the ring— seemed to have a contagious effect upon the assembled masses resulting in a mad stampede from the arena. I awkwardly pulled Geoffrey near me to keep him from being trampled in the melee and thanked him for helping the kid.

Geoffrey was more pale than usual and appeared pretty shaky as a result of whatever unholy energies he had expended on our behalf. He managed to grin, bat his eyes at me and then swoon. "Christ," I muttered, throwing him over my shoulder and heading into the ring to check on Eddie McCoy and seek a better vantage point from which to spot my partner.

I sat Geoffrey on a stool and hugged a very confused but victorious Eddie McCoy. Turning to peer across the bedlam I spied Towers standing over three crumpled bodies near the seats once occupied by Logan and his thugs. I guess they'd been trampled to death in the panic. Trampled or *something* like that.

Towers turned toward the ring and spotted me. He gave me the thumbs up sign and grinned.

Sonia's return led to a party, a double celebration including Eddie's triumphant victory. With a few loose ends to tie up, Barnes and me bowed out early.

Nature hates a vacuum, as does Arkham, and it wasn't long before another Mob Boss appeared to replace Logan's corpse, now chilling at the bottom of the river. Pickman he calls himself, and with our reputation, combined with the disappearance of his predecessor, the fellow gives us a wide berth. He has no interest in boxing but rather, art is his thing.

Since defeating the Iron Man, Eddie's career has advanced in leaps and bounds, so much so he recently moved his family up onto French Hill. Logan's safe, mysteriously appearing on Ma McCoy's doorstep, helped. Now, they want for nothing. The former owner of the mansion, the French Sorcerer, disappeared soon after Eddie's match with Whately. But that's another story.

Our friend Justin Geoffrey rents a wing of their home, but on one condition: that he remains vigilant around his experiments. Including our frequent visits, the family is protected both magically and by two big, well-armed thugs.

Barnes and Towers.

Skin Flick

I was tooling around through the sticks of Dunwich, having completed a job-related errand, when I spotted something strange. Yeah, I know that *strange* and Dunwich go together like mustard and Coney Island. But anyway, it was uncommon as hell to see a brand-new roadster parked in the middle of a field with its door open. I slowed my own heap to a crawl and pulled over to the side of the narrow, winding road to take a closer gander at the sight.

It appeared that the field had once been farmland but was currently growing nothing but some very healthy-looking weeds. I figured that a farmhouse must be nearby but couldn't spot one. I also figured that it or what was left of it might be beyond the thick trees that bordered the pasture.

". . . a hell of a note," I muttered, reaching into my pocket for my smokes.

After lighting up, I maneuvered my way through a rusty barbed-wire fence and ambled toward the abandoned car. Something about that open car door didn't sit right with me and my big nose was once again preparing to go prying into someone else's business. It's not that I'm generally a busybody but my line of work as a private investigator has sort of made such behavior a habit. My partner, a fellow named Trevor Towers, was back in Arkham probably flirting with our occasional receptionist Betty Polanski or else trying to avoid her voluminous mother who often filled in for her. With any luck there would be a logical explanation for the abandoned car and Trevor would just have to miss out on hearing another fascinating Riley Barnes adventure.

I crossed the weedy field and approached the car. A strong wind blew, causing the tall grass to sway, making me feel like I was wading through green waves. I reached the car and walked to the side with the open door.

"*That* don't look good," I whispered.

A woman's purse had its contents scattered on the seat. On the *blood-stained* seat. The blood was dry and rusty-looking and had probably been there for several days. The amount didn't indicate a fatal wound but someone had definitely been hurt. I took a stick and flipped through the items on the seat but found no identification. The car's tires had left a trail in the high grass and I followed it for a short distance to where it met up with a dirt road leading through the woods. Feeling adventurous and not wanting to deprive Trevor of a story, I began to follow the trail, first checking to see that the .38 securely tucked in my shoulder rig was loaded.

I walked only about a hundred yards into the woods before coming to a clearing. Sure enough, a decrepit wooden building stood half-heartedly in the open space, awaiting permission to fall down. I faded back into the trees and considered my options. A smart man would return to his car and report the discovery to the local constable. Not being a smart man—and knowing that the constable was dumb as a box of hammers—I removed my pistol from the holster and held it firmly.

Okay, Barnes, I thought. *Now what?*

Now what consisted of me walking quietly to the fly-specked window at the side of the house and peering inside. I couldn't see crap and everything was quiet as a graveyard. Taking a deep breath, I crept around to the front and stepped cautiously onto the warped wooden porch. The ancient lumber moaned in protest and I might as well have trumpeted a verse of *Darktown Strutter's Ball* to announce my presence.

Since no-one hollered from inside, I threw caution to the wind and aimed a kick at the door. It flew inward with a loud crash and I crouched beside it and waited for a response. I could've waited forever because nobody *living* was in the house. I entered the large room and waved my gun around as if *that* was going to do some good. It might've, if I'd had an inclination to kill flies; the room was thick with them. Their buzzing grated on my nerves but the sunlight and my presence seemed to prompt them on their way. I didn't know what to make of it and even less at what I spied on the large bed in the center of the room.

"Son of a bitch," I muttered, moving slowly toward the object.

At first I thought someone had left their clothing laid out neatly on the bed. I edged closer and the sky decided to lighten and give me a better view. I could've done without it. A woman's nude corpse lay atop the sheets. Well, that's true only as far as it goes. It was only the *skin* of the woman that remained. The bile rose up in my throat but I managed to keep down the greasy burger I'd consumed earlier in the day. After taking a few deep breaths outside, I returned to the grisly sight and did a more thorough examination.

I prodded at the remains with a stick—the things had really been coming in handy that day—and was amazed to find no tears in the skin. I was having a hard time believing my eyes but the damn thing appeared to be intact minus the important stuff like blood, bone and organs. I had scant medical knowledge but knew that what I was seeing should've been impossible. I mean, what consumes a person and leaves nothing but the skin? I thought of my partner and realized he was going to hear quite a story after all.

Only after a few shocked minutes did I notice the huge light that was broken on the floor. It was one of those big jobs like they use on movie sets.

What the hell? I wondered. Could someone have been filming something here? Filming whatever happened to the poor woman whose husk lay on the bed? Then things sort of clicked and I suddenly had a screwy idea about what happened.

I guessed that the woman had been brought to this out of the way place to engage in the sort of film work you didn't view at the local cinema. Something happened and she tried to scram. I figured that she must have made it to her car only to be subdued—accounting for the blood stains—and returned to the house. God only knows what happened after that but it was something that I had a hard time wrapping my mind around. There had been other tire marks, too, so it stood to reason that a number of people might've been involved in the woman's death.

I left the murder scene and stood grimly on the porch. The local constable would have to be informed but I damn sure wasn't going to do it in person. Walking back to my car, I decided that an anonymous phone tip was the way to go. I wasn't about to let some local yokel try to pin a murder rap on me

I spied a gas station not too far outside Dunwich and placed an anonymous call to the State Police. They could come down and deal with that bum of a constable. I gave them just enough information to find the place though they sure weren't happy with my lack of co-operation. After telling them what they could do with their unhappiness, I got back in the car and finished the return trip to Arkham.

Our office reception area was empty and I wondered what excuse our new secretary was currently using for her absence. I went to mine and Trevor's sanctum sanctorum and walked inside. Trevor was seated behind the desk and looked a bit green around the gills. My diagnosis was hangover since it would take a hell of a lot to shake a veteran like my partner. I spotted the metal film canister atop the desk and noticed a big 16mm projector set up in the corner of the office.

I grinned and said, "Is naked dames what they're currently prescribing for hangovers?"

He looked at me and grimaced.

"Hey," he said. "If you want to talk sick, wait until I lay this on you."

I was all revved up to tell him up about the horror I'd seen in Dunwich but he raised a big hand to silence me. My partner was seldom at a loss for words and usually had a storehouse of snappy insults to put me in my place so I was intrigued by his behavior, to say the least.

"Riley," he said, pointing to the film canister, "you gotta see this."

"Sure, Trev," I answered. "My story can wait."

I took a seat and remained silent as he went to the projector and got things ready.

I knew watching the film again would be hell on me. Even the thought of putting the gear together to watch the damned thing disgusted me. I borrowed the projector from the office downstairs, and was glad the owner would never know what kind of film had been used in it.

While getting the film canister from the desk I filled Barnes in.

"A guy came in here a little earlier, begging for our help." As I said this I lifted the lid from the canister; it seemed to weigh a ton in my hands.

"He told me to watch this," I continued. "And I suppose it's best you watch it too."

Barnes looked at me like I had something wrong with me. He wasn't far wrong.

I sat on the edge of the desk between him and the projector.

He'd taken the client seat. After letting the film roll, I clenched my fists to try and put a little strength back into them. I had little luck.

I've always thought myself a man of the world. Watching a monster brutally rape and kill a woman on screen proved I hadn't really seen much of the world after all.

The film was set in what looked like a large one-roomed cabin with a bed in its center.

Barnes hissed as the film began, I assumed because of the naked woman sprawled on the bed. He quickly educated me to the fact he'd just been in that very room, and he knew what was coming next.

Coincidences follow us like a bad cold.

Still he gasped and swore as we watched the naked man approach and then savagely rape the poor woman; a man that although looked human in appearance, kept shifting his form in an unnatural way as he assaulted her like some rutting beast.

It went on like that for a good ten minutes.

Then another man appeared on screen. Dressed in long monk's robes, his face was concealed by a round mask shaped like the moon but with a leering face at its center. He stood beside the bed and gestured at the woman in mockery, before again disappearing off camera.

The woman wailed and suffered silently, which in some ways made the film even more horrifying. I took a look at Barnes and saw a face pale and drawn with disgust.

My eyes drew me back to the film. Despite the fact I knew what was happening, I still found it difficult to watch, and who wouldn't? Certainly not Barnes, who sat cringing as the monstrous rapist sucked the life and soul right out of his victim. Monster? Yeah, because now its skin looked thick and mottled, darker than normal flesh. Muscles on its body bulged in all the wrong places, as if up until now it was only faking the human form, and had just given up on it.

Barnes began swearing but his words soon trailed off into silence. The man-thing on the screen, pressed down against the woman's quickly shriveling form, appeared to be sucking her essence right down his throat, his neck now bulbous and bloated as he gulped her down. His belly swelled against her now unmoving form.

There was nothing left inside her *to* move, nothing but a bare and empty woman-shaped sack to replace what had once been a living, thinking person.

I turned from the screen and darted towards the waste-bin. By the time I'd finished hurling, the film had ended.

As I used my handkerchief to wipe my dripping mouth I felt Barnes's hand on my shoulder. It seemed he had a stronger stomach than me, for as I stood back up I saw he was looking sick but not too worse for wear.

He must have known what I was thinking, for he said: "You should've seen how I was when I found what was left of her."

Barnes helped me up even though I didn't need his assistance; the man was just showing concern. Then, reaching over towards the desk, he retrieved the office bottle and passed it to me after taking a healthy swig himself.

The whiskey burned the insides of my throat and I felt better for it. As I dropped my soiled handkerchief into the fouled up waste-bin he said, "Trev, I think you need to fill me in on who brought us that damned film."

Barnes switched off the still-rolling projector while I went about disassembling the screen.

"The man that came," I said, "seemed pretty shaken up, but he had just watched *that*." I nodded towards the reel in Barnes's hands.

Barnes seemed as subdued as I'd ever seen him. I watched him replace the film gingerly back in its can.

I kneeled down to take the screen stand apart and continued. "This fella, Dafoe he called himself, said the film was made by some Hollywood director. He said that was him in the film, wearing that crazy mask."

I walked back towards Barnes with the equipment tucked under each arm and added the final bombshell. "The woman the beast had its way with was Dafoe's wife."

Barnes stared at me as I dropped the stuff down onto the desk. "And he thinks he's gonna be next."

Barnes swore under his breath before nodding at the film can. He said, "Then it seems we have a new client to deal with."

I agreed and reached for the bottle. My nerves needed steadying like never before.

We headed out early the next morning to Byron Dafoe's home, several miles west of Arkham. Much of the previous evening had been spent getting our things together for the job of protecting our client. If his suspicions were correct, he was going to need a *lot* of protection. Me and Trevor had seen some pretty terrible things during our short partnership but nothing that could compare to what we saw in that film. Sure, Herbert West's sick shenanigans ran a close second but we'd made pretty sure that he was now out of the running.

As the scenery rolled by, I asked, "Do you really think a professional filmmaker would be involved in this crap?"

Towers looked at me and shrugged. "Hard to say. They're plenty flaky out there from what I hear."

"Yeah," I replied, "but what was on that film goes way beyond flaky."

"Hellish," he said. "Beyond the pale."

I nodded in agreement and lit a smoke.

"Did you ever imagine we'd be going up against the kind of evil we've butted heads with in the past few months?"

"Imagine it?" He asked. "Shit, I didn't even know it existed. I've always had a pretty low opinion of the human race in general but never in my wildest dreams did . . ."

"Hey, is that the turn-off up ahead?"

Trevor peered through the thinning fog and nodded. "Yeah, I'm pretty sure this is the place."

I turned off the main highway and headed north through a thickly wooded area. After about half a mile, the woods thinned substantially and we moved uphill across an overgrown but woodless expanse until the road ended at an ominous iron gate. The gate was the only passage through a tall stone fence about seven feet in height.

"Well, now. This is a *welcoming* sight," Trevor commented.

"Yeah, just like returning home to Sing Sing."

A thick chain and lock held the gate shut.

"Now what?" I asked.

"Let me take a peep," Trevor said, opening the car door.

He passed in front of the car and inspected the lock. His broad back obscured my view but I could tell that his hands were busy. After about a minute, he turned, held up the open lock and grinned. I gave him the thumbs up to show my approval and waited as he swung the gate sections open. Once the entrance was clear, I eased the car through and waited for him to get back inside.

Trevor opened the door, eased onto the seat and grinned. "We'll need to bug our client about security issues."

"I sort of expected someone to be manning that gate."

"Me too," Trevor answered. "I guess we can find out what's shaking once we find Dafoe."

Dafoe's House sat atop the hill and seemed to look down at us. It was now light enough to get a good look at it. It was three stories in height and one of the most oppressive looking places I could imagine.

"It's even money whether Karloff or Lugosi greets us at the door," I said, trying to strike a humorous note and failing.

"What do *they* know of horror?" Trevor growled. "Their films are kid stuff compared to what we've seen."

"So true," I commented as we steadily approached the house. "What makes Dafoe think *we* can keep the boogie man away from the door?"

"Apparently we've got quite a reputation among the more *eccentric* set."

"Yeah, I guess so."

I pulled the car to a stop on the circular driveway and turned off the engine. Trevor frowned and said, "This is a lot of territory for two guys to cover."

"I thought it might be," I answered. "I spoke to Fred Massey and Willie Haynes about the possibility of lending a hand if needed."

"Good," Trevor said. "They're both pretty competent. I wish Geoffrey were still in the country. His angle on this might've been helpful."

"God, what a fruitcake!" I moaned. "Still, I have to admit that he's a regular encyclopedia where this screwy stuff is concerned."

"Well, we'll make the best of it."

"Maybe we don't need him anyway," I said. "Didn't you say Dafoe is supposed to be some kind of occult expert?"

"So he says," Trevor answered, "but who knows?"

"Yeah, there are lots of scam artists who claim to be."

Trevor looked at the building and grunted.

"Let's get started."

As we headed up towards the house, something came back to me that had been niggling the edge of my mind ever since I'd mentioned Justin Geoffrey.

It was relevant to our case, sort of.

I said, "You know, Geoffrey once told me about a movie made in Germany in the 1920's. It was some Dracula rip-off that had a real vampire in the lead role."

Barnes gave me an odd look and asked, "You know which one?"

"Can't remember the name," I replied, "but Geoffrey seemed pretty convinced. He said while he was abroad he even met some of the witnesses."

Barnes laughed, I thought because of the stupidity of my tale, but he quickly proved me wrong.

We were almost upon the house when he said, "Dealing with a vampire would be a piece of cake compared to what we saw in that skin flick."

He was right of course. He always is.

Dafoe was a tall fellow, cadaverously thin, and wore his white hair exceedingly short. It was about the length of Curly Howard's after six weeks between barbers. He sported dark circles beneath pale blue eyes and his skin had a jaundiced cast to it that made me hope he didn't have anything *catchy.*

We sat in a large room, adequately furnished with old but comfortable chairs. A small fire tried in vain to warm the chill that had descended upon us since entering the house. The walls were decorated with a garish assortment of masks and other objects, many of which left me clueless.

Dafoe caught me staring at an especially hideous mask and smiled.

"A rather meager example of my vast collection," he said. "It was once worn by an African shaman of reputedly fabulous power."

"To each his own," I answered. "My taste in art runs more toward the dogs playing poker type of thing."

He smiled sardonically and pointed across the large room to where Trevor stood. My partner was engrossed in the contents of a glass display case.

"Your associate seems to have found something of interest," Dafoe said.

Trevor turned to me saying, "Hey, Barnes, get a load of this."

I walked to where he stood and tried to see over his shoulder. "Am I supposed to guess or do you want to move so I can see?"

"Sorry," he said, nodding toward the contents with a grin. "You got any missing relations?" he asked. "That one sort of looks like you."

I stared at the collection of shrunken heads and smirked. "You're a real riot, Trev."

Dafoe excused himself and left the room with assurances that he would return shortly.

Looking at Trevor, I said, "I thought you said this guy was real broken up over his wife's death. It doesn't seem like it to me."

"You must be getting slow," Trevor answered. "Didn't you spot those needle marks on his arms? He's hopped up to the gills right now. Probably his way of coping."

I rolled my eyes. "Great, just what we need."

"Hey, even we needed something after watching that film."

"Okay," I said, "But you're in charge of dealing with him. I don't have the patience. You know how I feel about that shit."

"No problem," Trevor said. He started to say something else but Dafoe entered the room.

"Gentlemen," he said, "Is it too early for refreshments? I'm sure there's much you want to ask and talking is so much easier with lubrication of one's vocal chords."

"Never too early for us," Trevor responded.

We took seats and tasted our drinks. Trevor took up most of a small sofa and stared at the flickering fire through his scotch. "This is good stuff," he said. "But, if you're in danger we need to know all the facts."

Dafoe nodded. "Ask your questions," he said. "It's assuredly in my best interest to answer them truthfully."

"Why do you believe your wife was murdered?" I asked.

"I'm almost certain that it was motivated by the desire for revenge," he answered.

"You must have really pissed someone off."

"Yes, I'm afraid that I did," Dafoe answered, "though I never expected things to culminate in this horrible tragedy."

I noted that the bird had yet to refer to his wife by name. I found this curious.

"I was on the West Coast," he continued, "working as a technical consultant for a rather odious little film about black magic."

"What studio?" Trevor asked, sipping his drink.

"Starmont Pictures," he answered. "Frankly they were best known for producing a series of poverty-row stinkers, so wretched that even Lugosi declined to work for them."

"So how did you get hooked up with these guys?" Trevor asked.

"Money, what else?" he answered. "Abe Steinwitz, the studio owner, came into some big money and had aspirations of moving his studio into the big time. The problem was that he still *thought* small time. At least that's the only explanation I have for why he chose to hire a discredited, alcoholic director like Roger Bunning."

"I've heard of him," I said. "Wasn't he responsible for *The Ghastly Corpse Eaters?*"

"Yes, that's him," Dafoe answered, frowning.

"Never heard of it," Trevor said.

"It was quite the scandal," I replied. "Turns out they were using real corpses on the set. Bunning denied knowledge of it but it played hell with his career."

Trevor grinned. "Good to see you're reading something other than those pulp magazines."

I turned to Dafoe. "What led to you and Roger Bunning crossing swords?"

"The man was a willfully ignorant fool," Dafoe said. "Steinwitz insisted on authenticity for this particular film and Bunning was making up occult rituals on the fly. The man didn't know a black cat from a black mass."

"But you were there to provide the knowhow," Trevor said.

"Yes, and Bunning refused to listen to me. He was abusive, arrogant, and had me physically removed from the set on at least two occasions."

"And you went to Steinwitz?" Trevor asked.

"Yes, but only as a last resort."

"Well, what finally happened?" I asked.

"Steinwitz sacked Bunning and decided to scrap the entire picture. After that fiasco, Bunning was pretty much finished."

"Okay," I said, "I can see why he might want payback against you but what makes you so sure that he's responsible for your wife's death? *And* do you know what the hell that monster in the film is?"

"That mask in the film is an obvious taunt. It is one of a kind and came from my personal collection. I gave it to Bunning as a goodwill gesture before things completely soured on the film. As for the monster, *that* will take a bit of explaining."

Trevor finished his drink and set the glass down. He looked at Dafoe and said, "We're all ears. Lay it on us."

Instead of staying put, Dafoe decided to take our conversation elsewhere. After taking us back the way we'd come, he escorted us through a little museum of odd objects.

The ceiling and walls were painted a crisp white, the latter lined with glass-fronted cabinets filled with bizarre bric-a-brac. Between these stood even stranger things, with a long table at the room's center bearing more of the same.

Following Dafoe across the room we passed a tall, rusty Iron Maiden followed by a huge, wooden, man-shaped statue. Carved with big hair and medieval style dress, it had a five-pointed star upon its broad chest.

I said under my breath, "What is all this kooky crap?"

Barnes must have heard me for he made a quick, snorting laugh.

A door stood at the center of each of the room's four walls. Dafoe led us to the one to our right, which made us step around the table at its center.

It held a fake-looking brain accompanied by three swords and a very sharp-looking sickle. All had paper tags attached to them I didn't have the chance to read because Dafoe had already opened the door for us.

A silver-furred monkey suit and a gaudy gold sarcophagus flanked the door. Barnes stepped between them first, looked the monkey up and down and said, "Nice fangs, pal."

The room we followed Dafoe into was unlit, so his voice came invisibly from the darkness.

He said, "The suit is from the film, *The White Ape*, the sarcophagus a prop from *The Tomb of the Black Pharaoh*. Both one-of-a-kind rarities."

This at least explained the source of all of the weird junk, proof that as well as being a student of the arcane, our latest client was a film nut.

We remained in shadow for a few moments before a light appeared at the far end of what proved to be a library. The walls stood lined with bookshelves and tables stacked full with books.

Dafoe, obviously familiar with the darkness, had walked to the end of the room to switch on a lamp sat atop a wide wooden desk. There were two chairs before it, us heading for these as Dafoe stepped around the desk to his own.

The seat he took looked more like a throne, and an evil-looking one at that. The arms he rested his upon were carved in the shape of evil-faced lions, the backrest high, ornate and oval-shaped. It was painted red and gold and covered in weird shapes and symbols.

"Let me guess," I grinned. "Another prop?"

Dafoe stroked the lion beneath his left hand. "My most favorite prop at that," he said. "Excepting perhaps the golem in the main hall. This is the throne from *The Mask of Fu Manchu*."

With the only illumination coming from the desk lamp, the room wasn't exactly bright, and the chair looked creepier for it. The shadows also made our host appear a bit more sinister. An odd-looking statue, a hunched thing with wings, stood on the desk between Dafoe and us, completing the dark atmosphere.

Dafoe looked right at home, like an evil sorcerer from one of his films.

He said, "Sorry about the move, but this, my inner sanctum, is far more conducive for what I need to tell you both."

From the corner of my eye I saw Barnes nod. I steepled my fingers and became all ears.

Dafoe began with, "The universe is actually far older than you, or I can possibly imagine. This realm, and the universes beyond, bear life in abundance, although to look upon it would instill utter insanity."

Barnes and I shared a look that was part recognition that what he told us was the truth. We'd witnessed far too much weird already to truly question his claims.

He continued. "If you consider how long our humble race has lived on planet Earth, and imagine how far, technologically speaking, we've gotten already, can you imagine how our achievements will look in a few hundred years?"

"Pretty damned impossible to imagine," Barnes muttered.

"Their technology would seem like magic, their powers god-like."

Barnes added. "We've heard of these things being referred to as gods before."

Dafoe laughed. "Yes, but, unlike the paltry gods of humanity's religions, these beings actually answer prayers and sacrifice with gifts of power."

I said, "Like sending some beast to kill your wife?"

Dafoe sighed sadly before continuing. "The universe is full of monstrous entities like the Shoggoth, all ancient and powerful beyond human imaginings. I believe that my enemy summoned and controlled one of these blasphemies for the sole purpose of destroying my wife."

From the movie that we'd seen, it seemed Bunning had done a damned fine job of doing just that.

"Seems like a risky business for revenge," Barnes said.

"Risks are part of the game," Dafoe replied.

Game? I thought. *This guy is screwed.*

His next words did nothing to change my opinion of him.

"Many of the most maligned entities take a particular interest in our world. We can deal with them, if we're careful, and sometimes benefit thereof."

His comment reminded me of the King in Yellow and his mad, murderous worshipers. I wondered if Barnes was thinking the same.

Picking the statue up from the desk, Dafoe said, "But, the human race are as insects to their inscrutable minds, and to cross them is to bring upon us a wrath unimaginable."

Holding the statue so that we could clearly see its repulsive, tentacled face, he told us something that *was* difficult to believe.

"This statue, a depiction of the god Cthulhu, was actually sculpted on another world. It is a mere, tiny depiction of the god himself, a giant sorcerous evil which currently resides beneath our very own Pacific Ocean."

I finished making another sweep of the first floor and cursed my luck. Willie Haynes had been unable to assist with security because he was down with the flu and running a hundred and three degrees fever. Our other possibility, Fred Massie, was recovering in Arkham General from a gunshot wound sustained at the hands of a criminal's irate girlfriend. This left only the two of us to insure Dafoe's safety. We were confident in our ability to do the job but a little help would've been nice.

Trevor was on the second floor near Dafoe's room thumbing through a magazine when I returned. "All quiet?" he asked, letting his reading material drop to the floor.

"Yeah," I answered, "not that I'm crazy about roaming around in the dark through this museum of horrors. I wonder what Geoffrey would make of it."

Trevor grinned and said, "I think he would find it *oh so tacky*."

I took a seat and sighed. "Is our client all tucked in for the night?"

"He *retired* a few minutes ago," Trevor replied. "My guess is that he's in there self-medicating . . . if you know what I mean."

I nodded and said, "It's going to be a long night. Why don't you get a little shut-eye? I'll wake you if there's trouble."

"You won't need to wake me if it's the sorta trouble we *usually* get."
"Yeah, ain't it the truth," I replied.

"Some giant monster, asleep under the sea just waiting to come up and devour us all . . . damn, that just takes the biscuit." Barnes said, sat across from me in one of the plush seats of the upstairs lounge. Dafoe had retired for the night, leaving us on guard not far from his bedroom in case the bogeyman came a-calling.

We'd spent the last half hour talking about Dafoe and his alien worlds, the name of Cthulhu often coming up in conversation.

The doors and windows had been locked, and I'd even gone out to make sure the front gate was back in the condition we'd found it in.

I felt we were pretty well secured, all things considered.

"And what was that other thing Dafoe mentioned?" Barnes continued. "These monsters having avatars? Maybe Big Boss was one of those."

Big Boss was a gangster we'd come across, whom, despite not being as big and as ugly as this Cthulhu supposedly was, had been a monster of no small caliber.

Maybe because of my secure feeling, or perhaps because of my comfortable seat or the warming effects of the whiskey, I'd been growing sleepy for a good ten minutes.

So as not to be rude, I'd been grunting assent to Barnes's words, but my eyelids were fast becoming too heavy to resist.

I lit a smoke and Trevor nursed a glass of scotch as we talked for a while longer. We discussed avatars and about some of what we'd run up against in the past but it was obvious that Trevor was about to nod off. He was soon snoring contentedly but this didn't bother me in the least since I knew how fast he could respond if needed. Besides, the sounds he was making would probably scare any evil denizens back to whatever hell they came from.

I pulled a battered copy of *Baron Blood: Death Ace* from my back pocket and started to read. Before long I was locked in aerial combat, trying to maneuver away from the intrepid Baron and his deadly Spandau guns. I was soon destined to become another trophy on the Baron's victory shelf and put the magazine down before the inevitable conclusion. Rising from my chair, I turned and walked down the hall and past Dafoe's bedroom. All was quiet so I continued to the end of the corridor and eased back a heavy crimson drape in order to take a look outside.

A thick fog was rolling in and it would soon be impossible to see anything. "Well," I mumbled, "we've battened down the hatches and there's nothing to do but wait."

I still wasn't entirely sure that I believed Dafoe's tale of murder and revenge but intended on being prepared just the same. Would guns stop that *thing* we'd seen on film? I sort of doubted it but Trevor had brought a few other handy items just in case. My partner was ever resourceful in the ways of death and destruction. Turning from the window, I began to retrace my steps but suddenly stopped as something seemed to crash into the side of the house.

"What the hell?" I asked, turning back to the window.

I withdrew my automatic from its shoulder rig and clutched it tightly. The muffled sound of breaking glass came from behind the crimson drapes and a misshapen bulge appeared in the thick window coverings. I bounded several yards up the hall and yelled, "Trevor!"

His eyes were already open and he was getting to his feet.

"The window at the end of the hall," I growled.

A gun seemed to appear instantly in his meaty hand and he soon crouched beside me as we aimed our weapons at the bulging drapes. A large black-feathered head with a wicked beak ripped through the thick fabric. We opened fire and a hellish screech could be heard between shots as lead sent blood and feathers flying. In the middle of these fireworks, Dafoe popped his head out of the bedroom, glanced at our target and yelled, "It's a Byakhee!"

Trevor looked at me as if expecting confirmation.

I shrugged and said, "It's a damn big bird!"

The creature screeched again, pulled away from the broken window and disappeared from view. We heard loud thuds on the roof and the sound of wood splintering as it was wrenched loose.

Trevor grimaced. "Sounds like the bastards are all over the roof!"

I looked at him and said, "Take Dafoe out of here."

"Like hell!" Trevor answered. "*All* of us go or *none* of us go."

That was the ex-marine coming out in my partner. I knew

where he was coming from and that it was useless to argue with him. Still, I gave it a shot.

"Who's the senior partner in this chicken shit operation?" I asked.

"Screw you, Barnes," he answered. "You're not staying behind to play hero."

I grinned. "I'd go with you but it's *so* damp outside."

"Gentlemen," Dafoe interrupted, "I've made contingencies for such an emergency."

We watched him run down the hall, his open robe flapping behind him.

"What's he think he's doing?" Trevor asked.

I started to reply but stopped as Dafoe opened a hidden panel in the wall and pulled a switch. The lights flickered and an ungodly racket arose from the roof above.

Smiling hideously, Dafoe said, "There's an electric grid on the roof. They'll never get in *that* way."

No sooner were his words spoken when a section of the ceiling collapsed inward, almost blinding us with dust, sheet rock and smoke.

"Son of a bitch!" Trevor cursed, wiping at his eyes.

The smell of burning feathers made us gag as we tried to get our bearings and destroy the wounded Byakhee that flopped dangerously around the floor.

I emptied my .45 trying to kill the screeching creature but was having no luck

"Get away from it!" Trevor yelled from somewhere in the settling cloud.

I had planned to do exactly that when a singed, flailing wing knocked me across the room, causing me to crash into a suit of armor standing against the wall. I was seeing stars and little else but could hear Trevor yelling at me to "Watch out!" A bullet smashed into the wall nearby, prompting me to curse and wipe the blood from my eyes. The view that greeted me left a lot to be desired.

The pain-maddened Byakhee glared at me from blood red eyes and bobbed its head menacingly. Each bob of its half-cooked head sent its wicked beak closer to my face. My hand brushed against cold steel and a quick glance beside me revealed a sword. I grabbed for the antique weapon, thankful for any port in a storm. Trevor and Dafoe both screamed a warning and I instinctively raised the blade to defend myself against the downward slash of the Byakhee's deadly beak. I deflected the beak just enough to save myself but the impact had nearly deadened by arm. In desperation, I struggled to my feet and staggered away from the frustrated creature.

"Get down!" Trevor screamed.

Without hesitation, I threw myself face down and kissed the floor, knowing that my partner had something up his sleeve. The sound of the Thompson was sweet music to my ears as it sang its song of death. I glanced to my side and watched as the Byakhee danced like a puppet on a string as each bullet found its mark.

"I forgot about the Thompson," I said and stood to approach Trevor and Dafoe.

Trevor grinned. "It was in the case by the sofa."

Dafoe looked sheepish and said, "It seems my plan wasn't quite foolproof."

"I wonder how many got fried on the roof?" Trevor asked.

Window panes began to break throughout the house.

I felt sick. "Apparently not enough," I answered.

Dafoe, white as a sheet, said, "Quick, we can make it to the basement!"

I had just enough time to retrieve my .45 before we began our mad dash to the lower part of the house. Unfortunately, the fun was just starting. Our rush downstairs held another nasty surprise: we discovered two hulking things waiting down there for us, both of them looking suspiciously like the rapist from the death movie.

Dafoe squealed in horror.

Towers emptied the Thompson into them in a roaring hail of lead. This forced the creatures back but not down; it at least gave us room to escape. As we fled, Towers swore before dropping the now empty machine gun to the floor.

The door Dafoe led us to was made from solid-looking wood and held a row of locks along its right-hand side. It seemed pretty sturdy, which was great except we were on the wrong side of it. There were moments of tension as Dafoe produced a key fob from his pocket to search for the right keys.

With the injured monsters back up and coming closer, Barnes and I stood with our weapons ready as Dafoe continued his task.

Dafoe was quicker than our pursuers. He shouted, "Come on!" and we were hot on his heels as he disappeared through the door.

The door led to a small landing beyond which fell a steep flight of stairs. We were in darkness for a moment before Dafoe flicked a switch to illuminate a room below us.

Barnes had the door closed in a hurry. It made a solid, slamming sound before Dafoe drove home the heavy steel bolts lining its edge with quick, precise movements.

We were in the landing's cramped surrounds for only a second longer before Dafoe rushed past us to head down the stairs. Barnes and I were fast behind him, going down steps that were far too narrow and steep for my liking.

We'd gotten halfway down these when Dafoe, almost at the bottom, tripped and fell with a surprised yelp. The fall wasn't a long one and as I reached the bottom I found him spread-eagled on the floor of a room filled with wall-to-wall junk.

I stepped across Dafoe, quickly followed by Barnes. Turning to see that Barnes was checking on the man gave me the opportunity to finally reload my gun.

I emptied the chamber onto the floor and put four live ones in the barrel, the last of my ammo.

"He seems okay," Barnes said. "Just out for the count."

I hoped the door would hold, and felt glad it was the most reinforced in the house.

The basement though, a room lined with tea chests, boxes, and old furniture, had me a bit puzzled. I had to wonder why Dafoe had bothered with such security for such a junk-filled room.

I turned to Barnes. He'd bundled up his jacket as a pillow for Dafoe's head, the sword he'd been using to defend himself with laid out beside the unconscious man.

As he stood, I said, "You see something funny about this place?"

Looking round the room he shook his head, so I followed with, "The door. Why'd he have this so secure compared to the rest of the house?"

Barnes shook his head.

"This guy's a kook though. Let's just thank our lucky stars that he did."

Still, why would Dafoe have us run into a dead end where we might be trapped until either the creatures came for us or we starved to death? He might've been kooky, but suicidal?

I looked around us and soon found my answer. It stood beyond the stacked up chairs and wooden crates on the wall opposite the stairs.

"Hey, Barnes," I called. "Gimme a hand here." I then dragged away the stuff lining the wall to get a closer look at my discovery.

Maybe I'd finally learned something in my months of peeping, or maybe it was just dumb luck, but the outline of a hidden door, flush with the wall and painted the same color, had appeared to me like a lighthouse in a storm.

Barnes, removing the chairs and one of the boxes, was quick to see what I'd found.

"Nice work," Barnes said. "Can't see a handle though. But if in doubt, push!"

He pressed both hands against the door and did just that. To my surprise it fell forward on hidden hinges into the secret room beyond.

We picked up Dafoe together, me taking the rear as we led him into darkness. We deposited him to the floor and I quickly checked the walls and discovered a light switch.

The room I lit up was odd to say the least. The carpet was red, as were three of the walls. Not painted red, but covered in ceiling to floor length curtains.

"Damn, a freak room," Barnes muttered, but I was more interested in the other objects the light had revealed.

Two tall shelves flanked the door we'd come through, and these were lined with row upon row of film canisters. Just beyond where we'd dropped Dafoe there was a table with a projector. A chair stood before it and the whole scene had me thinking something was very wrong.

Barnes, already at the curtains, pulled the one facing the projector open to reveal a screen.

I took his lead and headed towards the curtain on my right, stepping around Dafoe to see if this one held a way out.

I dragged it open and my throat turned dry. Beyond, within a tall glass case, hung the lank shape of something horribly familiar. Suspended from a hook dangled the skin of a dead woman. She looked like a balloon without the air, her long black hair draped around a misshapen head that looked sad and eyeless. Its sagging chin touched breasts that were flaccid and deflated, the pipe thin arms and legs twisted around an empty torso.

I pulled the curtain further and discovered yet another empty corpse, this one a young girl. Her hair was the same color as the other sad husk's.

"I don't like the way this is going," I said. I turned to find Barnes stood before the projector screen, staring slack jawed at my ugly find.

Each case, or trophy cabinet rather, bore a labeled tag, just like the rest of Dafoe's collection. I knelt to examine these feeling unsteady on my feet and sick to the gut.

I uttered a sound of involuntary disgust as I read the paper notes attached by string to each body's right big toe.

The woman's read:
> *Ann Bunning – Died Broken*

The girl's:
> *Ellen Bunning – Died Screaming For Her Mother*

"Jesus, Trev, get the feeling we've been screwed?"

I couldn't have voiced Barnes's words any better myself.

"That and more so," I replied. I stood and backed away from the cabinets, their contents far too much for me to bear.

We stared at each other then back to the cabinets, Barnes looking exactly like I felt: pissed and disgusted.

Everything suddenly slipped into place. I realized the horror carried out against Dafoe's wife was only a small part of a much longer story of revenge and retribution; the evidence was right before us.

We turned to look down at Dafoe.

"Revenge," Barnes snarled. "Those monsters up there have been sent here for revenge against this piece of . . ."

His words were abruptly cut off by a loud, splintering crack from the direction of the other room. It seemed the monsters Barnes mentioned were on their way to finish the task.

There was no time to lose.

My first action was to step over Dafoe before rushing towards the only closed curtain. I mentally crossed my fingers as I pulled it aside. My wish came true, for just where I'd hoped it would be stood a door. It had a keyhole beneath its brass handle.

Probably locked, I thought.

I turned to Barnes to find him on his knees, doing something to Dafoe. He'd already removed the man's tie and used it to bind his arms behind his back. He was now removing the belt.

Dafoe started to moan. I could hear the things beyond his little snuff den screeching as they approached.

I hissed at Barnes, saying, "Get that bastard's keys from his pocket, we need to get out fast."

A second later the keys came jangling towards me. A second after that and I was working on the lock.

I fought a growing fear as I tried key after key, then Barnes was breathing down my neck, his breath fast and panicked sounding. I had the lock open on the sixth key.

"What do we do with him?" I said, nodding towards Dafoe, trussed up and now wide-awake.

As I stepped through the doorway he shouted in a pleading voice, "You can't leave me here! Don't you know what those things have been trained to *do to me*?"

"That's your answer," Barnes said.

I closed and locked the door and we charged up a flight of stairs, leaving Dafoe's wailing voice behind us. His screams turned louder, but not as loud as the monsters' roars.

Leaving Dafoe in the basement had me satisfied despite the fact the horrors might be after us next. Him being killed before the corpses of his victims seemed like a righteous retribution.

We made our way up the flight of stairs and I tried my damnedest to block out the screams coming from Dafoe. The bastard deserved what was happening to him but the sound of his agony only made me think about what his victims must have endured. In the darkness of the stairway I stumbled into Towers and cursed.

"Damn, Trev, you're moving like an old woman!"

"Pipe down!" he growled. "There's something at the top of the stairs."

Any welcoming committee at the top of the stairs *had* to be bad news.

Sounding braver than I felt, I said, "It's probably one of Dafoe's ridiculous props . . . a headless manikin or something."

"I don't think so," Towers replied. "It's moving."

I dropped to my knees, easing Trevor to the left with one hand while bringing my .45 out with the other. My finger was poised to squeeze the trigger when a terrific flash of light temporarily blinded me. "Son of a bitch!" I yelled, but the words were only in my head and had failed to leave my mouth. Trevor was uncharacteristically silent as well so I brilliantly deduced that he had been struck blind and was paralyzed as well. This didn't bode well for the continued existence of Barnes and Towers Investigations unless one of us could free ourselves from the strange force binding us.

Eventually my vision returned and I could see Trevor still frozen beside me from the corner of my eye. I could *see* him because there was an emaciated figure radiating crimson light from the landing at the top of the stairs.

"I have no desire to harm you," the figure said.

That would be a first, I thought.

It suddenly dawned on me that I'd seen pictures of the man—though looking more robust—in recent days. It was Roger Bunning!

Bunning took a step down the staircase and said, "I think you deserve an explanation before my spell of binding wanes and restores your freedom of movement. You should be able to speak now but I sincerely hope that you will listen because my time grows short."

I heard Towers mumble a curse as I cleared my throat.

"You're calling the shots for now," I gasped. "What's your story?"

"I would think it pretty obvious," Bunning replied. "Justice for my wife and daughter."

Dafoe's screams from the basement rose in pitch. "Shit, I'd say you've got that in spades," Trevor said.

Bunning smiled. "Yes, at the forfeiture of my soul . . . but it is a small price to pay."

"The bastard deserves what's happening," I stated. "But what you did to his wife makes you no better in our book."

"What I did?" he asked, shaking his head sadly. "I can't pass into the dark realm that lies beyond and allow you to believe that the Dafoe bitch's death was my handiwork."

"We saw the film," Trevor accused. "You were in it."

"No," Bunning replied. "Dafoe was the man in the film. I'm certain he concocted a wonderful tale for you but it wasn't true. He sacrificed his wife to save his own neck. It was the pupil turning on the teacher if you care to know the truth. It was her from whom he learned the dark arts and it was her who participated in the murder of my family. I didn't murder her but don't deny I would have done so had she still lived."

From his powers, and the way he spoke, Bunning really wasn't the witless occult dabbler Dafoe made him out to be.

"So we were duped," I said disgustedly.

"Yes, I'm afraid so," Bunning replied. "You are good and brave men that Dafoe chose to use in an effort to protect himself from my wrath."

"Huh . . . not the best choice on his part," Trevor said.

"I believe he made the right choice," Bunning answered. "Your intentions were good."

"Yeah," I said, "but we know what the road to hell is paved with."

"Do not sell yourselves short," Bunning said. "Not many men would have watched that film and marched off into battle against such horror."

"It's what we do," Trevor answered quietly.

I nodded in agreement and said, "There's still a lot we don't know about why this happened."

"I'm afraid there isn't time to go into details," Bunning answered. "The energy expended on bringing those things into this sphere has left me near death. Suffice it to say it's an old and familiar story of envy, greed and ego. As is often the case, it is the innocent who suffer."

"What now?" Trevor asked.

Bunning flashed a smile that chilled my soul.

"I'm going to go to the basement to bring this business to a close. I suggest you leave this house and forget you ever heard of Dafoe."

With that, the glowing figure made his way down the steps and passed through us on his way to the basement.

Several days have passed since our return from Dafoe's estate. It's been business as usual and sort of nice to be involved in some mundane, down to earth cases. Trevor has been spending time with that waitress at the *Arkham Kettle* and I've been beating myself up over hiring Betty Polanski to act as our office secretary. I've considered firing her but truth is I'm a little bit scared of her old lady.

I've also given a lot of thought to how many terrible things Trevor and I have witnessed during the short time we've worked together. There have been reanimated corpses, sea monsters, a deranged god-king dressed in yellow, and supernatural mobsters.

They are all horrible in their own way but there's one creature that has them beat hands down and that creature is Man. Man has a choice about doing good or evil yet all too often chooses the latter. Man can be pretty damn rotten at times. It's not something I like admitting or giving much thought to but it's there nonetheless. I see it when I look at my partner and I see it when I gaze in the mirror each morning. Trevor and I have both traveled some rough roads and done things we'd rather not talk about. Neither of us are good at apologies but I'd like to think that what we do is helping to balance the scales just a little bit.

Maybe it is and maybe it isn't. Maybe it's too late for guys like Trevor and me. Maybe we're already condemned to spend an eternity in Hell if such a place even exists. Still, it doesn't matter because we've made our choice and damned or not we choose to fight on the side of the angels.

I can live with that.

CONTRIBUTORS

The Authors

Glynn Owen Barrass lives in the North East of England and has been writing since late 2006. He has written over a hundred and thirty short stories, most of which have been published in the UK, USA, France, and Japan. He has also edited anthologies for Chaosium's Call of Cthulhu fiction line, and writes material for their flagship roleplaying game. To date he has edited the collections *Eldritch Chrome, Steampunk Cthulhu* and *Atomic Age Cthulhu*, for Chaosium, *In the Court of the Yellow King*, for Celaeno Press, and *World War Cthulhu* for Dark Regions Press. Upcoming books include *The Eldritch Force, The Summer of Lovecraft, Through a Mythos Darkly*, and *World War Cthulhu II*.

Ron Shiflet is a native of Texas and grew up under the influence of Howard, Smith and Lovecraft. He is the author of Looking *For Darla: Stories of Mythos Noir* and occasionally collaborates with Glynn Barrass on the Barnes and Towers stories of eldritch horror.

He has had short stories published in a number of publications such as *Arkham Tales, Frontier Cthulhu, Horrors Beyond* (both volumes), *Hardboiled Cthulhu* and many others. He also edited the anthologies *Hell's Hangmen: Horror in the Old West* and *Damned in Dixie: Southern Horror.*

Ron still writes occasionally but spends and inordinate amount of time reading alternative history and castigating the New World Order and its minions.

The Artist

M. Wayne Miller is a well-known name in the field of horror illustration. Not to be limited, he is equally adept with science fiction, fantasy, and young adult themes, welcoming the opportunities of each genre and, frequently, combining them all. Always open to new ideas and challenges, he continues his quest to learn and grow as an artist and illustrator. He can be contacted via his website at http://www.mwaynemiller.com